The Dream You Make

Christine Nolfi

DEDICATION

This one is for you, Dad.

Chapter 1

The school bus creaked to a stop before the small, white bungalow. Children's laughter carried on the springtime air.

Inside the house, Annie McDaniel reached for the book bag. She approached her nephew, to help steer his arms through the bag's straps. She gave no warning before touching Dillon.

The moment her fingers brushed his arm, he darted out of reach. Struggling on his own, he positioned the bag on his back.

His rejection hurt more than it should have, especially since she hadn't prepared him for the physical contact he dreaded. It was a foolish mistake. He was a five year old whose world had vanished in a burst of gunfire. The experience had left him frightened, skittish, a mere shell of a boy.

Despite her disappointment, she forced a cheery note into her voice. "Better hurry, Dillon. The bus will leave without you."

The gentle warning prodded him out the door. Head bent low, he trudged across the lawn. He climbed the steps of the bus without a backward glance.

Annie offered a half-hearted wave. There was no sense worrying about when, or if, Dillon would heal. It was a miracle he was a part of her life at all.

The school bus rumbled away. From the house next door

Miriam Di Nardo approached at a swift march, her helmet of salt-and-pepper curls capturing glints of sunlight.

They met in the driveway separating their homes. "I thought you'd already left for work," Annie said.

"On my way now." Miriam fiddled with her sedate gold earrings. She was dressed smartly in black pumps, a grey skirt and a matching blazer. "Ready for the interview?"

"I hope so." Annie smoothed down her pencil-thin black skirt, a recent find at a consignment shop. "How do I look?"

"Like a skittish colt. Ditch the nerves, dear. They won't leave the right impression."

"I still don't think this is a good idea." Even now, she wasn't sure how Miriam had talked her into applying at the marketing firm.

"Don't sell Michael short. He'll recognize your talents. You're a whiz on a computer, dear."

"Yes, and I own a greenhouse, meaning I'll need Thursdays off. Why should your boss agree to full-time hours over four days, not five?" She couldn't imagine how Miriam's boss would react once he discovered she wasn't merely a tech-head, but a business owner in her own right.

"Stop fretting." Miriam gave her unusual and distinctive snort of disapproval. "The minute you start talking computers, Michael will want you on staff."

"I don't have a degree."

"Who cares? You've taught yourself valuable skills in desperate need at Rowe Marketing. As for Green Interiors? Tell Michael about the greenhouse *after* you've gained his confidence."

"I'll give it my best shot." She wished she possessed a shred of Miriam's confidence. "I need to land a second job fast."

"It's not right that you have to fight for custody of Dillon." Miriam shook her head with disgust. "You're his aunt. He should be adopted by you."

"It won't happen unless I find steady work with medical benefits." The insurance she'd cobbled together since receiving temporary custody of Dillon only covered the basics. God forbid if he ever became seriously ill. The bills would eat through her meager savings.

Miriam pulled her into a rocking hug. "Now, perk up. You're a bright young woman. I'm sure you'll land the job." Drawing away, she added, "So I'll see you at 10:30 this morning?"

"On the dot."

"If Michael attacks with a dozen questions, just remember Dillon. You're taking on a second job to keep him here in Fairfax with you." Miriam started toward her car. From over her shoulder, she added, "Don't let Michael scare you. He's a hothead, but you deserve the job."

Working for a hot-tempered boss *did* scare her—a little. "Is he intimidating?"

"Most of the time he's great. But he doesn't like Fridays."

The warning lifted Annie's brows. "What's wrong with Fridays?"

***

Stalking into the men's john, Michael Rowe decided there was something downright malevolent about Fridays.

He despised how Fridays always brought unpleasant surprises. It seemed most of those bolts from the blue were disasters sent to derail him. He was a big guy—six foot, two inches in his stocking feet, and hard to knock down. Still, a staff of frantic employees could send the most stable executive right off the tracks.

From the last stall, the unmistakable sounds of retching echoed off the walls. A more sensible man would hightail it back to the sanctuary of the executive suite. Shrugging off the urge to leave, he rapped on the door.

"Bill, you dying in there?" he asked.

The toilet flushed. "Yes."

"Hang on, buddy. I sent the new secretary out to pick up antacids."

"You sent Bitsy to the drugstore?" Bill wheezed. "Are you crazy?"

Offended, Michael pulled back to glare at the closed stall. "Yeah, I sent Bitsy. So what?"

"She's an idiot, that's what. You never should have hired her."

"She types eighty words a minute."

"That's not all she does." Bill let loose a sickening belch. "Know why she needed a ride to work today? Her car is in the chop shop—third time this month. Haven't you noticed it in the parking lot? The blue Mercury?"

"The demolition derby model is hers? I sent her out in the company car!"

"Good thing the Beemer's insured. Bitsy's young, blind and brutal on all things automotive."

An image of the corporate BMW hurtling toward a tree accosted Michael. "Why didn't you mention she's a lousy driver?"

"It's never come up. Hey, I'm busy puking here. Go away."

On a groan, Michael changed the subject. "You shouldn't let Violet get to you like this. Every time she cries, you puke. It's got to stop."

"Give me a break," Bill shot back. "While you're conveniently holed up in your office, she bleeds tears all over the art department. Which works for me, but then she heads for copy and scares the crap out of my staff. What is it with artists? Why do they fall apart every time they finish a project?"

"No idea." Michael slapped the stall door in much the same way he'd slap Bill on the back. "If Bitsy isn't back in ten, I'll send Miriam out for the antacids."

"Thanks."

Returning to his office, Michael ran headlong into Terrence Kholer. Since it was Friday, Rowe Marketing's lead artist displayed all the signs of full meltdown. Nuclear reactors couldn't cause as much damage as Terrence when his core became unstable.

Terrence grabbed him by the lapels of his sports coat. "I'm going to kill Herman. I'll decapitate him! Do you hear me?"

Michael tried shrugging free. "Slow down. What did Herman do?"

"He's wrecked the computers again." The art director backed him against the wall, an impressive feat given that Terrence had a slight build and the physical strength of a fashion model. "He lost ten of the images I was working on when he crashed the computers. He's dead, do you understand?"

"Damn it, back off. Where's Herman now?"

Terrence snapped his hands to his sides. "Don't ask."

"Like hell. Where is he?"

"All right, all right—he's hiding under my desk. I heard whimpering." The artist shot off a smug look. "It's not my problem."

Which, Michael knew, meant it was *his* problem. "Is he breaking out in hives?"

"Gads—his face looks like a pizza with a double serving of pepperoni. The eruptions are volcanic."

"You scared the crap out of the kid again? If so, it's *your* problem. Crawl under your desk and drag him out. And get him the calamine lotion from Miriam's desk. You know where she keeps it."

The mention of Michael's secretary stamped fear on the art director's face. No one at the firm messed with Miriam. One glance from her steely eyes brought order to any situation.

Terrence fiddled with his mustache. "You want me to fetch the calamine from the dreaded gatekeeper's desk? Have you lost your mind? I refuse to go near her on Fridays."

Michael offered his most surly expression, the one that usually brought instant submission. "Now, listen up," he said. "I don't give a damn what Herman did. He'd run the computers just fine if you'd stop scaring the shit out of him. Drag him out from under your desk and get the calamine lotion. While you're at it, make Violet settle down. Is she still crying?"

"It's not my problem."

Irritation surged, but Michael battled it down. "Where is she?"

"In the cafeteria. Roaming makes her feel better when she's overwrought."

There goes breakfast. He'd planned to grab a granola bar from the vending machine before interviewing the tech applicant. No way was he going near the cafeteria now.

"Just take care of it," he snapped.

He walked away. To the left and right, employees inside offices chatted softly or worked at computers. The satisfying aroma of coffee spiked the air, mixed with the gardenia perfume Violet favored on her moodiest days. He didn't understand why Terrence's assistant chose an old-fashioned perfume better suited for someone's grandmother—it certainly clashed with her purple hair and punk rocker mien. Nor did he understand why the rest of the staff allowed the emotional girl to flood the cafeteria with tears when they ought to storm the Bastille and take the place back.

At Miriam's desk, within inches of the relative safety of his office, he spotted the new secretary shrinking into the wall. Bitsy's mousey hair looked wind blown. Recalling Bill's warning in the bathroom, he wondered if the corporate Beemer was strewn in pieces somewhere in Fairfax.

From behind thick glasses, Bitsy's eyes widened with the sort of quivering apology he knew he didn't wish to hear.

"Mr. Rowe—"

He held up a hand, silencing her. To Miriam, he said, "Notify the insurance company."

She picked up the phone. "I've already checked the company deductible."

"Good deal." He turned to Bitsy. "Did you get the antacids for Bill?"

"Yes, sir," she squeaked.

"He's in the men's john." When the secretary paled, he gave her the full force of his gaze. Confident he'd rendered her mute, he added, "March in there and slide it under the stall. Get moving."

After the girl stumbled off, he asked Miriam, "Has she arrived?"

"She's waiting. Her resume is on your desk."

Michael went inside the massive cave he called an office. If wide, open spaces and lavish accouterments were the ticket to intimidating employees he figured he'd done himself right. A slab of granite served as his desk. A wet bar was tucked into miles of cabinetry. The carpets underfoot were thick and inviting. He strode across with his frustration rising.

There wasn't time today to waste interviewing Miriam's friend for the post of Systems Analyst and General Dragon Slayer. He needed a Titan, some guy with an I.Q. of 200 and enough computer savvy to get the damn computers running and keep them running.

His patience thinning, he strode past the woman seated before his massive desk. He dropped into his chair without giving her so much as a once-over. He'd grown tired of interviews. Not one applicant had been qualified. He'd already decided to fly up to New York City with a stellar pay and benefits package, and steal an IT pro from one of the national ad agencies.

When he looked up, Annie McDaniel returned his gaze with a level examination from blue-green eyes. Mythical eyes of a compelling hue—green one moment, blue the next. Her skin was a translucent sheath framed by blonde hair, her features delicate and her mouth so pink that it called up an image of spring's first rose. He was still appreciating her eye-popping beauty when he realized she was waiting for him to speak.

"You're Annie McDaniel," he remarked, stupidly.

"Yes."

"Friend of Miriam's, right?"

"I live next door."

"You'd like to work in marketing?"

"That's the plan."

He dragged his hand across his scalp before drawing his attention to her resume. "Says here you work at . . . a greenhouse. Green Interiors."

He looked up in time to see her swallow hard. "Green Interiors offers horticultural design services to Virginia businesses," she said. "We bring in plants to soften the look of an office. Studies show that workers are more productive when surrounded by the natural world."

He liked the way her lips got pouty when she grew serious. "No kidding."

"It makes sense if you think about it."

"And here I thought all my employees need is a good paycheck and a swift kick in the ass."

The comment slipped out before he could check himself. She appeared horrified, which pleased him for reasons unknown.

"You aren't serious, are you?" she asked.

"I'm not sure." Michael rocked in the chair. "I'll get back to you."

Despite his sour mood, he liked how indecision relaxed the faint lines in her forehead and softened her mouth. Annie McDaniel was wasting his time but she sure was pretty. All she was missing were translucent wings and fairy dust.

His impolite appraisal sent wisps of pink across her cheeks. "It seems you're in no mood to conduct an interview." She gave a questioning look. "Should I go?"

A sudden, genuine smile lit his face. "I wish you would."

She bounced to her feet. But she didn't leave. He sent a silent curse to the mischievous god of Fridays.

Gingerly, she sat back down. "Mr. Rowe, I spent thirty minutes driving in heavy traffic to get here. I understand you're busy. Would you at least extend the courtesy of reading my resume

7

before I leave?"

"We don't grow petunias here," he replied tightly. "This is a marketing firm. If you're ready to move up in the world, why not take your shovel and gardening gloves to one of the greenhouses in the area?"

"I have other abilities if you'd just read on."

"I don't have time. I'm sure you understand."

She rose, and he sensed deliverance. Now she'd bolt for the door. They always did. It was nothing to be proud of, but he'd perfected the art of closing the interview.

But his satisfaction was short-lived. A combative flush spread across her cheeks. She curled her fists, her knuckles showing white and her legs trembling the slightest bit beneath her secondhand skirt. Hell, this was new. Never before had an applicant mustered the courage to stand up to him. The disappointment in her eyes had been replaced by . . . what? He wasn't sure.

Whatever it was, it didn't bode well for him.

She jabbed her finger at the resume. "Please stop baiting me. News flash—I have expertise with computers. It doesn't match up with the horticultural gig, but what do you care?"

The outburst was stunning. Floundering, he tried to form a retort.

He was still trying to get his neurons to fire when she asked, "Are you always this grumpy?"

He blinked. "Grumpy? Hell, I'm being damn polite."

"You're surly, actually. No wonder you can't find an employee."

He bristled. "News flash—I have fifty employees."

"You must pay well. Your personality wouldn't lure anyone into your employ. If you're always this temperamental, it might be more than I can tolerate."

Was *she* always this blunt? He leaned back in his chair, off-balance from the rude line of comments. "It's Friday, deadline day," he said, pulling himself together. He motioned to the door, thirty paces away. "Hear that?"

She lifted her nose like a hunting dog. "Someone is crying."

"I've got a puker, too. Down the hall in the john. Your buddy, Miriam? She seems all sweetness and light, but trust me—she's been ballistic since 9 A.M. I should douse her with Valium." He snapped up his wrist to examine his watch. "It's 10:42. By noon, some maniacal client will be on the phone scaring the daylights out of the secretaries. Rowe Marketing isn't the best place to park your gardening gear. There are easier jobs."

Her wispy, feminine brows rose. "Are you trying to frighten me?"

He saw no reason to lie. "You bet."

"I'd still like an interview."

"Then sit back down." Pleased by her spunk, he offered what he hoped was a malevolent smile. "You've got my attention. Thrill me."

She rattled off a list of software products she'd mastered and the social media platforms she understood. He mentioned the Rowe Marketing website, which picked up viruses so frequently it was on life support, and she assured him that old plug-ins were probably to blame. *What's a plug-in?* An image of a hundred electrical sockets danced through his brain, with the mess of computers, printers and light tables all plugged in to keep his fussy art director happy. He pushed thoughts of Terrence from his brain and encouraged the valiant Anne McDaniel to continue, in part because her knowledge *was* impressive, but also because she was so nice to look at.

She had guts, he'd give her that. Most applicants showed signs of stress by now. Five minutes into one of his interviews, the average slob was perspiring.

He pulled from the reverie when she stopped. "Are you listening to me?" she asked.

For a split second, he struggled to get back on track. "Yes. No. I'm looking for a computer guy," he rapped out.

"Or woman."

"Whatever." He scanned the resume. "Your computer skills are self-taught?"

Some of her confidence evaporated. "Yes."

"No college?" When she rubbed her lips together in a fetching display of frustration, he set the resume down. "You seem sincere. However, I need someone with proven computer experience *and* the credentials to back it up."

"You're sure?"

"You bet. No degree, no job."

The comment doused the light in her eyes. Regret gave Michael a swift poke in the ribs as she mumbled a few words in leaving. She hurried out with her head held high, and he considered calling her back.

Ditching the idea, he got back to work.

***

Sunlight spilled across Miriam's desk and the tidy reception area. Thankfully Miriam was nowhere in sight. Annie blinked back tears then spun in a circle in a desperate attempt to remember the way out of Rowe Marketing. A corridor to the left and another to the right—which one led to the elevator? Anxious to escape before she succumbed to full-throttle weeping, she chose the corridor to the right.

Employees streamed past. She'd just reached the elevator when an angry howl erupted from one of the offices.

Annie nearly jumped out of her skin. A young man with an unfortunate case of the hives hurtled toward her.

Despite her dismay over losing the job, she let out a laugh. She couldn't help herself. The man—a kid, really—was something to behold. Pink glop covered the welts on his face. He looked like he'd been dunked in a vat of Pepto Bismol.

Scudding to a halt, he shouted, "Terrence is going to kill me!"

Sniffling, she swiped at her face. "Who?"

"Terrence the terrible. Something went wrong with the install." The kid stole a glance over his pink spattered shoulder. "I don't know why the computers went down. If everyone would stop downloading crap from the Internet, we wouldn't get so many viruses."

"Did you run a virus check?"

"Tried to." Wild-eyed, he added, "Don't tell anyone, but I didn't want a job in systems. I was trying to get my foot in the door, see? I'd like to work on Bill's team, in the copy department. They weren't hiring so I talked my way into this stupid job."

His desperation started her grinning. Rowe's resident IT guy was a fake? "Do you remember when you last tuned up the Macs?" she asked. "Prior to this particular install?"

He gave a quizzical look. "What?"

She rolled her shoulders. The kid was out of his depth,

swimming the deep seas before he'd learned the doggie paddle. "Can you show me the computers?" She gestured down the corridor, where employees had begun popping their heads out of doors.

"Show you . . . yeah, sure." He grabbed her arm and tugged her down the hall. "Think you can fix them?"

She let him drag her into an office boasting artwork on every wall. The monitors of a dozen widescreen iMacs were dark. Artists huddled in groups. One frantic fellow with a mustache and too much jewelry shrieked at no one in particular. Edging past him, Annie licked her lips in anticipation. She pulled up a chair to the first computer in the row.

"Reboot," she instructed the young man. When he stared with puzzlement, she asked, "What's your name?"

"Herman." He wrung his hands. "I tried. I can't reboot."

"Soft boot or hard?"

He scratched his nose, stopped, and stared at the pink goo on his finger. "What?"

"Hard boot it is." She did the honors, and wavy bands of color lit the screen. She checked the disk utility and discovered a bounty of duplicate files. There was also a virus.

When she frowned, Herman said, "I saw the virus. I don't know how it got in."

"When did you last update the definitions?"

"Huh?"

Shaking her head with disbelief, she updated the software then ran a tune-up program. Moving down the row of workstations, she purged the virus and dumped old files. By the time she'd finished, a crowd had formed behind her.

"Show me the program you were trying to install," she said to Herman.

He did. She worked quickly, her fingers streaming across the keyboard in a ballet of knowledge and experience. She'd been playing around with computers since childhood—long before her father had died, leaving her the greenhouse, and before her sister ran off to Baltimore.

If life had been different, she might have taken more than a few online courses. Maybe she would've earned a degree as a systems analyst. Not that she didn't love the greenhouse and watching life sprout and unfurl beneath her care. She cherished the years she'd spent building the small enterprise with her father.

Wrapping up, she rose. The crowd parted.

She found herself face to face with the man a few inches taller than the rest.

"You're hired," Michael said.

"Thanks." She swept past, victorious. At the door, she paused. "I'll need Thursdays off." She waited as he opened his mouth then closed it again. "Great."

Beaming at the crowd, she walked out.

Chapter 2

Annie skipped up the bungalow's steps and went inside. Landing the job made her feel buoyant, alive.

It wasn't yet noon. Dillon wouldn't return from kindergarten for several more hours. Mulling over her options, she stuck her head inside the fridge and grabbed an apple. Should she stay at the house and finish the April accounting for Green Interiors? Or drive to the greenhouse and make a few plant deliveries? Other chores required attention. Dinner should be prepared or at least defrosted. The growing laundry pile was trickling out of the laundry room. Whittling it down would take hours.

How quickly her life had changed.

Eight months ago she'd lost her estranged sister in a shocking murder on Baltimore's mean streets. Weeks of petitions followed, before Annie received temporary custody of the nephew she hadn't seen since his infancy—Dillon. Prior to his arrival in Virginia, she'd barely been making the mortgage and covering the bills with the income generated by Green Interiors. Now she'd added more responsibility in the form of a job at Rowe Marketing.

Could she manage to juggle everything, including her new parenting responsibilities? She *had* learned to rely on Miriam for advice. Just memorizing the childhood vaccination schedule proved mind-boggling. The schoolwork Dillon brought home from the kindergarten class at St. Mary's demanded her full attention each night. Dillon's language skills were far below his classmates' and teaching him to read took hours of repetition.

All her new responsibilities paled beside Dillon's night terrors. Several times each month his piteous wails rang through the slumbering house. Annie would sprint down the hall and find him choking back sobs. It took an hour, sometimes longer, to calm him. She'd stroke his clammy face and murmur soothing words to assuage the grief he was too young to dispel.

It was the only time, day or night, Dillon welcomed her touch.

Like her young nephew, Annie suffered her own share of nightmares, of a man standing in the shadows and Toria screaming for help. The man lifting his hand to reveal the glint of a handgun . . .

Even though Annie's life had never been easy, this was the first time she'd wrestled with nightmares. She'd survived her share of emotional upheavals—losing her father had been difficult, and Toria's murder was an agony. Yet she'd never suffered the illusion life promised an easy road. Nor did she expect to banish the loneliness she felt when her father crept into her thoughts, or the soul-killing pain she encountered while imagining Toria's last moments of life. Yet Annie understood the past was simply that— over, finished. It was more sensible to focus on the present, and the possibility of creating a better future.

It might be foolhardy, but she even believed the situation with Dillon would improve. The hollow-eyed boy who greeted her each morning might blossom into a happy child. The silence lapping across the house in a wave of heartbreak might one day recede.

Besides, everything *was* turning up. Thinking about her new job started her humming as she tossed a load of Dillon's clothes into the washing machine. The plant deliveries would have to wait.

She'd just begun washing last night's dinner dishes when Miriam entered. "I heard about your incredible feats in the art department," Miriam said by way of greeting. "Even Michael thought you were amazing."

Annie rinsed a plate and set it on a towel beside the sink. "He did?" Michael Rowe didn't seem the sort of man quick with compliments. "During the interview, he said you should be doused in Valium."

"He would say that."

"Is he always temperamental?"

"Most days he's nice. It's the end of the week. All those deadlines. He's exhausted."

"I still can't believe I landed the job."

"Rowe employees and their dependents receive full medical coverage. Dental, too."

"We'll have dental coverage too?" She marveled at her good fortune. Dillon's recent dental bills were staggering. In February the pediatric dentist had extracted two brown, rotting baby teeth. His sinus infection had cleared up immediately, and he'd begun gaining much-needed weight.

Applying at Rowe Marketing had seemed impractical. Thank goodness Miriam had won that particular battle.

"I may have misjudged Mr. Rowe," she said. "Given the health benefits, he *is* generous."

"He'll seem different tomorrow. Friendlier."

"Mr. Rowe expects me to work on a Saturday?"

"You need to stop by for an hour or so, to get acquainted with the lay of the land." Miriam leaned close, smiling. "Call him Michael, dear. He doesn't stand on formality. And don't worry. I'll give you the grand tour. I don't usually work Saturdays but I'll make an exception for my favorite neighbor."

"How old is Michael?" Annie wasn't sure why she'd asked.

Miriam gave an appraising glance. "Now there's a coincidence. He asked the same thing about you. He said he couldn't believe he'd hired a teenager to run the systems. He's four years older than you—thirty-six." Miriam's eyes twinkled. "Handsome, too. Don't you think?"

He was a gorgeous specimen of male beauty with an athletic build, ebony hair and deep blue eyes. Not that she'd discuss his attributes with Miriam. If she did, the teasing would never stop.

"I had trouble getting past his brusque personality," she said. "His looks don't factor in. Not as long as the paychecks are good."

***

15

Dillon, his uniform of navy blue pants and light blue oxford shirt sporting wrinkles and dirt, trudged down the steps of the bus. He'd barely cleared the sidewalk when Chip Wilson leapt from the steps like Peter Pan taking flight. Chip was a sunny child with enough energy to lasso the moon. He also attended kindergarten at St. Mary's Elementary School.

The bus pulled away, and Annie waved at Chip. Dillon, dragging his feet across the grass, failed to acknowledge her.

Chip waved both arms through the air. "Hi, Mrs. McDaniel!" In a child's parlance, Annie's role as Dillon's foster mother elevated her to married status.

"Bye, Chip," Dillon interjected, without turning around.

"Hey!" Chip halted on the sidewalk. "I'm coming over, right?"

"Sure."

Chip flung down his book bag and spun in a joyous circle. "Great! I'll tell Mom." He looked to Annie. "Is it okay, Mrs. McDaniel?"

She chuckled. In a world full of miracles, Chip Wilson was a special blessing. "Please tell your mother first," she replied. "I have ice cream for you boys."

He gave the thumbs up before sprinting across the street. Dillon came up the steps with his head hung low.

"Bad day at school?" she asked.

He paused in the foyer. "It was okay. Sister Bernadette gave me a pear and cookies."

No matter how full Annie made Dillon's lunch sack, the teachers at St. Mary's plied him with extra food. So did the neighbors. Annie, of course, kept the fridge stocked with nutritious offerings at all times. By some unspoken agreement, every adult who cared about Dillon was on a mission to end his status as an underweight child.

"We're having hamburgers for dinner." She reached out to tousle his golden brown curls, but thought better of it. Dillon rarely welcomed affection. "Do you want burgers tonight? Or do you prefer something else?"

He slid a bashful glance. "I like burgers with lots of catsup." He lowered his eyes.

"I know you do. Since the dentist went to town fixing all

those cavities, you like all sorts of things."

"I liked the pear Sister Bernadette gave me." The admission hung in the air, whispery and tentative.

"Then I'll buy a whole bag of pears. We can afford it. I found a second job."

He toed the floor as if waiting to be excused. There was no sense in expecting him to shout for joy. At age five, he couldn't understand why her new position at Rowe Marketing mattered.

He didn't even know about the custody battle, or how hard Tom and Dianne England in Baltimore were fighting to adopt him. She was still waiting for him to ask why they'd stopped visiting at the end of March. She felt guilty about cutting off the visits but her attorney had advised her to break contact.

The Englands wanted Dillon—and they'd made it clear that if they won, Annie would never see her nephew again. In their view, Toria's reckless life and her ghastly murder warranted breaking off all contact with the past.

Meaning Annie, Dillon's only biological relative, would lose him from her life.

The prospect never failed to fill her with anger. And fear— she'd already grown to love Dillon. He'd begun to take root in his new life in Fairfax. Yet the Englands wanted to drag him back to Baltimore, to a world where he no longer belonged.

After he went to change into play clothes, she returned to the kitchen to make two bowls of ice cream. The doorbell rang. On the other side of the screen door, Chip bounced on the balls of his feet.

She made a mental note to ask the boy's mother to watch Dillon tomorrow while she went into work for Miriam's grand tour. The prospect of seeing Michael Rowe whirled excitement through her, which seemed foolish. During the interview they'd traded barbs instead of pleasantries. Still the anticipation persisted, impossible to brush away.

"You sure look happy, Mrs. McDaniel."

Startled, she regarded the freckle-faced boy at her hip. "I guess I am."

"How come?"

"I got a new boss." She backpedaled. "I mean, job."

Chip rocked on his heels. "Which do you like better?"

Both.

Tamping down her emotions, she nudged him toward

Dillon's bedroom. "Why don't you fetch your buddy," she said, "before the ice cream melts?"

Chapter 3

Strolling across the expanse of his office suite, Michael savored the morning silence. Even though it was Saturday, he'd already walked his mangy excuse of a dog, eaten a light breakfast, and arrived at the office before eight A.M.

Nothing beat Saturday's slower pace. Few employees came in, and those who did were close to deadline and too busy to badger the boss. Today was no exception. He planned to wrap up his own work by noon and take in a game of golf.

At nine-thirty voices drifted down the corridor, signaling Miriam's arrival.

She popped into the doorway. "Would you like coffee?" she asked. "I'm making a fresh pot for us."

"Then have it in here." He assumed the "us" meant Annie McDaniel had accompanied her to work.

He was correct, of course.

While Miriam busied herself in the reception area, Annie appeared in the doorway. Dressed in jeans and a gold T-shirt, she seemed hesitant to enter. Her shoulder length hair hung in a loose ponytail, accenting her high cheekbones and extraordinary eyes.

"Please, come in." He let his attention linger on her hair, catching sunlight in a shimmering display. "I don't bite."

Warily she stepped inside and came across the mile of carpeting separating them. An uneasy silence wound between them as she chose one of the chairs facing his desk. In the reception area, Miriam clattered china.

He was still searching for a way out of the impasse when she said, "Is it true your staff crashes the computers all the time?"

Good save. He liked how she chose to get right down to business. The cool tone of the question suggested she wanted to forget the barbs they'd traded yesterday. As did he.

"The staff crashes the computers with alarming predictability," he admitted. "It's been hell for months. New equipment, new programs. I hope you can network it all together."

"Why not stop your employees from making purchases until the problems are solved? While you're at it, implement a company policy. Tell everyone to *never* open attachments in email if they don't know the sender."

The suggestion would solve some of the problems. Unfortunately she hadn't yet made the acquaintance of Terrence Kholer and his squad of feckless artists. They were kids in the electronic candy store, purchasing software whenever it promised to improve the design process or just seemed fun to use. And email? Just last month Terrence's sidekick, Violet, infected every computer in the art department when she opened mail from Hong Kong. The gullible girl had believed she'd won a Chinese lottery.

"Once you meet the artists, you'll understand." Odds were they'd have Annie fleeing for the exit. "They never warn us when they load something new into the system. Then everything crashes."

"Which is reason enough to check with IT before installing anything new."

Terrence, check with IT? He couldn't wait for his new Systems Analyst to meet The King of Excess. "If it looks good, Terrence buys it. He's our lead artist, and not the sort to resist something he craves." Michael rocked in his chair, intrigued by her spunk. "You ask a lot of questions. It might get on my nerves."

She lifted her shoulders in a careless shrug. "You'll get used to it. Or begin to hate me. Your choice, totally."

"You don't care if we're at each other's throats?"

The question, a challenge, seemed to amuse her. "We need to forge a working relationship," she said. "Your personal opinion of me? I don't care what you think."

"You don't pull any punches, do you?"

"Not usually."

He fought down his pleasure. How often was *anyone* this honest? Her disdain for artifice was a refreshing alternative to the 'yes man' mentality of most employees, who were intent on sugaring the boss. Under different circumstances he would've already asked her out for dinner.

He switched topics. "Would you like to see your new office?"

"Of course."

Confident she'd follow he walked across the suite. Confusion settled on her face as he paused beside the ceiling-high bookcases that framed the wet bar twenty paces from his desk. After a moment she spotted the door to his left.

Distress bloomed on her features. "My office is connected to yours?"

The apprehension in her voice came as no surprise. He'd been short-tempered during yesterday's interview. Was it any wonder she dreaded the prospect of working in close proximity?

"Working nearby won't be like the seventh circle of hell." He beckoned her inside. "We'll get along fine."

If his office suite was palatial, her room was invitingly large with a U-shaped desk at the back wall. The desk faced a leather couch paired with a coffee table hewn from the same grey granite of his desk. Like so many other areas on the fifth floor, one wall was constructed of glass, lending a pastoral view of rolling Virginia hills and cloud-studded skies.

There was more, of course. Never one to scrimp, he'd outfitted the workspace with an iMac and an HP unit that did everything but the grocery shopping. He believed success arrived by offering employees the best tools and a comfortable work environment. Creativity demanded nothing less.

"I thought you'd stick me in a cubicle with a desk and a stack of technical manuals," she said. "This is where I'll work?"

"You bet."

She rested her fingers on the computer's sleek monitor. "This is amazing." A sweet, wistful note colored the admission.

"If you say so. I think of technology as the bane of my existence."

"I love computers." The words came out in a sweet, wistful

tone.

"Sure, they speed everything up. They also crash or send data to the wrong place at the wrong time."

"Computers don't do that; *people* do."

"Yeah, blame the people." He grinned. "They must be at fault."

"They are! Why blame an inanimate object for human frailty? We demand all sorts of conveniences then become angry if we can't work new software or program a new appliance. It's a good thing VCRs lost the battle with digital recording. I never could teach Miriam how to tape a movie."

The banter brought heat to her eyes, making her even more attractive. Evidently she didn't know he was joking. He saw no reason to pull her down from her soapbox, not when voicing her convictions made her so fetching.

"People won't take the time to read the manuals," she was saying. "They get impatient, start tooling around, and then become furious when something doesn't work. I mean, c'mon. Everything comes with a guide. If you need more help, there's Google."

Michael grunted. She'd described him perfectly. "I don't have time to read a manual every time I order some gadget."

"Sure you do."

"Think what you'd like. I'll keep my cell phone but don't care for computers. We should pitch the bastards off the nearest cliff and go back to making art the old-fashioned way. Say, with a sketch pad and a pocketful of pens." He paused as she feathered her hand across the iMac. "Are you going to pet that beast all day?"

"My monitor at home is the size of shoe box. And it's not high-res."

"You're kidding."

"I think it was born when Carter was in office."

"Replace it," he suggested, amused by the exaggeration.

"Sure, boss—as soon as I catch up on the bills. Say, by the time I'm forty."

How many bills did she have? "Are you married?" he asked, knowing full well it was none of his business.

"No." She lifted her hand from the monitor and stared. "Why?"

"You mentioned having so many bills."

"Meaning marriage is expensive? Thanks for the tip. I'll avoid it."

"I meant a husband could help—in theory, at least." He thought of something else. "Unless you hook up with a gambler."

She looked at him like he'd grown a tail. "The next time I'm tooling around on eHarmony, I'll avoid the guys roosting at the blackjack table."

"Good plan."

She angled a hip. "Anything else you'd like to know? My favorite color is green and I don't believe in astrology."

He searched for a witty retort but came up empty. Why push for details regarding her private life? How she handled her finances was none of his business. Maybe she held credit cards at every department store in Fairfax. She might be one of those women who bought enough shoes to fill three closets.

After his performance yesterday, he didn't want to make her any more uncomfortable than she already was. He'd hired her. They were now working together. Developing a productive relationship was the first order of business.

Which was a problem. It had already dawned he was attracted to her something fierce.

***

Miriam set the pewter tray on the coffee table. With a darting glance, she read Michael's face. He seemed nervous each time his attention strayed to his new employee, but also upbeat as they chatted in lowered voices. There was no mistaking how much he enjoyed Annie's company. Perhaps he even respected her, which came as no surprise. Michael never failed to recognize a valuable asset.

Pity the girl didn't hold herself in equally high esteem.

Some lives suffered one cataclysm after another. The lucky breaks were rare. Still, a series of heartbreaks hadn't turned Annie into a cynic or, worse, shaped her into a cruel and callous woman. Despite the trials and the obstacles that had plagued her for years, she clung to optimism. Even with Dillon, a child so emotionally scarred he might never heal, Annie played down the difficult days and reveled in the rare moments of happiness. Just yesterday she'd appeared in Miriam's kitchen right after dinner with the boy in tow and a sheaf of artwork under her arm. Dillon had begun using brightly colored crayons in his kindergarten class, a startling departure from the greys and browns he usually preferred. The way Annie had shown off his drawings, you'd think a box of crayons held the power to repair his heart after a horrifying loss.

It was Annie's loss too, though she hid her grief well. Now all she needed was an opportunity—finally—to build a future with the boy. Miriam prayed Rowe Marketing would afford the well-deserved chance.

"Coffee, dear?" Miriam asked her.

Annie sent a longing glance at her office. "Would you mind if I passed? I'd like to familiarize myself with Rowe's systems."

"It's Saturday." Michael's voice held a hint of surprise. "I don't expect you—"

Annie waved away his objections. "I know. Don't worry about it, okay? I can't stay long but I would like to get a head start."

Approval burnished his features. "Go ahead."

With a murmured farewell, she retraced her steps. The door to her office closed with a soft click. Shrugging it off, Michael settled into one of the chairs facing the couch and rested his legs on the coffee table. His casual posture was a source of pride for Miriam, a sign of how much he trusted her. With the rest of the staff, he rarely let down his guard.

"What do you think?" she asked.

Michael drank, considering. "She'll do."

"That's it?"

"All right, Miriam. She's great. Untested, sure, but a good addition to the team. I'm reasonably confident she'll stop mayhem from raining down."

"Reasonably confident? Oh, Michael—she's brilliant."

"You're exaggerating."

"Guess again." She slung her legs up onto the coffee table so they were sitting toe-to-toe. It was a breach of business etiquette the other employees wouldn't dare. But she'd earned her privileges. She'd been with Michael since the marketing firm's opening day.

Aware she'd piqued his interest, she said, "If Annie had attended college, she'd be writing software today or teaching grad courses. She's just like Sam."

"Sam?"

"Her father. Gone now. He was the same—sweet, quirky, brilliant. The man knew enough about plants to work at the Royal Botanic Gardens."

"You mean The Kew, in London? I've been there. Miles and miles of flowers."

"It's true what Annie told you—she *did* teach herself every software program listed on her resume. She's a natural scholar when something piques her interest."

"I thought she was stretching the truth," Michael admitted. "How long have you known her?"

"Since she was a child. Our wild little Annie. Funniest kid on the block." Miriam set down her coffee. "Maybe *wild* is too strong a word. She was independent, while Toria was shy. Even though Annie was much younger, she stood in as Toria's protector."

"Toria . . ?"

Sadness enveloped Miriam's heart. "Annie's older sister. Their mother died when Annie was three and Toria, nine. The girls and Sam had to make do. You can imagine—Sam's grief nearly did him in. He was trying to keep his greenhouse running while caring for the girls. By the time Annie was eight years old, she knew how to help with dinner and clean the house. She took charge while Toria—well, Toria was always chasing a rainbow."

"Meaning Annie was more sensible?"

Though he wanted to hear more, Miriam pursed her lips. She wasn't sure how to proceed. Annie was close in age to her own children, an adult who valued her privacy. The sad facts of her life weren't meant for public consumption. Now the desire to protect Annie's private life warred with Miriam's need to ensure her success at Rowe.

Michael pulled his legs off the coffee table. "You're leaving something out. I can see it in your eyes."

"I've already said too much." She took a sip of coffee.

"Nothing will change my opinion. I like Annie. She's a great fit for the company."

"Give it a few weeks. Your admiration will increase."

She let the comment linger between them, tantalizing and fresh, like a burst of spring air. Michael's dark brows lowered over his blue eyes, his features sparking with impatience and a boyish curiosity she'd always found endearing. He'd suffered his own share of heartbreak, privately and without self-pity, and it dawned that he wasn't so different from Annie. They both managed to soldier on, even in the most trying situations.

"Annie's sister . . . Michael, she had a lot of issues, especially with men." Miriam chose her words with care. "It started back in high school. Toria bounced from one bad romance to the next. She managed to finish college but the problem worsened. She followed a man to Baltimore and stayed with him for a year. He beat her. The next boyfriend was no better."

Disgust and sympathy mixed on Michael's face. "You're saying she was drawn to abusive men?"

She nodded. "Annie tried to drag her home to Fairfax, to no avail. She *did* manage to help Toria secure a job in Baltimore. The job lasted but there were other men."

"How many?"

"The police aren't sure."

"The police?" He swung his attention to Annie's office. The door was safely closed. Lowering his voice, he asked, "What aren't you telling me?"

There was no simple explanation. Annie had grown up without a mother. She'd buried her father while in her mid-twenties, a time of life when she should've been immersed in school and dating. After Sam's heart attack, she'd struggled to stop the greenhouse from going under, only to have Toria's murder to face just as Green Interior's prospects were beginning to improve. Now she was fighting for permanent custody of a nephew scarred by the life he'd led with his self-serving mother. And Toria—complicated, heartbreaking Toria—had made so many bad choices, Miriam couldn't begin to list them. She didn't expect Michael to understand.

She willed herself to continue. "Eight months ago, Toria was murdered."

Shock competed with the surprise on his face. Just as she'd suspected, he appeared incapable of absorbing the information.

She hurried on. "Toria used cocaine. She was gunned down during a drug buy. The police think one of her lovers might be the assailant. They aren't sure."

The summation of a life lost was crisp and brutal. Michael sank into his chair, his eyes unfocused as he tried to process the information.

Pulling himself together, he asked, "You're saying Annie's sister was a drug addict?"

"She abused a variety of substances. The police found cocaine and pot in her apartment. She also drank to excess. I have no idea how she managed to hang onto her job."

"And Annie?"

"After a few years, she gave up trying to turn Toria's life around. Doing so was too stressful on her father, and she was very protective of Sam. She'd come back from Baltimore after another attempt to talk sense into her sister, and Sam would be a wreck for weeks on end. You can imagine—like any devoted parent, he blamed himself for Toria's reckless choices."

"How was he supposed to control an adult daughter?"

"He couldn't. No parent can. The sorrow was too much. I'm sure it contributed to the heart attack that killed him."

The last of it deepened the compassion in Michael's gaze, and Miriam wondered if she should mention Toria's son. Sooner or later, Michael would learn Annie had a dependent on Rowe's company health plan. Not that he'd notice soon—he rarely visited the HR department.

She was spared making the decision. Annie came out of her office scribbling notes on a pad, her concentration complete. Michael gestured for her to join them, his expression kind and his attention unwavering. The girl's eyes widened as she came to him, as if he were drawing her forward with the crackling intensity of his interest.

The exchange lifted Miriam's spirits. There was something between them, a natural connection between kindred spirits.

Silently she said a prayer. Wasn't it time Annie caught a rainbow for herself?

Chapter 4

"**R**eady for the tour?"

The query sent Annie's cup rattling into the saucer. Michael planned to do the honors? Surely he had more important tasks.

The look of disbelief on Miriam's face confirmed she'd reached the same conclusion. "Now wait one minute. I came in to show Annie around." She began collecting up china like a proper yet peeved hostess. "Michael, you have tons of correspondence to deal with."

"It'll wait." He sent a winning smile that barely dented her displeasure.

"Since when do you enjoy the post of chirpy tour guide? You're not chirpy. Ever."

"Give it a rest." To Annie, he said, "Miriam thinks she's my mother. I have a mother, but I don't keep her on speed dial. I'm not stupid."

"Yeah, yeah, yeah." Miriam sent an impish glance Annie's way. "Usually new employees don't get face-time with Michael for months. He believes in treating each newbie like a *persona non grata* until they've proven their mettle. Or some such nonsense."

Michael frowned but merriment glinted in his eyes. "Don't *you* have a pile of correspondence to deal with?" Her maternal and slightly disapproving tone didn't bother him in the least. "Plow through it while I show Annie around."

With that, he strode out and marched into the corridor. Annie trotted after him. She spied offices with miles of cool grey carpeting and sleek desks nestled in shadow with the computer's screensavers unfurling pretty colors. The lights were on in an office further down, and a Sherlock Holmes impersonator in tweed stood before a light table comparing strips of film. A girl in thick eyeglasses raced down the corridor with an armful of packages. She looked like she was fleeing Genghis Khan and his vicious Mongols.

"We're split between marketing and advertising accounts," Michael was saying. "We develop a number of print ads but have won the most awards for our packaging concepts."

Catching up, Annie matched strides. "Packaging?"

"Companies need more than a good ad campaign to guarantee sales. Take cereal, for example. When you're in the grocery store, you've probably noticed how many brands are packed on the shelves."

"It's hard *not* to notice."

"Packaging influences the brand you buy. Like most consumers, you aren't aware that your decision is based on how successfully the packaging lures you."

The man was having so much fun expounding on a topic he loved, she wavered. Yank him out of fantasyland? A cruel option, but an irresistible one.

"I'm a predictable consumer," she said. "Anything whole grain works for me. Price is my only motivation. If a cereal is on sale it gets my attention."

The remark brought him to a stop in the center of the art department. "You never take in the packaging? The slogans? You only shop price?"

"Basically . . . yes."

"You're a marketing nightmare. You never try new brands?"

On her budget? "I don't."

He looked at her, astonished. "Consumers like you could put me out of business."

She pulled away from the delicious lights warming his eyes. "Cereal," she prodded. "You were saying?"

"That packaging is everything." He led her across the room.

"Let me show you."

Despite her earlier misgivings about working for a temperamental boss, Annie found herself fascinated by Michael—and by the creativity of the art department. Artists' renderings were everywhere—tacked to the walls, lying near the blinking computer monitors, littered across drafting tables. A man was scanning a full-color drawing for a children's cereal. The image popped onto the computer monitor to his right. The bold type screamed, Chocolate Goblins!

In another corner, a beautiful, sixtyish woman with stark white hair drew her pen across a sketch of a rose intertwined with the lettering, *Worthin*. It was an instantly recognizable logo for one of the largest shampoo and hair-coloring firms in the U.S. Once, when it had been on sale, Annie had tried the rich, herb-infused shampoo.

"How many clients do you have?" From what she'd already seen the list was impressive.

"We're just shy of one hundred clients." Michael steered her before the woman. "Most accounts aren't as large as Worthin. Do you like their products?"

"The shampoo is wonderful. Fragrant, but light. Better than perfume."

"The owner, Isabel Worthin, insists on using ecologically sound ingredients. She works with local tribes in South America. An extract doesn't make it into a product unless the plant can be reseeded in its natural environment."

Annie loved horticulture. She knew she'd like Isabel Worthin as well. "You handle all of their packaging?"

"You bet." Michael paused to take in her amazement. "Are you impressed?"

"Who wouldn't be? I thought Rowe Marketing catered to a local clientele here in Virginia." She thought of something else. "Do you have clients outside the U.S.?"

"A few are in Asia, even more in Europe. Most are in the U.S. and Canada. Time spent traveling poses the biggest hassle. Even with electronic design, I have to meet face-to-face with every client at least twice a year."

She pitied him. "You must live out of a suitcase."

The woman working on the Worthin design swiveled to regard them. "Michael, are you planning to introduce us?" She possessed a voice as elegant as Baccarat crystal.

"Forgive me. Lisbon, this is Annie McDaniel, our new Systems Analyst and Girl Friday. Annie, this is Lisbon Tate, our most distinguished artist and the only creative type at the firm you'll *ever* understand."

Lisbon held out fingers polished a subtle shade of pink. "A pleasure," she said.

Annie clasped her hand. "Your artwork is stunning."

Lisbon glanced at Michael with the same easy familiarity Miriam displayed around him. "Have you warned your new Girl Friday about Terrence? I suspect the answer is no." She patted Annie's shoulder. "We'll try to protect you."

The comment didn't reassure. "Who's Terrence?"

Michael cleared up the mystery. "You saw him yesterday—the flashy guy with the mustache? He was screaming while you performed CPR on the computers."

The man had reminded Annie of a skinny rooster decked out in high fashion and far too much jewelry. "Should I worry about him?"

"I'd pray," Lisbon said. She reconsidered. "Or try voodoo. I'm thinking about making one of those dolls and buying straight pins."

"I think I'll just avoid of him." It seemed the wisest strategy.

"Good luck," Michael said. He nudged her back into the corridor. "Tour's not over yet. Let's visit the copy department and a few other areas."

With a shrug, she followed him out. It didn't make much sense to worry. How much trouble could one artist be?

* * *

On her first day at Rowe Marketing, Annie never had the chance to harbor a bad case of nerves. There wasn't time.

The firm's artists and copywriters used a dizzying array of software. Programs were selected based on a single user's preference. If a program wasn't compatible with other software, who cared?

Problems more bizarre abounded. For reasons she had yet to decipher, the interoffice e-mail neglected to purge deleted messages between co-workers. Outdated mail reappeared with irritating frequency, and the Internet service was just plain flaky. Sometimes messages got through. At other times mail bound for Rowe Marketing returned to the sender as undeliverable. Strangely, every single piece of Spam got through.

Angry clients were up in arms about incoming viruses. No wonder—Rowe's staff downloaded so much junk, the computers resembled a hospital emergency room during flu season. Outbound attachments had mucked up client computers in Chicago, San Francisco, London and Paris. Inside Rowe, the writers in the copy department refused mail from anyone in art. Shipping, fed up with the entire affair fiasco, demanded printouts in lieu of email.

Sorting everything out would take time.

Annie spent the morning jumping from computer to computer cleaning hard drives. By the time she tiptoed through Michael's palatial digs and hunkered down in her own office, she found the floor littered with technical manuals. Young Herman, desperate for leadership, had located every tome at the firm.

Where to begin? Smoothing down her skirt, she sat on the floor in as ladylike a pose as possible and began digging through the mess.

Towers of clunky manuals soon filled the floor. Creating a sense of order reminded Annie of the best years with her father, before her sister Toria had reached puberty and sent their lives into chaos. Sam McDaniel might have owned a greenhouse, but he'd cultivated a scholar's love of learning with equal relish. Random facts, books checked out from the Fairfax library, articles gleaned in *Scientific American* or *The Economist*—he'd treated the amusing anecdote and deep theory with equal respect.

The house Annie now owned still teemed with bookshelves neatly arranged and dusted. The crates brimming with magazines were long—now, without her father to share responsibility for Green Interiors, she'd let the subscriptions expire. These days the wooden crates Dad had painted in calming earth tones were stuffed full of Dillon's toys.

By the time she'd finished sorting manuals, her back ached. In Michael's office, Terrence Kholer whined about one of Rowe's clients, a national bakery headquartered in New York. From the sounds of it, he was having a full-blown temper tantrum.

No wonder Lisbon had warned her about working with

Terrence. Every time Annie appeared in the art department, he flitted like a pesky fly on a pound of manure. She'd try swatting him away with soft words then stern comments. Nothing worked. At wit's end, she'd tried to ignore his complaints.

She'd already discovered more useless software and files on his iMac than on any other computer, much of the junk pilfered from the Internet. Terrence was a modern-day pirate sailing the electronic seas in search of bounty in the form of graphics, music, and the occasional movie. Convincing him to delete the mess might start a war.

Running from the thought, Annie chose a manual at random and began reading.

Chapter 5

"Three weeks and counting. Are you planning to read them all?"

At the sound of Michael's voice, Annie shut the book. She'd been reclined on her office couch with her shoes kicked off and her temples throbbing.

Most of the staff was gone for the night, and Miriam had offered to take Dillon to a movie. The invitation of babysitting gave ample time to work late. Annie had jumped at the chance.

Yawning, she sat up. "I have to read them all, Michael."

He loosened his tie. "You'll go blind, reading all that stuff."

His attention lingered too long, like a caress tingling across her skin. "Why are *you* here so late?" Unable to forestall her curiosity, she added, "Isn't someone waiting, a wife or a girlfriend? Someone who's irritated because she made reservations and you're late?"

The blunt line of questioning seemed to please him. "There's no one waiting. Not now."

"Meaning there was someone recently?"

A combative and very masculine air surrounded him. "What about you? You're not married. Is there a boyfriend?"

"There was, two years ago. I sent him back to the wife he'd

divorced. They sent an invite to the nuptials, but it seemed bad form to attend."

"Nice work. You're more efficient than eHarmony."

"I give it my best shot."

"So your time is your own?"

She considered Dillon, a topic she still hadn't broached with her new boss. Was it superstition? She rarely discussed the custody battle with anyone but Miriam for fear she'd hurt her chances of making Dillon her own.

Trying for a light note, she said, "I lead a full life. A boyfriend will have to wait."

A silence full of promise lengthened between them. The air crackled with an expectancy that sent hope whispering through her heart. No, it wasn't sensible to consider dating Michael. They'd spent the last weeks engaged in a subtle flirtation while doing their best to disregard their growing attraction. By some unspoken agreement, they never lingered too long and kept conversations short. Until now.

Steering back to safe ground, Michael asked, "How's the greenhouse?"

"Making due with my squad of teenage helpers. By the way, thanks for giving me Thursdays off. Your understanding is appreciated."

"I don't understand. Not that I'd trample your father's memory." At her questioning look, he added, "Miriam tells all. You ran Green Interiors with your father before his death. Nice of you to keep his dream alive even if it *is* at my expense."

She matched his playful tone. "You get your money's worth the other four days of the work week."

"Nothing has crashed since your hiring. You're doing something right."

Stretching, she shook the stiffness from her shoulders. "I'm doing *everything* right. Ask your staff to do the housekeeping chores, okay? Any dolt can run the program no matter what they tell you privately."

"When it comes to technology, they're your employees, not mine." His pirate's grin nearly took her hostage. "If you demand obedience, send out a memo."

"May the memo contain threats?"

"You bet. Send the biggest threat to Terrence. Something

mentioning death by torture."

"Every time I go near his computer, he gives me a hard time. Yesterday he chased me out of the art department. Something about a deadline and how I was destroying his flow."

"Don't let him intimidate you. Terrence is a handful but he's also brilliant."

"What about his sidekick, Violet? Her violet hair is a stand-out."

"Don't even go there. You've never seen her cry. Not yet, anyway."

"That bad?"

"Like a wolf howling on the prairie. It unnerves Bill and the other writers."

She laughed. They shared a quiet moment before Michael started out. "Don't work too hard." He studied her for a moment. "How long *are* you staying?"

She dropped the manual back into her lap. "As long as it takes."

***

With flourish, Miriam placed the platter of brownies on the kitchen counter. "I love the first day of summer vacation," she announced.

At the stove, Annie flipped another hamburger. "Yeah, but I'm on to you. Summer gives you three months to get the neighborhood kids sugared up. They know school's out by the cartloads of chocolate chips and cherry sprinkles trailing from your house."

"I like to bake. Kids like to beg." Miriam held her palms skyward. "What else can I do with my time?"

"Haul goodies to your daughter's house?"

"I've given up on my grandchildren. They've thrown me over for cell phones and FaceBook." Snagging a brownie, Miriam asked, "Anything new with the custody hearing?"

"No date scheduled yet. I have begun the home study's paperwork."

Last week Annie had received a packet of forms from Pete Johnson, the social worker at New Beginnings Adoption Agency.

It was the first step in her attempt to adopt Dillon. No father was named on her nephew's birth certificate, making him eligible for adoption. Once the home study was complete a hearing would decide permanent custody.

In Baltimore, Tom and Dianne England were also completing a home study to demonstrate their willingness to parent Dillon. Annie's late sister had first met Dianne England when they'd both worked in the secretarial pool at Bing's, a small department store in Maryland. After Toria's murder, they'd hired counsel to battle for the right to make Dillon their son.

Trying to keep the anxiety from her voice, Annie said, "The Englands are still petitioning for visitation."

"For heaven's sake, why? The judge granted you several months with Dillon. Why don't they wait for their day in court?"

"They're determined."

"Are you worried?"

The possibility of losing Dillon was difficult to contemplate. He was her flesh and blood, more her son now than her nephew. He'd become the best part of her life, and they'd begun to build a life together. A five year old couldn't process the rupture in his world caused by his mother's murder, but Dillon was making progress in fits and starts. He wept less frequently. He loved his kindergarten teacher, Sister Bernadette, and his irrepressibly cheerful friend, Chip. True, Dillon's attempts at eye contact were rare, but he'd let her help him into pajamas on those rare days when he was too overcome with exhaustion to refuse. She'd gather him close to inhale the scent of his just-washed hair and brush her knuckles across his soft skin. Those moments gave her the strength to keep fighting.

Drawing from the reverie, she said, "I'm more angry than worried. If I'd forged a relationship with Dillon while Toria was still alive, I wouldn't have to fight for him. I can see why the Englands think he should become their son."

Miriam planted her hands on her hips. "You *did* try. Toria cut off contact right after Dillon was born. She didn't even attend Sam's funeral."

"I should've tried harder, especially after Dad died."

"You're too hard on yourself, dear."

Annie turned off the stove. She glanced out the window at Dillon and Chip, running in circles across the backyard. They'd built a tepee with gardening poles and brown paper grocery bags. Dillon released a rare wave of laughter.

Miriam smiled at the impromptu game of Cowboys and Indians. "Amazing, isn't it? Time may heal all wounds, even for Dillon. Having a best friend doesn't hurt, either."

Annie fetched dishes from the cupboard. "He *is* happy with Chip."

"And with you, even if you're too blind to see it."

"He doesn't flinch as much if I touch him. Progress, right?"

"Your patience is paying off."

She placed the hamburgers on plates, considering. "My attorney, Will? He says I shouldn't feel bad about the Englands. But I do. Why won't they agree to an open adoption? Can't they let Dillon love me and them as well?"

"I admire the sentiment, but you're too generous. Just because they were willing to bail your sister out of a thousand scrapes doesn't mean they were close to Dillon."

"They've known him since he was a baby."

Miriam waved the comment away. "The Englands have every intention of taking him away from you. Don't you dare forget it."

How could she? Tom and Dianne England wanted to erase every vestige of Dillon's complicated past—everything, including her. The documents filed with the Virginia Court made their intentions clear. If they won custody, she'd never see Dillon again.

Miriam sighed with frustration. "If you've decided to wallow in guilt over the Englands then tell me this. Does Dillon miss them? Does he mention them?"

"No, never. When the court cut off their visitation, I was sure he'd be upset. He wasn't."

"You see? He doesn't miss them because he's settled in a new life with you."

The comment gave hope. "I do want what's best for him." She put the plates on the table, stopped. "He's been through so much. I just want to keep him safe and prove to him that I'll always love him."

Miriam dug condiments from the fridge. "The boy loves you too even if he doesn't know how to express his feelings. He also has Chip, a fun, engaging playmate, and me, his Nana Miriam. He has St. Mary's and a host of wonderful teachers. Annie, he has a whole new world full of people to love and protect him."

"But I can't offer him a father." Despite Miriam's optimism, Annie knew her single status could influence the custody battle's outcome. "Tom England has me over a barrel on that one."

"True, but consider another possibility. Dillon may wish to forget the Englands. He'll always grieve the loss of his mother, but they *are* tied to a past he may wish to forget."

"I've never looked at it that way."

"You never think about the past at all. I'm still waiting for you to discuss Toria's murder. You can't keep your emotions bottled up forever."

"I'm not ready yet." The great, lumbering guilt that slept inside her stirred. If she engaged in a discussion, she'd have to face a world of regret. Escaping the possibility, she took napkins from the holder and buried the memories deep in her heart. "Once I'm done battling the Englands in court, I'll think about Toria's murder."

"No, you won't. My dear, you avoid any topic sure to bruise your emotions."

The observation nudged the hard seed lodged in Annie's heart. No, she didn't want to examine her deepest emotions. She'd lost her father to a heart attack and Toria to a murder tied to her poor choice in men or drugs or both. She was at risk of losing Dillon to a Baltimore couple better equipped to parent him. If she dared to explore her emotions, she'd drown in despair.

Miriam appraised her with motherly concern. "Annie, I've known you all your life. I knew Toria, too. You aren't just grieving—you're angry with her. Heaven knows you have reason."

Annie held her hand up like a traffic cop. "Please, just stop. Okay?"

"Well, aren't you?"

"I'm not angry with Toria."

"C'mon, now. From childhood right up to Dillon, she always left you holding the bag. She bounced through life breaking things—mostly her own heart—and relied on you to pick up the pieces. Here you are now, trying to heal her son. Dillon deserved a stable home, but what did he get? A mother who abused drugs and paraded the worst sort of men through his life. She dumped him with babysitters and the Englands. The boy deserved better. Doesn't that make you angry?"

Pain darted through Annie's chest, swift and startling. "Don't do this, Miriam. I'm not ready."

"I'm here when you *are* ready."

"I know." Needing to drop the subject, she called the boys in.

The women ate in companionable silence. Chip and Dillon chattered on about the adventures they'd planned for the long summer break, including Cowboy Camp at the end of June and Icky Science Camp in August. They held a burping contest then competed to see who could whistle the highest notes. The noise cleared every bird from the trees out back.

After the last speck of food disappeared, Miriam fetched the brownies. "You may each have two," she said as the boys lunged for the plate.

"Nana Miriam, you're the best!" Chip said.

"Thank you, child."

"I never get stuff like this at home. My big brothers are hogs." Gooey crumbs framed his mouth. "I bet you make better brownies than my mom. But don't tell her. I don't want her to feel bad."

Miriam drew a finger across her lips. "It's our secret. I don't want to hurt your mother's feelings, either."

"She's good at stuff like meatballs."

"I'll bet they're the best meatballs in the land," Annie said.

"They are. Hey!" Chip grabbed Dillon's arm and shook hard. "What can your mom do?"

The query brought the women's heads up. It was clear Chip had forgotten that Annie was Dillon's aunt—not his mother. And he wasn't the only one who'd forgotten.

It seemed Dillon had too, as he scrunched up his face to ponder the question.

After much thought, he stuck his hands into his curls and rubbed lightly. "She does this," he said, referring to how Annie stroked his hair during those rare moments he allowed her near. "It's nice. I like it more than ice cream, even."

Tears sprouted in Annie's eyes. She wrestled the urge to nestle Dillon close. He looked adorable tousling his own curls.

She let the moment pass. It was too soon for full-out displays of affection.

Hugs would have to wait.

Chapter 6

Striding into the elevator, Michael pushed the button for the fifth floor. The doors slid shut, and the elevator hurtled skyward with a *swoosh* of sound. He went through the day's mental checklist. It was Wednesday, hump day, but it wasn't yet seven A.M.

Art needed to finish the new avian logo for Beele Electronics before transmitting to the company's headquarters in San Francisco. Other clients required TLC. Nicholas DiRameo, the New York bakery king, was growing restless awaiting the new packaging concepts for the Giant Chips cookie line. Michael made a mental note to call this morning and beg for more time.

In the darkened reception area, he paused. The door to his office was ajar. Inside, lights blazed.

What the hell? He found Annie before his office bookshelves with two software manuals cradled in her arms. She was looking at the assortment of framed photographs set upon the shelves.

"You travel a lot," she said.

"An understatement." Michael stopped before he got too close. Her floral perfume was much too appealing. "What time did you get in?"

"Six-thirty, I think."

"Too early, I think."

"I don't work Thursdays," she reminded him. "If it's one of those days when I have the opportunity to arrive early, I do. Is it all right to come in before everyone else?"

"No problem. Workaholics warm the cockles of my heart." He followed her line of vision back to the photograph she'd been studying. "Golf outing with the guys. Palm Springs, two years ago."

In the shot, he stood with three other men on the eighteenth hole. It had been a great trip. Sun, golf and on several nights, a few too many beers.

She lingered on the next shelf, and he liked the wonder revealed in her careful movements. "And this?" She picked up a photograph in a chunky oak frame.

"Whitewater rafting, Colorado. Last year." Enjoying himself, he added, "Only one friend came along. High adventure makes the other guys gutless. They blame it on their wives, but trust me. They're cowards."

"Whitewater rafting *does* sound dangerous." She picked up a silver frame. "What about this one? You're alone, Michael. Did you lose the last buddy?"

"Chile, three years ago." Any reminder of his divorce was a sure prescription for the blues, but he refused to dwell on his divorce. Besides, the trip through Chile's Los Lagos Region had been spectacular. "I hiked near the Osorno Volcano. Beautiful country. Camping and fishing in Lake Todos los Santos."

"You traveled alone?"

"You bet."

Giving into the temptation, he surveyed her profile. She'd worn her hair down today and it pooled light around her shoulders. Same grey blazer she wore much too often but she'd paired it with a pink skirt he hadn't seen before. Not that today's choice mattered. If Annie wore a sack, she'd still look stunning.

He motioned to the manuals in her arms. "Do you ever take a break? You do, on occasion, go on vacation. Don't you?"

She let out a throaty laugh, making the hairs on the back of his neck jump to attention. The tenor of her voice reminded him of a rich Pinot Noir, his favorite wine.

"Not often," she admitted. "I've visited Florida. Washington D.C. is a no-brainer because it's close. Nothing better than spending the day on The National Mall checking out the museums."

"That's the extent of your travels?" She didn't get out much.

"You, on the other hand, have been to the ends of the earth. I'm jealous."

"Are you?"

"Who wouldn't be?"

"Most people." *Most happy people.* He discarded the thought before it found a way into his heart.

She wagged another frame in front of his nose, and he leaned close. "Paris, the summer I graduated from college," he supplied. "A graduation gift from my parents."

Her eyes grew dreamy. "I'd love to travel the world. Maybe someday, when my life is more settled."

The wistful declaration started his pulse thrumming. She looked undeniably feminine, with her eyes distant and her mouth pursed. Standing this close was dangerous. Her alluring perfume was making him dizzy. The now familiar warning thumped through his ribcage. *Danger! Danger!* Ceding to common sense, he strode to his desk.

Following his cue, Annie set down the last photograph and started for her own office. "See ya." She gave a flirty wave then disappeared inside.

After she'd gone, he tried to concentrate on work. It was never a good idea to think too much about Annie. At least not in the flowers, dinner, I'd-like-to-see-you-in-the-buff way he'd been doing lately. Sexual fantasies were natural but, hell, he'd picked the wrong target for his desires. Annie was an exemplary employee. The staff loved her. He needed to think about raising her salary instead of fantasizing about what she looked like in the raw.

No wonder women think men are animals. We have sex on the brain.

Michael grimaced. *Maybe not all men. Just this animal.*

He caught himself grinning, cursed, then booted up his computer. Any number of interesting and attractive businesswomen in Fairfax would happily fill out his social calendar. His new star employee was off limits.

At 9 AM, Miriam entered. "Terrence is wrestling with insecurity today." She placed a steaming cup of brew before him.

"Thanks for the tip." Michael took a sip, frowned. "Where is he?"

"On his way in."

"Already? The day's just begun."

Fists clenched, she straightened her stout frame. The posture made her look like a linebacker for the New York Jets. Not that he'd tell her. It was luck enough his gatekeeper guarded his domain jealously.

"Should I keep him out?" she asked.

Michael rubbed his chin. "If you try, will it get physical? Planning to knock Terrence to the ground? Anything of that nature?"

"Of course not!"

"Then to hell with it. Send him in."

Miriam sucked in an impatient breath. "Are we in one of our moods today? If so, I must know immediately."

It made him crazy how she implied he had the emotional balance of a kid in puberty.

"Miriam, I am not a 'we'. You make it sound like I arrived with my evil twin."

"There *are* two of you—Michael-the-valiant and Michael-the-moody." She pursed her lips with displeasure, but mirth flickered in her eyes. "So? Which is it today?"

He let out a curse, which started her blinking. "I'm fine, trusted gatekeeper. On top of the world. Ready to sing show tunes, in fact. Satisfied?"

"No." She headed out. "But it'll have to do. I'll send Terrence in."

A squabble broke out in the reception area. A shuffle of feet, then Terrence flung himself into the room.

Today he wore purple velvet pants reminiscent of Mick Jagger in his prime. Terrence's white shirt was so snug, his rib cage made a wave pattern down to his belly ring. Heavy gel kept his hair stiff and straight as it skimmed his shoulders like chunks of yellow cardstock. The mustache he was proud of also wore a hint of gel, but his heart-shaped beard did not. Michael wondered if his lead artist had topped off the look with a touch of lipstick.

"Michael! We *must* discuss DiRameo Cookies. I'm at wit's end!" Terrence gestured wildly, his gem-studded fingers catching the sunlight.

Squinting to save his eyesight, Michael nodded with feigned

compassion. "What's the problem, sport?"

"I can't decide on the soul of this line of cookies. Is it the comfort food from day's past when Mother greeted you at the door with baked goods?"

"Not my mother." A retired surgeon from The Cleveland Clinic, she now lived on some of Florida's finest golf courses. "Get to the point. I don't have all day."

The artist placed two drawings before him. "Which do you prefer? I can't decide."

Michael studied one then the other. The first comp had a retro feel blended with a smart, modern typeface. The second was a departure from DiRameo's current brand but with appealing splashes of neon pink framing the logo.

"They're both good. Hell, they're both great." He shrugged. "Why make me choose? This is your area of expertise."

Terrence went still—an odd sight for a man with the metabolism of a ferret. "Don't you *want* to pick a favorite?"

"How can I? This may be the best work you've ever done." He drew the words out like a warm blanket for Terrence to wrap himself in. "I'm proud to show both concepts to Nick DiRameo."

"You don't *despise* them?" Terrence clasped his hands together like a kid who'd won sweets for life. "They're good?"

"They're great." Michael paused before dropping the bomb. "Now, come up with the other designs. We need four concepts."

"We do?"

They'd danced down this path countless times. It seemed a sadistic ritual they both craved for differing, if mysterious reasons. Michael knew the drill. First, stroke Terrence's ego. Then pound him into submission until he created The Holy Four.

"How many reminders do you need? We always show clients four concepts." Terrence made a strange mewling sound, and Michael added, "Listen up. I'm in a good space. Don't piss me off. Come up with two more concepts. Put your nose to the grindstone and work."

"But four concepts! You ask too much of the muse."

"Screw the muse. If he misses the deadline, I'll rip off his wings."

Terrence flapped his arms. "Must you resort to threats? Do you think it'll help my flow this close to deadline? It won't!"

From the doorway, Miriam snorted. "Terrence, shut up." To

Michael, she said, "Bill is next. Shall I send him in?"

***

Annie finished typing the memo and logged on the Internet. She tried firing up her concentration. Total fail, and she stared at the computer screen with exhaustion. Voices streamed in and out of Michael's office.

Recalling the photographs she'd discovered on his bookshelves, she marveled at all the locales he'd visited. It was all terribly exotic and faintly romantic. He was very much a man of the world.

He was also kind. Several times in the last month he bought the entire staff lunch—a refreshing change from her brown bag lunches. Last week he'd instructed Bitsy to order a cake large enough for a wedding. It had warmed Annie to join the others in the cafeteria to sing Happy Birthday to every employee born in June.

The man had more marvels than a magician. When Lisbon complained of a backache, a masseuse arrived to give chair massages. The refreshing scents of eucalyptus and spearmint hung in the air for hours. On the anniversary of the death of Miriam's husband, a dozen red roses appeared on her desk. No one knew what was written on the card, but Michael's thoughtfulness had propelled a grateful Miriam into his arms.

Remembering, Annie rolled a pencil back and forth. The man had decency down to a science. He was also tall. She had to crane her neck just to look up into eyes so dark a blue they resembled the ocean at dusk. Worst of all, he wore the most intriguing cologne, some combination of citrus and sandalwood. Finding excuses to stand near him was becoming an addiction. He smelled downright delicious.

Funny, how life worked out. Given his rude behavior during her job interview, she'd expected to hate him.

Annie bit down on her lower lip. The problem was, Michael didn't think too highly of *her*. In private chats he'd cut the conversation short—something he never did with the other employees. The man actually gave some of them bear hugs. Oh, she understood the reasons. They'd started at mild flirtation but she'd moved on to an adolescent crush on the boss. It was an understandable predicament for a healthy thirty-two-year old woman who'd forsaken dating until life settled down. Between parenting Dillon and work at Rowe and Green Interiors, there wasn't time for a relationship.

Maybe he's having second thoughts about hiring me. If she was wallowing in a schoolgirl crush a decade too late, it was time to nip it in the bud. They'd merged into an effective team. It was enough.

Returning to work, she gritted her teeth. Then why worry?

***

Hours later, she was still trying to shake off the blues as Dillon and Chip played in the living room.

Wooden blocks covered the cramped space. A haphazardly built castle, complete with a moat, sat in the middle of the room. Action figures fought a pitched battle against the plastic farm animals she'd purchased at the church's used toy roundup. The boys had snatched her pink hairbrush from the bathroom for a makeshift slide on the side of the moat. A plastic cow perched beside it, evidently to draw courage before squaring off before Luke Skywalker.

"Who's winning?" She dried her hands on the dishtowel as she approached.

The boys, deep in their fantasy world, didn't respond. Finally Chip's head lifted. "We're saving the princess," he said. "The cow's evil."

"Really? He looks like a decent fellow."

"Oh, he's a bad guy." Chip shimmied on his belly to the side of the moat. "He captured the princess. Luke Skywalker will save her."

"What princess?" The two plastic pigs and three goats beside the castle probably didn't count. Best guess? The farm animals were soldiers.

"Right there, Mrs. McDaniel. See?"

Chip dipped his nose behind the castle. A crayon drawing of a girl with blonde hair was stuffed inside a window. Annie reveled in a moment's pride—the artistry was familiar.

"We didn't have a real princess," Chip said. "Dillon made a picture."

"It's beautiful! Dillon, when did you draw this?"

"Last night."

"While we were at the greenhouse?" She'd repotted several fig trees. He'd been content to play at a table amidst the greenery.

Dillon moved the plastic goats into a tighter formation. "Yep."

"It's the best drawing of a princess I've ever seen." She hesitated then gave into the urge to tousle the curls crowning his head. After a few precious seconds, he crawled out of reach.

Returning to the battle, he walked Luke Skywalker up the hairbrush to face the evil cow. Scooting in from behind, Chip grabbed the cow and began making snarling noises. Chip let Luke Skywalker win. The cow hurtled through the air, landing with a plunk at her feet. She picked it up and handed it over.

"Thanks," Chip said. "He's only bad this time. Next time, he gets to be good."

"Who'll be the bad guy?"

"Oh, Dillon's gonna draw something. Right, Dillon?"

"I like to draw stuff."

They bumped shoulders and Chip said, "You're real good at drawing. Better'n anyone."

"You are," Annie chimed in.

The compliment didn't alter Dillon's flat expression. She longed for a real connection but he was still more ghost than boy. At least he enjoyed playtime with Chip, who'd become a guardian angel, concocting games or chattering nonstop when Dillon seemed trapped in silence. Chip had already done more to heal Dillon than all the doctors, teachers and Annie, combined.

She retraced her steps toward the kitchen and the stew simmering on the stove. "Give a shout when you boys want a snack, okay?"

"Hey!" Chip said. "Don't you want to know who the princess is?"

"Oh. Sure. How foolish of me." She recalled Chip had a crush on Beatrice, a classmate at St. Mary's. "Is it a girl whose name begins with a B?"

"Not even close." He swatted air. "C'mon, Mrs. McDaniel. Try harder. *I* didn't draw the picture. *Dillon* did."

The emotion churning on Dillon's face seemed a burden. He lowered his head to the floor and began rolling like a log down a hill. Curious, she returned to him.

"Who is it?" she asked.

He rolled back toward the castle, and Chip tackled him. "Go on, Dillon—tell her!"

Dillon's gaze lifted and found hers. The wonderment on his face snatched the breath from her lips. She'd never seen him look so happy.

His voice, when it came, was as gentle as rain. "It's you," he said. "You're the princess, Annie."

Chapter 7

Becoming Dillon's princess gave Annie hope that his attitude was improving. Yet throughout the following week, her mood remained low.

Working two jobs became a grind of missed sleep, slapdash parenting and general grogginess. As she ran through another program, Annie wondered if she should apply for Social Security. She felt about ninety years old.

It was a rare good fortune that Dillon never taxed her energy. With a playmate across the street and a summer bursting with activities, he seemed content to share a quick meal or spend thirty minutes at the playground while she sat nearby in a stupor. Chip's mother Shelley organized a weekly slumber party for the boys, and Miriam spoiled Dillon with trips to the amusement park. In lieu of rest, Annie used the time to stay on top of her workload at Rowe.

The obvious solution—close down Green Interiors—wasn't worth contemplating. She couldn't bear to give up a business her father had spent a lifetime nurturing. Which left the obvious question: if she won custody of Dillon, did she want to continue at Michael's company?

She stifled a yawn. *Lord help me, I do*. Despite the long hours she loved the job. Add in the medical benefits, something Green

Interiors wasn't yet profitable enough to afford, and she *was* in a bind. The two-job carnival act wouldn't end soon.

With newfound determination, she launched another program. It was after six P.M. but she was still mired in updates. With Terrence downloading half the attachments in the universe, the computers were always at risk of infection.

Terrence. Now there was someone she'd like to stuff into Miriam's oven. Right next to her latest batch of brownies.

"What's so funny?"

Startled, she snapped out of the reverie. Michael stood before her desk with his blazer slung over his shoulder. She hadn't heard him enter.

Logging off, she gave her full attention. "I thought you'd left."

He raised his briefcase like a kid at Show and Tell. "Left and returned. I forgot a report." He frowned. "Why are you still working?"

"Terrence pulled down a playlist for his iPod. It came from a site in Thailand. I'm beating back the bugs."

"It might be easier to beat Terrence. Try a baseball bat."

"Don't tempt me."

"Go home, Annie. It's been a long day."

"I will . . . after I secure the gates."

Muttering under his breath, Michael took the mouse from right under her hand. The gesture was nearly intimate. For the briefest interlude, he rested his hand on hers. It was enough to send electricity whipping up her arm. Would he also shut down the computer to drive his point home? She wasn't sure, but she wished he'd step away before her pulse went any higher.

He read the emotions warring for prominence on her face. Irritation, amusement, lust. Fatal attraction at the office, he mused. If they were both infected, he hoped one of her programs could purge it.

"Come on," he said, trying for a cool note. He backed off. "It's quitting time." Recently he'd begun perspiring like an ape if he got too close.

"I'm fine, Michael. Don't wait for me."

"If I don't, you'll make a night of it. Tomorrow I'll find you catatonic on the floor. Every last computer will purr like a Ferrari but I'll have to haul you to the ER."

"An exaggeration."

He crossed his arms with faint impatience. "*Why* do you work so hard? If you're under the impression I'm a slave driver, you need to cultivate better powers of observation. You've been here for more than a month and haven't let up. Enough with the heroics."

"I only work four days. I have to work harder when I'm here."

"Not this hard." Swinging away, he paused before the couch. Outside the setting sun turned the countryside to flame. "You're impossible to peg. Most of the time you're quirky and approachable. But you're damn stubborn too."

"All right, I'll go." She closed the program and came around the desk. Just as he'd done a moment ago, she kept a safe distance.

Were they equally bitten? He weighed the possibility as she swept up her purse and licked her lips, all the while casting glances that pinged off his chest without reaching his eyes. She *was* nervous. Which, ridiculously, shot him full of adrenaline. God, he was a fool. The last thing he needed was an office romance. Or maybe it was the first thing, since he'd never had one.

Stick to the rule. No sexual encounters with a woman on staff.

The mandate barely cleared his brain when his imagination skirted the edict. A flurry of enticing images followed. Like ditching the stale conversation and kissing her. Or running his palms over the tiny hairs on the damp skin of her throat. If touching her was part of the plan, he was all in.

He didn't shake free of the daydream fast enough. The titillating content of his musings sizzled through the air. On some unconscious level Annie picked it up. Her movements became jerky as she retrieved her blazer from the couch. She tangled one sleeve while thrusting her arm down the other, imprisoning herself.

Grinning, he took hold of the blazer's lapels. "Need help getting dressed?" he said with the finesse of a drunkard. His mouth went as dry as the Sudan.

"Sometimes." A smiled etched onto her lips. "Thanks for your help."

"Anytime.*" All of the time would be nice.* "Ready to go?"

"I'm forgetting something." She lunged for the desk, nearly tripped, and came back up with her briefcase.

A pheromone charged silence accompanied them on the ride

down in the elevator. They did their level best to find fascination in the floor, the ceiling, and each other's shoes. If the damn lift broke between the fifth and ground floors, he was pretty sure they'd strip down to their skin before a repairman arrived. Fighting off the fantasy, Michael dredged up the memory of last year's root canal.

The doors slid open and he asked, "Why *do* you need Thursdays off? Can't you do the greenhouse thing on weekends?"

"I make deliveries on Thursdays. Most of my clients aren't around on weekends. Law firms, accountants—you know. I use the weekends for tasks inside the greenhouse."

He stood back to let her pass. "Meaning you're on the go seven days a week?"

"Usually."

"Your body isn't a machine, Annie. You should take better care of yourself." When her mouth curved wryly, he added, "Close Green Interiors. Sell out to a competitor. You'll do better at my firm."

"It's not that simple."

"Sure it is." He pulled open the door. She waltzed through and he added, "Your work ethic is commendable. Kudos for keeping your father's dream alive. I get it. Take your emotions out of the equation and look at the numbers. Rowe pays better. You have benefits and a company retirement plan. This isn't a hard decision."

"Michael, my parents opened the greenhouse right after they married. I lost my father three years ago. My mother? All I have of her are a few memories inside the greenhouse while she worked with the plants."

"It's a greenhouse, not a monument."

"Shouldn't we protect the things we hold dear? Old photographs, a quilt your grandmother made by hand—a greenhouse your parents built?" The explanation drove anguish into her eyes. "It doesn't matter how tired I get, or frustrated. Entering Green Interiors is like finding shelter. I draw strength from every happy memory of a time when we were a real family."

Evidently he was mistaken. The greenhouse was a monument, or perhaps a talisman. Were the memories of a happier past a refuge in a difficult life?

"Point taken." She hadn't mentioned her sister, recently murdered. She'd lost Toria and her parents. She'd lost enough.

"I'm out of line. Forgive me."

A troubling silence accompanied her across the lot. "There's nothing to forgive." She stopped before a beat up truck he hadn't realized was hers. "How could you have known?"

He tried to dredge up a light farewell. The conversation had grown heavy and he didn't want to leave her upset. But his mind emptied out as he noticed the lock of hair clinging to her cheek. He hooked it behind her ear. The gesture wasn't standard operating procedure, but nothing about his feelings was within normal parameters. Another reason to end the cozy interlude.

"Have a good night, Annie." The smile on his face felt flimsy and raw. "Come in late tomorrow. I'll pretend not to notice. You need the rest."

"I'll try."

"I'm not asking—it's an order. Sleep in."

"Okay."

From over his shoulder he saw her trace the path on her cheek he'd just touched, as if memorizing the precise journey his fingers had taken. She seemed flustered, the color rising on her skin and her mouth hinting at pleasure.

It was victory enough.

Chapter 8

On Jefferson Parkway, Will Blaine's law firm was located in a classically southern outdoor mall. A fountain gurgled before the man-made pond. Window boxes brimming with red geraniums framed the picture window. Shifting the truck into park, Annie took a moment to enjoy their cheerful color. She felt alert and well rested for the first time in recent memory. Twice in the last week she'd taken Michael up on his offer and had slept in. Work hadn't suffered, and everyone on staff appeared relieved the resident tech head was feeling better.

Reflecting on her conversation with Michael in the parking lot, she suffered a tinge of guilt. He wanted her to make a permanent commitment to his firm. She'd hated disappointing him. It had been obvious that he'd assumed the greenhouse was a dying business. She'd neglected to reveal that Green Interiors was bringing in an increasing stream of cash sure to make the business solvent in a year or two. Once she reached the goal, she'd have no choice but to let one of her jobs go. No matter how much she'd come to love the staff and her duties, she wouldn't choose to stay at Rowe.

Beside her, Dillon popped the last French fry into his mouth. "Are you finished?" she asked. "What about your milkshake?"

He belched. "All done." He remained serene despite the evidence of his bodily functions.

Unbuckling his seat belt, she thought of something else. "You were a big help during last night's plant deliveries."

"I like carrying stuff for you." Pride laced his words. "Your plants are nice. They smell good."

"I'm glad you approve, munchkin."

On a whim she'd stopped by the Wilsons' house. He'd agreed to cut short playtime with Chip to accompany her on a last-minute delivery. Without complaint Dillon carried the lighter hanging baskets into the accounting firm and seemed happy to pitch in. For his efforts he'd received a treat of chocolates from the freckle-faced receptionist.

Annie had earned her own treat—the knowledge her nephew enjoyed making the rounds with her. Never before had he chosen her company over Chip's.

Helping him from the truck, she skirted around the rectangular sign set artfully in the strip of sod bordering the sidewalk, *William Blaine, Attorney. Family Law Specialist.*

She didn't have an appointment. Will, however, never seemed to mind if she popped in.

In the lobby, legal files stood in stacks on an Arts & Crafts desk. The row of filing cabinets to the left gave the reception area a cramped appearance. There was no one in sight. A common occurrence—Will's secretary was eight months pregnant.

Dillon placed his hands on his hips. "Mr. Will! Where are you?"

"In here," came the light-hearted reply.

Together they sauntered down the hallway. They found Will at his desk with his glasses perched on the tip of his nose. He was reading a legal tome. Other books, papers and pads covered the desk.

"I was in the neighborhood making deliveries," she said. "Thought I'd stop by."

Will snapped the book shut, sending a plume of dust skyward. "Actually, there is news." He smiled at Dillon. "Hey, sport. Want the toy box?"

Dillon stepped forward, hesitated. "Okay."

"It's in the corner of the reception area right next to the shelves."

The boy sensed Annie's regard and stared at his tennis shoes. "Can I play out there?"

She smiled. "Go right ahead."

He trotted out, and Will said, "Did you receive the material from New Beginnings? We need to get going on the home study."

"I have the forms, but haven't received a call. I was wondering when we'd start."

"If I hadn't pulled strings, you'd wait until Christmas for the assignment of a social worker. All those overseas adoptions—the folks at New Beginnings keep busy."

The Virginia Court required a home study before entertaining an adoption request. Annie knew the process would take several months, with a social worker visiting her home for a thorough understanding of her living arrangement. The process made sense—the State wanted assurance a child and a potential parent were a good match.

In cases like hers, the process usually went smoothly. She was Dillon's biological aunt. Since his birth certificate did not list a father, the court would favor adoption by next of kin. Unfortunately, the case was more complicated than most. She'd only visited Dillon once before Toria's murder, right after his birth. By contrast, Tom and Dianne England had documented proof of a longstanding relationship with Dillon, including photos of day trips and other occasions.

"We should have the home study wrapped up in about two months," Will was saying. "You'll need five hundred dollars to start."

Beneath her breath Annie whistled. "That much?"

"Is it a problem?"

"Of course not." In truth five hundred dollars would clean out her savings. "I'll get the money together."

"New Beginnings has assigned Pete Johnson. Great guy, older—Pete has three adopted and two biological kids."

"I look forward to meeting him."

"He'll ask for health records to prove you're in good shape. You'll also need a physical to prove you're in good health. Set up an appointment for a physical. Oh, and photocopy last year's tax return. I'll draft the letter to the court stating why you wish to adopt Dillon. Pete will help you draw up a fire exit plan for the house."

"A fire exit plan? My house is the size of a shoebox. If we ever smell smoke, we can climb out the nearest window."

"I know it seems like overkill."

"It *is* overkill."

"You'll also need to post a diagram of the house on your fridge. Dillon must understand where to exit in case of an emergency."

The home study was beginning to sound daunting. "Anything else?" she asked.

"There's more." When she slumped in her chair, he sent a look of apology. "I don't make the rules, kiddo. This is Virginia law. Pete will walk you through each requirement."

The friendly banter made her hesitate before asking the next question. "Bottom line, what will all of this cost?"

Will appeared just as hesitant to reply. "Two thousand dollars, give or take."

She sucked in a breath. "Meaning it *might* cost more?" Dreams of seeing Green Interiors become profitable disappeared. She couldn't buy more plant stock or think about advertising when the cost of keeping Dillon was so high. Not that she'd have it any other way.

She wondered if Michael was correct. Should she close a business she cherished, one that kept the memory of her parents alive? Kept her dreams alive too, since she happened to love working at the greenhouse. The best memories of her childhood were shaped in peat moss and dew-studded roses. No, she couldn't bear to give it up.

More importantly, *how* would she raise two thousand dollars for the home study?

Will sensed her confusion. "We don't have to use a private adoption agency. We talked about it weeks ago. County social workers can complete the paperwork for a fraction of the cost."

"A public social worker will take a year to get to my case. It's too long to wait."

"I agree. If we don't move quickly, the Englands might convince a judge to transfer custody until the final decision is made."

"I'm not sharing Dillon. He's mine, Will. My flesh-and-blood—"

Embarrassed by the outburst, she ground to a halt.

"Your *son,* Annie?" Will's eyes warmed with sympathy. "I'm glad you've made the emotional leap. I wasn't sure you would."

"What's that supposed to mean?"

"You seem averse to risk. Forgive me if I'm out of line, but I think you've lost so many people you've loved, you aren't quick to make an emotional investment." He gentled his tone. "Annie, relationships don't come with guarantees. People leave, people die . . . and people arrive in your life when they're least expected. Even if you've had more losses than most, there *is* one boy who deserves your devotion."

Emotion clogged her throat. "He has it."

"Good to know. It'll help with your new social worker. Pete needs to see how much you love Dillon—how you have every intention of becoming his mother."

Tears burned her eyes. She refused to let them fall.

Will let the silence lengthen. After a long moment he said, "One more thing. As you know, Tom and Dianne England were furious when we cut off visitation in March. They've petitioned the court for resumption of their visits with Dillon."

Fear shot through her heart. "Were you expecting this?"

"I'm not surprised. The court wasn't moved by the England's petition, at least not yet. You'll continue to receive an opportunity to bond with Dillon without interference."

"When we do face the Englands, must Dillon attend?" Thrusting a young child into the middle of a court battle was heartless. She couldn't imagine the damage it would do to Dillon.

"I'm trying to keep him out of the proceedings. The court hasn't decided, and the Englands are demanding he appear. They're convinced Dillon will support their claim that they've been an integral part of his life."

"That's absurd. He barely speaks to anyone but Chip." Putting Dillon through the ordeal would set him back by months. He'd only recently begun to smile and give more than monosyllabic replies. Didn't the Englands understand the damage they'd cause by insisting he attend?

Grimly, she decided nothing good would come from wallowing in fear—or anger. "I've taken up enough of your time." She slung her purse over her shoulder. "I'll wait to hear from Pete."

"Good enough." Will returned to his reading. He looked up

suddenly. "Annie?"

She turned around. "Yes?"

"How's the job search going? Found anything to supplement your income?"

"I have." She flapped her arms. "Can we go into it later? You've given me a lot to think about."

"Sure thing. Just keep at it."

She crossed her arms, mildly offended. "Meaning you think I'll bail out of the new job?"

He flashed a grin. "It's no secret you love your greenhouse. Hard to imagine you sticking to anything that takes you away from it."

"I'll stick like glue," she promised, heading out to fetch Dillon.

* * *

Bill Gibb's shoulders sagged. "You think I'm a perfect idiot, don't you?" He peered at the computer program as if it were a planet in an uncharted constellation.

Annie chuckled. Rowe's lead copywriter was one of the nicest people on staff even if his computer skills needed improvement. "I think you're wonderful," she said.

"You're not angry?"

She moved the mouse, clicked. "It's my job to retrieve files you've inadvertently deleted. Give me a sec. I'll find them."

Terrence stormed in.

"There he goes," Bill muttered. "He's hell-bent on terrorizing my staff because they haven't finished the slogans for DiRameo Cookies. I never should've delegated the account."

"You were following Michael's orders," she reminded him. "He said your stomach couldn't handle the project."

"Ulcers. My lot in life. Next time around, I'll find a job without deadlines."

"Your stomach would be fine if Violet didn't cry at the drop of a hat and Terrence used a normal tone of voice." She closed the program. "Don't tell anyone, but I harbor dreams of putting Terrence through a Cuisinart."

The notion delighted Bill. "How often do you puree him?"

"Several times a week. Fortunately, he stays out of my hair. Most of the time anyway. If he didn't, fantasy would become reality."

"Don't count your blessings just yet. Terrence *will* send you to the brink of insanity. It's his special talent."

"I hope not." She rose.

On tiptoes she skirted Terrence. He'd backed two members of Bill's staff to a wall with his high-shrieked complaints. Sticking around to watch him verbally reduce them to rubble didn't appeal.

Which, she realized, gave reason *not* to head back to her office. Violet was still raining tears before Michael's desk. The sound of her snuffling spun Annie on her heel. But not before Miriam latched onto her sleeve.

Miriam pushed her toward the door. "Get in there and save him."

They tussled, and Annie broke free. "Miriam, you go." Annie glimpsed Violet's flailing arms. She looked like a scarecrow on fire though you couldn't see flames. "I can't do it. Her tears make my molars ache."

"Where's your courage?"

"I left it in the copy department. Right next to Bill's antacids."

The sobbing increased, wafting past with the scent of desperation. "There isn't enough time to finish The Holy Four," Violet wailed. "Please tell Mr. DiRameo we need more time!"

More sobbing erupted from inside, and Annie squared her shoulders. "Oh, for Pete's sake." She shoved Miriam out of the way. "I'm going. If I'm not back in five, get your butt in there and help."

She was spared an intervention. Streaming tears, Violet lunged out, pinged off Annie's shoulder and shot down the corridor. One of the artist's hoop earrings had come loose and flapped on the shoulder of her retro glitter jacket. She looked like a grief stricken David Bowie, but with more makeup. Odds were she'd head for Bill's area and work off her angst by roiling his stomach.

Waltzing inside with a great deal of relief, Annie regarded her irritated boss. "Forget about dousing Miriam with valium on Fridays," she said. "Violet is the one who needs sedation."

"What she needs is a good, swift kick in the—" Rubbing his

forehead, Michael cut off. He switched track. "Have I mentioned you look better? Off death's door?"

"Amazing what eight hours of sleep will do."

He picked up the phone. "Remind me to get you up to speed on the DiRameo account. The new packaging designs take precedence over everything else."

"Will do." She tipped her head to the side. "Is DiRameo a big account? We should replenish Bill's stock of antacids."

***

"**A**nnie, it's after five. You promised to take Dillon to the zoo."

The mild rebuke brought her head up. "Thanks for the reminder," she said to Miriam. "I lost track of time."

"Don't make your little boy wait." Miriam shrugged into her light summer sweater. "I'll see you tomorrow."

"Good night, Miriam."

Annie logged off and collected her things. With school out for the summer, she didn't have to keep Dillon on a strict bedtime schedule. He'd taken to sleeping in until a few minutes before she left for work. Some days he was still in pajamas when Shelley Wilson escorted him across the street for a day of playing with Chip. A welcome convenience, especially since Chip insisted on clearing out one his bedroom drawers for Dillon's shorts and tee shirts. They were beginning to act like brothers.

Tonight, however, a play date with Dillon's best friend wasn't on the agenda. It would be just the two of them. Dillon had seemed excited about the excursion all week, and it was a perfect June night at the zoo. A light breeze kept the exhibits cool. The sinking sun gave the grounds a pretty, golden glow.

Two giraffes stood near a high wall in their enclosure, drawing squeals of delight from a gaggle of children. At the Birds of Prey exhibit, a Bald Eagle swooped through the air. The African-themed exhibit echoed with the chatter of a dozen monkeys. Throughout it all, Dillon seemed to enjoy himself.

When he appeared tired, Annie suggested a stop for ice cream. They ate dripping cones on the bridge above the enclosure featuring pink flamingos, lush hibiscus, and tall palm trees.

On tiptoes, he peered over the wall at the exotic birds trotting past. "They look silly." It was the first complete sentence he'd uttered all night. "How come their legs are sticks?"

"It's the way God made them." Real conversation was rare, and she searched for a way to prolong it. "Can you imagine walking on legs like sticks? They *do* look silly."

Nodding, Dillon finished his cone. "What animals are next?"

A hint of excitement rimmed the question. Any display of emotion gave reason to hope his heart was mending. Dillon was still too somber, but he did express fleeting moments of joy.

She finished her cone. "It's getting late. Let's skip the Reptile Building."

"Can we go next time?"

"Whatever you'd like." She checked the map. "The lions are right up the hill, over there. Ready?"

"Yep. I'm ready."

He walked beside her with his curls bouncing. A rivulet of ice cream dripped from the corner of his mouth, but she squelched the impulse to wipe it away. He still wasn't keen on being touched too often by anyone but the roughhousing Chip.

High atop the zoo, the lion's enclosure gave a breathtaking view of the exhibits below, the giraffes lumbering across the grass, the monkeys and the eagles in separate confines. Behind a stand of trees, the sun inched toward the horizon. Shadows bled across the pavement.

It was past eight o'clock, and the exhibit was empty. Sparrows fluttered in the trees searching for bits of seed before settling in for the night. Inside the enclosure, a lion paced restlessly between the boulders. A lioness with tawny fur lazed by the man-made pond.

"Aren't they wonderful?" Since childhood she'd loved the lions best of all. She'd spent enjoyable afternoons here with her father and Toria. "I used to come here when I was your age, Dillon. We always saved the lions for last."

Awareness prickled up her spine. The largest male had noticed them. He was near enough to pick out the burnt gold of his eyes, the focused gleam of a predator. He stopped pacing, and she smiled at Dillon. "Isn't he beautiful?"

There wasn't time for Dillon to respond. The great cat lifted its head and sent a thunderous roar into the night. Startled, she jumped. Then she laughed.

Dillon burst into tears.

"Sweetheart, don't cry." She knelt in a flash. "He won't hurt us."

Tears spilled down the boy's cheeks. Each one pierced her heart as cleanly as a knife. Without considering her actions, she pressed his damp face to her breast.

Hoisting him up, she struggled for balance. He held on as if he'd never let go.

Contentment spilled through her. "Shhh. It's okay," she said, rocking him. She buried her face in his hair. "I won't let the lion hurt you, not ever."

Dillon snuffled against her neck. "P—p—promise?"

She covered his wet cheeks with kisses. "I promise."

Nestled close, he hid his face beneath her curtain of hair. Careful not to fall, Annie started down the hill. Carrying him was as easy as breathing.

Her heart had never been so full. In an instant it had filled with joy and hope and love.

Like Dillon, she began to cry.

Chapter 9

"Do you need help tying your shoes?"

At the table, Dillon squirmed like a child with ants in his pants. He picked at the tangle of knots on his tennis shoes. "They're stuck," he muttered.

Last night at the zoo he'd welcomed her affection. The experience was a milestone in their relationship, tangible proof he'd begun to trust in her ability to comfort and protect him—to mother him. Recalling the satisfaction she'd felt as Dillon clung to her, she approached the table with newfound confidence.

She got to work untangling the knots. "I can fix this."

His gaze latched onto hers. "They won't tie good today."

"You sure did a number on the laces, didn't you?"

"Yep."

This morning Dillon had elected to take a bath instead of a shower. His fresh, soapy scent filled her nostrils. She took her time tying one shoe and then the other, glad for a moment of closeness.

When she'd finished, he asked, "Are we going to see the plants today?"

"Sorry, cowpoke. I'm going alone—but not until later." Giving into the urge, she ran her fingers through his curls. "I thought we'd hang around here this morning."

"It's Thursday. We always go on Thursday."

Opening the fridge, she paused to consider breakfast options. "You have summer camp today. Don't you want to go?"

"I forgot." He hopped down from the chair and joined her at the fridge. It was sheer heaven when he leaned against her legs, as if it were an old habit. "I don't want to miss camp. Chip chases me. It's fun."

"You chase him, too."

"He's faster. *I* want to be faster."

"Your legs will grow long. One day you'll be as fast as the wind." She couldn't help but add, "You'll be tall, like me."

Dillon peered up at her, gauging her height. "You're tall for a lady."

"I'm five-eight, but you'll be taller. Your grandfather was six feet." She found a yogurt and handed it over.

"That sounds big."

"It is." She grabbed an orange from the fruit drawer.

Taking the fruit, he tossed it from hand to hand. "Will you be here when I get home?"

The question warmed her. "Of course. You're my favorite guy in the world. Who else would I hang around with?"

The comment brought a rare, genuine smile to his lips.

***

The intercom continued to flash. Michael entertained visions of taking a hammer to it. For the tenth time in ten minutes, Miriam was trying to reach him. Thursday was shaping up like a balmy day in hell.

Herman, Rowe's long-suffering graphics assistant, had crashed all the design programs during an install. He'd been trying to impress Annie by taking care of business on her day off.

After the lynch mob of artists took chase, Herman raced for cover and knocked over someone's coffee. One of Terrence's preliminary sketches for DiRameo Cookies was ruined. Terrence was still chasing the stricken kid, lobbing insults and throwing the place into an uproar.

The secretary with the chop shop car had gone home sick. Violet and Bill Gibbs were arguing in the corridor. Lisbon was trying to maintain her composure by downing Bill's antacids and avoiding the raging hordes.

From the looks of the place, you'd think it was Friday.

To top it all off, a none-too-pleasant call had come in from San Francisco. The president of Beele Electronics had informed Michael that Terrence's new avian logo looked like a vulture with the company's product clenched in its claws.

And to think, it was only Thursday. Who knew what delights tomorrow might bring?

The blinking intercom seemed to have a voice: *Answer me! Answer me! Answer me!*

Pulling to his feet, Michael stalked to the glass wall behind his desk. He stared at the Virginia countryside five stories below, the canopy of trees and summer-green hills. A Zen-like calm refused to materialize.

Why would it? Throughout the morning's mayhem he'd let visions of Annie creep into his thoughts.

Frustrated by his lack of self-control, he rubbed the bristly stubble on his chin. He never should've hired her. He'd been drawn to her from the start. Though she'd behaved professionally from the get-go, he'd begun avoiding her in a self-protection strategy better suited for an adolescent. He pawned her off on Bill or Lisbon, as if they were responsible for teaching her the ropes. He dumped Herman on her without detailing goals and expectations for either of them.

He should've walked her through every job that was near deadline.

If Annie shared his pipedreams of striking up a relationship, she sensibly avoided dwelling on fantasy. She treated him with the same civility she displayed toward every other man at the firm.

On one level, her disinterest intrigued him. On another it stirred something in Michael he thought had died after Jen walked out on him.

Pride? Maybe. *Determination?* Heaven help him.

After the divorce he vowed to avoid entanglements. The women he dated lived for their careers and never talked of commitment. They enjoyed his company and the pleasure he gave them in bed. The no-strings-attached strategy wasn't a source of pride. Some might argue it was reprehensible. But no matter what Jen had done to him, he couldn't go to his grave an abstainer.

The door to his office opened, snapping him from his musings. Miriam held a sheaf of yellow slips, urgent calls he needed to return.

"Where have you been?" he barked, ridiculously.

Miriam flinched. "I've been trying to save Herman. He's barricaded himself under Terrence's desk with reams of paper. Terrence is trying to dig him out."

"Damn it! I'm sick and tired of the theatrics!"

She made the peace sign. "What can I do to help?"

"Call Annie. Tell her to get in here. She'll fix the program, and Terrence will calm down."

Miriam blinked rapidly. "I'm sorry, Michael. She won't pick up."

"Why the hell not?"

"On Thursdays she waters everything in the greenhouse. She won't have her cell on her."

He clawed his scalp. "Get the address for Green Interiors. I'm bringing Annie in *now*."

***

The morning's tender moments with Dillon made Annie's mood bright. The grueling hours of work ahead couldn't dull her optimism. Nor did Green Interior's overdue electric and water bills, which she'd just opened when Shelley arrived to take Dillon to camp. The next installment for the home study was also due. She hadn't yet cobbled the money together.

Did it matter? Dillon had allowed her to tie his shoes. And last night at the zoo, he'd rushed into her arms. In each instance, he'd let her into his heart. Not permanently. No doubt he'd experience setbacks. But he'd taken the first, tentative steps toward her love.

Inside the greenhouse, pots of ferns, philodendron and ivy hung from wooden rafters. Long wire mesh tables ran in cramped rows beneath. The air was rich with the organic scents of damp earth and the heady, floral perfume of gardenias in full bloom. She cradled a white, waxy flower and made a mental note to deliver the plants to Fairfax Bank & Trust this afternoon after she finished watering everything in sight.

Hurrying to the office, she flicked on the lights. A nicked and battered oak desk, a garage sale find, stood against the back wall. On top, bills and correspondence were tucked beneath a white ceramic flowerpot. The rotary dial phone, an antique her father had adored, sat by a vase of daisies.

She was working hard to put Green Interiors back on sure footing. They'd lost too many clients during the years when her father's health declined. Some, like Fairfax Bank & Trust, had returned. Now her life had changed again, and Dillon was the cherished center of her days.

"Annie?"

The familiar male voice spun her on her heel. Her heart thumped as Michael negotiated the center aisle.

"I let myself in." He sent a smile rife with apology. "I hope you don't mind."

"It's fine." She tipped her head to the side. "Why are you here?"

"There's a problem at the office."

"Michael, I can't come in today."

The comment put a scowl on his lips. "We're in dire straights. Herman crashed the computers."

"I left him instructions to stick to maintenance." Desperation ate through her pleasant mien. "Why don't I call, and walk him through a quick fix?"

"You're kidding, right? It's not possible."

"Why not?"

"He left work."

"Call him back in!"

"Miriam tried. He's not answering."

"Why did you let him leave?"

"I didn't. He walked out." Michael's jaw twitched. "It's more accurate to say he ran out. Terrence got the broom from the janitor's closet and chased him."

"Don't share the rest." Brushing off her frustration, she readjusted her expectations for the day. "Okay, this is what I'll do. Give me until one o'clock then I'll come in."

Relief settled on Michael's features. "I owe you."

She followed him out of the office. He took in the jungle of plants in the greenhouse's organized rows.

"What do you think?" she asked.

"Looks like you know what you're doing." He favored her with a shatteringly confident smile. "Which is a pity since it's time to sell. Rowe Marketing needs you, Monday through Friday."

"Let's not have this conversation again," she said, recalling their conversation in the parking lot. They'd already settled it.

"Why hang onto your father's dream? Annie, if you want a raise—"

"I've worked hard to rebuild Green Interiors," she cut in. "I can't let it go."

"Aren't you happy working for me?"

Pride, and the lightest hint of injury, wound through the question. Did it matter if her loyalties were split between her own business and his? "I love working for you," she said. "Michael, I do. But I love Green Interiors more. It's *mine.*"

"How long can you work two jobs before you burn out? You have to choose, and I don't want to lose you."

The sincerity rimming his words sent the sweetest ache through her. Surely he meant he didn't want the firm to lose her. Yet she sensed something deeper, a declaration buried inside the comment.

"You won't lose me," she said, giving in to the lie. "I need the job, and I enjoy working for you."

Emotion churned on her face. It was enough to warn Michael off. Why press when it was clear she wouldn't give in? He resisted the truth but it came to him all the same—Rowe Marketing provided Annie the means to rebuild her father's dream, a dream she now claimed. She was ambitious, as driven to chart her own course as Jen.

She doesn't look anything like Jen.

He despised the comparison but it arrived all the same: Annie was similar to his ex-wife. Beautiful. Talented. She put professional considerations first. Which was only part of the problem—he knew he was too hard on her, unreasonably pushing her when he ought to show more consideration for her feelings, pressing her for information when it wasn't his damn business. He'd never behaved this badly with a woman and was ashamed of behavior he couldn't quite manage to control. But he damn well needed to learn.

Yet even as he warned himself off, he found his attention narrowing on the open collar of her simple pink blouse, to the beauty mark beneath her collarbone. It was a strangely erotic blemish nestled above the swell of her breasts. He'd like to trace the blemish with his fingertips, and memorize the terrain of her skin before sampling her mouth.

The intensity of his desire bore no resemblance to the emotion he'd once harbored for Jen. They'd evolved slowly from friendship to courtship, sensible in their attraction.

And this? He tried drawing away but couldn't muster the willpower. Despite the twin gifts of intellect and ambition, Annie seemed vulnerable. The need to protect her from the troubles she refused to share appealed to everything male about him. The desire was swift, illogical, too potent to deny.

"I didn't plan to interview with your company," she said, nudging him from his thoughts. "Miriam insisted. She knew I needed additional income, and benefits."

"Are you trying to expand the greenhouse?"

"Not this year. There's too much going on."

"Too much . . ?"

Nervous laughter bubbled from her lips. "You know the drill. Just when you think life is dull, everything changes. I wasn't making ends meet."

Michael nodded, at sea. "There's no shame in searching for stability."

"A steady paycheck helps."

"Are you in trouble?" He hadn't meant to ask about her finances. Nearly hadn't dared.

"No. No, I'm not," she replied, but he caught the tension woven through her words. She nodded at the miles of greenery surrounding them. "It's hard making the bills when you're self-employed. I've never been good at hounding companies for payment. The waiting is hard."

He mulled over the explanation. She needed help. Rowe Marketing couldn't afford to lose her. His attraction? He'd get over it.

Coming to a decision, he flipped open his wallet and counted out fifteen hundred dollars.

"Consider this an advance." He pressed the bills into her palm. "At some point, I hope you will close the greenhouse. In the meantime, get caught up on the bills."

A startled gasp escaped her. "I can't take this. It's too

generous."

Her resistance started him grinning. "It's just an advance, not a back-room bribe," he said. "I expect to see you at the office this afternoon."

She bobbed her head. "Will do."

Her surrender pleased him more than was reasonable. "Great. I'll see you later."

***

The radio's R & B tune choreographed the steady movement of the afternoon traffic. Humming along, Michael tapped his fingers on the steering wheel in tandem with the music. He felt like opening the window and singing at the top of his lungs.

He'd completely lost his mind.

Somebody get me a straightjacket.

With bemusement he reflected on his faithful gatekeeper, Miriam. He left her babbling at his retreating back. An afternoon of client calls, none of which had been returned by her usually responsible boss, would've sent her over the edge. The staff? They were on the verge of rioting like peasants storming the castle. Of course, there were other worries—like the vulture logo for Beele Electronics that Terrence needed to revise.

What had Michael done to take charge? He'd stormed out in search of Annie. He'd found her all right, and their moments together allowed him to soar in defiance of gravity.

No wonder he craved a hard game of tennis. He needed to work off some steam.

He needed to feel something more reasonable than elation.

He also needed to see Annie again, with her pale blond hair and elfin smile. Why did her skin remind him of apricots? Soft, with just a hint of color. He liked how her eyes shifted from green to blue like a storm-swept sea.

He liked blue—and green. He liked them a lot.

A straightjacket, please.

With effort, he threw off the sugary emotion. The traffic stopped for the light, and he snapped off the radio. Horns blared and engines rumbled. Find the nearest florist and get Miriam a dozen roses? After grilling her on Annie's whereabouts, an apology was in order.

Stop thinking about Annie. Think about Jen, instead.

He did, and the process of dredging up the most painful moments of his life dulled his mood. The debacle of his marriage never failed to yank him off a cloud. Yet in the slice of a second, it was too much. The memories rushed him in a wave of sorrow.

The light turned green. He couldn't see it.

He saw the blood instead. The sickening, crimson pool spread across the bathroom floor. He recalled the gasping wails that should've been Jen's, the tortured voicing of all they'd lost.

But he'd been the one who'd sobbed like a child.

In the car behind, a man stuck his head out. "Hey, buddy— the light's green. Are you going to move it?"

Blinking, Michael stared at the light. Struggling from the memory, he sped away.

Chapter 10

Miriam returned the phone to the cradle. Bill and Lisbon, her partners in crime, crept into the reception area.

"Worked out a plan?" She eyed them devilishly.

"Sending him out of town might stabilize his hormones." Lisbon fiddled with the silver bangles encasing her wrist. "He's been terribly lonely since his divorce, but we can't let him fall in love with Annie. What if his attentions compel her to leave? This is the first time I've been able to send email to clients without a glitch. I refuse to go back to The Stone Age."

Miriam nodded in sympathetic agreement. "He doesn't know the trouble he's in."

Bill rubbed his stomach. "My ulcer could use less excitement." To Miriam, he said, "You haven't mentioned Michael's crush to Annie? Ask if she'll ward him off? We'd hoped you might."

"Do I look nuts?"

"You *are* her next door neighbor."

"And the reason we're in this mess," Lisbon added in a faintly accusatory tone. "You encouraged her to apply for a position at Rowe."

Miriam brushed off the comment. "Annie has proven her worth. Yes, she's beautiful. No, she doesn't understand the depth of Michael's attraction. She's a geek with a complicated private life."

Bill frowned. "I don't follow."

"Even if she *is* aware of how Michael feels about her, she won't encourage him. There's too much going on in her life. She's not looking for romance."

Lisbon pursed her lips. "And Michael?"

"The Bedouin?" Miriam snorted. "He's as freewheeling as an Arab traipsing across the Sahara. Since his divorce from Jen, he's more likely to pack up his tent and travel the world than settle down. Love will never ensnare him again."

Relief melted the anxiety on Bill's face. "Maybe you're right," he said. "Once he realizes how he's behaving, he'll take one of his offbeat vacations. To Patagonia or Tibet. Which works for me, as long as he's not gone too long."

Miriam stared at the phone. "I should check if his shots are up-to-date."

"Good thinking," Lisbon said.

Miriam drummed her fingers on her desk. "Until he comes to his senses, let's stick to the plan. Find an excuse to cart him out of town."

"We're on it," Bill said.

Miriam jerked her chin at the closed door to Michael's office. "The pheromones in there have reached toxic levels. I'm worried it's contagious. The new secretary, Bitsy? Yesterday she was batting her eyes at Herman. And that's not all. I find myself less inclined to beat Terrence to a pulp, maybe because he's sugared the art department with Barry Manilow music and chocolates. This ain't good, children."

The specter of love reared its head, and Lisbon shivered. "Heaven help us all."

***

"**C**'mon, Michael. Listen! Move the mouse to the icon like this. Click once. A dialog box will appear."

Annie's fingers flew across the keyboard. Michael knew he was no slacker at a keyboard, but he'd never seen anyone type so fast.

My fingers could do a nice minuet right across her breasts.

Ditching the thought, he gave himself a mental kick in the

keister. *Get a grip, man.*

Launching into self-protection mode he shot his rabid-bear look, which was usually reserved for employees who'd missed a deadline. He hated using it on Annie. She'd done nothing but come close enough to allow him to savor the tiny pulse point at the base of her neck. It was beating fast.

She yanked her fingers from his keyboard. "Anyone can run a compression protocol. Let me know if you need more help."

"You bet."

Lisbon and Bill came in unannounced toting frowns and bad vibes. Ignoring them, Michael lingered on Annie. She shifted from foot to foot searching for a way to leave. Today she'd worn a yellow dress and matching pumps. She looked like a sun goddess.

Her gaze slid to the others. Tongue-tied, she tried to retreat to her office. *Smart woman.* If she left, there was a chance his temperature would return to normal. If it didn't, he'd ask Miriam to throw a bucket of ice water on his head.

Knowing Miriam, she'd be game.

Annie's attention ricocheted off the walls. Then she lasered him with a fierce curiosity that put goose bumps on his skin. Never one to run from a battle of the sexes, he lasered right back.

Wow. If she kept looking at him like that, he'd fetch the ice water for himself.

The others approached and Annie murmured, "If you'll excuse me . . ."

"Please stay," Michael heard himself say. "Show Lisbon and Bill the new compression protocol."

Lisbon paled and Bill gasped. *What was their problem?*

Then Lisbon rushed the desk like a ballerina stalked by predators. "Michael, let the girl go. Annie, dear, do you mind showing us later?"

"I have time now," Annie said. "It's no bother, really. I'll teach you in a flash."

Happy to help, Michael pushed his keyboard toward her. The others appeared trumped and none too pleased about it. Michael, on the other hand, was happy to slide Annie all his Aces.

Bill held up his hand. "Hold on. We're here because we need face-time with clients. We're wrapping up a few projects."

"Should I accompany you?" Michael hated asking. He already knew the answer.

They nodded in tandem. "You have to," Bill said. He rubbed his stomach, which was evidently roiling.

"Sure thing. Where are we headed?"

"Seattle then San Francisco," Bill said. He smiled like a tourist held at gunpoint. "We'll return in a week."

"Or longer," Lisbon put in. "Ten days, tops."

Michael knew he was missing something. But with Annie standing this close, his powers of observation were fuzzy.

He rubbed his temples. The thought of traveling for ten days oddly displeased him. However, keeping the clients happy was important.

"When are we leaving?" he asked Bill.

"How about tomorrow?"

"That soon?" When Bill's eyes narrowed, Michael added, "I'll have Miriam book the flights."

"Good deal."

"Everything's settled," he said, to Annie. "Except dinner."

She tottered on her stylish heels. "Michael, it's four o'clock in the afternoon."

"Tonight. If I'm going out of town, I need to get you up to speed on the accounts. I've been putting it off. We'll discuss them over dinner."

She appeared ready to refuse. "What time should we meet? And where?" The doubt in her gaze surrendered to bliss.

"I'll pick you up at eight."

"You don't mind driving?"

"Not at all."

"Great." Floating on a proverbial cloud, she disappeared inside her office.

Michael wheeled his attention to the others. They'd crept to the door separating his office from the reception area. Behind them, Miriam hung off the edge of her chair. Lisbon, appearing ill, leaned against Bill. Stranger still, Bill was mouthing a prayer. Michael had thought the guy was an atheist.

Miriam recovered first. "Should I begin dialing?" she asked. "Book flights? Reserve hotel rooms? Make tonight's dinner reservations for you and Annie?"

Michael scratched his head. He felt miserable for reasons he didn't dare analyze. *You could always get me a—*

"Should I get you a straightjacket?" she said.

He cursed, loud. "I'll make the dinner reservations," he snapped. "Take care of the other items in whatever order you prefer."

Chapter 11

Miriam returned the phone to the cradle. Bill and Lisbon, her partners in crime, crept into the reception area.

"Worked out a plan?" She eyed them devilishly.

"Sending him out of town might stabilize his hormones." Lisbon fiddled with the silver bangles encasing her wrist. "He's been terribly lonely since his divorce, but we can't let him fall in love with Annie. What if his attentions compel her to leave? This is the first time I've been able to send email to clients without a glitch. I refuse to go back to The Stone Age."

Miriam nodded in sympathetic agreement. "He doesn't know the trouble he's in."

Bill rubbed his stomach. "My ulcer could use less excitement." To Miriam, he said, "You haven't mentioned Michael's crush to Annie? See if she'll ward him off? We'd hoped you might."

"Do I look nuts?"

"You *are* her next door neighbor."

"And the reason we're in this mess," Lisbon added in a faintly accusatory tone. "You encouraged her to apply for a position at Rowe."

Miriam brushed off the comment. "Annie has proven her worth. Yes, she's beautiful. No, she doesn't understand the depth of Michael's attraction. She's a geek with a complicated private life."

Bill frowned. "I don't follow."

"Even if she *is* aware of how Michael feels about her, she won't encourage him. There's too much going on in her life. She's not looking for romance."

Lisbon pursed her lips. "And Michael?"

"The Bedouin?" Miriam snorted. "He's as freewheeling as an Arab traipsing across the Sahara. Since his divorce from Jen, he's more likely to pack up his tent and travel the world than settle down. Love will never ensnare him again."

Relief melted the anxiety on Bill's face. "Maybe you're right," he said. "Once he realizes how he's behaving, he'll take one of his offbeat vacations. To Patagonia or Tibet. Which works for me, as long as he's not gone too long."

Miriam stared at the phone. "I should check if his shots are up-to-date."

"Good thinking," Lisbon said.

Miriam drummed her fingers on her desk. "Until he comes to his senses, let's stick to the plan. Find an excuse to cart him out of town."

"We're on it," Bill said.

Miriam jerked her chin at the closed door to Michael's office. "The pheromones in there have reached toxic levels. I'm worried it's contagious. The new secretary, Bitsy? Yesterday she was batting her eyes at Herman. And that's not all. I find myself less inclined to beat Terrence to a pulp, maybe because he's sugared the art department with Barry Manilow music and chocolates. This ain't good, children."

The specter of love reared its head, and Lisbon shivered. "Heaven help us all."

***

"C'mon, Michael. Listen! Move the mouse to the icon like this. Click once. A dialog box will appear."

Annie's fingers flew across the keyboard. Michael knew he was no slacker at a keyboard, but he'd never seen anyone type so fast.

My fingers could do a nice minuet right across her breasts.

Ditching the thought, he gave himself a mental kick in the keister. *Get a grip, man.*

Launching into self-protection mode he shot his rabid-bear look, which was usually reserved for employees who'd missed a deadline. He hated using it on Annie. She'd done nothing but come close enough to allow him to savor the tiny pulse point at the base of her neck. It was beating fast.

She yanked her fingers from his keyboard. "Anyone can run a compression protocol. Let me know if you need more help."

"You bet."

Lisbon and Bill came in unannounced toting frowns and bad vibes. Ignoring them, Michael lingered on Annie. She shifted from foot to foot searching for a way to leave. Today she'd worn a yellow dress and matching pumps. She looked like a sun goddess.

Her gaze slid to the others. Tongue-tied, she tried to retreat to her office. *Smart woman.* If she left, there was a chance his temperature would return to normal. If it didn't, he'd ask Miriam to throw a bucket of ice water on his head.

Knowing Miriam, she'd be game.

Annie's attention ricocheted off the walls. Then she lasered him with a fierce curiosity that put goose bumps on his skin. Never one to run from a battle of the sexes, he lasered right back.

Wow. If she kept looking at him like that, he'd fetch the ice water for himself.

The others approached and Annie murmured, "If you'll excuse me . . ."

"Please stay," Michael heard himself say. "Show Lisbon and Bill the new compression protocol."

Lisbon paled and Bill gasped. *What was their problem?*

Then Lisbon rushed the desk like a ballerina stalked by predators. "Michael, let the girl go. Annie, dear, do you mind showing us later?"

"I have time now," Annie said. "It's no bother, really. I'll teach you in a flash."

Happy to help, Michael pushed his keyboard toward her. The others appeared trumped and none too pleased about it. Michael, on the other hand, was happy to slide Annie all his Aces.

Bill held up his hand. "Hold on. We're here because we need face-time with clients. We're wrapping up a few projects."

"Should I accompany you?" Michael hated asking. He already knew the answer.

They nodded in tandem. "You have to," Bill said. He rubbed his stomach, which was evidently roiling.

"Sure thing. Where are we headed?"

"Seattle then San Francisco," Bill said. He smiled like a tourist held at gunpoint. "We'll return in a week."

"Or longer," Lisbon put in. "Ten days, tops."

Michael knew he was missing something. But with Annie standing this close, his powers of observation were fuzzy.

He rubbed his temples. The thought of traveling for ten days oddly displeased him. However, keeping the clients happy was important.

"When are we leaving?" he asked Bill.

"How about tomorrow?"

"That soon?" When Bill's eyes narrowed, Michael added, "I'll have Miriam book the flights."

"Good deal."

"Everything's settled," he said, to Annie. "Except dinner."

She tottered on her stylish heels. "Michael, it's four o'clock in the afternoon."

"Tonight. If I'm going out of town, I need to get you up to speed on the accounts. I've been putting it off. We'll discuss them over dinner."

She appeared ready to refuse. "What time should we meet? And where?" The doubt in her gaze surrendered to bliss.

"I'll pick you up at eight."

"You don't mind driving?"

"Not at all."

"Great." Floating on a proverbial cloud, she disappeared inside her office.

Michael wheeled his attention to the others. They'd crept to the door separating his office from the reception area. Behind them, Miriam hung off the edge of her chair. Lisbon, appearing ill, leaned against Bill. Stranger still, Bill was mouthing a prayer. Michael had thought the guy was an atheist.

Miriam recovered first. "Should I begin dialing?" she asked. "Book flights? Reserve hotel rooms? Make tonight's dinner reservations for you and Annie?"

Michael scratched his head. He felt miserable for reasons he didn't dare analyze. *You could always get me a—*

"Should I get you a straightjacket?" she said.

He cursed, loud. "I'll make the dinner reservations," he snapped. "Take care of the other items in whatever order you prefer."

Chapter 12

Dillon surveyed the cosmetics strewn across the dresser. "That's a lot of stuff," he said.

"Sure is." Annie rimmed her mouth with lipstick. "I'm trying to look pretty. I'm not sure it's working."

"You *are* pretty."

"You don't say?" She grabbed for his body, nicely encased in fuzzy pajamas with dinosaurs stamped on the fabric. Giggling, he darted out of reach.

Returning her attention to the mirror, she analyzed the work in progress. A touch more eye shadow wouldn't hurt. A bit more blush, to cover the nerves turning her skin an unsavory white. She snapped open the compact and fished out the brush. From behind, Dillon's soft hand settled on her forearm.

"Annie, it's a good song."

She'd learned Dillon-speak, a language cryptic and sometimes nonsensical. Getting from Point A to Point B might require a quick jog around C, D and E. Dillon meant he wanted her undivided attention.

She readily gave it. "What is it, sweetheart?"

"Chip's Mom. She says we're half done with summer. We have to remember school. If we don't, we'll forget everything."

"Are you're remembering right now?"

Dillon toed the ground. "Mr. M, mostly. He's got a song."

Last year's kindergarten class had learned a letter person for each member of the alphabet family. Mrs. A's apple. Winking Mr. W. The zipper on Mrs. Z's raincoat. Amused, she waited as Dillon swayed back and forth to the music he'd drummed up in his head.

"I'm Mr. M with my munchin' mouth. My mouth goes munch, munch, munch. My mouth goes munch, munch, munch . . ."

She tugged him into a bear hug, mid-munch. She took in the soapy smell of his just-washed hair, mixed with the unmistakable aroma of Miriam's famous chocolate cake. When had she begun to love him so much?

A mother's love.

She wasn't sure when the change had occurred, but she no longer viewed Dillon as her nephew. With every passing day it became harder to think of him as her late sister's child at all. Toria was gone. Dillon now belonged to Annie. She couldn't love him more if she'd carried his heavy promise beneath her heart for nine months.

If the Englands won custody, how would she survive the heartbreak? In a deep, cold place in her soul, the answer was frighteningly clear. If they won, she'd never heal. She'd spend a lifetime broken by the loss of Dillon.

Pulling from her embrace, he tumbled out of the bedroom. Trish, the most responsible of the teenagers who worked part-time at Green Interiors, announced 'tooth brush time.'

Water splashed in the bathroom. Dillon struck up another rendition of Mr. M, this time with a faster beat. Trish sang along. More giggling, and he reappeared in the bedroom. Annie pulled him into her arms for a quick peck on the cheek before he trotted off to bed. After he'd gone, she went to the kitchen in search of her purse.

"It's on the counter," Trish offered. The lanky teenager gave Annie the once-over. "By the way, you look fabulous."

"You think so?" Annie smoothed down the simple black dress. She didn't feel fabulous. She felt awkward and unprepared for dinner with the boss. "It was this or one of my business uniforms."

"The Dollar Store specials? You're killing me with the discount shopping."

The teenager ambled over to the table. One of Miriam's

chocolate cakes sat on a bone china platter. What were they celebrating today? Annie wasn't sure. Whatever celebration Miriam had devised as an excuse for more baking, she'd been successful. The cake was half gone, pillaged by a voracious teenager and a rambunctious child.

Trish shaved off another healthy slice and grabbed a fork. "Miriam brought over the cake while you were in the shower. She left a message."

"What is it?"

"She said you owe her for the straightjacket she's buying."

"Are you sure that's what she said?" Obviously the message was garbled.

Trish chewed thoughtfully, unaware of the smudge of chocolate smeared on her chin. "She said something about putting a man in a straightjacket—Michael, I think. He's your boss, right?"

"Right." Divining the message wasn't worth the effort.

Annie slung her purse over her shoulder and buttoned her trench coat all the way to her neck. She cinched the belt tight.

Earlier she'd decided to wait outside. All evidence of Dillon had been cleared from the yard, the tricycle wheeled into the garage and the makeshift tepee folded up and placed at the side of the house.

Pacing in the center of the driveway seemed a logical choice, and she took in gulps of air as she scanned the street. Even if she did seem like a fidgeting sentinel posted at the gate, at least Michael would think she was eager to be punctual for their business-cum-dinner affair.

This isn't a date. It's a business dinner with the boss.

She studied her cheap shoes, already sporting feathery lines in the fake leather. Even if this were a date, she was no great catch—a woman past thirty, up to her eyeballs in debt. Add in a custody battle for her nephew and a home study sure to peel away her privacy, and what did you get? Demands sure to crimp any man's privacy.

The conversation necessary to woo Michael was easy enough to imagine. *Michael, I'd like to begin seeing you socially. How do feel about stopping at the jail and being fingerprinted? After the FBI runs your prints, we'll begin dating . . .*

The soft hum of a car engine snapped her from her depressing thoughts. The silver Mercedes glided into the driveway.

She got in and Michael said, "You didn't have to wait outside."

"It was no bother." She prayed Trish wouldn't come to the window to wave goodbye. Explaining why she had a babysitter would lead to a conversation about Dillon. And maybe the FBI. "Where are we going?" she asked.

"The lady should choose."

"Do you like pizza? The place on Longview is good." She peered at the house. "Let's just go. How about Tasty's Chicken? It's right around the corner." The restaurant was one of Dillon's favorites.

"Perhaps I'd better decide." Michael pulled out of the driveway. "Your culinary experiences require expansion." He gave a quick appraisal of the trench coat. "You look like a spy."

"And here I was trying for a Katharine Hepburn impersonation."

"Trust me, you're reaching."

She fingered the buttons. "This was my father's. A well-worn memento of my favorite man in the world."

"You loved him very much." Michael sent a swift, sidelong glance before returning his attention to the road. "He must have been a good man."

"Decent and true. A Boy Scout to the end. Well, a Boy Scout in love with ficus and the occasional fern." Annie stopped, embarrassed. "But enough about me."

"Please, continue. You never talk about yourself."

"You're prying."

"I can't help it," he muttered, shaking his head with bemusement. "I can't decide if it's modesty or if you're suspicious by nature. Whatever the case, I *would* like to know more about you."

Something forthright and male came across in the statement. Was Michael trying to bring their attraction out into the open? She hoped not. Becoming involved with the boss wasn't a smart career move no matter how much the possibility appealed.

"Do you like lobster?" he asked, breaking into her thoughts.

Despite the worry lingering in her heart, she offered a splendid smile. "I'd rather grown used to Guido's fare."

"The pizza man will have to wait."

He pulled his cell phone from his blazer and made

reservations. While he did, she breathed in his tempting cologne and dined on the sensual curve of his lips. He possessed a hard mouth that softened unpredictably and seemed fashioned for kissing. What woman could resist his confident sexuality?

He's your boss. Stop thinking about him that way.

It was a relief when he steered the conversation to the upcoming DiRameo cookie campaign. The company would soon unveil the new and improved Giant Chips chocolate chip cookie with its snappy new packaging, compliments of Rowe Marketing. Afterward they discussed projects for Beele Electronics and a new account in Seattle. By the time they'd reached the restaurant, she'd ditched her illicit thoughts even though she was stuck with the anxiety.

Red carpeting swept from the curb to the restaurant. A white-gloved valet helped her disembark. The vestibule of glossy parquet led into the dining room with its scintillating chandeliers and tables set with white linens. Vases of dusky pink roses added subtle color. Sapphire blue carpeting dampened the sounds of chatting guests at the candlelit tables.

The anxiety returning, Annie faltered. Thank goodness she hadn't worn her corduroy slacks. The secondhand black dress had been a last-minute decision, the closest she had to party clothes. More than a few of the female diners wore cocktail dresses of silk or velvet. Several women were done up in evening gowns.

"You look great," Michael said, leaving her with the distressing sensation he'd read her thoughts.

She smoothed down the trench coat, banishing imaginary wrinkles. "I'm missing a strand of pearls or a feather boa. Look. The lady over there is wearing one."

"She's wearing the only feather boa in the place."

"Are you sure you wouldn't prefer pizza? A nice pie with double cheese?"

"Relax." Michael grinned. "Who says feather boas are the height of fashion? If you ask me, they went out with the Charleston." He led her across the dining room.

They reached the table, and she eased out of his grasp. "Shouldn't we wait to be seated?"

"I prefer a corner table." With a commanding glance, Michael signaled the waiter. He did that all the time, summoned people and made his opinions known without opening his mouth.

"You're a regular?" His monthly dining bill must be higher than her mortgage.

He pulled out her chair. When she scrambled onto the seat, he bent to her ear. "Annie, your coat."

"What?"

"Your coat. Give it to me."

Nervous tension washed her mind clean of thought. "Why?" she asked.

His gaze danced. "I'll hang it up for you."

Embarrassed, she got to her feet and snapped to attention like a good soldier. She let him unbutton her coat, his movements languid and unmistakably suggestive. If he'd undressed her in public, she couldn't have felt more exposed. Desire pooled in her belly.

"You aren't planning to salute me, are you?" he murmured.

She swayed nearer. "I'm not sure. I'll get back to you on it."

"Annie, ditch the nerves." He brushed her hair from her eyes. "We'll discuss Rowe's accounts. You *are* dressed appropriately. Relax."

Following the suggestion became easier once their cocktails arrived. Michael relieved the tension by keeping the conversation on business. Worthin planned to launch a series of new hair products before the holidays. The cereal brand Chocolate Goblins was developing a ghost game contest for kids across the U.S., Canada and Mexico. Several of the Rowe artists were putting the final touches on the game board, which would be enclosed in packages of the cereal.

The waiter appeared, and she declined an appetizer. Michael ordered a shrimp cocktail for himself and lobster for them both while they continued to discuss Chocolate Goblins.

"I don't think chocolate should be part of a child's breakfast, but it is a catchy promotion," Annie said. "Glow in the dark game pieces, and a chance to win with every purchase. It is a darling concept."

Michael thanked the waiter, setting the shrimp cocktail before him. "I spent a lot of sleepless nights dreaming it up."

"Ghost Game was your idea?"

"Who else? I don't get paid for screaming at the staff. That's just one of the perks."

"Then you're both brilliant *and* an evil contributor to

89

chocolate addiction in children."

"It's just cereal," he said. With relish, he bit into a shrimp. "Not heroin."

"Oh, yeah? Ever seen a kid on a sugar buzz?"

"I'm an only child, my parents' late-in-life surprise." He chewed thoughtfully. "I don't know any children, unless you count whiny artists."

"A kid high on sugar isn't a pretty sight, I can assure you."

He paused as steaming lobsters were placed before them. When the waiter had gone, he said, "I think you're exaggerating."

She considered Dillon's behavior after a typical birthday party, the type of celebration that began with goodie bags loaded with candy bars, and ended with cake and ice cream. Send enough glucose singing through his veins and he was capable of running until midnight. Sugar buzz hardly described it.

Michael sent a questioning glance. "Is this something you have experience with?" he asked. "Kids high on sugar?"

"Not really."

"You sound like an expert."

"Everyone knows kids and sugar don't mix. Not unless the adult in charge is stoked up on enough caffeine to last the night."

The guarded note had returned to her speech. He'd hit a nerve—but sugar? Was Annie a food purist, like the accountant he'd dated last summer? The woman had lived on tofu and spinach salads. Somehow he didn't have Annie pegged as a nutritional activist. He'd seen her order burgers and fries with the staff even if she did prefer a brown bag lunch.

Brushing it off, he began shelling his lobster. He stopped when he noticed her gaping at her plate.

"I don't know how to eat this," she said, her expression temptingly open. "It looks like it's still alive."

He battled down his amusement. "You live two hours from the ocean and you're afraid of shellfish? Consider moving to a land-locked state. I hear Nebraska is nice."

She lifted a steaming, crimson claw then placed it back on her plate. "This thing isn't dead. How do you know it won't crawl off my plate?"

"It's dead, I assure you."

"I see movement."

"You're imagining things."

She had the air of an eight-year-old girl lost at the circus. "I can't maul a defenseless animal. Don't get me wrong—I'm not ready to sign up with Vegetarians Anonymous. But this lobster wants off my plate."

He watched, flabbergasted, as she placed her linen napkin over the lobster. The napkin's corners were tucked beneath the plate. No doubt the funeral shroud lent the crustacean enough ceremonial protection to enter the next world unhindered.

The waiter, midway back to refill their water goblets, halted.

A look of warning sent him away. Then Michael returned his attention to the funeral proceedings.

Perhaps they should bow their heads and pray. Waft sticks of incense above the deceased. If it made Annie feel better, he'd recite a eulogy for all the lost lobsters of the world. As it was, she'd begun turning a not-so-savory shade of green.

He came to a decision. "Let's go." A sheepish grin took his face hostage. "Let's make our escape before we have to deal with any corpses at nearby tables."

She brightened. "We're leaving?"

"Aye, mate. We're out of here. Unless you'd like to stay and bury the poor bastard."

"Can I let the waiter do it?"

"No problem."

She leaned deliciously close. "We aren't making a run for it, are we? Even if we didn't eat the food, we *did* order it."

And to think, he'd wanted a straightjacket for himself. He should ask Miriam to order a second one for Annie. It wasn't polite, but he let her go on in her soft, conspirator's voice.

". . . so we have to pay for our meal. I can't steal my uneaten fare from this establishment."

She reached for her purse. Did she plan to pay for the meal with a portion of the advance he'd given her at the greenhouse? Stopping her, he clasped her wrist. He encased the delicate bones between his thumb and forefinger and relished the soft, damp skin.

"Annie, I have an account." He led her past the staring patrons. "The company, remember? I entertain clients here."

"Omigosh. I'm an idiot."

"You're nothing of the sort. Dining with you is the most fun I've had in a long time."

The truth struck him hard. He was thirty-six years old, past the age when he might delude himself about such matters. He was attracted to her, unreasonably so.

Which, naturally, placed a thousand roadblocks in his path. Annie was his employee, not his alluring and unpredictable date. Yet he couldn't hold on to the worry, not when it took all of his energy to stop from laughing outright. She was so pretty and so very amusing.

Annie was intoxicating to all of his senses, a heady wine in an irresistible, feminine package.

He had a sinking suspicion the package came, like all women, with a warning label: *Consume at your own peril.*

Chapter 13

They drove in a comfortable silence.

A fast moving July shower had come and gone. The air smelled sweet and the temperature had fallen to a balmy sixty degrees.

Casting shy glances, Annie wondered if her ignorance in matters of shellfish shocked Michael. Oh, she ought to be embarrassed, terribly so. Given the energy buoying her up, the notion was impossible to entertain. Michael's amusement in the restaurant had erased the tension bounding through her. He'd practically chortled when she'd refused the lobster, a response that made her as free as the summer breeze shuttling through the car's windows.

The garish lights of a fast-food window beckoned. At the drive-through, Michael ordered hamburgers, shakes and fries. Back on the road, he tossed the bag on her lap and handed over a milkshake. Within minutes they were pulling into the parking lot of Jefferson High where Trish and the other Green Interiors staff attended school.

It seemed a lifetime ago since Annie, too, had been educated at Jefferson High. Those years had been easier—and nothing like the hardships that followed. The opportunity to waltz slowly into adulthood never arrived, not with Toria's penchant for trouble and Dad's health problems. Assuming control of the greenhouse consumed the next several years. Then she'd endured the grief of Toria's murder, and the mad rush of settling Dillon into a new life here in Fairfax.

And now the Englands, determined to win custody of Dillon, threatened to tear her world down.

Too many torments dulled the possibility of reveling in the fleeting years of young adulthood. Dillon had provided the only happiness. It was foolish—dangerous—to allow Michael to fill her with an even greater joy.

Yet his proximity was reason enough to rejoice. It lifted her up, allowing her to believe in the power of flight. She could soar above it all, beyond the heartache, the pain, and the past burdened by too many responsibilities.

Light from the high school stadium spilled across the street. A baseball cracked against wood. Fans roared.

Michael parked in the stadium's lot. "Sounds like the home team's winning."

On the field, the batter flew around the bases. Sure enough, the Jefferson Eagles had scored a run. The boy rounding third base looked vaguely familiar to Annie, a tall kid with light brown hair and a hawkish nose. It dawned he was the senior Trish, her babysitter and part-time employee, had a crush on. Whenever Trish worked at the greenhouse she chattered about him nonstop.

Following Michael's cue, she got out of the car. "The boy rounding the bases? He's a senior, one of the best players on the team."

"He sure can hit."

"Yeah, and he's trying to score with Trish, a girl who works at Green Interiors. I'm hoping he strikes out." Horrified by the blurted remark, Annie bit into her hamburger. It tasted like cardboard. Swallowing, she added, "That was awfully crass. I shouldn't be discussing sex with you."

Shut up, shut up, shut up!

Above the car's hood, Michael slid a look dark with mischief. "We can discuss anything you like."

"How about we find a big pit instead?" She brought the milkshake to her lips and swallowed a gulp of tasteless goo. "Find a shovel. Bury me alive."

Clearly at a loss, he rubbed his chin. She stood before him with her trench coat flung open, a Katherine Hepburn imposter, as some sweetly unintelligible battle raged across his face.

"Annie, are you afraid of me?" he asked. "I can assure you I'm harmless."

You're as safe as heroin. "I know."

"The restaurant I can understand. It was . . ."

His voice trailed away as she cradled the shreds of her pride. "More than I'm accustomed to? Full disclosure—the best meal I've ever had was at The Olive Garden. Five-star restaurants are beyond my budget."

"That isn't what I meant."

"It's what you're thinking. I can see it in your eyes."

He dragged his hand across his scalp. "I meant it wasn't my intention to make you feel uncomfortable. Full disclosure—I was showing off."

"You're good at it. By the way, the silverware would make anyone nervous. Who needs three forks?"

"The third was a shrimp fork. Next time I'll teach you everything from the shrimp fork to the sorbet spoon." Softly, he added, "I'd like to teach you."

He left with his pronouncement sinking into her heart and started up the hill overlooking the ballgame. Lamely she followed. Rounding a garbage can, he tossed in his uneaten food and continued skyward with his fists shoved into the pockets of his blazer.

The grass was damp from the rain. He didn't seem to care as he settled high on the hill to face the ball game. "Your house is a few blocks away," he said, nodding at the line of trees behind them. "Was this your school?"

Cradling the milkshake like a lifeline, Annie sat beside him. "It's a wonderful high school. Great teachers, a nice art department."

"Were you a good student?"

"Straight As, mostly."

"But you chose not to attend college."

"I took a few courses."

"Weren't you motivated to continue? Obviously, you had the grades to succeed."

He stopped the interrogation when she stubbornly glued her

attention on the ball game. Was it wrong to grill her like this? *Probably*. Embarrassed, he searched for a neutral topic.

Surprising him, she said, "I wanted to stay in college."

An opening he gladly took. "But you didn't." When she remained silent, he added, "I apologize if I'm prying. Your life *is* mysterious."

A small huff of exasperation issued from her lips. She stretched out her legs and crossed her ankles. She seemed lost in her own counsel and the secrets she jealously guarded. Michael's attention followed in swift pursuit, skipping lightly over the bare skin of her lean calves then further up, to where the slight swelling of her thighs disappeared beneath the hem of her black dress. She'd recklessly forgotten to button the trench coat, and it lay in crumpled waves beneath her hips. The breeze fluttered the hem of the dress and her thighs shifted, daring him to look away.

Awareness sizzled through his veins—of the tiny breaths she took, and the mix of roses and spice in her perfume. The desire he felt was nothing like the craving he'd easily sated in casual relationships. Never had he encountered a hunger so pure and unrepentant. He felt powerless simply because Annie reclined beside him.

It was a dangerous proximity.

Why did he bring her here? Why torture them both with the pretense they'd embarked on a budding relationship full of excitement and discovery? She deserved better from him. Ashamed of his behavior, he donned a businesslike mien. He'd wait one more excruciating minute for her to finish her milkshake then suggest he'd drop her at home.

Finding the willpower to follow though would've been easy if their evening together hadn't revealed so many new splendors, like the dusting of freckles across the bridge of her nose. They were nearly translucent like a dash of color an artist would use on the mesmerizing portrait of a woman. He wanted to run his hands through Annie's silken hair, and memorize every curve of her face. He wanted to ravage her mouth, and bunch the sun gilt of her hair in his fists until the color blinded him of reason.

At risk to his heart, and at the prodding of his common sense, he determined to get to his feet. He'd barely shifted when Annie's veil of hair fell back. She looked at the stars overhead and began speaking in a voice as lush as lilacs.

"From elementary school onward, I had nearly perfect scores," she was saying. "When the other kids were nervous about an upcoming test, I'd be excited. I mean, really charged up about taking the test. I loved the learning, devising science projects and writing papers. I loved it all."

He let her voice pull him out to sea. "What was your favorite subject?"

"Gosh, I never took a class I didn't like."

Never? He was smarter than most but he'd had to slog through Calculus in college.

"I skipped third grade, which was hard. The friends, I mean. Missing them." She studied the clouds hovering near the moon like ardent suitors. "The elementary school told Dad I should skip eighth grade, too. I vetoed the idea."

"Why?"

Drawing from the deep slumber of memory, she smiled. Her features were gently swollen to within a breath of lust. "Well, I'm fairly tall for a woman but I've always been skinny," she said. "I looked so much younger than the other kids."

He dared a glimpse of her full breasts, set above the sloping indentation of her waist. "You aren't skinny," he managed gruffly.

"I'm not thirteen now. Back then, the older kids made fun of me. The skinny brain. Dweeb girl. You can imagine."

The hurt registering in her voice sent anger whipping through him. "They shouldn't have picked on you." He recalled her first day at Rowe, and Miriam mentioning how Annie had taught herself all the programs listed on her resume. He hadn't believed it. And now? "You should've received a scholarship to college. You deserved it."

"I got several. Dad wanted me to go right away, but I had to wait for Toria."

Toria—her older sister. He recalled Miriam mentioning Toria's penchant for ill-fated romances, and her murder in Baltimore.

"Why did you have to wait for your sister?"

The question hung between them. Above, starlight glittered. In the stadium below, the fans were back on their feet. The cheering barely reached Michael's ears as Annie shut her eyes. When she opened them again, sadness brimmed on her face.

"We had an agreement, a pact between sisters," she said.

"Toria promised to come back and help Dad at the greenhouse after she finished college. Not permanently—just until I got a chance to get started. We never talked about it much, but we both knew Dad was slowing down. We had no idea his heart was giving out."

Listening to the tale, Michael understood. His heart was doing the same.

"One thing led to another and Toria met a guy from Baltimore her senior year. She graduated and went to live with him."

"She never returned to Fairfax to keep up her end of the bargain?" He thought of something else. "Why didn't you go to a local university? Commute from home?"

She laughed, but the sound was rife with sorrow. "I did, for a semester. One day I came home from classes and found Dad unconscious in the greenhouse. Blood everywhere—he'd struck his head on a bench. We couldn't shut down Green Interiors and let him retire, and he couldn't manage without my help. Toria had run through his savings long before we knew about Dad's failing heart. There wasn't anything left."

The explanation was depressing, and common. An adult child's proclivity for trouble putting a middle-class family in financial peril. A second, more responsible child trying to hold everything together. A man self-employed for a lifetime without the savings for first-class medical care or a retirement he sorely needed.

"Did you hate Toria for leaving you in the lurch?" He couldn't fault her if she did.

"Sometimes, I suppose. Not all of the time. If I ran into a friend from high school who'd just finished a law degree or landed a plum management position, well, I *did* hate her then."

"It's understandable." Everything proud and protective and male within him wanted to bellow at the heavens. He wanted to cradle her close, this temptress with starlight skimming in her head, this beautiful, brilliant woman.

On the ball field another home run brought shouts from the stands. The coach slapped a redheaded boy on the back. The commotion seemed a mile away, a world away. Another batter up, and the opposing team stood silent and vaguely demoralized.

Drawing his attention from the action, Michael said, "You

should attend college now. It's been a few years, but the scholarships can be renewed. I can help you with the paperwork."

"Whatever you say, boss. Naturally, I'll have to quit Rowe Marketing if I'm going to dazzle the college profs."

Losing her would be difficult on so many levels. "An education is more important," he agreed, tamping down the pain. "You deserve to fulfill your potential."

Startled by the suggestion, she searched for a suitable reply. Was he serious? He'd change his tune if she found a way to mention Dillon, and reveal the financial pressures she now thought of as commonplace. But the conversation had already grown heavy. She'd rather shrug off the sad musings of lost chances. Once she'd felt deprived of the opportunity to chase her dreams. It had seemed Toria received every opportunity while Annie was saddled with the drudgery.

The first time she took Dillon's small hand in hers, she'd let the anger go.

"Get the degree," he was saying. "Close the greenhouse. I understand it's a monument to your father but your future is more important. If you can't reactivate the scholarships, sell your house and use the money for college."

"I like my house."

"It isn't wise to give up on your dreams. You have a yen for computers—become an IT chief for a Fortune 500 company. Bring home six figures and buy a bigger house."

He seemed irritated, and his shift in mood left her baffled. "I don't want a bigger house." Dillon adored visiting his Nana Miriam next door, and dashing across the street to play with Chip. "I grew up there. Dad put in the perennial garden decades ago and it's perfect—"

"Damn it, buy new flowers! Don't you want something better from life?"

She flinched beneath his callous tone. "Of course I want something better! But I can't plan too far ahead." She couldn't think past the looming custody battle. "I've learned to be patient— a virtue, I thought. I'm not willing to chase impossible dreams."

"You've learned to settle for less than everything."

His cold analysis hurt more than it should have. "What have you settled for, Michael? Happiness? The word that comes to mind is jaded. All you have is your work."

He looked positively rabid. "I have a good life."

The conversation had gone far enough. She got to her feet. Michael did the same, glowering like an unfed bear. His blackening expression brought stinging tears to her eyes. She walked away before he could see how deeply he'd cut her. Faster now, she rushed across the damp grass, which had probably left a wet patch on the back of her coat. *Good.* Let him stare at it. Let him critique her old clothes and blissfully dull life—*what had gotten into him?*

She hit a patch of mud, and her heels sunk deep. Tugging off her pumps, she followed the wild, raging impulse and tossed them over her shoulder. Hopefully they'd hit Michael on the head.

A grunt from behind, and she suspected he'd bent to retrieve her shoes. "Annie, wait—"

The husky entreaty of his voice propelled her down the hill. She refused to continue a discussion about her house or college or the life he *thought* she should lead.

"Annie, please—" He cut off. A string of expletives issued out. He directed every one at himself.

Stunned, she swung around. "I would have settled for bastard." The cool tone of her voice mocked the pain settled in her chest.

"Fine. Bastard it is." He jogged midway down the incline to reach her. "I'll settle for bastard."

"Stay away from me."

"No."

Her shoes dangled from his hands, giving him the dizzying advantage of height. Annie dared to lift her eyes. Their gazes battled, and heat rippled between them. The sweetest yearning followed.

Michael dropped the shoes and took hold of her.

So palpable were his emotions, she expected him to shake her. But his touch was gentle. She let her eyes drift shut to better experience his breath fanning across her forehead and the touch of his hands wending up her arms. When she dared to look at him, the consuming agony in his eyes was unexpected. A storm built on his face. She parted her lips, an invitation.

He captured her mouth. His kiss was gentle, urging her to respond. Quickly.

Arching close, she slid her hands beneath his blazer. Against her palms his heart beat wildly. The kiss lengthened and she moaned with pleasure, her simple, heady response to his lovemaking quickening his mouth upon hers. She twisted against the need. His lips weren't enough. She needed the feel of his hands, taking ownership of her body.

Pleasure flooded Michael's senses. She'd gone pliant in his embrace, fitting soft curves against his shuddering torso. At fear of drowning, he broke off the kiss.

There wasn't a way to apologize. He wouldn't know where to begin.

She stared at him blankly, and he said, "I'll take you home."

She swallowed. "All right."

He walked stiffly to the car, conscious that she chose to trail a step behind. He didn't dare the pretense of opening the passenger door. The lure of physical contact was too great. It would be difficult enough on the short drive to her house.

When she refused to look at him, he reached over and buckled her in. "Can you forgive me?" he asked. "I had no right—"

"I'm glad you kissed me." She pinioned him with a defiant look. "It's not your fault. It's no one's fault."

"I'm your employer."

"We're both consenting adults. You didn't do anything wrong." She offered a brave smile. "Forget it, okay?"

A rebuttal formed on his lips. Letting it die, he turned away from the passion lurking in her eyes. A passion mirrored in his blood.

Squashing the emotion, he started the car.

Chapter 14

"**W**here's our Girl Friday?"

From her vantage point in Michael's office, Annie spied Terrence Kholer rooted in the reception area staring down his nose at Miriam.

Rowe Marketing's lead artist had his assistant in tow. Annie still hadn't decided who was more bizarre—Terrence, with rings on every finger and a faintly disapproving air when speaking to mere mortals, or Violet, just as skinny, but with punk rocker violet hair and black leather slacks.

Miriam, whose grandmotherly appearance belied a spine of steel, sent the pair a dismissive glance. "Terrence, you've been badgering Annie all morning. The handholding must stop."

"Stop playing the dreaded gatekeeper and let me through." Terrence flicked his wrist as if batting away a fly.

Annie approached. "It's all right, Miriam." She turned to Terrence. "What's up?"

"It's the compression utility. I can't remember how to use it." He gestured wildly. "Really, dear, I don't have time to read a tutorial."

"It's simple. Follow the directions in the dialog box." She'd run him through the process countless times.

"There are so *many* icons. How can I remember which one to click?"

"The icon looks like two, teeny-weeny hands smashing something."

He flashed gem-studded hands. "It's the smashing part I don't like. What if the program destroys my art? What if something goes wrong?"

"It won't." She followed him back to his area. "There's no need to worry. I archive your files every night before I leave."

Twenty minutes later, she finally returned to the reception area. Miriam had vanished. Humming, she wandered into Michael's office.

In less than two months, she'd become indispensable. The computers ran without a hitch. If one of the artists seemed on the verge of cracking, she'd appear with pastries and cafe lattes for all. She kept up with the IT demands of Bill's staff, and knew every housekeeping program used at Rowe Marketing. She'd even taken Herman under her wing.

It turned out that he learned quickly. If a lesson were presented in a relaxed way, he got it down without problems. Herman admitted he'd rarely offered to take on new tasks because, "Everyone screams at me." Recalling his admission brought a grin to her face. They'd bellowed at her, too. She'd learned to shout back. Now the staff stood in awe of her. Even Terrence deemed her worthy enough to view his sketches. So many successes, but Michael wasn't around to see any of them.

His trip out West with Lisbon and Bill had drawn out longer than expected—eleven days and counting. Lisbon and Bill planned to fly back today, but Michael had left a message with Miriam that he was going on to New York City. No one knew why he'd extended the trip, or when he'd return.

It was for the best if he stayed out of town. They'd ended their dinner with an argument and a wonderful kiss.

He'd flown out the following morning.

Annie slumped in a chair and propped her feet on his desk. The desk was without photographs or even an engraved penholder. The entire, overlarge office was sterile. Which was why, on the fifth day of his absence, she began bringing in flowers from Green Interiors and her own yard. Each day another vase found its way onto Michael's desk or his bookshelves, slender flutes of purple delphinium and lush bouquets of salmon-hued tulips. Redbuds and white roses and a pale pink amaryllis she'd expertly forced at the greenhouse had also arrived.

Okay, so she was up to seven vases. This morning a fragrant bouquet of apricot roses had found a home on the coffee table.

She let her attention linger on the phone on his desk. Michael called Miriam regularly to check in on the troops. The contents of those conversations were never shared. How many more days before his return?

Not that it mattered. Whenever he *did* return, he surely wouldn't mention that one, shattering kiss. They'd both known it was a mistake, the disastrous outcome of an office flirtation. Better to forget, and move on.

Voices rose in the corridor. Pulling from her reverie, Annie went to investigate. Hopefully Terrence hadn't returned with another problem. Or Violet, his computer-illiterate sidekick.

"You rascal—slow down!"

A wave of barking resounded through the reception area. She discovered Miriam being wrenched forward by a runaway leash. At the end of the leash was a dog. At least Annie thought it was a dog. Beneath the thick hair, perhaps a small bear lurked.

"No, boy—slowwww!"

Miriam dug in her heels as she noticed Annie. "He's happy to be here," she said through clenched teeth. "Blasted dog. I don't know why I insist on rescuing the beast from the kennel."

"Oh, but he's lovely!"

The leash slipped and the dog bounded into her arms. Annie fell with a shriek. The mutt proceeded to slather her with wet, eager affection.

"Good boy, it's okay—calm down. Oh, he's darling!"

The commotion brought Terrence in to investigate. Spying the love fest on the floor, he wrinkled his nose. The dog stuck *his* nose in Annie's armpit. She toppled backwards with the pooch *yap, yap, yapping* his love to her.

"Gads." Terrence sniffed. "It's the Thing. Miriam, how could you?"

"It's been over a week since Michael left. You know the rule."

"What rule?" Annie asked, from beneath the dog.

"The Thing. It's Michael's." Terrence shivered theatrically.

"We kennel it whenever the master is away. Miriam insists on a jailbreak if Michael's been gone too long. Our dreaded gatekeeper is sentimental."

"Stop complaining," Miriam said. "This afternoon I'll return him to the kennel. Until then he'll nap beneath my desk."

Struggling into a sitting position, Annie chortled as the dog gave her a sloppy kiss on the cheek. She ran her fingers through his mountain of hair. "He's gorgeous!"

Terrence gasped. "He's a mutt. Some blasted varmint Miriam talked the master into getting from the Humane Society, if you can imagine. Of all the silly ideas. I loathe dogs. They're loud and they smell."

Annie brushed back thick wads of fur, unearthing a pair of brown, adoring eyes. "He's perfectly clean. Just bathed, I think. Oh, you *are* sweet." She looked up, beaming. "What's his name?"

Miriam crossed her arms. "Michael couldn't decide. We gave him two weeks. Nothing."

"Michael? The brilliant idea man?"

"It was three years ago—he was running a deficit of imagination." Terrence shrugged. "He couldn't create anything much less name a dog. Heavens, it was an awful time. Miriam thought the mutt would cheer up the old sour puss."

"Michael, a sour puss? What happened?"

"Don't ask." Terrence sighed. "He wasn't his typical hotheaded self, mind you. He was awful *all the time*."

The pooch draped a paw across her arm in loving possession. "What did the staff name him?" she asked.

"Lucky," Terrence supplied.

"Why?"

"Because he's lucky we haven't shot him."

She looked up, astonished. "Why would anyone shoot such a wonderful dog?"

Terrence waved his hand before his nose as if banishing an offensive smell. "He pees."

"Not anymore, he doesn't," Miriam said.

Terrence flailed his arms. "Lucky peed on the floor not one foot from my chair. A big, yellow dog-spot. It was a violation of the worst sort."

Miriam nudged him away from her desk. "Terrence, you're a ninny. It's been over a year since his accidents. I told you, I've trained him."

"Accidents? As in *several?* Lucky peed in my sacred space more than once?"

"Stop sniveling. The cleaning service took care of it." Miriam struck a haughty pose. "Really, Terrence—if you're planning to vomit, do it in the men's room."

The two women shared a look of triumph. Obviously Miriam liked the dog, too.

Annie ran her fingers through Lucky's Sheep Dog hair, admired his German Shepherd snout, and laughed at his Golden Retriever tail, thumping the floor with joyous abandon. She cooed in the dog's ear. The music must've been good because he dropped his head into her lap for a snooze.

During childhood she'd desperately wanted a dog. Dillon did too, and he hadn't inherited Toria's allergies. If Annie won permanent custody, she'd select a puppy at the Humane Society's Shelter—with Dillon's help, of course.

The idea was too delicious to resist. "Miriam, don't take Lucky back to the kennel," she said. "I can keep him until Michael returns."

Miriam placed the leash on her desk. "Lucky does like you. I've never seen him fall asleep in anyone's lap except Michael's."

The comment warmed Annie to the tips of her toes. It wasn't realistic to hope for a relationship with Michael, but she could share a love of his dog. It was something.

The phone on Miriam's desk rang. "If you two love birds will excuse me." She took the call then looked up. "Annie, it's Michael. Line three."

"He wants to talk to me?" Not once in eleven days had he asked for her.

"Line three. Hurry."

Inching out from beneath the dog, she went into Michael's office and snatched up the phone. "Michael?"

"Yeah, it's me."

She heard the commotion of traffic, and what sounded like a foreign language. "What is that?"

"Singing," he replied with palpable irritation. "I think the cab driver has found God." A long pause and then, "How are you, sport?"

Sport? The impersonal, jock-buddy greeting doused her

excitement. Did Michael think she was on speakerphone with everyone listening? "I'm fine," she said.

"The staff hasn't eaten you alive? No disasters to report?"

"Everything is super. I transmitted the new *Worthin* designs to New York for Isabel's approval. There aren't any disasters to report."

"Good deal." Beneath the cabbie's singing, Michael's tone was cool and businesslike. A long, excruciating silence then, "When I get back tomorrow, we need to talk."

Her throat went as dry as Wyoming in July. "No problem."

"I'm bringing Nicholas DiRameo. He's ready to see the new cookie campaign. Miriam has the details."

"Right."

"We'll talk after the meeting."

"Right."

"Oh, and Annie?"

Hope soared inside her. "Yes?"

"I'm sorry about what happened last week. You've forgiven me, haven't you?"

She gripped the phone as hope vanished. "Of course," she rapped out.

"Great."

With that, Michael hung up.

Chapter 15

Isabel Worthin waited.

The president of Worthin International and high priestess of New York society rested her fingers on the side of her still remarkable face as Michael spread the packaging concepts across her desk in his commanding way, taking charge as only a confident man does, without ceremony.

She'd known power longer than most, and still enjoyed watching each sex grapple with it, equally to be sure, but with subtle, unmistakable differences in style.

Young men like Michael never relied on etiquette. He launched in without apology, certain of his innate superiority to within a shade of arrogance. Or perhaps he crossed the line, knowing his sexual charm and smooth grace made any woman inclined to forgive. And Isabel—wealthy, powerful and past her seventieth year—was a woman, after all.

Even as Michael discussed the Worthin designs in a no-nonsense tone, she understood he'd come to her for another reason entirely.

For her counsel, no doubt.

More than three decades separated their ages, but they were very good friends. Both maintained a level of grace and virtue despite the gift of beauty and the seduction of power. She knew Michael valued her opinion on the most important aspects of life. Whatever the problem he grappled with, he'd come to her for advice. He was terribly proud, and so she allowed him to arrive at the heart of the matter at his own pace.

With an intuition rare in a man, he sensed her calm study. Of course, he was far from average.

He splayed one hand across the rendering of the Worthin logo. Indecision fought for advantage on his face. Drawing back, he sent a fleeting, devil's smile. Ever composed, Isabel let the silence lengthen.

He seated himself before her marble desk. "It's a woman," he said.

"Naturally. What other problem would haunt you so?"

"She works for me."

"That *is* unfortunate."

"I can't fire her. She needs the job, benefits. The staff loves her."

"Give her ample severance pay."

"It wouldn't be enough."

"For her, or for you?"

Impatience better suited for a cruel emperor took hold of his features. "For me, damn it." He looked up defiantly. "I'm consumed by her. Every hour. Every minute."

"Then sleep with her. Work the girl out of your system. A liaison with an employee is ill advised but if you choose, risk the lawsuits. Get your fill."

Distress filtered across his face, surprising her.

"Is that your advice?" he asked.

"Are you asking what I would do if equally consumed?"

"I am."

She withdrew her fingers from their resting place on her cheek, and lowered them to her lap. "I would walk away. Hand out severance pay, a generous sum. It's only money and neither you nor I have a want of that. I would remove the temptation from my path."

Stone-faced, he nodded. A hint of disappointment bloomed on his lips. "You would," he said, the comment bereft of hope.

The light went out of his eyes like a candle snuffed. Her heart shifted. For one, startling moment she pitied him even though he wasn't the sort of man a woman risked pity on for very long.

"You're still young, Michael. Younger than you think. Find a playmate, someone to help you forget this woman. Release yourself in sensual pleasures until she no longer holds power over you."

"As you would do. Perhaps have done."

She held him in a stern gaze. "I've felt as you do—obsessed—but have never become involved with men in my employ. Lawsuits are a nuisance, emotional entanglements a curse. I don't allow such problems the opportunity to destroy my focus. I keep my sex life separate from my ambitions. Never would I alter this strategy."

"Never," he echoed, lost.

Shutting down the conversation, he collected his briefcase. Stiffly, he rose. He seemed as placid as a summer lake. She marveled at how he buried the torment inside his regal heart.

She wasn't fooled. He murmured a few words in leaving, and she let him start for the door. "Michael."

Wearily, he turned back to her. "Yes?"

"In matters of the heart, there *is* one time when I chose to disregard my philosophy."

"But you said—"

"Just once." She wiped the impatience from her face and reached for the gold-framed photograph of Theo, taken in his prime. He'd died nearly a decade ago.

"Just once," she repeated, and the memory of bliss made the grief as fresh as on the day she'd buried Theo.

Michael hesitated, his eyes dull. "And?"

"Dear boy, don't you understand? It was Theo." Tucking the memory away, Isabel smiled. "I married him."

Chapter 16

"**A**nnie, please, please, please! Can I keep him?"

Dillon hopped up and down like a kid on a spring. Lucky spotted him, and streaked from the car. Yapping, yipping, the dog landed a paw on each of Dillon's shoulders and slathered canine adoration across his face.

Dillon grabbed a wad of fur and tugged Lucky off the steps for an impromptu game of toss. Everything he threw, the dog caught. A stick. A baseball. The garden trowel Annie had forgotten in the flowerbed.

"Look! He knows how to catch!"

"Yes, but he might still have accidents. Don't get him too excited inside the house."

"We aren't going inside the house. Not ever!"

Dillon rolled his newly rounded belly across the dog's back. The sight was immensely pleasing. Paychecks from Rowe Marketing were bringing in enough money to add treats like steak to the menu. Dillon was becoming quite a carnivore, and she hoped he'd continue to gain weight. Wouldn't the pediatrician be proud of her efforts? She giggled as Lucky marched around the grass with Dillon slung across his back like a sack of potatoes.

"He's not ours, sweet pea." She leaned against the doorjamb.

"Lucky is only spending the night."

On a shout, he dropped to the ground and rolled until his curls were tangled with twigs. He jumped back up and nuzzled the dog's ears. "Gee, he sure is furry. Where are his eyes?"

"Search long enough and you'll find them."

The rumble of a car engine brought the conversation to a halt. The familiar red minivan parked in the driveway. Her attorney Will Blaine got out.

He took in the roughhousing on the lawn. "What's this? A new pet?"

Annie chuckled. "Actually, he belongs to a friend. We're dog-sitting."

"Be forewarned. Looks like Dillon's in love."

"No kidding." She ushered him inside. "Guess what? The second job is working out. I can finally pay the rest of your retainer."

Will followed her through the foyer. "I didn't think it would stick. No offense, but I assumed you'd run back to Green Interiors."

"I'm not closing Green Interiors but I *am* planning to keep the second job for awhile." She began making coffee. "I'll be honest. It's rough working two jobs."

"What about Dillon?"

"One of the teenagers at Green Interiors babysits, and Miriam helps out. So does Chip's mother."

"Chip is the boy Dillon plays with?"

"He lives right across the street." Annie flipped on the coffee maker. "I'm not getting enough sleep, but the new job comes with great medical and dental. And my boss lets me work four days, not five. I have Thursdays off to catch up on work at Green Interiors."

Will's brows rose. "Nice boss."

"Basically I'm working seven days a week, but who cares? Dillon's happy. I'm even putting money away. Not much, but it's a start."

A rap at the door caught their attention. Miriam entered with a platter of chocolate chip cookies.

"Sorry to intrude, kids." She set the cookies on the table. "I saw Will drive up and decided to be a pest."

Annie fetched a third coffee mug. "You're nothing of the sort."

She brought three cups to the table. In the yard, barking drew nearer. Dillon's laughter followed. More barking, and Dillon rounded the side of the house with Lucky.

Will set his briefcase on the table and leafed through documents. "I heard from Tom and Dianne England's new law firm today."

The note of warning in his voice pulled Annie's attention from the happy scene outside. "What do you mean, new law firm?" she asked.

"They've moved to one of the biggest firms in Baltimore. Frankly, I'm concerned."

"Oh, dear," Miriam whispered.

Annie, reaching for a cookie, thought better of it. Did Will have more bad news?

He placed several documents before her. "The Englands' new counsel gave an indication of the argument they'll make at the custody hearing. This has led me to conclude . . ."

He stopped, and Annie knew he was reluctant to continue. "It's all right, Will," she said, although it wasn't. "Tell me your conclusion."

"I have several personal questions about your late sister."

"What does Toria's murder have to do with this?"

"Not her murder—her life." He studied his notes, his brow furrowing. "To your knowledge, was Toria intimate with a number of men?"

The line of questioning was unwelcome. "The Baltimore detectives have suggested her murderer might have been a drug dealer she was intimate with," Annie said. "Seven men have come forward claiming to be her past lovers. None are persons of interest according to the police."

"She was intimate with seven men?"

"I don't know if it's true or not, but Dillon *is* illegitimate. Toria and I weren't close. She was always battling with our father or with me. By the time Dillon was born, we'd both given up on having a normal relationship with her. I don't know much about her life after Dillon's birth."

Adjusting his glasses, Will continued scanning the documents. "So you weren't aware Toria left Dillon in the Englands' care for up to a week at a time? That she did this more frequently when involved in a relationship?"

The questions were stunning. "I had no idea. I thought they babysat once in awhile, that's all."

"Did you know she left Dillon alone in her apartment unattended when going out on a date?"

The room swayed in sickening waves. Lightheaded, she tried to make sense of the awful questions. Only a monster would leave a small child without proper supervision. What if Dillon had been injured while unattended? At age four—or younger—he couldn't possibly have taken care of himself. In all the months Dillon had been with her, he'd never once mentioned Toria leaving him alone. Annie chastised herself for letting her sister break off their relationship. If she'd insisted on staying in contact, she never would've missed the signs of neglect.

"Annie?"

"I'm okay, Will. Go on."

He did, in a voice softened with compassion. "If you'd known Dillon was without stable, adult supervision, what would you have done?"

The question snapped her out of the stupor. "I would've rescued him," she said, with heat. "I would've convinced Toria to let me take him back to Virginia. For a few months, maybe longer." She cut off as a memory edged to the corner of her mind.

Her father, exhausted after Toria stayed out all night. Their argument at dawn shattering the silence. Annie leaping into bed and throwing the blankets over her head. Toria storming off, and her father trying to calm his eight-year-old daughter with the gift of a synthetic rabbit foot, a forgotten toy from a long-ago trip to the circus. "The rabbit foot will bring you luck, Annie. Carry it in your pocket. It'll make you feel better"

The memory lay deep beneath the sediment of her life. Now it nagged persistently. Were there other, equally grim memories? She didn't possess the tools to unearth them. She didn't know how to dig.

Miriam placed soothing fingers on Annie's forearm, drawing her back. "Honey, do you need a moment?" Miriam asked.

"I'm fine." Annie regarded Will. "Really, I am."

He looked to Miriam. She nodded her assent, and he said, "Annie, why didn't you have an ongoing relationship with your nephew?"

Miriam grunted with disapproval. "Will, you've forgotten

something. Toria moved to Baltimore and refused contact with her family. After Sam died, what was Annie supposed to do?"

"No, Miriam. Will's right," Annie said, needing to take possession of the truth. "I should've tried to stay in Toria's life, especially after Dillon's birth. I knew she immersed herself in one meaningless affair after another."

Miriam was having none of it. "She was a grown woman, six years older than you. How were you supposed to control her?"

"I should've done something. Toria didn't care that Dillon was fatherless. I should've known she didn't care about him at all."

Will leaned forward. "Were you aware your sister was bipolar?"

A hard pebble of memory scraped against Annie's heart. "I've heard the phrase before. I'm not sure where. What is it?"

"Someone with a bipolar disorder fluctuates between manic highs and depressive lows," Will said. "When manic, an individual seems to have limitless energy, and might engage in dangerous behavior."

Miriam caught on fast. "You mean how Toria dated indiscriminately without using birth control?" Anger worked across her features. "It burns me up to think she never tried to figure out Dillon's paternity."

"Her sexual behavior could fit the manic side of bipolar disorder," Will said.

Annie tried to dispel the anxiety jangling inside her. "What about the depressive side?" she asked.

"An individual may become closed-off, even suicidal."

During Toria's teenage years, she'd come and gone at odd hours to avoid contact. "Do you think Toria *was* bipolar?" she asked Will.

"The Englands claim they have proof. They took her to a psychologist when Dillon was three years old."

Annie closed her eyes, allowing yet another ugly memory to surface. "I brought Toria to a psychologist several years before Dillon was born. A man she was dating had beaten her. I'd gone up to Baltimore to visit without calling first. I found her crying in her apartment. It was the day after he'd moved out."

Miriam sucked in a startled breath. "Good heavens. Why didn't you tell me?"

"I didn't think Toria was mentally ill. I thought she needed a professional to teach her how to make better choices."

Will jotted a note on the margin of a document. "Your desire to intercede might help in court. Unfortunately, we're in one of those 'we-say, they-say' situations. The Englands claim Annie was aware of Toria's condition. Clearly she wasn't. If you know a sibling has mental health issues and your sibling has a child—well, it brings us to a grey area in U.S. Family Law."

"How so?" Annie wondered.

Will was eager to explain. "You want the judge to look kindly on your request to become Dillon's adoptive mother. U.S. law provides for blood relatives to stand first in line. However, if an outside party can demonstrate the biological family is negligent, or in some other way cannot provide adequately for the child, other alternatives for the adoption will be entertained."

He paused long enough for Annie's blood to run cold. Guilt followed. In the strictest sense, she *was* negligent. She hadn't fought to stay in Toria's life. Dillon had suffered as a result.

"In addition, you're single," Will was saying. "The Englands can show the court a long, stable marriage. And let's not forget that Dillon lived with an allegedly unstable parent. If half of what the Englands say is true, he needs counseling. They've suggested you can't afford his therapy."

"I'll find a good psychologist," she replied, angry the Englands implied she'd refuse Dillon anything he required to heal. "How long do you think he needs therapy?"

"It's a question best answered by a child psychologist after several visits with Dillon."

"C'mon, Will. Best guess."

"Two years of counseling, twice a week to start. That's eight hundred dollars a month." He frowned. "It would help our cause if you can indicate to the court your willingness to begin sessions."

Miriam gasped. "She can't afford it!"

"Many psychologists will work on a payment plan. That's not the problem." He placed the photocopied bank statement before Annie. "The Englands have already set up an account for Dillon's psychological care."

Annie snatched up the document. "They did?"

"They've set aside twenty thousand dollars for his therapy. I also have a letter . . . here. You'll see it's from one of Baltimore's leading child psychologists. Mr. Breckenridge states Dillon will become his patient, should the Englands receive custody."

Miriam peered at the letter. "I've heard the name. Is Breckenridge an author?"

"He's well-published, an expert in child development." Will flipped through his notes and produced a letter. "The other issue? Tom and Dianne England's work histories. Both earn a sizeable income while Annie has been trying to salvage a greenhouse once run by her father. The unpredictable income of Green Interiors versus steady employment—the judge won't fail to see the difference."

"But Annie took your advice," Miriam protested. "She's found a second job."

"She did mention she'd stuck with something."

"She's now at my firm, Rowe Marketing."

Will sat back in his chair, clearly pleased. "Annie, you're working for Michael Rowe?"

"Do you know him?"

"He's a member of my country club. Great connections. He sits on the boards of several local charities. Is the job permanent?"

Miriam jumped in. "Michael thinks she's doing a great job. He's already thinking about promoting her. Oh, yes—he won the lottery when he hired our Annie."

"A job with an established company helps," Will agreed. "However, there's still the issue of the psychologist. If we can show Annie has already hired the best services for Dillon, it will take the wind out of the Englands' sails." To Annie, he asked, "Is there any way you can set aside ten thousand dollars?"

"Be serious. How will I come up with the money?"

"A second mortgage?"

"I took out a second for Green Interiors after Dad died."

Miriam asked, "Should I try to put together some cash?"

The offer was generous and unrealistic. "You can't afford to pillage your retirement account," Annie said, moved by the sweet offer. "It could take me years to repay you."

Will snapped his briefcase shut. "One last thing. I'm petitioning the court to request a continuance. We won't be ready by August. I want the custody hearing moved back to the middle of September."

Annie's heart plummeted. "We have to drag this out?"

"We need more time." He paused in the doorway. "Annie,

think about the money for a psychologist. If there's any way to set up a bank account, contact me immediately."

"Ten thousand dollars." She smiled wanly. "I'll wrack my brain."

"Do that. I'll be in touch."

Nodding, he left her with a deep stillness shutting down her heart. *Ten thousand dollars*. It was an unimaginable amount.

Chapter 17

Morning dew misted the rose bushes and left shimmering marks on the hydrangea's heavy bloom clusters. With July approaching its demise, the perennial garden was awash with color, the air fragrant and warm.

From the driveway, Dillon's laughter mixed with Chip's chatter as they climbed into Shelley Wilson's car for the drive to day camp. Abandoned by his favorite boy, Lucky flopped down in the flowerbed. He sniffed the coral daylilies mashed beneath his paws.

"On the grass, buster." She grabbed for a mound of fur. Catching her drift, Lucky bounded forward and sat obediently at her feet.

Absently she gave the dog a pat. Next week Dillon would celebrate his sixth birthday. Should she break down and get a dog as cuddly as Lucky? Given yesterday's conversation with Will, it seemed premature. What if Tom and Dianne England got custody but refused to take a dog too?

Just as difficult to contemplate was the Englands' assertion that Toria had been bipolar. Was it true? Mulling it over, Annie gathered a bouquet of roses for Michael's office. Tonight she'd surf the web and read up on the disorder. She also wanted to contact Jefferson High and ask for a meeting with the school's Guidance Counselor, Gerald Dunlop. A clue regarding the illness might be hidden in Toria's high school transcripts. Assuming, of course, Annie could persuade Mr. Dunlop to allow her to read them.

She reached Rowe Marketing at nine o'clock in a reasonably upbeat mood. She had a good job, and was managing to keep Green Interiors running part-time. No, she wouldn't lose Dillon. The possibility wasn't worth entertaining. The ten thousand dollars . . . well, she'd have to think of something.

Throughout the morning she worked on the computers in the art department, encouraging every neurosis Terrence harbored. It allowed her to bury the depressing thoughts about the money she didn't have, the Englands—even her feelings for Michael. She wasn't prepared to see him again, not after his jock-buddy comment during their phone conversation. It had been easy to pretend their office flirtation would wane before he'd kissed her. Clearly it was a mistake. How would she mask her emotions when he returned?

At eleven-fifteen, Miriam came in. The area had filled with commotion as employees worked in small groups or alone, scanning artwork or drawing sketches. The buzz of activity was loud, but Miriam silenced them all.

"Okay, gang. I just spotted Michael's car outside. He's on his way up with Nicholas DiRameo." She turned to Terrence. "Are the sketches ready?"

Terrence sighed. "When am I *not* prepared? Of course they're ready."

"Good. New York's bakery king doesn't look happy."

Terrence's bravado slipped. "What do you mean?"

"Let me put it this way. I hope that crazy hair of Violet's is a wig. Put it on, trade places, and let her face Nicholas."

"My hair isn't a wig," Violet said, missing the point.

"Violet, shut up!" Terrence grabbed Miriam's shoulders. *"Why* is Nicholas in a foul mood?"

"The flight was late. A woman in first class dropped her suitcase on Nicholas. Nasty bruise, I gather. Then Michael fell asleep on our man's shoulder."

"On the plane?" Terrence roared. "Michael doesn't sleep. He's invincible!"

"Not today." Clearly Miriam was enjoying herself as Terrence swooned. She clapped her hands. "Now, everybody, Terrence has a big presentation in Michael's office. Help him gather his things. If you'll excuse me, I need to make the boss a big, healthy pot of Papa Joe."

She hurried out with Annie following. "Is it true, what you said about Michael sleeping on the plane?" Annie didn't believe a word of it. "You were kidding, right?"

"It's true. Straight from the horse's mouth."

"Michael told you he fell asleep?"

"You got it."

"Didn't he apologize to Nicholas?"

"No chance yet. Nicholas was so furious, he refused Michael's offer of a ride. He took a cab. Looks like they've arrived in tandem."

They'd entered Michael's office. Annie rushed to look. In the parking lot below, Michael was gesturing to an older man who'd stepped out of a yellow cab. She lingered on Michael's wide shoulders and wind-blown hair. She'd missed him something awful.

Miriam gave her a push, breaking the spell. "Get crackin'. This is your first meeting with a client. It'll be a doozey."

"But you'll be there to steer me through."

"Not for all the tea in China." Miriam started for the reception area. "I'm the dreaded gatekeeper. I never sit in on meetings. Frankly, I'm too old for the chaos. Clients screaming—"

Fear pitched through Annie. "Screaming?"

"Terrence weeping—"

"Weeping?"

Miriam winked. "Welcome to the world of marketing."

With that, she was gone.

Annie tried to move. No dice. Her feet were glued to the carpeting. Elmer's glue, a big tube. Anxiety had stuck her to the carpeting and she couldn't budge.

Where was the manual? *How to Survive a Catastrophe in Five Easy Steps.*

"Annie!"

Annie jumped. Terrence flew into the room with a handful of sketches clenched in his fists. He promptly hurled them at her.

But she came unglued a second too late. Papers spun through

the air like white kites set loose on a summer wind. On a yelp, Terrence careened into the sofa.

Springing back to his feet, he snatched at papers in mid-flight with Annie's frantic assistance.

Which, naturally, was how Michael and the client found them.

Snapping to attention, Annie flinched as a paper *boinked* off her head. Terrence stumbled into her shoulder.

Michael halted in the doorway, glowering.

The last papers fluttered to the ground. Surveying the mess, Nicholas muttered beneath his breath. It sounded like choice words in Italian.

Terrence, with his unerring artist's eye, glanced around the room. He looked like he'd never seen the place before—which he hadn't since Michael's absence. He preferred to drag Annie back to his area and not chat in here.

She watched with horror as Terrence sniffed. That slightly-offended-wrinkling-thing he did with his nose. The flowers. He was taking in vase after vase of flowers on every available surface.

"This place looks absolutely funereal," he said.

Nicholas frowned. "Has someone died?"

Michael looked to Annie. "Not yet," he growled.

Omigosh.

She opened her mouth but her voice wouldn't work. She felt like a trout flung on the beach.

Nicholas squinted impatiently at his watch.

Michael moved. He went swiftly across the room, taking long strides that sent his minions scattering to retrieve the papers on the floor.

"Coffee's almost ready," Miriam called gaily, from the safety of the reception area.

Michael paused beside Annie. She came back up with a handful of paper and he leaned close. "Remind me to shoot Miriam," he muttered.

"Sure, boss."

He pinned her with a fiery glance. "This afternoon, with a Gatling gun. One of those big guns from The Civil War."

"Of course."

A muscle danced in his jaw. "Right after I line you and Terrence up."

Yikes.

Her mouth formed an O and he added, "Get moving. Seat Nicholas. Fetch coffee. And while you're at it, shake some sense into that idiot from the art department. Go!"

She rushed to do his bidding, all the while marveling at the way his eyes had moved across her face. Yep, he was really, really peeved. But there was something else there, too—something from the other night when they'd shared a kiss. The tiniest flame, leaping from the back of his eyes. And his mouth had almost revealed amusement. *Don't even think about his mouth during the meeting.*

Ushering Nicholas to the couch, she quietly inquired as to how he preferred his coffee. Cream? Sugar? She steered Terrence to a chair and gave him a push down onto the cushion. Then she stacked his artwork on the coffee table between the two men. She bowed slightly, like a good butler, and went to fetch the coffee.

The pot had finished brewing. Standing beside it, Miriam was doing a nice impression of a Roman statue, circa 300 B.C. Through some weird force of nature all the gaiety had vanished from her face.

"The dog," she said.

Annie stopped. "Lucky?"

"I always fetch him when Michael returns from a trip. Seeing the mutt after a rough meeting calms Michael. You left the dog inside your house, right?"

Oh. Oh, no!

Miriam started doing a Terrence-the-terrified impression. "It rained this morning," she said. "A nice, big storm. You know that, right?"

"Uh—"

"You left the dog in the house, right? Not outside?"

"Gosh, Miriam. I think I left him outside. Dillon ran Lucky, we sang an alphabet song, Shelley took the boys to camp . . . um, I think I left him outside. Just leave him at my house. We'll clean him up later."

"I didn't get this far by disobeying Michael's edicts." Miriam shook her. "Your house key. Give it to me. And cover for me until I return."

Can't I run for cover, instead?

Voices rose inside Michael's office. A shout. Silence.

Employees tiptoed up the corridor to listen. More shouting, and they scurried away like mice.

Annie grimaced. *Guess that makes me the lead Mouseketeer.*

She tried yogic breathing but it didn't help. Reining in the nerves, she gathered up coffee and cups and marched back inside.

Michael was seated beside Nicholas in a hunched posture, his elbows resting nicely on his long legs. He wore a classic navy blue suit and a red silk tie. A muscle on his neck bunched then relaxed. Placing the coffee before him, Annie sighed. A stray lock of hair tickled his forehead as he leaned forward to survey the sketches on the coffee table. She'd like to smooth his hair back into place or maybe mess it up even more. She wasn't sure which option was more enticing.

Of course, there was his mouth to consider, his lower lip resting under pearly teeth. Was Michael nervous? Maybe. If only those were her teeth, nibbling gently on his lower lip, tasting the soft pillow that appeared so stern one moment before softening the next.

You aren't going to think about his mouth, remember?

Terrence placed a sketch before Nicholas. The New York Bakery King murmured his mild approval. Michael rubbed his brow. His temples throbbed.

Hell, what a day. He'd earned a full-blown headache. Not that he'd get the aspirin until Terrence sealed the deal. Rowe's lead artist finally had everything under control.

No more surprises. They might just survive the meeting and keep the client if nothing else went wrong.

Which is why Michael knew he should've ignored the flutter in his stomach. It nagged persistently, throwing his inner antenna on alert. That keen sixth sense of his.

He lifted his eyes and locked onto Annie. She was standing stock-still in the center of the room staring right back.

He knew, instantly, that he needed to cut off the interchange. Somehow he couldn't manage it. An indefinable emotion whirled through his chest. It was brought on by the vulnerable, open way she was gazing at him.

As if she adored him.

Women always looked at him, right?

Yet her eyes carried a profound message, and a mesmerizing joy. As if he were the only man in the world and she'd never before seen the likes of him. As if she were entranced by the very proof of his existence.

He cursed his pulse, which obligingly kicked up a notch. His lead artist had managed to elicit another satisfied grunt from the client, and all he could do was listen to the *boom, boom, boom* of his heart.

A straightjacket, please.

He watched as awareness tickled Annie's shoulders and she realized they were stuck in sexual staring match. Her eyes widened with shock, as if he'd glimpsed her naked. Which, come to think of it, he wouldn't mind doing.

"Don't you have work to do?" he asked.

Her tiny Adam's apple bobbed up and down in her throat. "You bet," she said, aping his favorite saying.

She spun around, took a step, nearly tripped then brought herself upright by grabbing the edge of his desk.

Panic gripped him. A platter of Miriam's chocolate chip cookies sat on top.

He raised a hand in warning. Too late. The generous girl picked up the platter.

"Miriam brought these in this morning." Annie trotted toward them like a merry hostess. "I had a bunch at home, but most were gobbled up. Good thing it was a double batch."

Michael fell back against the couch.

Nicholas favored her with an approving nod. "Aha! Someone on the staff with gumption." He reached for a cookie and thanked Annie. She thanked him back. "My chocolate chips, the cookie that launched my company. Giant Chips—I still like the name, don't you? My grandfather came up with it in 1922. We've considered changing the name from time to time. I worry about losing customer recognition. Our cookies *are* a national favorite."

Michael ran his fingers up his cheek and rubbed hard. "Annie, put the cookies back on the desk."

She appeared hurt by the suggestion. "I don't mind sharing. Honest. Here, Nicholas—have another, please."

"Why thank you."

"I love chocolate chips, too. They're so gooey. Terrence, a cookie?"

"Gads!"

"Miriam baked them last night. They're fresh." Annie

munched, her attention settling on the fake sunshine that was Michael and skipping right over the storm brewing on the client's face. "You know Miriam—no store-bought confections, no siree. If it isn't home-baked, it isn't good enough."

Nicholas spat out the cookie. "Of all the—"

Barking. From the corridor. It shot through the reception area like a cannon.

Michael shut his eyes. He sensed doom in the shape of a beast with four paws. Lucky had arrived.

"No, noooo! Come back, you rascal!"

Lucky bounded into the room, covered in mud, and spotted Annie. With a *yip, yip, yippity* hello, he jumped at her from behind and sent the girl, the cookies, and a gallon of mud on New York's Bakery King.

Chapter 18

Silence. At ten minutes after five P.M., the employees had dashed for the exits.

Nicholas DiRameo had also stormed out dripping mud and muttering choice words. Michael let him go. Far better to let Nicholas fly back to New York—and cool off—before trying to salvage the account.

Now the place resembled a ghost town. Only Annie remained.

Miriam had abandoned her with a comment about telling Dillon she'd be late. Who was Dillon? A man Annie dated?

Jealousy gripped Michael. The boyfriend probably knew she feared lobsters. The bastard was surely privy to all sorts of engaging secrets about her. Maybe he was her soul mate, some eccentric guy who lugged around potted plants and tech gear.

Maybe Michael would wring the guy's neck if he ever went near her again.

Cursing the ridiculous thought, he took in the vases of flowers scattered around his office. Twelve days out of town . . . but he counted only seven vases. Hadn't she missed him the other five days?

A straightjacket, please.

Next he appraised Lucky, sitting at attention by his desk.

Before fleeing, Miriam had also garbled something about the mutt spending last night with Annie. Had the dog slept at the foot of her bed? He really *was* lucky.

Mud speckled the dog's fur and covered most of his snout. It wasn't the strangest part, not by a long shot. Someone had pulled the mangy Sheep Dog hair on his head into two rubber bands. Not the best styling job, no way. One rubber band neatly encased a whole lot of hair and also his right ear. It gave Lucky the appearance he was listening for something to the right of him.

The other rubber band contained only muddy hair. Brown, adoring eyes—which Michael had never before glimpsed—were trained on him as if to say, *What do you think of my new hairdo, pal?*

Stranger still, there was a contraption hanging around his furry neck. A variety of items hung from the necklace of green florist wire. A limp rose bud. The slimy remains of a banana peel, and a Lego man. Two tiny ghosts, which must have been pressed from a Play-Doh stamper.

Had Annie done all this? Flowers? Legos? Ghosts made from Play-Doh? Maybe she also channeled spirits on her day off.

With an impressive degree of composure, she walked toward him. Michael tensed. He ought to read her the riot act but something different hammered away at his insides. Maybe he couldn't stick to anger because her black dress displayed a nice smattering of mud and a few paw prints, too.

During the trip he'd barely slept. He'd missed her sun-drenched hair and her low, husky laughter, which made the hair on the back of his neck jump to attention. No wonder she had him dropping his defenses down around his ankles. It was as if she'd caught him in red polka dot boxer shorts, which he didn't own, but might have appeared on his body through the aid of divine, and mischievous, intervention.

"I can explain everything," she said.

He'd just bet. Perhaps she'd explain why heat enveloped him the moment she neared.

"Don't try," he replied.

"I'd like to."

"Whatever."

"It's all my fault."

A fan of lashes hid her eyes as she smoothed down her dress, drawing him to appreciate every curve and hollow of her body. Big, big mistake. He'd do better to stare at the dog, plopping down for some shut-eye.

"Terrence contributed," Michael said. Heat pummeled him full force.

"I ruined everything."

"Miriam helped. She knows not to combine Lucky and baked goods. It never turns out well."

"No, it's my fault. Totally."

The sincerity of her words threatened to fell him. The urge to tug her into his arms grew strong.

"Spare the others," she was saying. "I'll understand if you fire me."

"I'd rather not."

"Then *what?*" She looked to be imagining the worst of fates. Like the guillotine.

He mulled it over. "I'd rather kiss you," he said.

The pronouncement cleared the fear from her eyes. Happiness edged in and took over. "Why?" She looked confounded.

"Damned if I know."

And he didn't, not even when he drew his thumb across her mouth, relishing the way his touch parted her lips. He went deeply into the kiss, without pretense, with nothing but a direct communication of his emotions. In response, she wrapped her arms around his neck. He brought her in close.

Against her lips, he said, "Let's go to my house." He nipped at her ear. "I'll make dinner. Stay the weekend. Stay Monday. We'll call in sick."

"I can't."

He chuckled at her very feminine refusal. "You can't go to my house or you can't spend the weekend?"

"Neither." The need in her eyes mirrored his hunger. "But I'm tempted."

He dragged his mouth across the velvety skin of her cheek. "Then come with me. Later we'll kick ourselves for breaking the rules."

"Michael, we have to wait." She untangled from his arms and stepped back. "I can't start a relationship, not yet. There are legal ramifications."

"What's that supposed to mean?"

"I can't go into it."

"News flash—we're already in deep. Maybe it's time to follow through on our desires."

"I'd like to, very much." But the glow left her face. She studied him with glistening eyes. "I have to get through the next few months. Afterwards, we can decide what to do."

"You're asking me to wait?"

"I guess I am."

Ice crusted over the heavy drumbeat of his heart. "What's going on in the next few months?"

"Would you mind waiting for the details?"

"I deserve an explanation."

She released a soft, ragged expulsion of air. "Michael, I've recently learned my late sister had serious mental health issues. It's a lot to digest. I don't know what else I'll discover, but it won't be good. Not to mention it's the end of the day and we've probably lost the DiRameo account."

"Not lost. I'll apologize to Nicholas, fly to New York if needed," he assured her. She began trembling, and he frowned. It seemed she'd gone from fire to ice. He shrugged out of his blazer and flung it across her shoulders. "Annie, you're freezing."

"I can't stop shaking."

He led her to the couch and steered her onto his lap. "You came in here to apologize and all I can think about is my own needs. I'd planned to tell you we couldn't start dating. The best laid plans."

"Michael, stop it. I want to be with you too." Despite her distress, amusement colored her words. "You aren't going to blame yourself, are you?"

"I'm a man. I know where this leads." Considering, he landed a kiss on the top of her head. "Here's a suggestion. Stop keeping so much to yourself. Bottle everything up, and it's bound to cause problems."

"You sound like Miriam," she said, and he experienced a moment's relief when her trembling eased. "I *have* been upset. This last year has been awfully hard."

When she paused, he dispelled the urge to press. Eventually she'd share her troubles. He just didn't know when.

She relaxed fully against his chest and let her eyes drift shut.

Burnt orange light streaked fire across the office. Shadows draped the room, blackening the desk and placing strokes of charcoal on the bookshelves. Peering through the graying air, Michael sifted through the questions still wrapped in mystery.

His life was built on action. He knew how to target a problem then solve it. The emotions now burdening him cautioned against moving too fast. How to proceed?

This last year has been awfully hard. What had she meant?

Doubt threatened his heart, but he pushed it away. "Annie?"

"Hmmm?"

"I need to know. Is there someone else in your life?"

"Not in the way you imply. I have responsibilities."

"To another man?"

The pride in his voice brought her head up from its resting place on his chest. She thought of Dillon, who was probably singing an alphabet song for his Nana Miriam. He'd sing to her throughout dinner and clear the kitchen of sweets afterward. Next she considered Toria, and the revelation of mental illness that was probably the reason why their shared adolescence had known more sorrow than joy. Finally she thought of Michael, and how he deserved the explanation she wasn't yet strong enough to give. But she needed the truth, all of it, no matter how much it would alter the foundation of the life she thought she knew. She couldn't reveal everything until she did. And she had to come to terms to what she'd done to Dillon. She'd left him with a negligent parent when she should've provided safe harbor.

"This doesn't have to do with another man." She tried to continue, but the shame of how she'd let Dillon down precluded it.

"Annie, I know your problems are financial in nature. It's no secret." He eased out from under her. "Work for me full-time. I'll raise your salary by twenty thousand."

"Let's not do this again, okay? Five days a week means closing Green Interiors. Your offer is generous, but I can't shut down the greenhouse."

"Can't or won't?" When she refused to answer, he added, "If dating your boss is the problem, I'll help you find another job. I don't want the firm to lose you, but I'd rather help you transfer than lose you from my life."

"You won't lose me." She pushed the hair from her eyes, frustrated. "If I change jobs, it'll look like I'm incapable of pleasing my employer."

"You please me just fine." Despite the depressing nature of the conversation, pleasure danced across his mouth.

"Don't joke. I can't afford to lose my job."

"Damn it—I don't want you to work somewhere else. But I do want to start seeing you."

"In a few months. Please, Michael. All I ask is a little patience."

He clawed his fingers across his scalp. "I think the well is dry." A grin overtook his features. "By the way, it's impossible to take you seriously with my dog's paw prints all over your dress."

The black silk sported a crazy design of Lucky's prints. "Looks like you both left your mark on me," she said, pulling off his blazer before the mud transferred.

He went to the wet bar next to the office's bookshelves. "We both like you a lot."

"Good to know."

He made sandwiches and poured ginger ale for her and whiskey for himself. Returning, he said, "Come to think of it, *why* does my dog like you so much? And why are you making him necklaces?"

"Yesterday Miriam organized a jailbreak. I offered to let Lucky stay at my house for the night."

"And the necklace?"

"I plead the fifth."

"You would." He placed the sandwiches and the drinks between them. "I can't date you, but the pooch can spend the night? There's something wrong with this picture."

"Well, he doesn't pry into my life."

"He just needs lessons."

She gave him a playful nudge. "I hate the thought of Lucky pining away for you in a kennel," she said. "He can stay with me whenever you travel. His home away from home."

She whistled, and Lucky's head popped up. He bounded past Michael and plopped down on her feet.

Michael shook his head, clearly impressed. "I think he likes you more than he likes me."

She unwound the rubber bands from the dog's ears. "I'll bet I give him more kisses than you do."

"I wish you'd give me more kisses."

"Will you be satisfied if it ends with a Milk Bone and nothing more?"

He bit into his sandwich. "No way," he said between mouthfuls. He jabbed a finger at her plate. "Eat."

Digging in, she was glad for the simple act of sharing a meal with a man she'd begun to care for deeply.

Still, the nagging thought persisted. Would Michael wait for her?

Chapter 19

Tucking the last geranium into a pot, Annie continued to wrestle her doubts.

Was she throwing away an opportunity to begin a relationship with Michael? Would he wait for her? For the past few days, they'd managed to remain cordial if distant. Michael never mentioned the conversation they'd had in his office, but she caught the hint of longing in his voice, the note of stress regarding the unanswered questions about her private life. Even if she found the courage to tell him about the custody battle, what right did she have to expect understanding? She couldn't explain without being entirely truthful about how, before Toria's death, she'd neglected to forge a relationship with Dillon.

The phone's shrill ring carried through the greenhouse. Setting the pot aside, she hurried to the office.

"Hey, kiddo. Hope I didn't catch you in the middle of deliveries."

It was Will. "I'm about done for the day," she said. "What's up?"

"They've set our new court date—September 13th."

Unlucky thirteen. An inauspicious omen if ever there was one. Lightheaded, she dropped into a chair. "Will we be ready?"

She heard a rustle of papers then Will said, "Pete Johnson is almost finished with your home study. Your prints cleared the FBI. The job at Rowe Marketing helps, and I've been able to locate the psychologist you brought Toria to see when she first moved to Baltimore. There are still some odds and ends to finish, but we're prepared."

She caught the hesitancy in his voice. "Anything else?" she asked.

"One more thing, actually. The Englands haven't simply hired Tyrone Breckenridge to become Dillon's psychologist in the event they win custody. Breckenridge will attend the hearing. He's quite the celebrity. I'm concerned about the positive impression he'll make on the judge."

The news was disheartening. "What should we do?"

"Can you set up the account for Dillon's psychological care? It would help."

The desperation in Will's voice was new, and disturbing. "It's only the middle of July," she said, refusing to consider defeat. "Give me a few days, a week. I'll think of something."

"Do that. Oh, and Annie?"

"Yes?"

"I read the transcript from the Englands' legal counsel regarding Toria's bipolar disorder. I believe their assertions are true." A beat then, "You really didn't know?"

"I didn't."

"You don't recall your sister seeing a psychiatrist during her adolescence? Or later, while attending college?"

"Will, if Toria was diagnosed with a bipolar disorder, my father kept it secret. But I *do* think there's someone who might know—the guidance counselor from Jefferson High. I've been meaning to talk to him."

"Keep me posted if anything turns up. And think about the money. It would help our cause."

Fear clogged her veins. If she couldn't locate the money, would she lose Dillon forever?

"I'll think of something," she promised.

***

Legal ramifications, Annie had said. What had she meant?

In a vain attempt to dispel his agitation, Michael paced in a restless path. He'd spent the day hunkered down with work or running roughshod over the employees. Nothing stopped his thoughts from tugging back to Annie.

Legal ramifications. Was Annie married? Did she have a wedding band conveniently tucked away?

The night of the lobster fiasco when he'd asked her out to dinner—she'd waited for him in the driveway. Had there been evidence of her marital state inside the house, photographs and mementos?

Did you tangle with a married woman?

Michael dropped his face into his hands. *Not possible.* Annie was secretive, but infidelity was beyond her. She possessed a streak of honesty impossible to miss. She was arguably the most genuine person he'd ever met.

Then what was she hiding?

What legal ramifications came into play if two single, consenting adults chose to have an intimate relationship? His inability to decipher the mystery only heightened the anger simmering inside him.

Why didn't I keep my hands off of her?

Muttering a curse, he snatched up his keys and stalked through the empty reception area. It was time to drive home and take a cold shower. Or visit the club. Eighteen holes of golf— would it be enough to banish her from his thoughts?

Punching the elevator's button, he paced like a wounded panther. In the lobby downstairs, his heels echoed across the lonely expanse. He'd already reached the door when the memories engulfed him.

They were unexpected and painful. He let them overtake him, unbidden and despised, until the wracking, familiar pain sliced through him.

Before their divorce, Jen used to meet him here in the lobby.

Jen.

He'd thought she'd forever cured him of feminine entanglements. She was as hardworking a professional as he, a spitfire in public relations he'd met through a client.

They'd both been thirty-one when they'd wed and wildly successful in their careers. Complimentary ambition, tennis, and comfortable sex seemed enough to cement a marriage. During the first two years everything was fine, if rather predictable. Michael considered himself fortunate.

Until Jen became pregnant.

Long hours and busy work schedules precluded a serious discussion about children. The pregnancy—a careless accident during a weekend in Cancun—shocked them both.

They'd discussed everything from their investments to the best country club to join. They talked shop, and compared their growing client lists in a friendly, competitive way. The only topic they'd missed was whether or not to bring children into the world.

After the initial shock wore off, Michael grew excited about the prospect of fatherhood. Ballet lessons and a pony for a girl. Or Little League and soccer for a boy. They already had everything else—money, great jobs and what seemed a stable marriage.

Whenever Jen worked late, he increasingly took to wandering through the baby department of local stores. The mysterious world of womanhood, the layettes in shell pink and robin's egg blue, began to mean everything. It was a world of wonders, where a pair of baby booties fit snugly in the palm of his hand.

Something inexplicable grew within him, a fine thread of hope. He began weaving it into a tapestry of love.

One child wasn't enough. If Jen agreed, they'd have two. Or more. He didn't care as long as he had years of fatherhood ahead. It was an ambition he hadn't known he possessed, much less coveted.

Michael began to view himself as a father, strong and ethical, a good role model for their children. He began to dream, a host of dreams beyond the paltry ambition he'd funneled into the art of getting ahead.

The dreams ended abruptly.

Jen discovered the evidence of a shopping expedition— blanket and booties he'd lovingly tucked into the back of her lingerie drawer. Her fury was immediate.

In stunned silence, he listened as she railed at him for getting her pregnant, as if she'd had only a cursory involvement in the affair. The baby would ruin her career. Her recent promotion was in jeopardy. And she had no intention of giving up the six-figure income she took pride in earning.

Every time a tirade blew past, he deluded himself into believing she'd come around. She needed time to get used to pregnancy. She needed a few weeks, maybe longer. Rowe Marketing had already made him a millionaire, and they didn't need her income. If she preferred, he'd build her a PR firm in their home. Or he'd pull back, send half of Rowe's clients packing and teach his daughter how to play baseball better than the boys. He'd take his son on camping trips and help him catch frogs and salamanders and dreams.

Each suggestion met with cold, clinical cruelty. Every discussion ended in a battle.

After a month, she viciously dispensed with every possibility and felled him with the truth. She didn't want the baby. She wanted him to discuss a solution he couldn't bear to contemplate.

Heartbroken, Michael worked punishing hours. Jen began staying out late with friends as if she weren't carrying their child, as if the problem would disappear if she ignored it long enough.

It did, with gut-wrenching efficiency.

One morning he found her crumpled on the bathroom floor. She'd miscarried. They waited for the ambulance with nothing for company but Michael's howling tears and Jen's cruel silence. Even after the divorce, he'd been inconsolable.

Stop thinking about Jen and the baby.

It took some doing, but he pulled free of the memory. Blinking, he cleared his head. He took long strides through the deserted parking lot and yanked open the driver side door of his Mercedes.

Never again.

The agony of betrayal was too great, the promise of disappointment too predictable. Why take another chance?

But he had. Briefly, he'd forgotten the credo that had steered him though. He'd thrown away every tacit resolution when he'd held Annie in his arms.

Only a fool risks his heart twice in one lifetime.

Whenever Annie neared, she made him forget. Her sweet humor and honeyed kisses lifted him up. Her genuine spirit and stormy gaze lulled him into believing in a better outcome.

Her secrets yanked him back down to earth.

Jamming the key into the car's ignition, Michael brought the engine to life. The car hurtled forward.

He was in purgatory, and he didn't like it.

Chapter 20

Worrying about ten thousand dollars she couldn't raise wasn't enough to dampen Annie's mood. Not today.

At the table, Dillon bounced on his chair. Miriam set the cake before him. With a whoop of joy, he leaned close to blow out the candles.

"I'm six years old!" he shouted.

Chip bumped his shoulder. "Did you remember to make a wish? It's okay if you forgot since this is your first cake."

"Sure I remembered."

"Is it a secret?"

Dillon scrunched up his face. "I know the rule," he said. "I won't tell anyone."

At the kitchen counter, Annie collected plates and forks. Her favorite teenager on the *Green Interiors* staff stood at her elbow. Trish looked confused.

Lowering her voice, she asked, "Didn't the little guy make a birthday wish last year?" She glanced furtively at the table. "Why does Dillon's buddy keep reminding him of the rules?"

Annie shrugged. "Don't worry about it."

"C'mon. What gives?"

She reached for a handful of napkins. "This is Dillon's first birthday cake," she said. Trish looked at her with astonishment and she added, "He told Miriam several days ago. It's nothing to get up in arms about."

"You must be kidding. How does a kid get to age six without green frosting and candles?"

"Sorry to say, it happens."

"That's awful. It should be illegal or something."

Giving a teenager a life lesson bothered Annie, but she plunged in anyway. "Not all parents are as great as yours," she said. "My sister, Dillon's mother? She had emotional issues and abused drugs. If I had to guess, I'd say she forgot when it *was* Dillon's birthday."

"Still hard to believe."

Regret sifted through Annie. Toria had been gunned down, her life brought to an awful end. The memory was still an agony.

Tucking it away, she said, "Parenting skills are learned just like anything else. Some adults never get the lessons down." She gave Trish a quick hug. "Don't worry about it. From now on, Dillon *will* have a wonderful birthday each and every year."

At the table, Miriam sent a look of impatience. "C'mon, ladies. It's time to cut Dillon's birthday cake."

***

Michael punched the intercom—again. Where was Miriam?

Muttering a string of oaths, he stalked into the reception area and found her sorting paperwork at her desk. The cropped strands of her hair stuck out like a porcupine's quills.

She ran her fingers through her hair yet again. "Michael, you must stop bothering me," she said, without looking up.

He gritted his teeth. "I call because I need you."

"I'm not Lucky. I won't play fetch every ten minutes."

"What the hell does that mean?"

Sighing, she penned a notation in the corner of a document. "You've been badgering me all morning. I've been to your office so often I've worn tracks in the carpet. Long-distance sprinters aren't forced to do this much running."

"But it's Friday. You know the code. I'm always crazy on Fridays."

She hunched her linebacker body over the desk and dropped her chin onto her hands to study him with exasperation and that singular, motherly impertinence that never failed to irritate.

"Michael, it's not Friday. It's Tuesday." She released a sigh as his brows lifted. "There's a calendar on your computer. Start using it."

"Right." He tried to backpedal, gave up, and stared.

"Do you need an aspirin? Does your head hurt?"

"No, no. I'm fine."

"Gum? Candies?"

"Thanks, but no."

"More coffee? You've only had three cups. Another hit of high-octane fuel might dehydrate you enough to make you resemble a prune."

The sassy remark raised his hackles. "Jump in a lake, Miriam."

She offered a smile infused with saccharin. "I should, you grouchy Bedouin. You've put me in hell."

"I won't badger you for the rest of the morning. I'll yank the intercom out of the wall. Satisfied?"

"That's not what I'm talking about."

His keen sixth sense went on alert. Michael plastered on an expression of sheer aggravation, that trusty look he used to drive people off. He hated the ruse, but he knew she meant Annie.

"I realize your private life is sacrosanct," Miriam said. "You lord over your emotions like a vicious bear. Enough! We need to talk."

"About what?"

The exasperation vanished from her eyes, leaving only the maternal wisdom he knew to fear. "Are you being a good boy?" she asked.

The question took him off-guard. Regrouping, he said, "I'm thirty-six-years old, far past the age of Tom Sawyer. I think you've finally done it, Miriam. You've gone right off your rocker."

"Spoken like a true Bedouin. Insult me again and I'll smack you with my ruler."

"You're shitting me."

She dug through paperwork, and came up with a shiny ruler. "Guess again," she said, waving it around.

It dawned she was serious. The situation's humor might have

made him laugh on a normal day. But he'd been lugging around a burdened heart for days, making his trusted gatekeeper miserable. She had every right to put him in his place.

Ashamed, he said, "I haven't been myself lately. Can you forgive me?"

"Michael, I've known you since you were a fresh-faced boy straight out of college. With all honesty, you're one of the finest men I've ever met."

"Can't say I deserve the accolades at the moment, but it's nice to hear."

"In many ways, you're like a son to me. I love you . . . as much as I love Annie."

Mention of Annie brought the agony rearing up inside him. Thankfully she was still helping Bill at his desk. Working near her had become a torment, especially since she'd made it clear they couldn't begin a relationship. At least not yet.

Miriam pressed on. "She's nothing like Jen. She's been through more than you can imagine. And I suspect the two of you have been trading kisses like careless teenagers. I *do* understand."

He fished around for a retort. Nothing came to mind.

"Find a way to make it stop," she said. "You can't have one of your three-week romances and break Annie's heart. Not now, not ever. She's sweet and bright and nowhere near as strong as you think. If you crush her, Michael, I will never forgive you."

He swallowed. "I wouldn't forgive myself," he replied gruffly.

Miriam lowered her eyes to the paperwork, but not before he was jolted by the unshed tears pooling in her eyes. "Then we understand each other?" she asked.

He filled with self-loathing. "Yes, we do." He'd never hurt Annie. She meant too much to him.

Midway across the office, he stopped as Annie darted inside. A study in purpose and concentration, she veered around him. For days now, she'd remained aloof as if she'd severed the connection between her emotions and her intellect. If she was as troubled as he was, she'd learned to hide it.

She came around the side of his desk. "Can I get on your computer? It won't take long." When he nodded, she dropped into his chair and wheeled close to the granite desk. She looked fragile surrounded by the masculine accouterments that fit him so well.

She typed quickly. "This morning our ISP reconfigured the Wi-fi."

He was too depressed to decipher what she meant. "Run that by me again."

"Our internet service provider made changes to our wireless connection." She shot a look of disbelief. "Don't you remember? I explained last week."

"Right."

At risk to his heart, he closed the distance between them. On the computer, dialog boxes popped open. Four, five, some minimized, others maximized and reset.

When he paused directly behind, Annie forced herself to continue typing. His spicy cologne tickled her nose. Then he rested his hands on her shoulders and she gave up the pretense.

The gentle way he kneaded her shoulders contained a welcome message. "Does this mean we're friends again?" she asked. They'd been avoiding each other for days. "We'll find a way to muddle through?"

"No problem."

She managed to smile. "We won't hurt each other?"

"Never."

Relieved, she rose and faced him. He wound his arms around her waist, and she said,

"Please be patient, Michael."

He rubbed his nose across hers. "I'm trying."

"It's hard. You don't have a lot of patience."

"Never did."

"Find some now. Focus."

The heat in his eyes sent a shudder through her. "I'm not like you," he said in a voice thick with desire, and her emotions rose like a storm. "I don't wait for life to happen. I go out and get what I want."

"You mean *take* what you want." The storm building in her increased, and carried gale winds. She fought it down. "You can't. Not this time." She reflected on the impending court case, and her struggle to keep Dillon. Nothing, absolutely nothing would come before her little boy. "Let me get my life settled. Once I do, we'll explore a relationship."

She went up on tiptoes and repeated the lesson she'd just learned, rubbing her nose across his with sweet emotion. The muscles in his arms relaxed and his hold loosened. She drank in his scent, as if it were a potion from which to draw strength.

With regret, she returned to work.

Chapter 21

At Jefferson High School, Annie stepped into the disorganized cubbyhole that served as the guidance office. "Anybody home?" she called.

Avery Dunlop's shock of white hair bobbed from behind a filing cabinet. "Annie McDaniel, is that you?"

"The one and only." He appeared, nattily dressed in tweed with the familiar pink carnation stuck in his breast pocket. Grinning, she added, "Wow. I feel like a kid again. Mr. Dunlop, you look exactly the same."

"You're an adult now. Call me Avery." He tweaked her nose then wrenched open the filing cabinet. "After you phoned, I started searching for your sister's transcripts. Not an easy task, I don't mind saying."

"Have you found anything?"

"Not much yet." He slammed the cabinet shut. "Most data is kept in the cloud. Don't worry. I keep original documents like any good pack rat. C'mon."

In the basement, industrial grey pipes for the school's plumbing system snaked overhead. The smell of dampness mixed in the air with the faint odor of chlorine bleach. Avery unlocked a metal door and led her inside a room bursting with wall-high stacks of boxes.

"Let's get started," he said, pulling one down.

"Are we checking all of them?" The prospect was daunting.

The guidance counselor dragged a chair to the center of the room. "I hope not," he replied. "The boxes are dated. Find the years Toria attended Jefferson High."

Searching, they lost track of time. Boxes lay in a haphazard circle on the cement floor. The wall of documents had been whittled down to nearly half its original size.

During their phone conversation, Annie had given Avery every detail about Toria's ill-fated life and the battle to keep Dillon. It had been easy. During her high school years, he'd been an adult who practiced the art of listening well. Never judging, he offered the teenagers in his care the guidance they needed. Adulthood hadn't changed the dynamic, and she'd found herself spilling all her troubles.

"Almost there." He rifled through the yellowed transcripts. "Don't give up—we'll find Toria's records."

"I'm sure we will," Annie said, even though she wasn't.

"We're close. I can feel it."

"You're silly."

"The kids say I'm psychic. Psychic Dunlop."

"We called you other names." She sent an affectionate glance. "I apologize for each and every one."

From behind tufts of white hair, his eyes danced. "I heard them all, you know."

Groaning, she shoved the box away. "You did?"

"You thought your big mouth didn't echo in the halls? It carried far and wide."

"I'm so sorry." Humiliation washed over her. "You were one of the kindest adults at the school. I should've treated you better."

"Annie." He gave a penetrating look. "You were an angry kid. I was needling you, trying to reach past the anger."

Struggling to her feet, she grabbed another box. "I was feisty, maybe. High-spirited. I don't recall being angry."

"Still bottling it up, I see."

"Bottling *what* up?"

He regarded her with discomforting interest. "You grew up without a mother. Your father was a good man, but he was too preoccupied with his greenhouse and his books. He died, leaving you with a business that was barely solvent."

She didn't like the turn of conversation. "True enough," she said, hoping he'd stop.

Cheerfully he continued. "Let's not forget to factor Toria into the equation. Six years older than you, she was a troubled kid if ever there was one." Avery stacked documents on the floor as if he needed a way to keep busy. Finally, he added, "In her senior year, she told me about the deal she'd made with you."

He meant the pact between sisters. Annie would take care of their ailing father while Tora left for college. Then Toria would do her part—but she never did. The betrayal still hurt.

"Toria mentioned our pact?" she asked, despising the waver it her voice. "It was a secret."

"Annie, she told me all about it. She never planned to hold up her end of the bargain." Avery hunched over one of the boxes in determined pursuit of the transcripts. "Now, do the math. How old were you when you agreed to the pact?"

She resisted tallying the numbers. "I've never really thought about it."

"You were in seventh grade. You should've been in sixth, but you'd skipped third grade. My dear, you were one the brightest children ever to grace the halls of the Fairfax school system."

"The world is full of smart people. So what?"

He eyed her with irritating humor. "By sixth grade, you were running the cash register in your father's greenhouse. He had you requisitioning supplies when you were barely out of short pants."

"I wanted to help."

"Kids want all sorts of things. Adults should set limits so kids aren't burdened."

"What are you trying to say?"

"I'm saying your past doesn't inform your future unless you decide it should. Chase any dream. Be anything you want. Life isn't fair, and it's certainly kicked you around. Kick back. Find a big rainbow, and chase it."

The words struck hard. "Dad always called Toria the rainbow chaser. I'm not like that at all."

He pushed a box to her and waited until she started flipping through files. "Think again. You have every right to find a big, beautiful rainbow, and chase it."

They were quiet for a long time as she weighed his advice.

Aching, and a little cold from sitting on concrete, she got up and stretched. With the last of her fading determination she took down another box.

And spotted the thick folder of her sister's transcripts right on top.

"Found it!"

With a grunt, Avery came to his feet. He tossed the ring of keys into her lap. "Lock up when you're finished," he said. "I'll be in my office waiting to photocopy whatever you need."

Nodding with gratitude, she flipped through the documents with an inexplicable sensation tripping up her spine.

School grades. A few Fs, mostly Ds and Cs. Two yellow forms dealt with Toria's suspension from high school. More report cards, and a lime green permission slip to join the tenth grade basketball team.

The psychiatric evaluation was in back.

School Principal Beatrice Parks and Guidance Counselor Avery Dunlop were notified by Samuel McDaniel, parent of eighth grade student Toria McDaniel, that Toria was taken to St. Luke's Hospital for a psychiatric evaluation on April 2nd . .
.

The document rustled as Annie gripped the edges.

. . . bi-polar disorder was diagnosed. Lithium has been prescribed to control the fluctuations in Toria's behavior. Mr. McDaniel has assured school officials that his daughter will begin treatment immediately . . .

The words jogged something deep in Annie's mind, a memory long buried. She looked through the file and found the paperwork dealing with Toria's second suspension from high school. Lightheaded, she read each word carefully.

. . . Principal Beatrice Parks has determined suspension will continue until the 10th grader resumes the regimen of Lithium prescribed two years ago . . .

Toria had stopped taking the prescribed medication? Why hadn't Dad insisted she take it?

Hungry for the truth, Annie continued reading.

. . . School administrators learned from Mr. Samuel McDaniel of his struggle to control his daughter's behavior. He conveyed that his deceased wife, Alice, had also received a diagnosis of manic-depressive syndrome early in their

marriage. The late Mrs. McDaniel discontinued treatment and took her own life by an overdose of sleeping pills . . .

For a blinding moment, the words didn't register. When they did, shock lanced through her.

Her mother had taken her own life? Shuddering, Annie let the document flutter to the cold cement floor. Tears burned against her eyelids. She blinked them away. Her father hadn't revealed the brutal truth. He'd betrayed her trust with a fiction about how her mother had died in a traffic accident.

He'd kept Toria's illness a secret, too.

Swallowing down the hurt, she organized all the paperwork. She placed the file at her feet then covered her face with her hands.

Annie cried for a long time. All the pent-up fear she'd harbored since Toria's murder—that Dillon wouldn't bond with her, and the Englands would take him away—it all burst forth. She wept for her father, who'd lied to protect her or because he didn't have the words to convey a tragedy of losses. She cried for the mother who chose death when Annie had been a toddler, and for Toria, her maddening, destructive sister.

She cried until her throat burned, the sounds of her despair a hollow music in the closed room. When she'd finished, she ascended the stairwell to the high school's first floor.

Avery was waiting. He'd cleared the mess of sports gear and papers from the couch, just as he would've done when she attended the high school. The familiar ritual was an invitation to sit, stay, and share your troubles. Annie took a seat with her sister's file gripped in her hands.

The sympathy on the guidance counselor's face was almost too much to bear. "Now you know your family's real story," he said. "Do you want the entire file copied?"

"Yes."

Gently, he eased the folder from her grasp and carried it to the copy machine. "Did you know Toria and your mother shared the same illness?" he asked.

She examined the sensation of emptiness overtaking her. It seemed they were discussing nothing more threatening than what they'd had for breakfast. She wondered if she was in shock.

"My father lied about it," she said. "I thought my mother died in a car accident. I never heard about her disorder, or my sister's."

The copy machine threw bands of light across Dunlop's

bifocals. "Any questions?" When she refused to respond, he added, "C'mon, now. You've always had courage. Ask anything you'd like."

Her shoulders sagged. "Will I become mentally ill like my mother and Toria?"

"Probably not. If you want my personal opinion, it'll never happen. Ask me why I'm sure, Annie."

"How can you be sure?"

"When you were at Jefferson High, we brought in a psychiatrist to test you. He did—four times over six years. You thought he was in training to become a Guidance Counselor. We didn't want to scare you. By the way, your Dad was behind it. He wanted you tested."

She recalled a young man in wire-rimmed glasses and a keen sense of humor. The tests he'd asked her to complete were fun, story problems and fill-in-the-blank games.

"What did you find from the tests?" she asked, worried.

"He found no evidence of bi-polar disorder in your profile, no evidence of mental illness whatsoever. However, he did reveal some rather intriguing facts."

Dread embraced her. "What's wrong with me?"

Avery chuckled, easing her concerns. "You're fine, kiddo." He placed another sheet in the copier and pushed the button. "Now I'm not crazy about numbers, at least not when they're used to pigeonhole kids. But sometimes numbers *do* tell the story."

"What kind of story?"

"What do you know about IQ?"

"Not much. It's a gauge of intelligence."

"Personally I hate the blasted tests, especially if a kid has low scores. Human intelligence is malleable—we can become smarter by reading often or playing number games. Yet in some instances, an IQ test is quite revealing . . . "

She waited as he marshaled his thoughts. Another page went in, and the copy machine whirred. In the corridor a boy with ebony hair ran past, evidently late for a class.

Avery pulled her back to the topic at hand, asking, "Do you know the normal range for IQ?"

"I can't even guess."

"It's between 90 and 110. An IQ denoting mental retardation is below 70. Genius IQ? It's 140 and above. To give you some perspective, it's thought Einstein's was somewhere around 160." Smiling, he added, *"You* have an IQ of 160."

"I score in the genius range?" Absorbing the facts would take time. She was numb from everything she'd learned about her family secrets.

"There's a correlation between mental illness and genius." Avery placed the photocopies in her lap. "Scientists are still trying to work it out, but in some families with inherited illnesses like bi-polar disorder, other relatives may display genius-level intelligence. Some studies indicate family members with bi-polar may also have high IQ scores. This was true in Toria's case."

"And my father. He was also very bright." She recalled his yen for crossword puzzles and anagrams. A worrying thought dawned and she quickly asked, "What about Dillon? Is he at risk for mental health issues?"

"He's more 'at risk' of inheriting your high IQ." Avery sobered. "Actually, it's unusual both your mother and Toria suffered from the same illness."

They'd both struggled with demons. Silently Annie sent a prayer heavenward. Wherever their souls now resided, she hoped they'd found peace.

Avery regarded her closely. "Can you handle all of this?"

"It'll take some time." She gave him a quick hug. "I appreciate everything you've done to help."

"If you need a sympathetic ear, I'm here."

Warmed by the offer, she hugged him. "I just might take you up on it."

For now, she needed to return home and read the file again before calling Will.

Her attorney would want to know his suspicions were correct. The Englands were telling the truth about Toria.

Chapter 22

"**A**re you finished yet?" Terrence wrinkled his nose. "This is taking forever."

Nearing the limits of her patience, Annie rolled the tension from her shoulders. "I'm still compressing files."

"How much longer?"

"Not sure."

"Can you estimate?"

The shreds of her composure frayed. "No."

"Would you at least *try?*"

A growl erupted from her lips. Startled, Terrence flinched.

She rose then jabbed a finger at the chair. "Take a seat. It's time you learned to use a computer properly."

Aghast, he stared down his nose. "Gads! How dare you talk to me like this."

"I'm serious. Sit down NOW."

His gums flapped as she grabbed his thin, velvet encased shoulders. With one swift push she landed him in the chair.

From the corner of her eye, she caught a glimpse of the usually subdued Lisbon punching the air. *You go, girl!* Other artists stopped working. A pen clattered to the floor somewhere to Annie's left. The place went silent.

She put Terrence back into her sights. "Now," she snarled, "put your hand on the mouse."

He worked his jaw. "Who do you think you are?"

"DO IT."

He tried scrambling off the chair, but she pushed him back down. From the secretarial pool, people hurried in. Elbows knocked and heads craned. Herman rushed in with network cables swinging around his neck like a noose. Lisbon put a finger at her lips as if to say, *Silence, children. Let's watch.*

"Gosh," Herman whispered, "I didn't know Annie had a temper."

Well, she did. She'd straightened to five foot, eight inches of fury. Terrence spluttered, his eyes flashing with indignation and fear.

"Put your hand on the mouse," she told him, "or we're trading punches."

"Okay, okay." He dropped a shaky hand on the mouse. "A fist-fight, indeed. Now what should I do?"

"Click the icon on the screen. The teeny hands, you ninny. Do it."

He clicked. A dialog box popped open.

"Now read the flippin' screen."

"I'm reading, hold on, just give me a sec . . ."

"Hurry up, you nitwit from hell!"

"Okay! It says to click here. And then . . . here."

"Can't you read any faster?"

"I'm trying," he whined. He suffered another of her glowering looks then added, "You're scaring me."

From the crowd, Bill said, "She's scaring me, too."

Annie didn't care. Spinning like a kite in the wind, she stared down the whole lot of them.

In unison, they raised their fists and cheered.

***

From her desk, Miriam said. "So you finally did it. You slayed Terrence-the-terrible. Congratulations. Art lost a bundle, but Bill and I did well."

Annie swiped the hair from her forehead. "You were

gambling that I'd fight with Terrence?"

"Bet's been good since the day you were hired." Miriam shrugged. "I always knew you'd win. You're a fighter. Was Terrence injured?"

"It wasn't a wrestling match. You watch too much TV."

"No blood on him? Bruises? If you'd come to blows, it was worth another fifty bucks."

Annie angled her chin. Somehow it seemed insulting that a fistfight with Terrence wasn't worth more. "I didn't strike him," she said. "I just lost my temper, okay?"

"You've been doing that a lot lately."

There was no denying the truth. Since meeting with Avery at Jefferson High, she'd been struggling with a host of emotions.

After the shock wore off, she'd battled an ungovernable rage. She was angry at so many people——her father, for lying about her mother's death, and the Englands, for threatening to take the child she loved. She was mad at Will for pushing her to find ten thousand dollars for Dillon's therapy. She was furious with Terrence for his incessant nagging, and Michael for reasons she couldn't pinpoint.

She was even angry with Miriam, although it didn't make much sense.

Tired of everything, she said, "I want to hit someone." She kicked the wall instead.

"Didn't I say you keep too much in?"

"Now I know why I'm mad at you, too. You're too damn wise. It makes me bananas the way you have the whole world figured out."

The confession didn't dent Miriam's calm. "In case you're wondering, Michael was also in on the bet. He won a hundred bucks." She studied her newly polished nails. This week she'd gone with fire engine red. "Pity he's not here to cash in."

"What are talking about? I saw him an hour ago."

"He's gone. Poof. No more Bedouin."

"Where is he?"

Miriam moved on to a close examination of her wrists. She looked like one of those women in a 1970s dishwashing commercial, noticing how soft and creamy an hour of scrubbing dishes had made her skin.

Annie leaned over the desk. "WHERE IS HE?"

"Calm down! He was talking about a trip to the Rockies. He's planning to hike the trails or some such nonsense."

"He's in The Rocky Mountains?" With Michael, anything was possible. She'd seen the photographs for proof.

"I vetoed the idea." Flipping open the appointment book, Miriam rapped lightly on the page. "He couldn't traipse off to climb every mountain, as it were. Not with next week's schedule."

"Where *did* he go?"

"Florida, to visit his parents. He's planning a few days of fly-fishing with his father."

The explanation made her miserable, and she shuffled off. She paused in the center of Michael's office to examine the contents of her heart. It was troubling to discover a new emotion mixed in with the rage.

Loneliness.

***

Dillon charged into the kitchen. Pete, the social worker from New Beginnings, sauntered in behind him.

"Hey, you." Annie captured Dillon in a tight embrace. "Are you done talking to Mr. Johnson?"

"All done." Dillon pressed his face into her hair. "You smell nice."

"It's my latest perfume. Potting soil with furniture polish mixed in."

"Lemon!" Dillon gave her an Eskimo Kiss. "I like lemon. Can I spray the polish?"

"Later." Annie hoisted him onto her hip. "Want to help with the dishes?"

"Sure!"

Balancing him gingerly, she let him splash through the soapy water until they were both soaked. "Okay, you've done your chores. You're off the hook. Go outside and play with Chip."

"One more Eskimo kiss," Dillon begged. After she rubbed her nose gently across his, he glanced over his shoulder, at Pete. "Annie's friend taught her to Eskimo kiss. I like Eskimo kisses."

Pete eyed her with interest. "A *friend* taught you?"

At a loss, she nudged Dillon out the door. She'd shown him

the Eskimo Kiss when she was really blue. He'd been nestled on her lap, watching cartoons, and she'd been dreaming of Michael. Without thinking, she mentioned a nice thing a friend had shown her. Then she'd given an Eskimo kiss.

Funny, but she'd never before had one. Not until Michael had shown her how.

Pulling from her musings, she said to Pete, "It's nothing. A friend of mine likes to give Eskimo kisses."

Dropping the subject, he collected his things. "I'm all set. You'll have the completed home study in a couple of days. I'll forward a copy to your attorney."

She escorted him through the foyer. "Thank you—for everything."

"I'll see you in court in September." He shook her hand. "You're doing a great job. And the psychologist? It's going well?"

"Dillon began sessions two weeks ago. He's even begun discussing his mother's death in a tentative way. It seems to help."

"He needs counseling to fully heal." Pete hesitated. "Can you afford the sessions?"

"The money isn't a problem." A lie, but she *would* find a way to continue. She'd do anything to ensure Dillon's wellbeing. "We're managing."

Pete walked out into the hot August air. Watching him go, she became aware of another emotion sifting through her heart.

Not rage, which rose whenever the Englands crashed into her thoughts. Or loneliness, because she missed Michael. No, this was another emotion altogether.

The fear had returned.

***

The cool, marbled lobby reeked of money. First Bank & Trust was the largest financial institution in Fairfax, the last stop on a disappointing journey.

Crystal chandeliers hung from the ceiling's gilded fresco. Cherubs bounded across the walls as if playing the music of heaven. Annie moved forward on heels as wobbly as toothpicks, the scruffy black pumps making an embarrassing amount of sound. A bank teller motioned her forward then told her to wait. Mr.

Bartholomew would see her in a moment.

Tension stole the dampness from her throat. Every other bank in the county had turned her down. If she failed here, it was over. There would be no money set aside for Dillon's long-term therapy. She couldn't demonstrate to the court she had the resources to keep him in counseling for the long haul.

She'd face the Englands with their world-class psychologist at their side. By comparison, she'd have nothing to sway the judge except her unwavering love for Dillon.

A middle-aged man, plump and dressed superbly in blue pinstripe, strode to her. With a shuttered glance he took in her old dress and cheap purse, and she experienced doom.

Mr. Bartholomew assured her the bank rallied behind the small business owner. *However, in these difficult economic times and given that Green Interiors has already used the equity line on your house, we must decline to loan another ten thousand dollars . . ..*

Murmuring farewell, Annie wandered into the glaring August day. She stood high up on the bank's marble steps with her emotions adrift. People hurried down the street to appointments and meetings and happier lives. Briefly she felt nothing, not even the sun licking her skin.

She examined her heart. It had become a strange habit.

The loneliness was gone. So was the fear.

She was left again with only the rage.

Chapter 23

Tanned, rested, and more relaxed than he'd felt in months, Michael rode the elevator to the fifth floor. The return flight to Dulles International had arrived at 8:30 P.M. On a whim, he'd decided to stop at the office to put in a few hours. At the least, he'd chip away at some of tomorrow's workload.

Time spent in Boca with his happily retired parents always put him on an even keel. They'd plied him with food and pleasant conversation, and Pops took him fishing on the Atlantic's aqua waters. The salty air was salvation, the sun hot and good. He'd come back rejuvenated. A little sunburned, sure, but more upbeat than he'd been in weeks.

The muffled sounds of typing in Annie's office threatened to shatter his mood. The rest of the staff had left hours earlier—why hadn't she? More importantly, had she missed him during his absence? There were no vases of flowers on his desk or the coffee table, no sign at all that she'd been in his office. Not that a homecoming gift was necessary—she'd made it clear they wouldn't begin a relationship anytime soon.

He booted up his iMac. "Hey, Annie!" he called. "Did you change the settings on my computer?"

"I did updates. Some of the settings are different."

He floundered, his patience slipping. *"Everything* looks different." Some of the icons weren't even remotely familiar.

"They're all there. They're simply rearranged."

Channeling Boca's relaxing beach, he tried again. Nothing. A new program popped up on the monitor. It was utterly foreign, something used to match Pantone colors.

"I'm lost here," he called, with heat. "I have to write a proposal for *Beele Electronics*. I don't have all day."

"So write it!"

Scowling, he stalked into her office. As usual she looked fetching even though the anger emanating from her was impossible to miss. A ponytail encased her silky, blond locks. She had on a lipstick that reminded him of Florida's coral, and the yellow dress that made her look like a sun goddess.

Her concentration was so complete he considered waving his hands in front of her face. "I need some help," he said.

Her eyes narrowed on the screen. "Take a number. Everyone needs help."

"It's nice to see you, too."

"Whatever."

The dismissive remark nicked his composure. "Aren't you going to say hello?"

"I'm glad you're back, Michael. Everyone missed you, and I'm happy to report the firm didn't burn down during your absence. Now, I need to install this program." She shot daggers then returned to work. "So beat it."

It took a moment for the surly remark to register. "What did you say?"

The danger thickening his voice didn't draw her attention. "I said go away," she replied. "If you leave, I can finish installing this friggin' program."

If she'd slapped him, he wouldn't have been more stunned. No one, not anyone who worked at Rowe had the audacity to tell him to hit the trail. Not if they wanted the paychecks to keep coming.

"Why are you deliberately baiting me?" he demanded. "I was in a good space. If you're looking for a battle, you've found it."

She smirked, as if daring him to blow his stack. "News flash—I've been in a bad space for days. Feel free to join me."

"Tell me what's wrong."

"No, thanks."

"I'm giving you five seconds." He leaned over her desk to ensure she couldn't miss the warning in his eyes. "Then I'm throwing you out of the building. Want to lose your job? Think it over, sweet pea. If I were you, I'd start talking."

She flinched, but her attention remained glued on the monitor. Damn if she wasn't calling his bluff.

Trumped, Michael pulled his palms off the desk. It made him perfectly crazy to think she'd won. He wouldn't fire her no matter how rude her behavior because she meant too much to him. And she knew it.

Wrong thought, pal. It's hard to be crazy about a woman when she wants nothing to do with you. The urge to hoist the keyboard right out from under her and slam it against the wall nearly got the better of him.

"Sit there in your pissed off state and keep all your secrets bottled up." He enjoyed a moment's victory when the comment stabbed color into her cheeks. "I'm tired of trying to figure out what goes on inside your stubborn head. You're selfish, Annie. You act like you're carrying the weight of the world, but you refuse to let anyone help. You have a martyr complex a mile wide."

With that, he stalked out. Maybe the battle had been lost, but only because he hadn't brought in the proper weapons. If she kept it up, he'd finish this with a severance package. Then he'd take Annie to the nearest window and drop her out on her head.

He was still devising ridiculous, imaginary punishments when she charged him from behind.

She came like lightning. Shoving him with surprising strength, she released a growl of pure rage. The impact hurtled him forward, and he stumbled. Righting himself he swung around, amazed by her irrational behavior.

She stood with fists clenched, breathing fast. "You want to know what's wrong? My whole life's a mess. Where should I start?"

"Anywhere you like. Tell me the entire sob story."

Instantly he regretted the jibe. The agony in her eyes was too great. He should try to pacify her, not goad her on.

"It's no sob story. I've worked hard, but I'll probably lose Dillon. And I've just discovered how gutless my father was. He lied to me—lied about so much—and I can't forgive him."

"Who's Dillon?" She shook her head, an angry refusal, and he asked, "What did your father lie about?"

"My father is dead. How can I be angry with someone who's gone?"

"Annie, you aren't making sense."

Rage shuddered across her shoulders as she began gesturing wildly. "He lied about my mother and Toria. He pretended Mom died in a traffic accident and that my sister was just irresponsible. He didn't tell me they were struggling with depression. He should've told me. Why didn't he trust me with the truth?"

Michael tried capturing her flailing arms. "Slow down—I'm listening."

"Don't touch me!" She shoved him away. "I'm so worn out, but I can't get past the anger. I can't find my way around it, it's too big—"

She cut off suddenly. The torment bent her over like a body blow. She took in gulps of air that didn't seem to sustain her. Michael's heart overturned.

Clammy perspiration sprouted on his skin. He was sick with apprehension. It seemed impossible to break through her suffering, break past it and offer comfort.

He reached for her. "Don't shut me out. It's time you learned to trust me. Let me help."

The heartfelt suggestion went unheeded. "Avery said life kicked me around." She drew tall, her face lit with fire. "I want to kick back."

She flew at him, shoving hard against his chest. He stood like a bulwark in the storm. His refusal to budge seemed to offer some relief from the tumult she was experiencing, as if his solid footing would help her find her own. He understood how helpless she must feel, how cast about by misfortune and a life that seemed only to offer failure.

She looked at him fully now, her chest quaking beneath the brunt of her emotions. "I want to chase rainbows, too. I don't know how." She buried her face in her hands. "My life is work, and worry and a million lost chances. It's too late."

"No, baby. It's not."

"Every time I pick up the pieces something else falls apart. I can't fix everything. It's too much. There's never enough time."

"You can make your life better." He grappled for sensible words to reach past her despair. "I can show you how if you'll let me."

"How can you fix what's already done? Toria was sick and before her, my mother. Toria never came back, and Dad died. I didn't understand what was going on. I should've. Why didn't Dad let me help? His heart gave out—his heart broke because he lost Mom, and then Toria."

Her disjointed comments were difficult to follow. "Annie, I'm sure your father only did what he thought best. He was trying to protect you. Let it go, sweetheart."

The love he tried to offer seemed yet another burden she couldn't carry. Her knees began to give way. Michael sprinted to her, catching her a split second before she fell. She was lifeless, a rag doll in his arms.

He brushed his mouth across hers. "It's not too late," he murmured, glad for the tears welling in her eyes, an indication he'd broken through. "Life isn't easy, sure. You have to fight."

"I'm tired of battles I can't win. I'm tired of losing."

He scattered kisses across her hairline. "Let me help. I won't let you lose."

"Help me now, Michael."

He lifted his head. With dismay he realized she was fumbling with his tie, trying to pull it off. She seemed hungry for anything capable of unburdening her heart, if only for the briefest interlude. The possibility that he might provide sanctuary warred with a more obvious truth—she was too distraught to make sensible choices and he refused to take advantage.

"Annie, we aren't making love." Certainly not in his office, and not while she was overcome with grief. "Let me take you home. We can talk about everything tomorrow. You need rest, and time to calm down."

"I don't need to rest. I need you." She dragged her mouth across his neck, drawing a shudder. You need me, too."

"No, not like this. You aren't yourself."

"I don't want to be myself. I don't want to think about tomorrow, or the next battle. The next time I'll lose." She rested her palms on his shoulders in a subtle urging that brought his eyes back to hers. "Michael, I don't expect anything from you. I want to forget my troubles—and I want to love you, as much as I'm able.

Let me."

How long had she run from this longing? She was tired of hiding from her desires, tired of pretending she didn't crave everything Michael had to offer. He was here, now, a man more generous than any dream lover she might fashion. For once she needed something for herself, a victory to cherish through all the defeats in her life.

Brooking no argument, she slid off his tie. He watched with hooded eyes, his emotions impossible to read. When she began unbuttoning his shirt, he stopped her. Their gazes dueled.

With a defiance matching her own, he pushed her hand away and peeled off his shirt. His pupils dilated as he tried to slow his breathing. She took in the sight of his naked torso, the peppering of black hair on his muscles, the rise and fall of his rib cage.

Annie lifted her hands. He stood perfectly still as she roamed the broad muscles and springy hair, the secret hollows separating each of his ribs. Touching him calmed her mind and, freed of the drudgery of thought, she let her senses expand to take in his musky scent and the nearly imperceptible sound of the rush of air he'd locked in his lungs.

"Michael, you're beautiful," she murmured.

He regarded her for a long moment, and she knew he was weighing a decision sure to alter both their lives. The care he took before choosing moved her heart into her throat. This was a man worth having, a man decent and wise, and she filled with a calm so complete it erased her grief for a welcome moment.

Pivoting away, he crossed to the door and locked it. He moved with patient, animal grace. Returning, he undid his belt. His eyes never left her face.

Pain clenched her heart as she studied his open, tortured expression. He was so beautiful and strong. Yet she understood: he would not press his advantage. He'd given her all the power, like a gift to use as she pleased. The knowledge sent longing pitching through her in irrepressible waves.

Swiftly, she drew away and slipped off her shoes. She unzipped her dress and let it fall to the floor in a rippling puddle. Michael sucked in a desperate breath. She unclasped her bra and shimmied out of her panties, daring him to look away.

Keeping pace, Michael shrugged out of his clothes. Yet he waited until she loosely draped her arms around his waist. Skin to skin, she let her eyes drift shut to better explore every sensation.

It was more than he could bear. She was so soft, pressed close to the storm building inside him, a tumult of need. She moved against him, liquid heat.

Passion, fierce and hypnotic, compelled him to lift her into his arms and carry her to the couch. He pressed her down beneath him and rained kisses across her skin, claiming every inch of her. The control he prided himself on maintaining slipped loose as hunger overtook him. More pleasure, more intense, and she cried out his name.

Nipping at her ear, he said, "If you keep voicing your pleasure, I won't be able to control myself." When her eyes drifted open, he added, "I want to be able to control myself for a while longer."

She studied him with softly hungering eyes. "Don't wait," she said. "I want you *now.*"

Her capitulation brought a low growl from deep inside him. Gripping her hips tightly, he hoisted himself slightly off the cushions. She opened her eyes as passion stole the last of his composure.

Nothing prepared him for the shattering bliss of possession. She was his for this one, perfect moment. His senses loosened as he took in the evidence of his domain, the feverish parting of her lips, her blond hair tumbling across his fists, the startling depths of her eyes. Rapture gripped his heart. For this moment, he possessed the passion in her blood, her cries, her limbs wrapped like vines around him. She belonged to him. For this moment, no more—and the thought made him despair for something deeper than mere carnality.

"That's right, Annie. Let me love you—"

He wondered at the strangled timbre of his plea, the desperation rimming the obsessive lust clouding his brain. After his divorce, he'd given up. Now he found a greater glory.

Need me.

Michael gentled his lovemaking to allow him to memorize the curve of her cheek and the scent of her skin.

Need me as much as I need you.

Afterward they lay still, taking in ragged breaths. She nestled into the hollow of his shoulder, allowing him to weave lazy circles across her collarbone. The minutes wound out, one after another.

Finally he forced his eyes open. "We can't stay like this," he said, with regret. It was closing in on midnight.

From beneath him, she looked around, dazed. "Where are my clothes?"

"All over the place. Just like mine."

She started to shimmy out from beneath him, but he held her still. "Annie, wait. Tell me about your parents and Toria. Why are you angry?"

Lovemaking had built a wall of trust, and she answered without delay. "My father let me believe the fiction about my mother dying in a traffic accident," she said. "I recently found out that my mother took her own life. It was a suicide, Michael."

The flat, emotionless statement brought him into a sitting position. Annie did the same, and he carefully he rested his hand on her back. "I'm sorry," he said. "About your mother—about all of it."

"I deserved the truth."

"When you were old enough to hear it." The reasons why her father chose to shield her were easy to understand. Any good father would protect an impressionable child from sordid facts. "How did you find out?"

She explained about the trip to Jefferson High to hunt through her sister's transcripts. Wrapping up, she said, "I can't rehash everything now. It's a lot to process. I'm still trying to sort myself out."

"It's fine. We can talk later."

It wasn't, but he didn't stop her from collecting up her clothes and making herself presentable. He followed with the full force of what they'd done barreling into his brain. They'd made love in his office, breaking every rule he'd ever set for himself with regard to women employees.

"Stop it, Michael."

He looked up.

Annie stepped into her heels. "I seduced you. It wasn't the other way around." She smoothed down her hair, a hint of impatience gleaming in her eyes. "I hate it when you act as if you're responsible for everything we do."

"What *are* we doing?" Reconsidering, he clasped her shoulders. "Strike that. You need to know what I'm doing. I'm falling for you. Not the best strategy given that you work for me, but I can't worry about that now. I want to see where this leads."

His declaration sent tears to her eyes. "We will," she promised. "Let me get some things sorted out first."

"Is that another of your famous evasions?"

"It's my way of saying I'm sleepy and feeling better than I've felt in months. I'm not ready for a blow-by-blow of every crisis in my life. Not this late at night."

He wouldn't beg. Ever. "You know how to try my patience, Annie." Hurt, he dropped his hands to his sides. "You know that, right?"

She cradled the side of his face. "I'll see you tomorrow." She kissed his cheek.

He let her go, leaving him alone with his doubts.

Chapter 24

"**L**ast throw, boy." Michael hurled the Frisbee across the park. His dog zoomed past in pursuit.

After a sleepless night, Michael had left the house at dawn to clear his head. It was upsetting to lose sleep over a woman who wouldn't share her troubles, or her deepest emotions. He chastised himself for doing so. Instead of roaming the park with Lucky while replaying the memory of making love to Annie, he needed to get to work. Lisbon had asked him to review the packaging concepts for the Voom hair products before Isabel Worthin's annual visit with the Rowe staff.

Lucky bounded across the grass. They tussled, and Michael wrenched the Frisbee from the dog's teeth. "Go get it, pal," he said, sending it aloft yet again.

By the time Lucky was worn out and panting, Michael had worked himself into a state of edgy irritation. When would Annie learn to trust him? Last night he'd only deciphered the merest fragments of her life story, enough to understand her late father had kept too many secrets from his younger daughter. There was no question betrayal left marks, even scars. He needed to get to the bottom of it.

Tail wagging, Lucky hopped into the Mercedes' back seat.

Michael shoved the key into the ignition. It was Saturday, and the weekend loomed before him. Waiting until Monday to see Annie seemed an impossible hardship.

Before he might think better of it, he flipped open his cell and punched in her number. When her machine picked up, he said, "I'm coming over. If you aren't out of bed, I'll wait. We need to talk."

***

Shock worked past her early morning grogginess. Annie replayed the message with her pulse beating in her throat.

Dillon padded down the hallway. "Morning, Annie."

His pudgy cheeks were sweetly flushed from a restful night's sleep. Thank goodness he was already dressed. He'd chosen green shorts and a purple tee-shirt.

"Hey, sweetie." She banished the anxiety from her voice. "Why don't you go over to Chip's house to play? I'll call his mother. I'm sure she won't mind."

Dillon rubbed his eyes. "Should I eat breakfast first?"

"Mrs. Wilson will make you breakfast, honey." Dialing, Annie suffered a moment's embarrassment at the babbled explanation she offered Shelley. Chip's mother readily agreed for Dillon to come right over.

From the front steps, she watched him walk across the street. She'd just finishing waving to Shelley, waiting on her own steps, when the familiar Mercedes glided into her drive. Tension made her muscles feel atrophied, and she wound her arms around her waist in a defensive posture.

A second later, she peered down at her clothes. Or bathrobe, to be more precise, since she'd been awake for less than twenty minutes.

There wasn't time to change.

With a sheepish glance, Michael eased his tall frame from the car. Barking erupted from the Mercedes' passenger side. Inside the window, Lucky's tail beat a healthy rhythm as the dog bounced across the seats. The second the dog was freed from his prison, he cut a tight curve around the car's bumper and shot straight into Annie's arms.

Given the nerves rattling through her, the affection was

168

welcome. "Hey, Lucky." She ruffled his fur.

"Two uninvited guests for the price of one." Michael stuffed his hands into the pockets of his jeans. "I'll bet this isn't how you planned to start the weekend."

"It's fine." His apologetic tone was balm for her tattered nerves. "Come in."

He did, moving straight through the foyer and into the living room. "Nice place." His attention swept the room.

"Would you like coffee?"

"Sounds great."

They went into the kitchen. She rattled around at the sink, nearly dropping a cup. His appearance first thing on a Saturday was startling, but not exactly unexpected—not after last night. She still hadn't wrapped her brain around the idea that she'd seduced Michael in his office after a particularly bad bout of behavior that included raised voices and tears. Or her raised voice—if memory served, he'd remained calm while she acted like a child having a tantrum.

Once the coffee was brewing she turned, and ran right into him. She hadn't been aware he was standing so close.

He steadied her, saying, "And I thought *I* was wound up. You have me beat." He smoothed his palms across the lapels of her robe. "Nice look. Though I'm all for seeing you out of it, after we talk."

"Why don't you sit down?" She glanced at Lucky, pawing the screen door. "Does he need water?"

"He drank his fill at the park." Michael let the dog loose into the backyard. Returning, he lowered his face into the soft tangle of her hair. "You smell good."

"And look awful."

"You look great." He kissed her with a hot urgency that recalled last night's lovemaking.

The front door banged open, jolting them both. They pulled apart without a second to spare.

Dillon scampered past. If he found an unfamiliar man in their kitchen surprising, his sunny demeanor gave no indication. He disappeared around the corner.

"Chip wants to play baseball," he called from over his shoulder. "Where's my bat?"

Shock rounded Michael's eyes. There wasn't time to explain.

Annie dashed out.

"I'm not sure where you left it," she said to Dillon's retreating back.

She reached the living room on a prayer Michael would stay where he was. Once Dillon returned to Chip's, she'd give a full explanation—something she would've done weeks ago if she'd had the courage. But not while her nephew was rooting under the coffee table for lost sports equipment.

"Oh, I 'member." Dillon turned on a dime and headed out. "In my closet, right?"

It was a surreal moment as he sprinted toward the hallway and Michael approached. They exchanged looks; then Dillon skipped past. Speechless, Annie raised her palms skyward.

"Found it!"

Dillon popped from the bedroom and sped out the front door. He left a deadly silence in his wake.

Struggling for a way to break it, she said, "That was Dillon."

Michael's face was as placid as the sea before a storm. "You've got my attention," he replied. "Start talking."

***

He listened in a cold, analytical silence to her tale about how her nephew had arrived after her sister's murder. When she'd finished, Annie stopped pacing and dropped into a chair. A shred of pity ate through his anger at all she'd kept hidden. She looked frightened and disconcertingly fragile. Revealing the boy's existence and the upcoming custody battle was surely the most difficult work she'd ever done.

As well it should be.

"Why didn't you mention him earlier?" Michael asked, outraged by everything she'd kept from him.

"I tried to."

"I don't mean yesterday. The night of our first date, you met me outside. Why didn't you ask me in? Introduce me to Dillon? Or later, at the office—you had a million opportunities to bring it up."

"I wasn't sure how you'd react."

"Were you ashamed of Dillon?"

"Of course not! I didn't think it proper to discuss him with my boss. The custody battle is a private matter."

Her *boss?* "You've got to be kidding." They'd been intimate less than twelve hours ago.

Clearly she preferred to forget their interlude.

"I hardly knew you, Michael," she snapped. "I wasn't ready to discuss the custody battle."

"Well you damn well know me now. In several different positions if memory serves."

The mention of their ardent lovemaking lit the tiniest flame in her eyes. Extinguishing it, she replied, "I didn't mean to mislead you. The last months have been rough, and I'm a private person. Maybe I have trust issues. I don't know. But I am sorry."

"I'll just bet you are." He tried to assimilate everything she'd told him. "You didn't have contact with Dillon before your sister's death?"

"I wasn't sure how to—"

He cut her off with brutal efficiency. "You mean you didn't care enough to try?"

"You aren't listening."

"Why didn't you mention the work you're doing to adopt him?" Rising, he began pacing where she'd left off. Hell, he could answer that one for himself. "You thought I'd fail a home study? I wasn't good enough?"

A tremor went up her spine, but he squashed any notion of pity.

"No woman has ever been ashamed of me," he said, hiding the hurt behind a savage tone. "Did you think I cared if a social worker dug into my private life? That there's anything I'm ashamed of? I graduated third in my class at Harvard. I own a successful business. I'm well respected in Fairfax."

"I wasn't ashamed of you." She went white, like a victim of a bloodletting. "I was ashamed of *me.*"

The small confession seemed to halt the earth's rotation. He could no longer hear Lucky's barking from the back yard or even the soft hum of the refrigerator. The truth shifted something in Annie's gaze, and he wondered if she was afraid of what she'd revealed.

"I should've done more to help my sister." She brushed the hair from her eyes then balled her hands into tight fists. He sensed movement, in her heart or her mind, but she remained still. "I should've known how much she was harming Dillon. I didn't care because I was sick of dealing with Toria's messes. I blamed her for Dad's failing heart. She'd brought him nothing but worry for more years than I cared to count. When he died, my love for Toria and her baby died too."

"You were heartless."

"Yes."

"You left a small child in harm's way. For the love of God— what if Toria had dragged Dillon along on the night she was shot? You might have buried them both."

"I didn't understand how precious he is."

Repulsed, Michael dragged his attention off her. "I don't have any siblings. If I did, I'd care about them. I'd never walk away from my own flesh and blood."

"How do you know, Michael? You've never had to deal with an unstable sibling. You don't know what I've been through." The admission bent her shoulders. "I might lose Dillon to the Englands," she said, her voice catching. "They forged a relationship while I pretended he didn't exist."

"I hope you don't lose him." Paltry words of comfort, but they were all he was prepared to give.

"The court will decide." She met his gaze with equal disdain. "Now you have the story. You should leave." She started for the foyer.

"You're throwing me out?" It hadn't dawned she might.

She flung open the door.

He rocked back on his heels. "When we made love, we got tangled up in each other's lives. Last night meant something, and you can't just shut me out. Not that I propose sex at the moment. We'd have a great time in the sack, but neither of us would like ourselves much, afterward."

"Get out."

Regret pricked him, full and deep. The emotion took him aback. But he couldn't back down, not while she was staring at him with loathing.

"You're so deep under my skin, I'm not sure how to work you back out," he said. "This isn't over."

***

He'd already thrown himself into the Mercedes and brought the engine to life before he remembered Lucky. For the love of God—where was his dog? Craning his neck, he scanned the summer bright street. Kids played on front lawns and a balding man two houses down was trimming his hedges. On a wave of oaths, Michael got back out to look for his dog.

A tickling sensation turned his heels due north. In the driveway next door, Miriam gaped at him. The stream of water from the hose she held missed the flowerbed and nearly hit his shoes.

Michael pointed a finger. "Not a word," he commanded. The hose joggled, and sent water across the front shutters of her house. "Damn it, Miriam—watch what you're doing."

Lucky's bark resounded from further off. He caught a glimpse of Miriam dropping the hose as he whirled around and spotted his dog racing across the street.

The boy, Dillon, raced after him.

"Lucky, come back! Don't go!"

The kid tried to grab hold of the mass of fur traveling at rocket speed. Michael did a second take. Someone had strapped a cowboy hat to Lucky's head.

Dillon.

The hat nudged a memory to the surface. Michael recalled a necklace of green florist wire and Lucky's ears squashed into bizarre ponytails. It was the day Annie had fallen headlong into Nicholas DiRameo, The New York Bakery King, with her platter of cookies and his mud-caked dog.

Michael winced. It was the day she'd fallen headlong into his heart.

Now he understood. Annie hadn't decorated his dog. Dillon had.

"Hey, Mister—can Lucky stay? Does he have to go? Can he play with me?"

Wading through the fog of bad temper, Michael tried to assimilate the questions rattling off like gunfire. Lucky plopped down beside him, joggling the cowboy hat on his furry head. The boy skidded to stop to look up, up, up Michael's body.

Michael blinked. The kid's eyes were exactly like Annie's, perfect blue-green gems. The realization gutted him.

Snapping out of the stupor, he found his voice. "Lucky has to go home," he told Dillon. "He's ready for a nap."

"I take naps sometimes." Dillon leaned against Michael's legs with a child's deliberate charm. "Can Lucky take a nap with me?"

"I'm sorry, buddy. We have to go."

"Where *is* Lucky's home?"

"About twenty minutes from here." Sympathy rained down in his chest, soft and unbearable. The kid looked mournful and ridiculously cute in his leather holster and cowboy boots. "Maybe he'll come and play with you another time. I'll see what I can do."

Dillon peered around him. "Nana Miriam! Can you get Lucky to stay?"

Wheeling around, Michael bumped into his valiant gatekeeper.

All things considered, he expected Miriam to singe him with one of her bulldog expressions. If she laid into him right in front of Annie's kid, it was no more than he deserved. This morning he hadn't been on his best behavior.

Without considering his actions, or the implausibility of a man of his height reacting in fear of a woman nearly twice his age, he took a hasty step back. She'd never kicked him, but this wasn't a normal day.

"Come here, Dillon." She held out a hand that was quickly grasped. "The dog has to go home. He'll visit soon, I promise."

She regarded Michael with enough compassion to gut him all over again. When she patted his arm, the shame he didn't welcome stole into his bones.

"Go on," she murmured. "Just leave."

Nudging the dog inside the car, cowboy hat and all, he followed her request.

Chapter 25

Late in the month, Annie's attorney arrived on a Monday afternoon. The visit was unexpected.

The day had been dreadful. Since the argument with Michael at her house, work at Rowe Marketing was less than enjoyable. He'd taken to treating her like a persona non grata, not that she'd behaved any better. Wearing a frigid cordiality like a coat of armor, she spoke to him in short, clipped sentences. The warrior pose didn't stop her from feeling like a wreck.

She parked before her house and heard little boy laughter coming from inside. Shelley Wilson had a key and must have picked up the boys early from summer camp. The hilarity emanating from her living room, however, didn't snag her attention. On the front steps, Will sat in a hunched posture.

"It's about the continuance I requested," he said, by way of greeting.

She sat beside him. "What's wrong?" He looked as blue as she'd ever seen him.

"Asking the court to push back your custody hearing to September was a risk. I didn't have a choice. We needed more time to look into the Englands' accusations regarding Toria's mental health. Legally, I've opened a door."

Her mouth went dry. "What do you mean?"

"Since the court granted our delay, the Englands want to visit Dillon. The judge has agreed."

"Tom and Dianne England are coming *here?*"

"Next weekend."

The awful news refused to sink in. "No, it's not possible."

"The judge granted six-hour visits each day, Saturday and Sunday."

"The court halted their visitation to give me time to get acquainted with Dillon. Why is the judge going back on his word?"

"To his mind, we've changed the rules."

"Dillon will be confused. He never talks about the Englands. He hasn't seen them in months—forever in the life of a small child. What if they take him for an outing and he's scared? I *can't* let them take him."

Sighing, Will patted her knee. "They'll arrive at 10 A.M. each day and return him at 4 P.M. I'm sorry, kiddo. It's out of my hands."

The screen door creaked open. Shelley sensed the glum mood. "Should I stick around and watch the boys?"

Annie put on a brave front. "That would be great. Thanks, Shelley."

"Can I get you anything? Coffee? Water?"

"No, we're fine. Just give us a couple of minutes."

The door closed softly. Inside, Chip shouted. More laughter, but it barely registered in the quagmire of Annie's thoughts.

Despairing, she shut her eyes. "The Englands are well off," she said. "They'll bring a million gifts on Saturday, every toy imaginable on a little boy's wish list."

"Like Christmas in August. Next month we'll bring Dillon into court and all he'll do is smile at them. Major gift-giving would snow any kid."

"The judge won't fail to notice."

"No, he won't. Watching Dillon react positively to the Englands . . . the judge might be swayed. Damn it all. Every time I think we've got this case won, the Englands throw another curve ball."

"Are you giving up?" Dread crawled her skin. "Does this mean I'll lose Dillon?"

"It means winning got harder."

Grasping at straws, she asked, "What about the ten thousand? If I can set up an account, will it turn the odds back in our favor?"

Will looked at her with disbelief. "You've been turned down by a dozen banks. You can't raise the money."

"I have to do something."

Mulling it over, he asked, "What about Michael Rowe? You're an employee in trouble. I don't know him personally, but he has a stellar reputation. Ask him for a loan."

"I can't." She refused to elaborate.

"It was just an idea. We *are* running out of options."

Between them, a pitiful silence grew. Annie listened to it as the fear crept into her heart.

***

"**R**ead this book. Wait! Read this one."

Reclining on Dillon's bed, Annie said, "Pick one, sweetie. It's almost bedtime."

On tiptoes, he sent a playful look. Finally he selected a book from the child-sized shelves beside his dresser and hopped onto the bed.

"I don't like sleepy time." He rubbed his nose. "There's nothing to do."

She wound her arm around his shoulders, encouraging him to snuggle close. "If you go to sleep right away, it'll be morning in no time. You can play with Chip."

"We have to play lots. It's almost time for school."

"Three more weeks."

"Summer got over too fast." He shrugged. "It's okay. I miss my teachers."

Annie sucked in a tremulous breath. If the Englands won, Dillon wouldn't return to the elementary school he'd grown to love. He'd move to Baltimore, to another world without Chip or familiar teachers. He'd lose everything tied to his life in Virginia.

Everyone, including her.

A simple way to broach a painful topic proved impossible. "Sweetheart, I need to talk to you about something," she said with false cheer. "Next Saturday we're having visitors. You haven't seen them in awhile."

"Who are they?" Dillon nuzzled to her breast.

She tightened her hold. "Mr. and Mrs. England. You used to call them Tom-Tom and Dianne. They'll take you out to play for a couple of hours on Saturday. Sunday, too."

"I think I 'member them. From my old house. We were friends."

"That's right. Months and months ago."

Would mention of the Englands lead to a conversation about Toria? With Liz, his new psychologist, Dillon had tentatively discussed his mother in the language of a small child. During the last visit, Liz had explained to Annie that children lived in the present, and rarely dwelled in the past. *When Dillon is older, it's likely he'll discuss Toria with you. It might not happen until he's a teenager or an adult. Adopted children survive a terrible break in their lives. Many will forge a new relationship with an adoptive parent over many years before feeling comfortable enough to discuss the past. Let him set the pace on how and when to talk about his biological mother.*

She treaded carefully, fearful of saying anything that might upset him. "Do you remember when you first came to live with me? Once I dropped you off at Will's office to see Tom-Tom and Dianne. They took you to a movie."

The pudgy hand on her heart curled tightly. "Why didn't you go with us?"

The truth was painfully simple. She'd dreaded meeting the couple determined to take him away from her. "I was scared," she said. "I knew they loved you very much."

"Nana Miriam loves me. She isn't scary."

"No, she isn't."

Something in her behavior spelled danger, and Dillon tensed in her arms. "I don't want to play with Tom-Tom and Dianne. Can you tell them to go away?"

"No, honey. I can't."

"Can *I* tell them?"

"Dillon, you have to see them. It'll be fun—promise."

She wrestled the urge to jump in and explain about the upcoming custody hearing. She couldn't bring herself to begin. Instead, she stroked his hair. It was wrong to burden a small child too quickly. His new psychologist had suggested waiting until the court date neared. After the Englands returned to Baltimore, Annie would find the courage to explain how the world she'd carefully built for him might soon be torn down.

On a smile, she opened the storybook.

***

Trish stepped out of Annie's pickup and brushed the dirt from her jeans. "That lady at the tavern sure is a pain," she said.

They'd spent half the morning delivering plants to The Blue Cock Tavern ahead of schedule. On a whim, Annie had called the office and told a stunned Miriam she wouldn't arrive until noon.

Flicking a pothos leaf off the seat, Annie recalled the terse conversation. She hadn't given a damn about showing up late. Yes, Isabel Worthin would arrive today. The entire staff was working on preparations for the new Worthin product line. But the prospect of another day of Michael's tight-lipped wrath firmed up Annie's resolve to spend several hours immersed in the calm of the greenhouse before facing him.

Heading inside, she said, "The woman who owns the tavern is elderly. You should be more patient."

"Yeah? Try being nice to some old bag while she's barking orders. I wanted to pop her in the nose."

"Trish!"

"Oh, c'mon. She was driving you nuts, too." The teenager headed for the fridge and the sub sandwich she'd stowed there earlier. "We should charge an extra fee for general aggravation. If someone makes us nuts, they should pay. Big time."

Exhausted, Annie fell into a chair wedged beside an overgrown palm tree. "It's part of the job. They buy, we deliver." She studied the tree—roots were peeking out of the pot's bottom and creeping across the floor. She really needed to repot the plant. "Sometimes we play interior decorator when we make a delivery. Customers don't always know where to put the plants they've ordered."

"You would defend the old bag."

"She's a good customer."

"I'm glad because my back hurts. Shit, I need a hot compress or something."

"Your language is out of line, young lady."

Unruffled, Trish took a hearty bite of her sandwich. "Blame my love-toy, Colin. He's turning me into a wild woman. Don't tell my mother. I'm eighteen now and it's none of her business."

Annie yanked her attention from the palm tree to the hormonally flushed teenager. "You aren't having sex with him are you?" The girl had toed the straight and narrow until now.

"Not yet."

"Keep it that way. Spend more time thinking about college, not boys."

Trish paused, her manner disturbingly mature. "Since we're on the subject, who have *you* been dancing between the sheets with?"

"As if I'd discuss my private life. Eat your sandwich."

"C'mon, boss lady. It's written all over you. Who's the stud?"

Annie had no intention of telling her young employee about the deeply gratifying sexual encounter she'd had with Michael. An encounter they'd never repeat. At this rate, the stars would fade before they managed a civil tone with each other.

"There's no stud." She went to the refrigerator and looked inside, glad for the diversion. "If there were, I wouldn't discuss him with a teenager."

"Why not?" When Annie favored her with a chilly silence, Trish added, "Lie all you want. I can tell you've been burning up the sheets. I have girlfriends, you know. Something's going on—it's in your eyes. You're moody all the time, and that means guy-heaven."

More like guy-hell. "You're imagining things."

"Have it your way." Trish took a swig of her bottled water. "You've got the look in your eyes right now. All haunted and stuff."

"Change the subject, please."

Maybe she *should* get to work. Facing Michael couldn't be any harder than an interrogation by an astute teenager.

Chapter 26

Isabel Worthin stood in the reception area chatting with Miriam and looking all the world like a model, even though she was more than seventy years old.

The silver hair was natural, Annie guessed, a pure, metallic color without the slightest hint of dull yellow. Isabel wore large diamond earrings, which would've appeared garish on a lesser mortal. The gems flashed with cold fire as she tipped her head back to laugh at the private joke she'd shared with Miriam.

Annie patted down her hair, and checked her fingernails for dirt. She'd just arrived, determined to maintain a calm demeanor no matter how Michael treated her today. She smiled in greeting.

"I suppose Miriam has already told you about Michael," she said.

Isabel regarded her with slightly slanted, honeyed brown eyes. "He's at the airport waiting for me." She laughed, a low, sensual note of amusement. "The poor boy. My plane arrived early so I took a cab. I didn't think to call him first."

"Already done," Miriam supplied. "He'll be back in twenty minutes."

"I'll wait in his office." Isabel sashayed away from Miriam's desk. Pausing, she regarded Annie. "Aren't you coming, dear?"

The invitation lifted Annie's brows. Why would Isabel Worthin deem her suitable company? Someone should find Lisbon since she was itching to reveal the new designs for the Zoom hair products. Or Miriam could stay with Worthin's elegant president. By comparison, Annie was out of her depth.

"Of course," she said, following.

Isabel floated into the office with the confidence of a woman in control of every situation. She seated herself then waited for Annie to do the same. "You're Michael's new assistant, aren't you?"

"I am, Mrs. Worthin."

"Please, call me Isabel. Everyone does." Emotion sparkled in her rapt gaze. "You've only been with Rowe since the spring? Do you like it here? Michael seems to think you do."

He'd discussed her with Isabel Worthin? The possibility was both heartening and disturbing. "I enjoy my job," she replied. "I still have a lot to learn about marketing. I work with computers. Forestalling crashes, integrating software. That sort of thing."

Something in Isabel's face prodded her on, and Annie found herself talking easily. She'd nearly relaxed when Michael's voice rang out from the doorway.

"Don't you have something to do?" Without awaiting her reply, he turned to Isabel. "How was your flight?"

Ignoring the question, she spread out her hands. "It was fine but I'm parched. A nice cup of tea is in order."

"I'll get it." Annie smiled.

She skirted past Michael, hurtling darts from his black gaze. Stepping to the coffee station beside Miriam's desk, she boiled water and dropped a tea bag into the cup. To her right, Miriam led a group of artists up the corridor. As lead designer on the Worthin account, Lisbon was at the head of the queue.

By the time Annie had returned, Terrence, Violet and Bill had appeared, and Isabel was immersed in conversation regarding the upcoming product launch.

***

"Why don't you knock off early?" Miriam whispered. "You need the rest."

While the meeting continued Annie had stayed on the fringes, ordering in lunch and racing to fetch renderings and other supplies. Coffee and tea were replenished, mineral water brought in. When it became clear Michael intended to glare at her all afternoon, she'd taken Miriam up on the offer to help with filing in the reception area.

"I'd love to leave early," she admitted. "I don't have the nerve to walk back through to get my purse." Annie placed a document inside the file. "Michael is peeved at me today."

"You did come in three hours late. What were you thinking?"

"I needed time to myself."

"What was he doing at your house last weekend? He won't explain. I wish you would."

"I don't have the stomach to go into it."

"I hope you *will* at some point." Miriam shut the file cabinet. "Should I go in there and grab your purse? The way Michael has been acting, it's best if you stay clear of him. If he so much as gives me a nasty look I'll belt him one. Which will delight Isabel. She knows Michael can be a stubborn mule."

The prospect of Miriam putting Michael in his place brought a weary smile to Annie's lips. "Trish is at the house babysitting Dillon. If I sneak out of here early, I can take the munchkin to the playground before dinner."

"Then it's settled. I'll grab your purse. Go home and spend time with your little boy."

**

Gobs of spaghetti sauce dotted the kitchen counter. Parmesan cheese trailed in a sloppy line across the floor to the table. A few wet strands of pasta dangled off the edge of the table, like droopy worms lined up in a row.

With a burp, Dillon finished the meal he'd helped cook.

"You need a bath." Annie swiped at the red ring around his mouth. She surveyed the splotches of sauce on his tee-shirt. "A bath with oodles of soap in the bargain."

"Do I have to?"

"Oh, yeah. It's almost bedtime."

"It's too soon."

She waited as he hopped down and padded into the hallway. "You never want to go to bed."

"Can I bring toys in the tub?"

"No stuffed animals this time. And no raisins. You know what I thought they were the last time I saw them floating in the tub."

"You thought it was poop!" He chortled.

"Don't do it again. Poopy tub water is a woman's worst nightmare." She marched him to the bathtub and turned on the tap. "C'mon—hop, hop, hop!"

He'd just kicked off his shoes when Miriam appeared.

Dillon squirmed free and into Miriam's arms. "Nana Miriam!" He scrunched up his face as she landed a kiss on his cheek. "Want to give me a bath?"

She chuckled as he helpfully tore off his clothes. "Ordinarily, I'd love nothing more," she said. "Your alphabet songs are enthralling, but we ladies need to talk."

She sent a meaningful look over his head. Evidently this wasn't a casual visit.

Quickly, Annie helped him into the tub. "I'll be right back," she promised. She tossed several plastic toys into the water. "No splashing, okay?"

"Okay."

In the kitchen, Miriam said, "The staff is going out to dinner, compliments of Isabel."

"Everyone is going?"

"Isabel loves the new packaging concepts. She's taking us to The Mark to celebrate."

The Mark was a premier Fairfax restaurant in the area's most exclusive country club. The only time Annie had been inside was to attend a friend's wedding reception.

"I'll skip the festivities and deal with the repercussions tomorrow," she said. "Michael isn't speaking to me, and it's not like I'll be missed. And what about Dillon?"

Miriam waved away the excuses. "Call Trish to babysit. We're driving to The Mark together."

"Trish left an hour ago. She has a date."

"She'll cancel." Miriam smiled confidently. "Tonight you'll avoid Michael and stick by me. You came in late this morning—and he adores Isabel. If you don't go, I'll never hear the end of it."

***

Set like a gem on one of Virginia's finest golf courses, The Mark teemed with activity.

In a gesture of flamboyant generosity Isabel had reserved the entire restaurant for cocktails and mingling, and instructed the restaurant to open up the large banquet hall in back for dinner and music. A five-piece ensemble played softly in the banquet hall amid lavish flower arrangements and festive table settings.

"What I'd give for a cocktail dress fancy enough to do this room justice." Annie had settled on a grass green linen dress purchased months ago at a consignment shop.

"Who cares about clothes? I want to dance." Miriam swayed her hips in zesty anticipation. "Darryl, in accounting? He looks dull but the man has moves."

The stodgy accountant looked about ten minutes from death, but what did Annie know? "If you say so. I hope he keeps your dance card filled all evening long."

They were swallowed up in the throng of Rowe employees. Inside the main dining area, the bar brimmed with laughter and cozy chatter as drinks were poured. Waiters hurried past, balancing trays of salad and appetizers.

Beneath the dais where the musicians played, the head table quickly filled with guests. Terrence stood chatting with Violet and Bill, his jewel-studded hands gesturing wildly. Annie glimpsed Michael politely seating Isabel then Lisbon. He looked dashing in a charcoal grey suit and cobalt blue tie. The sight of him made her miserable with longing. Not that her reaction made sense— Michael had every reason to be angry. She should've mentioned the custody battle long before he'd practically bumped into Dillon at her house.

Lowering her eyes, she followed Miriam to a table in back.

The secretary Bitsy, and Annie's sidekick, Herman, wavered nearby. Miriam motioned them forward. "Kids, sit with us." She began fussing in her maternal way. "Why, Bitsy, you look wonderful—such a lovely dress! Herman, you look dashing in your sports coat."

"Bitsy picked it out." Herman fiddled with his tie. "We went to the mall after work."

"She did you proud. It's very attractive."

The foursome ate dinner together with Miriam keeping the conversation afloat. Annie forced a bite of filet mignon into her mouth, conscious her old friend watched her like a hawk, searching for signs of distress.

When the waiters began clearing dinner plates, the music's tempo became lively. Employees swirled past with their husbands or wives or dates; the air steamed with a heady mix of perfumes. Still in a funk, Annie frowned as Miriam's eyes glazed over.

"What is it?" she asked as Miriam snatched up a napkin and began swabbing her face. "Are you ill? You've gone green."

"The filet." Miriam grabbed her water goblet, drank. "What was in the sauce?"

A creamy, brown sauce had been drizzled on the beef. "Is it important?"

"I think it had mushrooms. I'm horribly allergic."

Across the table, Herman fidgeted. "What should we do?"

"Nothing, dear. I need to go home, take something to settle my stomach."

"I'll drive." Annie leapt up.

She careened into Michael, rooted behind her chair. Strong fingers locked on her shoulders, and he spun her to face him.

"Searching for the exit?" He arched a brow.

She threw him off. "Miriam ate something that didn't agree with her. We're leaving."

His hostility morphed into concern. "You're sick?" he asked Miriam.

"Mushrooms," she croaked, grabbing the water goblet for another sip. "You know how they bother me."

"Isabel was having so much fun putting together the menu, I forgot to remind her of your allergies. Damn it all. Should I take you home?"

"I brought my car. Annie will drive."

"She can't."

Annie piped up. "Why not?"

He slid a frigid gaze her way. "Isabel asked you to join us. She enjoyed talking to you this morning." The disclosure hardened his jaw. "What *did* you discuss?"

"Nothing in particular." She returned his icy inspection with a guarded look. She'd be damned if she'd tell him anything. "Send my apologies. I'd love to stay but I have to take Miriam home."

"You drove together?"

"You catch on fast."

The tart response furrowed his brows. "I'll take her and drop you off later. We can't disappoint Isabel."

"Thanks, but I'd rather not hitch a ride with the boss."

"Stop being unreasonable."

"Stop baiting me. It's your favorite entertainment, but it's not much fun from the cheap seats."

He leaned close, his dark eyes glittering. "News flash—I've had about all I can stand."

He meant her secrets, and Dillon. "I've already apologized," she shot back, as the others listened in stunned silence. "I'll flail myself later. Don't ask me to rehash it here."

"Don't push me, Annie. You've used up all your chits."

"Go to hell, Michael."

At the table, Miriam belched. Her hand flew to her mouth. "Stop squabbling," she muttered from between her fingers. "I'll drive myself. I'm perfectly capable." She turned to Bitsy and Herman. "Will you kids take Annie later?"

Herman cowered beneath the dueling match between the boss and Annie. "Sure, we'll take her." He grabbed Bitsy, evidently to wrench her out of harm's way. "We're, uh, going to dance. Right, Bitsy? We love to dance. Annie, find us when you're ready to leave."

Abandoned, Annie watched them dash to the relative safety of the dance floor, Bitsy's fancy heels clattering all the way.

Miriam hoisted herself up on a moan. "Glad it's settled." She held her stomach with one hand and grabbed for her purse with the other. "I'll see you both later."

She scooted from the banquet hall before Annie could protest. The urge to follow was strong.

Reading her face, Michael latched onto her arm. "Don't even think it. You aren't skipping out. My staff worked hard for this shindig, and you aren't mucking with Isabel's plans." He tried tugging, but she refused to budge. "Are you coming quietly, or do I have to drag you?"

"What is this—a hold-up? Take my purse. I have a twenty and change."

"Are you finished?"

She ditched the comedy routine and searched for logic. The danger emanating from him started her heart banging around her rib cage. "I should go with Miriam. She's too sick to drive."

"She'll survive."

"Don't you care if she becomes violently ill?"

"At the moment? No."

"News flash—I don't particularly like you right now."

He swore lustily beneath his breath. "Stop arguing with me in front of my employees. I'm not interested in becoming fodder for gossip beside the water cooler." He winced. "Or on YouTube."

"Stop telling me what to do!"

"Whatever." He let go of her wrist and she tottered on her heels. "I hadn't planned on providing the night's entertainment but with you, babe, anything goes."

The urge to shove him to the ground nearly won out. Instead she darted past with her shoulders squared with military precision. He couldn't intimidate her if she refused to play along. A dozen curious faces bobbed before her eyesight but she kept moving. Sweet angels above, people *were* staring.

She made a beeline toward Isabel, who was waving like a long lost friend. The owner of Worthin had chosen a flowing silver gown for the affair and a necklace of sapphires flamboyant enough for a ride on the Titanic. It was doubtful she knew how much havoc her invitation had caused.

Terrence, to her right, launched his hands into the air. "There you are!" He propelled Annie into the chair he swiftly vacated. "That's right, that's right—make yourself comfortable. Isabel was telling us how she missed chatting with you."

Isabel waved him off like a pesky fly. "Did you enjoy dinner, Annie?" She leaned close, a co-conspirator amidst the night's revelry. "I saw Miriam rush out. It was the mushrooms, wasn't it? After all these years, you'd think I'd remember a food allergy."

"I'm sure she'll be fine."

"Let's hope so. Everyone else is having a good time, don't you think?"

"I do." The event was less than pleasant, especially after Michael roosted beside Lisbon like a vulture waiting for carrion. "I can't imagine what all of this cost, dinner for fifty employees and their guests. You must have spent a fortune. Of course, you *have* a fortune so it's probably not a big deal."

The words bubbled out in a rush. Luckily the observation merely amused Isabel.

Motioning to the waiter, she had wine poured for all. "I'm very rich, and haven't given much thought to the expense. I do enjoy hosting parties. Not New York parties with simpering society mavens and journalists poking around for gossip. I much prefer celebrations with genuine people like you, Annie."

From across the table Michael shot black arrows, but Annie clung to the light banter. "Are you all that wealthy?" she asked.

"My beauty empire is worth millions. I'm sure Lisbon or Bill can supply you with the worst part of the truth. I'm a lonely old woman, too ambitious or too driven for much of an interior life. In many ways, Michael and I are quite similar."

Mention of his name yanked Michael's attention from Annie. "Run that by me again," he said.

"Dear boy, we're both ambitious. Too much so."

"It's not exactly a character flaw."

"Oh, but it is. We're both adept at piling up money and making our mark on the world. In the end, what do we have?"

"Money," he supplied with thick sarcasm.

Isabel narrowed her regard, reducing him to the level of a fool. To Annie, she said, "When they place Michael in his casket, they'll pour all his money inside. He won't have anything else. Not love, certainly. He won't have children weeping over his grave."

Michael drained the whiskey from his glass. "Where's a violin when you need one? This is beginning to sound like opera." He appraised Isabel with hooded eyes. "You didn't have kids. You survived."

"A rather callous observation."

"The unvarnished truth."

"I might have considered children if circumstances had allowed."

"Hold on. I'm trying to visualize you with a screaming toddler." Michael flagged down a waiter and demanded liquor. After it was supplied, he added, "Sorry, Isabel. I can't conjure up the image."

Maybe it *was* time to knock Michael to the ground. His behavior was rude in the extreme. Annie was considering more violent options when Isabel spoke.

"Perhaps it *was* a mistake not to have a child." With fingertips, she drew lazy circles across the table's linen. "Looking back, I was busy building an empire. Who knows? I might not have had a talent for parenting. At least I had Theo and a few years of wedded bliss. Poor Michael. All he has are his millions."

The words dampened Annie's ire. Sure, she was still upset with Michael. He'd been treating her poorly for days. Yet the sympathy she felt was far more compelling. On the surface, Michael had everything—looks, success, power. But what did he truly have besides an adorable dog and a successful company?

He could have me. The thought proved impossible to outrun.

He could have me, and Dillon.

With effort, she brought her attention back on the conversation. "You're very wise, Isabel."

"Ah! Now you're flattering me."

"It's not flattery. You're the most beautiful woman I've ever met, and one of the kindest."

Isabel cradled Annie's cheek. "You *are* a treasure," she said. "I doubt you're even aware of your own gifts."

The compliment left her speechless. What gifts? Annie felt like damaged goods. She'd failed Dillon when he was a toddler. She'd ruined her chances with Michael. She was deep in debt, and about to fight a custody battle she deserved to lose.

The others murmured agreement with Isabel's compliment. Everyone except Michael, who was scowling, and Violet, spooning cheesecake into her mouth.

When Violet finished her dessert, Terrence leaned toward her ear. "Violet, I believe I'm on your dance card. Shall we?"

They walked arm and arm to the dance floor. Bill looked questioningly to Lisbon. On the dais, the musicians started into a slow number. Lisbon nodded, and Bill escorted her away.

Which left Annie, Isabel and Michael in a clumsy silence.

Isabel broke it. "Don't you want to dance?" she asked Michael.

Grunting, he rose. "Sure. Why not."

"I meant Annie. Perhaps she would like to . . ?"

"She won't."

"Have you asked?"

Annie snatched up her wine glass and drained it. "Oh, I'd rather not." She set it down with a bang and reached for Violet's untouched Chablis. "I'm exhausted. Long day. Isabel, you go." She dispelled with pretense, and chugged.

"Now, don't be frightened." Isabel motioned to the band. "Why, the music is lovely. Enjoy yourself."

Michael shifted in his chair. "Annie said she's tired."

"What young woman doesn't want to dance?" Isabel stared down her nose. "But not with you. Certainly not while you're glowering at her. I'm sure she's injured."

"I'm not doing *anything* to her."

Annie stiffened as he aimed another volley. Ducking it, she considered finishing the dregs from Lisbon's glass.

Indifferent to her desperation for more wine, he asked, "Am I in any way invading your space? Making you uncomfortable? Anything at all?"

A suitable retort died in her throat. Or maybe the booze made a quick comeback impossible to locate. Wine and warfare was not the best combo.

Isabel came to the rescue. "Michael, you're acting like a child." She patted Annie's wrist. "He's angry with you, isn't he? Don't lie. You've made him angry so now he'll brood. Men like to brood in private. Or in public, when they've misplaced their common sense."

"He's not angry," Annie lied. Where was Herman? It was time to leave.

Isabel tapped a jeweled finger on the table. "Ah, it's none of my business. Perhaps you fight all the time. It might be habitual."

Michael gritted his teeth. "We don't fight all the time."

"It's not my affair. Though I do wonder how you work closely together when you can't tolerate each other."

"I like Annie just fine!" he bellowed, drawing startled glances from couples on the dance floor.

Which was enough to launch Annie to her feet. "Let's dance." It was that, or have a blowout in front of everyone. She stared at him belligerently. "One dance, okay?"

He flung down his napkin. "You're the one who's exhausted."

"Well, now I'm just dandy."

"You were exhausted two minutes ago."

"It was a long two minutes. I've rested. Now I can dance all night. Waltz. Fox trot. I'll even have a go at the Tango if you lead.

Satisfied?"

Fuming, he hesitated. He appeared ready to spit fire or bellow at the top of his lungs. Which would drag them into a shouting match. She'd had enough.

Watching the exchange with a secretive smile, Isabel crossed her legs with the leisurely repose of grand dame having a marvelous time. "Are you planning to dance, or not?" she asked.

Chapter 27

If Annie had been furious before, now she was unnerved.

Michael pressed a hand to the small of her back to push her toward the dance floor, tripping her pulse and sending her forward in silent compliance. He seemed beyond rage, hovering in some netherworld for the irrationally ballistic. Perspiration glossed his brow. His features were burnished with a ruddy glow that under different circumstances would've been attractive.

"Isabel doesn't usually meddle like this," he muttered at Annie's back. "Why she gives a damn if we dance is beyond comprehension."

Annie moved through the sea of dancers parting to make way for their angry boss. "Isabel was trying to be nice," she said. "She's trying to patch things up between us. She knows we've been fighting."

"We aren't fighting."

She went rigid as he hauled her into his arms with the finesse of a lion dragging down a kill. "Stop with the denial, all right?" She tried to find a rhythm to match the song's slow beat. "You've had me in the dog house since you found out about Dillon. If a dozen apologies don't suffice, I'll send chocolates."

"I'm not going into it."

"Maybe you should. I'm sick of the dog house."

"Enough with the psychobabble." He jerked her in a circle then lowered his voice. "I'm not having a go at you in front of my employees. Change the subject."

"What would you like to discuss? The weather? World politics? Pick a topic and I'll jump right in."

"Shut up, already."

"Go on, Michael. Say it. Everything is my fault. Isabel's meddling, your crabby mood, my penchant for keeping secrets—everything."

"I'm not playing the blame game."

She laughed with disbelief. "Sure about that?"

In response, he yanked her tight against his chest. She tried drawing up her hands in a defensive posture, but there wasn't room to maneuver. Defeated, she flattened her palms on the crisp lapels of his suit coat. At a nearby table, two women from the accounting staff bent their heads close, giggling.

Thankfully Michael missed the interchange. "Okay, I do blame you," he said. Pulling her due east, he bumped a couple out of the way. "I'm not too proud to admit I'm also hurt."

"Mostly you're livid because I didn't tell you about Dillon."

"Meeting him *was* a hell of a shock—especially since I was thinking about stripping you out of your bathrobe. What if he'd walked in?"

She refused to honor the comment with a reply. Better to dodge any conversation about intimacy. It would only dredge up memories of their tryst in his office—an incredible experience she'd do better to forget.

Pity Michael was less inclined to let it go. Leaning in, he said, "In case you're wondering, I'm still coming to grips with our office sexapades. First you were so upset you scared the hell out of me. Then you lit me up like a Roman candle. And, of course, there's Dillon to consider. I've been having visions of burning in hell because some tyke almost caught me making love to his mother on a sunny Saturday morning. It's a lot for a man to deal with."

The way he freely admitted she *was* Dillon's mother won him several Brownie points. Even if Michael hadn't come right out and apologized for his oafish behavior, his tone *had* softened considerably.

She fixed him with a sober, searching gaze. "Try to internalize this, okay? I never meant to shut you out. No question, you had every right to know about Dillon."

"That's right."

"I know! This isn't about you—I'm ashamed because I should've done more to help him before Toria died. I took the easy way out when I let my sister cut off contact. I knew she had problems, especially with drugs, but I was sick of dealing with her abusive boyfriends and her scrapes with the law. The way I behaved was stupid and selfish and easily the worst thing I've ever done." Her voice threatened to break, but she managed to add, "I never meant to hurt you or Dillon."

The admission brought him to a stop. "All right then. You're forgiven."

"Gee, thanks."

"Cut me some slack, Annie. I've been on an emotional roller coaster since you walked into my life."

She nearly smiled. "You have control issues."

"No kidding. I'm trying to improve." Grinning, he drew her back into his embrace and resumed dancing hip to hip in a way that nearly turned her legs to butter. "I need time to get used to all of this. It's not easy thinking of you as some kid's mother when I've had this image of . . ."

Breathless, she looked up at him. "Of what?"

"Of us. A relationship. Long walks on the beach and candlelit dinners. I hadn't factored in a child right from the start. Not that I would've held off because of a home study that should've included me from the get-go."

Did he want to make their relationship work? She was trying to shape a response when his expression deepened. Lovemaking had given them too much knowledge, and she melted against him automatically. The music died away and couples moved from the dance floor. They continued swaying together as one.

Yearning rose in her blood. "We can sit down now," she said.

The musicians started into a ballad. Michael brushed his lips across her brow.

"We should." He sent a warm breath across her ear. "I can't."

Beneath her fingertips, his heartbeat raced. In some small part of her brain, she knew they'd caused a scene after all. Curious glances filtered their way. Muffled whispers sounded, further off.

Dancers quietly drifted on and off the floor as the band played one slow, romantic number after another.

They might have danced forever. It was heaven enough.

When it seemed she'd completely lost track of time, he led her back to the table. Terrence and Violet were gone; the others were deep in conversation. Without asking her consent, Michael swept up her purse and steered her outside.

They walked through the shadows to his car. She got in without a word.

Dreamily she watched the streets stream by, her thoughts centering on the quiet, brooding man beside her. Once they'd reached her house, he got out. She sensed he wasn't looking for an invitation to come inside.

When he finally spoke, his attention strayed to the moon, riding high in the midnight sky.

"Annie, I don't have anything against children." He leaned against the Mercedes. "I'm sure Dillon's amazing."

She joined him. "He's a great kid."

"I'd like to get to know him."

"You will."

"I'm divorced." When she looked at him, startled, he added, "I thought it was for keeps. Jen didn't feel the same. If she loved anything, it was my connections."

"I don't understand."

"Jen owns a PR firm in DC. Rowe Marketing had clients she wanted to tap. She lives in Georgetown now, lives for fashion, parties . . . she used me to get ahead."

The stilted explanation was terribly sad. What sort of woman used a man to further her career? Annie studied her feet, amazed by her own naiveté.

Lots of women.

"The divorce changed me in ways I'm not proud of," Michael was saying. "Living with someone like that eats away your ability to trust. It makes you suspicious of people's motives long after the damage, and the divorce." He paused as if coming to a difficult decision. His voice thinning, he added, "Jen got pregnant. Total blunder—we thought we had it covered. The pregnancy became a fault line in our marriage. I hadn't understood how much I wanted kids . . . Jen didn't. No kids, ever. She miscarried, and we split soon after."

At a loss on how to provide comfort, she rubbed his arm in soothing strokes. The cold facts bent his back. He looked old.

Somehow he continued. "I wanted the baby more than anything I've ever wanted. Not like ambition, going after a goal— it was like something sacred. Life would give me the chance to become a father. Why we didn't have the foresight to discuss children or how we felt about parenthood is beyond me. We were so busy conquering the world, it never came up. The thing is, relationships don't work without trust and communication. I want to trust you, Annie. We need to keep the lines of communication open."

"I understand."

"I don't think you do. And you should, for my sake. It's no picnic being knotted up inside."

"I don't want you knotted up."

"Do you want me to fall in love with you?" He prodded her into his arms. "Because I have. I'm sure of it."

The words rang through her, joyous and bright. Had she heard him correctly?

Overwhelmed, she struggled to voice her deepest wish. "I want this to work because I love you, too."

Her declaration erased the anguish on his face. "That's a good start for us and Dillon." He grew silent. After a moment, he added, "Given your upcoming court date, we have to be careful."

"Should I recall the home study? Ask the social worker to have you included?" She'd do whatever he chose.

"It's not the best option." He nuzzled her ear then drew back. "I've already looked into it."

"You did?" He was a thorough man. Of course he'd checked.

"I needed to understand how adoption works. Even if your social worker reopens the home study, there's another problem. The judge will push back your court date. The battle for Dillon will drag on."

"I don't want to drag this out."

"Then I'll stay on the sidelines until you win custody." He cupped her face, grinning. "By the way, stop giving me that look at the office."

"What look?"

"The one on your face. Like you're mentally undressing me."

She laughed. "I guess I am." The admission pooled heat in

her belly.

"I'm no superman. That look gets me every time."

To prove it, he crushed his mouth to hers. She cried out with pleasure, the sound igniting the fire they'd both tried to keep at bay. His palms lifted from her face and landed with a thud on the car, enclosing her between his arms.

She knew he didn't risk touching her. He wouldn't stop if he did.

Chapter 28

The alarm clock read five-fifteen. Sleep had eluded Michael for most of the night.

At his feet, Lucky rolled onto his back and whimpered for a belly rub that wasn't forthcoming.

Hours of tossing and turning hadn't sorted Michael out. Last night Annie had returned his affection with her own profession of love. Now the chill of the retreating night left him wrestling his worries. His experience with matters of the heart included a nasty divorce and years afterwards of meaningless dating. It wasn't the sort of history to inspire confidence. Add in his feverish attraction to Annie, and he wasn't exactly operating from a position of strength. Losing control of his emotions scared him most of all.

Second thoughts hounded him as he dressed and went downstairs. He cradled a cup of coffee grown cold by the time Isabel, who stayed at his mansion whenever in town, strolled into the kitchen.

"Have you been up long?" She filled the teakettle with water and placed it on the stove. "My flight doesn't leave for another three hours. You didn't have to rise early."

"I couldn't sleep."

"Because of Annie?"

Count on Isabel to get right to the point. "Yes, because of Annie." He waited while she prepared a cup of Earl Grey and joined him. "I'm not sure I can keep my distance, but I don't like being a home wrecker."

"That sounds a tad melodramatic. Since when are you a home wrecker?"

"She's trying to adopt her nephew." He explained then added, "With the home study complete, I need to back off until she wins permanent custody. It shouldn't be a problem."

"But it is?"

"She's a kid's mother, not casual date material. And what about me? I'm no great catch. I should have 'cynic' tattooed on my chest."

"That *is* a quandary. Did you discuss this with Annie last night?"

"I covered some of my concerns. Mostly I was thinking about making love to her against the side of my car."

Mirth waltzed across Isabel's face. "Oh, to be young again, doing it against the side of a Mercedes." She sipped her tea. "Though at my age, my yoga instructor wouldn't approve."

"You're a barrel of laughs."

"I *do* try. Give me that much."

"I don't know what to do about Annie."

"Options?" She understood his need to weigh the pros and cons of any decision. Michael was predisposed to avoid any risk he hadn't thoroughly assessed. "Surely you've worked out a few."

"The obvious solution? Stay the hell away until the adoption finalizes. I'm not crazy about that option. Second choice? Talk to her social worker and find out what sort of relationship we can have pre-court."

"We don't live in a Gestapo state. Surely you can take her and the child out to dinner without having to rewrite a home study." He looked wrung out, but she couldn't resist adding, "Give me a moment. I'm trying to imagine you with a child."

"I'd be great with a kid." He shoved his coffee cup away. "Stop smiling. It's not funny."

"Says you."

"I don't know why I talk to you, Isabel. Compassion isn't your strong suit."

"Swim with sharks, you must be a shark."

She finished her tea in a rapidly improving mood. If life had been different, if she'd met Theo before Worthin went international and middle age had arrived, wouldn't they have brought someone like Michael into the world? It was natural to think of him as her son. Even to dream a little.

Didn't she share his disappointments and successes like any parent? She loved him. Oh, she'd never actually said the words. For all she knew, Michael viewed himself as one of her rare friends, a trusted confidante. He might even believe his success in marketing her products had earned him the right to her friendship.

He was mistaken.

Although the facts were obvious, she asked, "Are you in love with Annie? I'm not talking about infatuation or simple passion. Do you love her in a real and lasting way?"

The query worked creases across his brow. She watched him grapple with his heart, this remarkable example of manhood felled so completely by his yearning for a singular woman.

A woman, Isabel had already decided, she liked very much.

"Yes, I'm in love with her." He clawed a jagged path across his hairline. "I'm crazy to feel this way."

"You'd be crazy to feel anything less. I'm sure she loves you, too."

"She says she does."

"Then stop acting like a coward. You're using the custody hearing to avoid the more serious issue." When he remained silent, she added, "What happens after court? Can you set the past aside and bring a better skill set into this relationship? Let go of the bad habits you learned in your marriage to Jen? It's time, Michael."

He gave a stiff nod.

She hurried on. "Because the real issue is your desire to marry Annie."

He laughed shortly. "Hold on, now. You're jumping the gun."

"Am I? Granted, you need time to develop your relationship. After you do, marry her." She patted his wrist. "In case you're wondering, I approve."

He laughed. "Good to know."

Should I ask Annie to marry me? He hadn't looked that far ahead. Jen had destroyed his ability to hope for anything better than the steady, stable life he'd built. She'd left his emotions brittle. She'd left him with a deficit of imagination.

No longer.

***

"**H**ey there, pretty lady." Michael closed the door to her office, lending them privacy.

"Where have you been?" Annie let him tug her into his arms. "Isabel's flight left hours ago."

"I spent the morning with your social worker. Nice guy."

She angled her neck to stare at him. "You saw Pete? Why?"

"To get the game rules. Seems I *am* allowed to see you and Dillon before your day in court. Pete suggests we stay to public places. Amusement parks, restaurants, that sort of thing."

"But you shouldn't come over to my house?"

"You've got it." His eyes lit with pleasure. "He also sent a message for you."

"Which is?"

"If the men you date are of this caliber, I apologize for scaring you from the dating scene."

It sure didn't sound like dignified, low-key Pete. "You're kidding."

"Am not." He shot her an engagingly boyish look. "I assured him that even though you're only two weeks from court, I'll do whatever it takes—get fingerprinted, give him access to my financials. Actually, I brought some stuff with me."

Stuff? "What did you bring to the adoption agency?"

He grinned like a pirate. "Bank accounts, the bio Harvard publishes on alumni . . . a donation."

She wrenched out of his arms, caught between horror and a bad case of the giggles. "Tell me you didn't try to bribe my decent, upstanding social worker."

He appeared genuinely insulted. "Thanks a lot. What do you take me for?"

"At the moment, I'm not sure."

"Pete runs an inner city baseball program. I read about it on the New Beginning's web site, and donated five thousand dollars." Michael tapped his temple. "Research, sweetheart. It closes the deal every time."

Laughing, she flew back into his arms. "Oh, I *do* love you."

Was it wrong to ask him to loan the money for Dillon's psychological care? Apprehension darted through her—ten thousand dollars was more than a simple loan—and there were his ex-wife's deplorable habits to consider. Jen had used Michael for her own financial gain. He might easily misconstrue the request.

"What's wrong?" He held her at arm's length. "You're hiding something."

Getting used to his sixth sense would take time. "It's nothing, Michael. Listen, I have a ton of work to dig through. Let's talk later."

"Open lines of communication, remember? We won't get our relationship off the ground without it."

She went to the wall of glass and searched the vista of green for a way to begin. They'd only just begun building a foundation of trust. Doing anything to put it in jeopardy was foolish.

"Annie, talk to me."

Relenting, she said, "I need a loan."

"For your attorney? Legal bills can be a killer."

"This isn't about Will's retainer."

In a halting voice, she explained about the twenty thousand dollars the Englands had set aside, and how she needed to demonstrate her own willingness to pay for long-term psychological counseling should Dillon need it. As she spoke, Michael's features hardened so quickly she felt weak with apprehension.

But she mistook the target of his anger. "The Englands put twenty thousand into an account for Dillon's care?" he asked.

"Earlier this summer."

"You're not borrowing ten from me," He remarked, as if they were discussing mere dollars, and not thousands. "I'm giving you twenty. We'll match them, dollar for dollar."

***

"Why the long face?" Miriam asked.

When Michael didn't reply, she padded into his office. For the first time in memory, he'd drawn the ceiling-high blinds across the wall of glass behind his desk. The near darkness filled the suite with gloom. She negotiated a path to his desk then paused to study the Slinky he rolled from palm to palm while unanswered calls flashed on his phone. She wasn't sure what was more bizarre—the ghostly feel of his office, or the glinting toy he held.

"Michael!"

Wrenched from his thoughts, he glowered. "What, already?"

Miriam jabbed a finger at the Slinky. "Explain."

"Haven't you ever seen a Slinky before?"

"Why are you playing with one?" Oh, he really had gone off the deep end. Head first, and right into the water. "Let me guess. Senility hits early in your family. Next you'll be drooling. Lord knows I'll be the one stuck dabbing at your chin. Should I put a gerontologist on speed dial?"

"Funny, Miriam. Keep it up, and you can do a stand-up routine with Isabel."

"What are you talking about?" she snapped, although she *could* imagine Isabel doing comedy. Most people were intimidated by her elegance and wealth, but Miriam knew better—or knew Isabel better, which amounted to the same thing.

Michael waved her off. "Go away," he said. "I'm brooding."

"You sure are. Mind explaining why you're playing with a child's toy?"

"It's for Dillon."

The admission stopped the next barb from leaving her lips. Lately he'd been insufferable, and she'd been dreaming about belting him soundly. The way he charged the employees like a mad bull or tested Annie's patience, why, who wouldn't dream of buying boxing gloves? This newer, softer Michael was rather disconcerting.

A squishy sensation pooled inside her. "You bought a toy for Dillon?"

"Starting out small makes sense—right?" He glanced at her as if, heaven above, he valued her opinion. "Sports equipment is too much for a first gift. I thought about getting Dillon a bike. Too expensive. I spent an hour shopping. This is what I came up with."

"Let me get this straight. You went shopping in a toy store?"

"That about sums it up."

The squishy stuff in Miriam turned to pudding. "So why the long face?"

"I was hoping to take Annie and Dillon out tonight. I was

looking forward to quality time with her boy. No can do. She has a meeting with her attorney. They're rehearsing for court."

"You can still see Dillon if you like."

Michael slapped the Slinky down on his desk. "I can? How?"

"He's coming over to my house, dear." Miriam straightened. Had she actually called the Bedouin 'dear'? "I'm having a picnic for my family. Would you like to join us?"

Nodding, he practically glowed. "You bet."

Chapter 29

"**M**om, should I get the door?" Tina asked.

Miriam's daughter swiped the brown, curly hair from her face. Petite like her mother, she was juggling her baby and the gelatin mold she'd just pulled from the refrigerator.

"I'll get it." Miriam hurried past. "It's probably Michael Rowe. I invited him to join us."

Tina stopped rocking the baby. "You invited your boss? Really?"

Miriam snorted. "Good heavens, it's a family picnic. Why the fuss?"

"Mom, the twins are home from college." Tina followed, with the baby cooing in time with her steps. "They'll talk about body condoms and sex toys. Or compete to see who can be the first to give Mr. Rowe a heart attack by slurping food up their noses. The twins are certifiable."

"It's your brother's problem. If he can't control his kids, what can I do?"

"Hide your boss from the mayhem?"

"Michael won't keel over because your brother raised a couple of hooligans." Miriam halted before pulling the door open. "And do call him Michael. He despises formality."

She found her visibly anxious boss twiddling his thumbs on the front stoop. The confident, mercurial owner of Rowe Marketing had morphed into the foot-shifting, tongue-tied replacement before her.

"Here." Michael thrust a bottle of wine into her hands. "Should I have brought food, too?"

"Of course not. Come in." Miriam scanned his white golf shirt and crisp navy pants. "Where's the Slinky?"

"In the car. If everything goes well, I'll grab it later."

"Everything *will* go well. Don't be so nervous, dear."

Midway across the foyer, he dragged her to a halt. "Miriam."

The poor thing, he was perspiring. "What!"

"Stop calling me 'dear'." His grin grew lopsided. "It's weird. "

"Fine."

She led him into the kitchen and introduced him to Tina. He finally stopped fidgeting, coming to a standstill before the bank of windows above the sink. More than twenty adults and children, the bulk of her extended family, had gathered in the back yard.

"Big family," he said, obviously hesitant to proceed.

"Go on out," she said. "You'll be fine."

"Maybe this wasn't a good idea. I'm an intruder."

"What? Are you packing a gun and pantyhose? Relax." Miriam bit her tongue before she slipped up and added 'dear.'

Tina handed over the baby. "I'll take him outside, Mom." To Michael, she said, "Why don't I get you started at the grill? You can get the meat on while I set the picnic tables."

"Yeah. Sure."

At the grill, uncooked hamburgers and steaks were lined up on a white platter. Barbecue tools hung from the grill. Spotting them, Michael tried throwing off the thousand pound gorilla sitting on his chest.

He picked up the long, two-pronged fork. "Where're the onions?"

Tina tipped her head to the side. "Onions?"

"Don't you want grilled onions? I can do them up on a grill pan with butter."

"Oh. Of course."

"And the A1?" He gave Miriam's daughter a sheepish look. His penchant for taking charge might not mix well at a family gathering. "Do you like A1?"

Tina grinned. "Doesn't everybody? I'll get that, too."

She returned inside and he got to work. Surreptitiously he surveyed the crowd, the adolescent girls texting on their cells and the men clinking beers. The gangly teenage boys nailing each other with cans of whipped cream looked thunderstruck when Miriam took chase with impressive speed. A nice family, he mused, slapping burgers and T-bones onto the flames.

"Your onions, sir." Tina set the onions and a grill pan at his elbow. "Want me to introduce you around?"

"Not yet."

"Nervous?"

He gave a quick glance. "My extended family consists of three people. Well, four, if you count my Aunt Edna. She lives in Paris, and doesn't visit often." He speared a steak and flipped it over. "My idea of a big group is a business meeting and . . . "

His voice evaporated. Far behind the throng, Annie's boy stood alone beneath a maple tree. Dillon was trying to toss a baseball skyward and swing a bat at the same time. The effort was clumsy, but the tyke didn't seem inclined to give up.

An indefinable emotion grabbed Michael around the throat. It was probably the damn gorilla, back for more punishment.

Tina carefully took the barbecue tong from his grip. "Let me take over," she said. "Help Dillon with the baseball."

Like a sleepwalker, Michael wove his way through the crowd. His ears buzzed—a nice compliment to the acid brewing in his stomach. Which struck him as ridiculous since he wasn't about to make a million-dollar marketing presentation. Tossing a baseball around with a kid was easy.

This wasn't just any kid, he reminded himself. This was Annie's Dillon.

The baseball rolled out of the boy's reach. "Need some help?" Michael scooped it up.

"Sure." Dillon lifted his shoulders in a careless shrug. "I need practice or I'll never get as good as Chip. He's great."

"Who's Chip?"

"My best friend. He's two months older. Maybe that's why he hits so good."

"He does, eh?" Michael wiped the sweat from his brow. "Why don't I pitch?"

"Sure."

He did. Slow pitches, some faster. A few girly-pitches to ensure the kid connected with the ball. When Dillon finally made contact, he gave out a whoop of joy that started Michael grinning.

Ten minutes later, it was a disappointment when the kid tossed down the bat. "That's enough, mister." He flapped his arms. "I'm getting sore."

"You aren't hurt, are you?"

"I'm okay." Dillon stared at him with sober curiosity.

Michael straightened, perplexed. He'd met precious few kids in his life. His only familiarity with childhood derived from conversations with other men. On the golf course, at business lunches—he'd never paid much attention. How to entertain Dillon?

He was still trying to work it out when the kid closed the distance between them. "Wow, you're tall." Dillon leaned in. Evidently he didn't know the rule about staying out of a guy's personal space. "You're like a tree. How tall are you, mister?"

"Over six feet, easy. And call me Michael."

"That sounds like a lot . . . Michael. How tall am I?"

"I'm not sure." He was pee-wee short. "You'll get taller."

"That's what Annie says." Dillon pushed against Michael's thighs. "Are you strong? Chip's dad is strong."

The unexpected physical contact nearly threw Michael off his game. But it was nice. It dawned on him that this wasn't so hard. Stick to guy stuff and he was home free.

"So Chip's your buddy?" he asked.

"My best friend in the whole world. Do you have a best friend?"

He thought of Annie. "I think so."

Dillon disarmed him with a smile. "Show me how strong you are."

"What do you want me to do?"

"Hold out your arm, silly. Don't you remember?"

Michael blinked. He had no idea where this was headed.

Then he *did* remember. How, during his own childhood, his father held out his arm for Michael to grab hold of. How his father had lifted him up then lowered him, over and over, until Michael believed he was a monkey swinging from a sturdy branch. Until he believed he could make his father's strength his own.

Thrusting out his arm, he winked. "Go on. Jump up and grab

hold."

Whooping, Dillon leapt into the air. His small hands barely wrapped Michael's forearm, but he managed. He whooped again as he was lifted toward the sun.

After the muscles in his arm burned, Michael walked the clinging boy to the picnic table resting in the maple tree's shade. Dillon hopped down onto the bench.

Now they were much closer in height, allowing a thorough examination of a child very much a baby still with plump cheeks and crazy curls. He was similar to Annie in many ways. They shared the same creamy skin tone. Both had a nose that upturned sweetly at the tip. And of course Dillon's eyes were like Annie's— the familiar, blue-green ocean Michael adored.

Annie loved the boy. She loved him with the full, fervent devotion a mother reserved for her child. Dillon meant everything to her, but she might lose him.

Memories Michael wasn't prepared to entertain barreled into his brain. With them came the shattering emotions he couldn't bear to relive. The fear, when he'd found his ex-wife lying on the bathroom floor after the miscarriage. The nearly insurmountable grief for the child he'd wanted and lost.

What if Annie loses Dillon? The loss would cleave her heart in two.

Shaken, he sat heavily on the bench. He stared at his hands as he wrestled with shame. Why hadn't he considered how difficult this must be for her—the waiting, the wondering? Until now, he hadn't fully processed everything she was at risk of losing. He loved Annie. It would be easy to fall for Dillon, too.

Maybe he already had.

Chapter 30

Saturday morning the grey Honda Accord pulled into the driveway at 9:57 A.M.

On a wave of fear she couldn't suppress, Annie walked outside. Months had passed since she'd last spoken to the Englands. If past history was any guide, she could expect an unpleasant visit.

Dianne England disembarked from the car first, smoothing her short red hair into place and casting dismissive glances at the street's working class homes. She wore pressed khakis, a white linen blouse, and a predictably stern expression. She relaxed the slightest degree when her husband came around the hood and took her hand in his.

Silver haired, with a gym rat's muscled build, Tom England seemed confident and nearly at ease despite the situation. Unlike his wife, who seemed content to study the street, his attention quickly landed on Annie. He regarded her with nerve-wracking intensity.

"He's ready to go, I presume?" Tom rapped out.

Evidently there would be no formalities, no pretense of cordiality. "I'll get him," Annie said, her stomach tumbling.

Dillon was rooted in front of the television. The morning

cartoons were on, something with a rabbit hurtling out of the atmosphere in a space ship. The volume was set too high, and she rushed over to turn it down.

"Dillon, honey, the Englands are here." Kneeling, she stroked his cheek. The familiar affection usually brought him around.

Not this time.

She was about to gently steer him to his feet when Tom's footfalls came from behind. Shocked, she swung around. The Englands barreled into the house without so much as an invitation.

"Dillon, my boy! Are you ready?" Tom's voice boomed across the living room.

Pinpricks of anger needled Annie's heart. "If you'll wait outside, I'll bring Dillon in a moment."

The softy issued command put ice in Dianne's gaze. She opened her large canvas purse and withdrew an iPad with a lime green cover. Pushing Annie aside, she wagged it before Dillon's nose.

"Darling, look what I've brought! I've missed you so much. Oh, my sweet boy—how are you?"

The lure of electronics brought Dillon out of his stupor. "For me?"

"It certainly is, cupcake."

"Chip has one—I've played with it. It's neat."

"Don't you want an iPad for your own?"

"'Course I do!"

"Here you go, darling." Dianne placed the sleek device into his outstretched hands.

Turning the iPad over and over, Dillon went to her. He left Annie kneeling on the floor.

"There are more surprises in the car," Dianne was saying. She rubbed her hands together with relish. "Oh, I had so much fun shopping for you! There's a new basketball and Legos and— Dillon, do you remember the red fire truck that made so much noise? The one I kept for you at my house? I bought you an even bigger one. It'll make all sorts of sounds. The big, red light on top flashes, too."

Dillon trembled like a kid on a sugar rush. "It does?"

"We'll bring the fire truck with us to the park. Tom-Tom will show you how to play with it. Are you ready to go?"

"Sure!"

Annie's heart pitched as Tom England took Dillon firmly by the hand. "C'mon, son," Tom said. "Let's go."

Dillon skipped out of the house. Annie couldn't find the strength to get to her feet, not with Dianne scanning the living room with unmistakable distaste, the old sofa and garage-sale rug, the plants, and the tiny television set. When her eyes swept downward, they brimmed with venom.

"He's my son," Dianne rapped out. "You can play all the games you'd like, but you won't win. Am I making myself clear?"

Annie tried to formulate a suitable retort. *Say something.* But she couldn't speak. She could barely breathe.

"You aren't much for small talk, are you?" Dianne's upper lip curled with disdain. "You're just like your sister—in over your head, and unaware of it. Tom, the fool, thought we could help her. She was such a mess, and he's always been stupidly soft-hearted."

The words crashed through Annie. The need to defend Toria—and to defend herself—sent a sickening heat through her chest. She managed to rise on unsteady feet.

"I despised your sister." Dianne released a cruel, short laugh. "Admit it. You hated her, too. She was a rock around your neck."

"No! She was my sister . . . I didn't hate her, I'd never . . ."

The words sunk into a confused silence.

Dianne smiled, triumphant. "Toria was a drug addict and a whore. And you? You didn't have the slightest interest in her or Dillon. You left that sweet, defenseless boy living in hell. Tom and I rescued him—not you. Never you."

"It's different now. I love Dillon. He means everything to me."

"Pity you didn't love him when he needed you most." At the door, Dianne hurled a last volley. "You won't win, Annie. Dillon is my son."

***

Sunday was worse. The Englands arrived twenty minutes early bearing more gifts. Dillon launched out of the house chattering about the fire engine they'd given him and the day's activities. An afternoon at an amusement park was planned, with rides and carnival games. It was as if the Englands had never left Dillon's life, and the easy way he clasped Tom's hand and hugged Dianne made the last months seem like an illusion. It was as if they'd never left his life at all.

Rooted at the kitchen table, Annie let the hours slip by. For the first time, she mapped out her life without him. It was a depressing task.

Michael called twice. The calls went unanswered. Making the attempt at conversation would have her wailing in seconds. She felt too raw to share her emotions with anyone.

In the early afternoon, the scent of cinnamon wafted into the kitchen. Slumped in a catatonic pose, Annie sniffed. She lifted her gaze and focused on Miriam, standing before her with a china platter.

"Get up." Miriam placed the freshly baked cinnamon buns on the counter. "That's an order."

Grudgingly, Annie got up and moved to the sink. She leaned heavily on the counter like a robot operating on the last of its power.

Miriam sighed. "Come closer. Heavens, I can't reach your head if you don't bend a little."

A hairbrush tugged at clumps of Annie's hair. "What are you doing?" She tried pulling away.

Miriam stopped her. "What does it look like I'm doing? I'm brushing your hair. There—much better. Don't move." She thrust a dishcloth beneath the sink's tap. "Didn't you wash your face this morning?"

"What?" Annie spluttered as Miriam swabbed her face with the wet cloth.

"How about your teeth? Did you brush them?"

"No."

Miriam pushed her into the bathroom. "Get going," she said, thrusting the toothbrush into Annie's hand. "I suggest using mouthwash afterward."

Annie trudged to the sink. While she brushed, Miriam disappeared down the hallway. Dresser drawers squeaked. The closet door banged open, followed by the sounds of hangers sliding down the rod.

Going to investigate, she leaned against the door jamb as Miriam selected blue jeans and a cotton shirt with a rosebud pattern. Tennis shoes landed with a thud by the bed. Stiffly, Annie unbuttoned the rumpled nightgown and pulled it over her head. The modesty she'd feel on a normal day wouldn't materialize. She was too low.

Miriam scooped the nightgown from the floor. "This is how you were dressed when the Englands arrived?" She hurled the dirty gown into the laundry hamper. "Good heavens, child. Don't you have an ounce of pride?"

"Not at the moment."

"I forbid you to let those people walk all over you. Find some backbone. I raised you better than this."

"You didn't raise me."

"Guess again. I've been part of your life for longer than you can remember. And I've always been here for you. I love you as much as I love my own children."

The heartfelt soliloquy put a faded smile on Annie's lips. "I love you too," she said. Miriam was shaking all over as if she'd caught a fever. "I don't mean to upset you."

"You think I'm happy with you acting like a zombie? Keep it together, dear."

"How can I? Dillon is thrilled to see the Englands. It's like they never left his life. He's picked right back up with them."

"Annie, he's six years old. Children don't understand devotion—or loyalty. If an adult showers a child with gifts, they become best friends. You've heard of Santa Claus, haven't you?"

"Santa comes once a year. He doesn't try to steal your kid."

"Enough with the pessimism." Miriam's gaze grew fierce. "You're special, Annie. You're special because Dillon loves you. Let him have his fun. When the Englands leave, he'll be back in your arms."

The words soothed, but they didn't banish the doubt. "I want to believe you," Annie said. "I'm not sure I can."

***

Beyond the gingham curtains, crickets sang a late summer melody.

Inside the tiny bedroom, new toys sat in stacks on the floor, on the dresser, and in neat piles in every available corner. The bright red fire engine stood in a position of prominence on the braided rug.

Annie sank onto the bed. Weaving through the mountain of toys, Dillon selected a storybook from the shelf.

He looked exhausted from the day's excitement at the amusement park. The soft curls framing his face were still damp from a quick bath, and he dragged his feet. Yawning, he ran his fingers across a selection of books. Evidently he was too worn out to delay bedtime, and he yanked down a book without glancing at the cover. With effort he crawled onto the bed then nuzzled beneath her waiting embrace.

The book was a well-worn favorite, *The Littlest Angel.*

Annie began reading in an animated voice. Coaxing him to reveal the weekend's events was tempting, but she knew it wasn't appropriate to pose questions. Still she wondered. Had he enjoyed every minute with the Englands? Would he miss them, now that they'd returned to Baltimore? And lastly, the question she'd never dare ask—did he love them more than he loved her?

Dillon broke into her reading, mid-sentence. "Annie?"

"What, sweetie?"

"Tom-Tom and Dianne told me something funny."

Wary, she set the book aside. "What did they say?"

He wriggled out from beneath her arm, his expression solemn. "They said I might be their son pretty soon. Next month, even."

His matter-of-fact tone left her wondering if he understood the ramifications. "Do you want to talk about it?"

"Not really." He burrowed deeper against her side. "Why do grown-ups make the rules? It's stupid."

"Sometimes it is."

"Tom-Tom says I'll be happy. He got a room fixed up for me."

"Sweetie, he shouldn't have told you. A judge will decide where you should live." She gave as simple an explanation as she could devise, adding, "Tom-Tom and Dianne don't get to make the rule. The judge will."

He seemed to take this in with admirable composure. Then he surprised her by saying, "My Mom went away. Where did she go?"

Sorrow burned the back of Annie's eyes. He meant Toria, dead now for more than a year.

"She's in heaven. I'm sure she's happy even though she misses you very much." There seemed no better explanation, and Dillon's eyes had grown dark.

"Didn't she want to stay with me?"

"Of course she did." Annie pulled him onto her lap and pressed her palm to his chest. "You know what? She's not really gone as long as you keep her in your heart. Can you do that?"

"'Course I can." He rubbed his chest in a slow circle. Finally he looked up. "Annie?

"Yes?"

"I don't want to be with Tom-Tom and Dianne. I want to be with you."

"I want that too, more than anything in the world! I love you, Dillon, with all my heart. That's why I'm trying to keep you here with me."

Silence wound between them. Outside, the crickets sang a frantic music.

"Annie?"

"Yes?"

"When I'm alone, I call you something secret. I didn't tell Chip. I didn't tell nobody."

The keeping of secrets was serious business for Dillon. "Do you want to tell me? You don't have to if you don't want to."

"Okay . . . Mommy." He leaned close to her ear. "Can I say it when we're alone?"

Annie opened her mouth to agree. A cry of joy burst forth, instead.

"Yes, Dillon," she said, cradling him against her breast. "Call me Mommy. When no one's around, I'll call you my son."

Chapter 31

"**W**ant to hear Mr. T and Mrs. S, too?"

Michael nodded in the affirmative. The encouragement started Dillon singing in a voice loud enough to carry across the park's kiddie playground.

Finishing, he planted his elbows on Michael's knees. "What do you think?"

Michael gave the thumbs up. "Best rendition so far." In the last thirty minutes, he'd enjoyed songs for most of the letters in the alphabet.

"Thanks." Dillon leaned sideways, ensuring he was directly in Annie's line of sight. "Did *you* like it?" he asked her.

"You know I love all of your songs. Life wouldn't be sweet without them."

Michael nuzzled her ear. "Life *is* sweet," he murmured, "especially when you're around."

The comment elicited the velvety laughter he'd grown to love. She wound her fingers through his, squeezing gently in subtle response. The interlude ended with a small fist pounding on his kneecap.

"Why do you do that?" Dillon shot tyke-sized daggers. Toothpicks really—but they hit the mark.

Baffled, Michael stopped running his fingers through Annie's hair. "Do what?"

Dillon pointed at Michael's fingers, still tangled in strands of gilt. "You touch Annie all the time."

The displeasure on the boy's face seemed tangible. Chagrined, Michael pulled his hands into his lap like a schoolboy caught stealing. With an impish glance, Annie scooted down the park bench.

Unfortunately, Dillon wasn't finished. "*Why* do you like touching her?"

"She's nice. I guess that's why."

"You make slurp-y noises when you kiss her. Did you know that?"

Michael blanched. He'd done his best to avoid public displays of affection. Well, at least the displays that involved kissing. When had he tripped up? He couldn't recall.

"Does it bother you?" If he'd upset Dillon, it was best to get to the bottom of it.

"It's okay."

"You're sure?"

"I guess." Dillon offered a skittish look, which was less than reassuring. To Annie, he said, "Michael never kisses me. How come?"

Bewilderment glossed Annie's face. Then she laughed, and they were both reaching for Dillon, poking fingers into his armpits and ruffling his hair. The boy howled with laughter as they tussled over his arms and legs before Michael, determined to win, dropped the boy on his lap.

"You want a kiss, eh?" He put a smacker on Dillon's cheek, drawing a chortle. Then he landed another right on his mouth. "There you go, sport. Keep me posted if you need more."

Without ceremony he dumped Dillon to the ground. Playing along, the kid rolled across the grass on a peal of laughter. The revelry brought Chip dashing toward them with Lucky bringing up the rear.

"Hey! What's going on?" Wheezing, Chip came to a halt.

Dillon rolled to a stop at his ankles. "We're being silly," Dillon said.

"Without me?" Chip toed the ground. "What're you doin'?"

"Michael's kissing me."

"Did he tickle your armpits first? My dad does. Or he gets my ribs when he slobbers all over me."

"Hey! I don't slobber," Michael said with mock indignation. "Chip, your Dad may be a Great Dane, but I'm not."

Annie giggled. Dillon rolled on down the hill.

Chip lifted his brows. "What's a Great Dane?"

***

Terrence snapped his briefcase shut, a fashionable number in aqua leather that beautifully accented his coral silk suit. Once he landed the frameless sunglasses on his nose, he looked like an attractive if quirky movie star. Angling her hip against Michael's desk, Annie smiled with approval.

"Are you ready?" Terrence asked Michael.

"You bet." Michael placed the airline tickets in his breast pocket. "Terrence, will you give us a moment?"

After the door clicked shut, Annie said, "You know we can't keep our relationship secret forever. Terrence will catch on. So will everyone else."

"Let's worry about telling the staff after we get through next week." Pulling her close, Michael switched topics. "I'll keep the trip short. I wouldn't go at all if I could put off the meetings at Pacific Salmon."

"Terrence needs you in Seattle. Don't worry—I'm fine."

"I hate to leave this close to your court appearance."

"Court isn't until next Monday. You'll be home on Sunday, right?"

"At noon. We'll go out for dinner. Tell Dillon he can pick the restaurant."

"Great." Knowing Dillon, he'd choose a fast food joint.

Michael canvassed her face. "Everything will work out. You've had temporary custody of Dillon for a year now. The judge will listen to the Englands' request, but then he'll order your adoption to proceed."

She tried to cling to his optimism. "Right."

Which must have failed, because Michael's brows lowered. "Don't get emotional. Stay focused."

"Sure thing."

He feathered kisses across her brow. "You won't lose Dillon. Don't give up hope."

This time, she managed a faint, fierce smile. "I won't," she said.

Chapter 32

Meetings at The Pacific Salmon Company dragged into Saturday afternoon. Michael was pleased to note Terrence was at the top of his game, regaling the company's marketing team with his edgy packaging designs. Terrence took the lead on a series of presentations then Michael took everyone to lunch at a trendy bistro on Seattle's waterfront. Afterward they visited the local print house he'd hired for Pacific Salmon's new packaging concepts.

Michael was exhausted and nervous when they boarded the return flight on Sunday morning. His thoughts centered on Annie's nine A.M. court appearance tomorrow morning.

The Boeing 737 descended into the Lambert-St. Louis International Airport without incident. As the plane taxied on the tarmac, Michael recalled the promise he'd made to take Annie and Dillon out to dinner tonight. During the weekend's snatched phone calls he'd done his best to relieve her stress by promising to drive her and Dillon to court Monday morning and provide moral support during the proceedings. He had no intention of letting her down.

And he wouldn't have, if all manner of chaos hadn't broken loose in the St. Louis airport when a man ran through the security checkpoint, shutting down the terminal and putting TSA on alert.

The pilot announced the delay.

Beside him, Terrence swabbed his face. "Why are they holding us up?" he snapped. "Can't they find the gate crasher and let us disembark? Gads, it's a hundred degrees in here."

A muscle twitched in Michael's jaw. It *was* hot. "Have patience," he said, even though he was privately in short supply. "The guy was probably late for a flight. They'll find him, and let us off."

"We've been trapped for fifteen minutes! We'll miss our connecting flight."

Michael's gut clenched. "We won't." They couldn't miss the connector. It seemed half the U.S. was finishing summer vacations and clogging the airports. What if they couldn't book a later flight and were stuck in St. Louis overnight?

Terrence waved a napkin before his perspiring brow. "The eternal optimist, aren't we? How can you remain upbeat when we're trapped?"

"We aren't trapped."

"We are!"

Unfortunately, Terrence's pessimism was well founded. The sloe-eyed flight attendant appeared to announce that Airport Security hadn't finished the sweep inside the terminal.

When she'd finished the announcement, Michael flagged her down. "May I phone my girlfriend?" he asked, brandishing his cell.

The woman offered a sympathetic look. "I'm sorry, sir. You'll have to wait until you reach the terminal."

"Which will be . . ?"

She hesitated long enough for Michael to glimpse doom. "I'm sorry, sir," she said. "I'm not sure."

Chapter 33

Dillon peered down the morning bright street. "Where's Michael?"

Locking the front door, Annie knelt before him. "Michael's plane hasn't come in yet." How many times would they have to discuss this? They'd been over this a dozen times since daybreak. "I'll drive us to the courthouse. As soon as his plane lands, he'll come, too."

In an uncharacteristic gesture, Dillon stuck his thumb in his mouth. "He promised to take us," he mouthed around the digit. "Why did he promise?"

Annie's throat tightened. "It's not his fault, sweetie. As soon as it lands, you'll see him at the courthouse."

"I want to see him *now*."

Oh, baby. Me, too. Annie tried to control the tremble in her voice. "Let's get going. Michael will be with us soon."

She continued murmuring words meant to soothe as she buckled Dillon in. Grimly, she turned the ignition.

"I don't want to go." Dillon struggled beneath the seat belt. "Let's stay home."

"Sweetheart, we have to see the judge."

"Let's run away. Can we? Please?"

His desperation tore at her heart. "We can't run away. We have to see the judge, and he'll decide if you can stay with me . . ."

The heartbreaking conversation dragged on for the better part of twenty minutes, with Annie wondering how she managed to keep her own fear at bay and Dillon becoming increasingly fearful. Within sight of the courthouse, he began cowering.

"Mommy—help me!"

The sound of gagging had her slamming on the brakes. The putrid stench of vomit filled the car's interior. She veered into the courthouse parking lot, grabbing for the knapsack on the passenger seat she'd had the wisdom to pack last night.

Dillon's curls wagged perilously as he tried forestalling the tears bucking through his body.

"Shhh—it's okay, sweetie. I'll get you cleaned up in a jiffy." Careful not to soil her navy suit, she lifted him from the truck and gently pulled off his polo shirt. "Let's get you inside. We'll finish cleaning up in the ladies bathroom, okay?"

His lower lip wobbled. "Okay," Dillon agreed.

***

"*Must* you push?" Terrence demanded. Squeezing sideways, he allowed Michael past in the plane's jammed aisle. "You've kept me up all night in that godforsaken airport, hauled me on a crack of dawn flight, and *now you've bruised me*. Look at my arm!"

"Shut up already." Michael yanked his carry-on down from the bin, nearly braining a redhead and drawing a glare. "I'm taking the first taxi out of here. You'll get our bags, right?"

Terrence rubbed his arm. "Yes, yes," he sighed. "I'll get the bags. Go to court. Go! Rescue Annie."

"It's a plan." Michael snapped up his wrist, and groaned. *If it's not too late.*

***

Judge Archibald Kirkland peered down at the proceedings with a slightly peevish, imperious air. Built like a barn and past eighty years in age, the judge possessed a big-boned face and thick bifocals that glinted over penetrating grey eyes.

Each time he regarded Annie, sweat broke out on her palms. He was terrifying, direct, needling Will and the England's attorney with sharp-tongued queries. A renegade, he was too powerful a judge to stand on custom or, some said, care much for legal precedents not bearing his name. Annie knew Will stood in awe of the judge. Over a long and illustrious career, Kirkland had written a large number of Virginia's family law statutes. Despite his standing, he still enjoyed presiding over the occasional custody hearing that impacted the common man.

Or woman, Annie thought.

For all the obvious reasons, a child as young as Dillon rarely attended a custody hearing scheduled to decide his fate. Due to the Englands' persistence, Judge Kirkland had agreed to allow the boy to participate—but only for a few minutes. For their part, The Englands each took the stand with calm indignation, detailing the negligence evident in Dillon's early childhood with chilling detail.

Throughout it all, they never so much as glanced at Annie.

Finally it was Annie's turn, and the judge waved her forward. "Miss McDaniel, please take the stand."

Her heart moved into her throat. She started for the witness stand with her thoughts wending back to Dillon. She'd been forced to carry him, sobbing, from the woman's lavatory and into Pete's waiting arms. As far as she knew, the social worker was still trying to calm Dillon in the adjacent waiting room.

Just as awful, Michael hadn't arrived.

"Miss McDaniel?"

Settling into the chair, she gave Kirkland her full attention. "Yes, your honor?"

"Now, you understand you're not on trial. You'll answer questions from the Englands' counselor. Afterward, your Mr. Blaine will also pose questions. Understood?"

"Yes, sir." With trepidation, she wheeled her attention to Leslie Yelverton. The England's attorney was a petite woman with a fiercely intent demeanor.

Immediately Yelverton cut right to the bone. "Miss McDaniel," she began, "let's start with Dillon's early childhood. I'm sure everyone in this courtroom would like to understand *why* you chose to avoid contact when intervention was clearly needed . . ."

***

The cab driver had one eye on the hundred-note bobbing before his nose and the other on the curb. He brought the cab to a screeching halt.

Michael flung open the door. He tossed the bill into the cabbie's lap then flew up the marble steps.

The courthouse hummed with activity. Above the throng, he heard a familiar voice. Annie's social worker hurried toward him with Dillon held firmly by the hand.

Dillon pulled free of Pete's grasp and launched into Michael's arms. He burst into tears.

The boy's piteous wails tore right through Michael. "Hey, Dillon. Looks like you're all shook up, buddy."

"Just like the song," Pete put in dryly.

How to calm a distraught child? Rocking seemed the best bet, and Michael easily hoisted the kid up. He danced in an awkward circle with the boy's damp face pressed to his neck. "Are you scared, Dillon? Want to talk about it?"

"I don't want to go inside."

"You can't run away, pal."

"No! I don't want to go in there!"

The last of it came out on a sobbing howl that drew curious stares from people rushing past.

Watching an innocent child deal with an awful situation would test any adult and Michael tightened his hold, determined to keep his notorious temper at bay. He could fantasize all he liked about punishing the Englands for insisting on Dillon's involvement, but it wouldn't help the boy.

He shifted Dillon on his hip, bringing them eye-to-eye. "Listen to me, pal. When you go in there, look at Annie or me. Understand? We'll be with you."

The child released a shuddering hiccup. "You'll stay? You won't run away?" He dropped his weary head onto Michael's shoulder. "Promise?"

"You bet. I won't leave you."

"Annie too?"

"She'll be there, Scout's honor."

An instinct he hadn't known he possessed compelled Michael to rub his nose across Dillon's cheek in gentling circles. He topped it off with an Eskimo Kiss that put the faintest hope in the boy's eyes. The affection they shared calmed them both.

He lowered Dillon to the ground. "One more," the boy said, nearing. He rubbed his nose across Michael's. "I like 'em." When Michael complied, he added, "Put one on my cheek too."

Warmed by the offer, Michael did. "You sure like Eskimo Kisses."

"Don't you?"

"I love them," Michael replied gruffly. He paused to savor the clean ache centering in his chest. "I love *you.*"

Dillon sighed. "I love you, too."

***

Annie felt like a cornered animal as Yelverton grilled her on Toria's reckless behavior prior to Dillon's birth. Dredging up the sad facts of her sister's life was a torment.

"We're waiting, Miss McDaniel. Please answer the question."

Annie swiped at her forehead. "Would you repeat the question?"

The petite attorney swooped down on the witness stand. Annie fisted her hands, unsure if she could withstand more questions designed to make her look incompetent and uncaring. She was granted a reprieve when the courtroom's massive doors swung open.

Michael walked in.

The tears she'd held at bay blurred her vision. From the bench above her, Judge Kirkland cleared his throat.

"You there." His gravelly voice froze Michael in his tracks. "This is a private hearing. Reporters aren't allowed."

"I'm not a reporter, your honor."

"Who are you?"

"Michael Rowe. Miss McDaniel works for me." When the judge appeared ready to throw him out, Michael added, "I'm dating Miss McDaniel."

The Englands twittered. Yelverton cast an impatient glance.

Kirkland peered down at Annie. "Do you mind if he stays?"

the judge asked.

Annie drank in Michael's encouraging smile before regarding Kirkland. "Not at all, your honor. I'd like it, actually."

"Fine." The judge motioned for Yelverton to continue, thought better of it, and held up his hand. His attention rocketed back to Michael, freezing him in place before he'd taken a seat.

"Rowe, you say? Michael Rowe? Are you the man who recently donated fifty thousand dollars to the Fairfax Boy's Club?"

"Yes, I did."

Will rose. "Your honor, I apologize. The documents before you do not include information regarding Mr. Rowe's donation."

The judge waved him off. "Sit down, Blaine. The Boy's Club needs the largesse." He set his sights back on Michael. "Son, was your contribution an effort to manipulate these proceedings?"

"It was a goodwill gesture," Michael prevaricated.

"I sit on the board of the Boy's Club with Miss McDaniel's social worker. I suspect you know that."

"I do, sir."

"Did Miss McDaniel ask you to make the donation?"

Will was back on his feet. "Your honor, I must apologize again. I should've pointed out the home study was recently amended. You'll find a note at the end by Miss McDaniel's social worker. Mr. Rowe is seeing my client socially."

Kirkland lowered his brows. "Don't interrupt me again." He stared Will into his seat. Appraising Michael, he said, "Answer me. Did you make the donation at Miss McDaniel's behest?"

"No, sir. She wasn't aware of my decision. Actually, when I told her, I lied. She thinks I made a significantly smaller donation."

"You lied to her about the true amount?"

"Yes, your honor." Michael cleared his throat. "I didn't want to unduly concern her by revealing the extent of my generosity."

Kirkland adjusted his bifocals, his expression stony. "Unduly concern her? Explain yourself."

Michael experienced the uncomfortable sensation he'd been stripped down to his skivvies in a front of the cranky judge. "I wanted to do everything in my power to help Annie," he said. "She's a fine mother to Dillon and an outstanding woman. Which is why I want to marry her. I just haven't found the opportunity to ask her yet."

The announcement brought a gasp from Annie. Yelverton

grimaced. Will's eyes rounded.

The judge grunted with mild approval. "I think you just did, son."

**

Miriam bobbed on a sea of indecision.

Why hadn't she skipped work and gone to the courthouse? She should've taken a personal day and stood by Annie for moral support. It was awful, not knowing how the hearing was progressing.

Taking a personal day would've been simple, if not for the Bedouin. That crazy Michael had phoned and demanded she stay put while *he* went to the courthouse.

Stay put? How could she remain hog-tied to the office on the day Annie needed her most?

"What's wrong with our dreaded gatekeeper? Bad hair day?"

The sight of Terrence stalking into the reception area nearly started her cursing, and she never used strong language. One look at his sniffling superiority nearly had her spouting oaths like a sailor on a shipwreck.

"Back from your trip so soon?" she snapped. "I'd hoped Michael lost you in the Seattle airport."

"You wish." Terrence stroked his mustache with twitchy fingers. "I came straight from the airport. We need to talk. It's urgent."

She took in his disheveled clothes and impervious air. Why did he have to badger her today of all days? He appeared utterly serious, despite the dab of red jelly edging his mouth.

Reaching into the bottom drawer of her desk, she produced a box of tissues. She wadded a tissue and flung it in his general direction. "Clean up before we talk. I won't chat with an artist dripping jelly donut."

"Gads, you're touchy."

Primly, Terrence wiped. He tossed the tissue down with a *sniff, sniff* of impatience. That blasted thing he did with his nose, an affectation Terrence alone believed made him superior.

Miriam raised a brow. "Well? What's up?"

"It's about Michael."

"What about him?"

"And Annie?"

"What about her?"

Terrence leaned across the desk, the smug possessor of secret knowledge. "Miriam, put it together. They fight, they make up, they fight some more—you left Isabel's party at the country club and missed the awful squabbling. It made Violet so weepy we left early. A tragedy—I hear Isabel poured champagne at midnight."

"What's your point?"

"Don't you *see?* Annie and Michael have incompatible personalities. Michael will lend moral support in court today, but what about tomorrow? They'll start fighting all over again. They can't work together!"

Miriam's patience evaporated. Granite wasn't as thick as this fool.

"They don't have incompatible personalities," she said.

"You're wrong. Honestly, we need a plan. What if we move Annie to another area in Rowe, somewhere far from Michael's office? I can't bear the thought of losing her."

"She won't quit."

"She despises Michael. If they keep fighting, she'll resign."

Miriam gritted her teeth. "She doesn't despise Michael."

"What if *he* despises *her?* Either way, it spells disaster."

"Figure it out, Terrence. Surely you've heard the gossip. The thing about gossip? Sometimes it's wrong—but sometimes it's right on the money."

Terrence rolled over a thought. Miriam swore she could almost see the levers in his brain whirling as he sorted it out.

"Gads! I just realized something." He gripped the edge of Miriam's desk. "What if they argue because they're falling for each other?"

In response, Miriam stood. Glancing around, she spotted the metal ruler beneath a stack of correspondence. She picked it up and *thwacked* him on the head.

When he stopped whimpering, she said, "Terrence, you're such a ninny."

***

The England's attorney, like everyone else in the courtroom, looked ready for a break.

"Perhaps your honor would like to recess for lunch?" she asked Judge Kirkland.

Peering down his nose, the judge snorted. Startled, Annie looked up. It was the same odd, crabby sound Miriam made whenever she was irritated or angry. Oddly, the sound left Annie feeling comforted for the first time in days.

"I want to see the child," Kirkland said.

Yelverton's mouth twitched. "We wish to present Tyrone Breckenridge next," she said of the well-published psychologist waiting in the air-conditioned luxury of his limousine. From what Will had mentioned, Annie knew Breckenridge expected to wrap up the hearing quickly then be on his way to a book signing in Richmond.

"The child," Kirkland said. "Bring him in."

The England's counsel shuffled through her notes. "Perhaps your honor would prefer to save questioning until after the recess?"

"Miz Yelverton, I'd prefer to leave the boy out of the proceedings entirely. Stop testing my patience and bring him in."

She motioned to the bailiff, who left the courtroom to do the judge's bidding. Pete Johnson walked in with a trembling and pale-faced Dillon on his hip. Dillon craned his neck, searching the pews for Annie. He couldn't find her at the front beside Will. She was grateful when he noticed Michael seated midway up the aisle. Dillon's eyes never left Michael's face as Pete carried him to the front of the courtroom.

Miraculously, Dillon settled into the witness chair without making a fuss. Pete whispered something in his ear, and her heart soared as he relaxed the tiniest degree. Pete remained standing by the witness stand, a small child's guardian angel.

For the first time all morning, Judge Kirkland did the improbable. He smiled. First at Pete. Then he smiled at Dillon. The webwork of lines comprising the judge's face eased into an arresting display of compassion.

"What's your name, child?" Kirkland asked.

Dillon threw a timid glance at Pete, who winked. Then he swiveled toward the judge. "I'm Dillon."

Kirkland leaned far over the bench, his huge body a swath of black robes. "Don't be nervous," he said. "Let me ask a few questions, and you can go."

A tremor spiked through Dillon, but it wasn't enough to dispel his curiosity. "What do you do when I'm gone?"

"I think."

"*Why* do you think?"

The question seemed to please Kirkland. "I'm good at it."

Something in the old man's expression caught Dillon's attention. In a calmer voice, he said, "I'm good at things, too."

"You are, eh? Like what?"

"I sing alphabet songs." Dillon peered out at the adults, and found Annie. The relief on his face was a gift she gladly accepted. "I'm not supposed to sing one now."

"You're not, eh? Why not?"

"She told me not to."

"Who told you?" The revelation swung Kirkland's head around. When his eyes locked on her, she nearly fainted. "The woman over there? Did she tell you not to sing?"

"Yep." Since they were talking about his Annie, Dillon evidently thought it natural to wave at her. She waved back, and he added, "She let's me sing at home. I sing real loud in the bathtub. It scares the birds outside. But she said it wouldn't be nice to sing in here."

"Maybe not," Kirkland agreed.

Yelverton rose. "If I may approach the bench?"

"You may not. Must I remind you that this is a hearing, not a trial?" The judge glared until she retreated. He motioned to her clients, seated tall and proud beside her. "Dillon, who are those people?"

"Tom-Tom and Dianne. They're nice."

"How so?"

"They buy me toys. Lots of 'em. I'll show you sometime."

"What about her?" The judge nodded toward Annie. "Doesn't she buy you toys?"

Annie felt sick as Dillon weighed the question. "Not much," he admitted because she'd taught him never to lie. Sitting up straight, he added, "We're on a budget."

"You are, now?"

"Yep." Dillon squirmed in his chair. "But she buys other stuff."

"Like what?"

"Food, mostly. She buys lots of food 'cause I was skinny. And she buys shoes that fit real good. See?"

Dillon stuck out his feet, allowing Kirkland to study the bright red tennis shoes. "Nice," the judge agreed.

"*I* like 'em."

For an interminable moment, the judge withdrew into his thoughts. When he again nodded to Annie, her heart nearly hit the floor. "I've got one more question for you, son. *Who* is she?"

Dillon offered a smile so broad it stretched from ear to ear. It was a silly question, but the big man wasn't so scary after all, and he knew to tell the truth.

"She's my Mommy," Dillon replied.

"You don't say." Kirkland cast a withering glance at Yelverton and the Englands. To both attorneys, he said, "Counselors, that will be all. I'll retire now to my chambers."

***

The decision came down in forty minutes.

They'd won.

Chapter 34

Annie bustled around the kitchen whipping up a batch of waffles. She'd barely slept a wink. It didn't matter—a long shower at dawn had invigorated her. Besides, she looked forward to this day like no other in recent memory. For months worry had weighed her down, making her jittery and defensive. Now? She felt reborn.

She'd won the custody battle. Judge Kirkland would finalize the adoption next week in a short ceremony at the courthouse. The Englands had no recourse, no other legal avenue to pursue. Dillon was now her son.

Pulling out the waffle iron, she let her attention stray to the telephone. She really *should* call Michael to ensure he'd received her message and would arrive this morning for breakfast. Last night she should've made a second attempt to reach him after she'd tucked Dillon into bed. Mind-numbing exhaustion sent the plan astray.

After she set the table for three, she put in another call. The way she'd bolted from the courthouse had surely hurt his feelings. Offering an apology seemed the best solution.

His answering machine picked up. She left another message.

Was he avoiding her calls? The minute the custody decision had come down, Dillon's nausea returned. He was stricken with a bout of the dry heaves in the courthouse so intense she'd been rocked with guilt. She'd believed a six year old couldn't possibly understand the gravity of the proceedings. She was mistaken— Dillon not only understood, he'd fallen apart the moment Annie had told him the news.

Taking a sick child immediately to the pediatrician was a no-brainer. What *had* been brainless was her refusal to allow Michael to accompany them. She'd left him standing on the courtroom steps muttering a farewell as she'd carried Dillon out. She should've accepted Michael's offer to take them. She hadn't, for the simple reason she needed time alone with Dillon. No social workers poking around her life, no attorneys threatening to take him away—she'd been struck by the realization that he belonged to her now, and she could do as she pleased.

Adding to her bad behavior, it wasn't until hours later as she tucked Dillon into bed that she recalled Michael's declaration in court. Why, he'd basically *proposed* to her midway through the proceedings. The prospect of beginning a courtship thrilled her even if it was too soon to consider marriage. Knowing of Michael's serious intent allowed her to consider dreams that would've seemed outlandish even a few weeks ago. A real family. A father for Dillon, and a husband for her.

Leave an apology on his answering machine? The decision was forestalled by the sound of footfalls in the hallway.

Dillon padded into the kitchen in a bright red Mickey Mouse tee shirt and his favorite purple corduroys hitched up with a green belt. "Mornin'." He plunked down in a chair. "What are you making?"

"Waffles. They'll be ready soon." She gave his choice of apparel the once-over. "Nice duds. Are you going to school as a cowboy?" With the adoption decided, he'd start back at St. Mary's Elementary with Chip.

"Yep. But I wish I didn't miss the first day. Think I'll have lots of homework?"

"No, sweetie. School only started last week. You haven't missed much."

In celebration of Dillon's adoption, Sister Theresa, the principal at St. Mary's, had declared today a special "dress down day." None of the children were required to wear uniforms. Miriam had stayed up half the night baking ten large sheet cakes. Shelley

Wilson planned to bring in ice cream for the students. The PTA would pass out balloons.

The festivities touched Annie deeply. She hadn't realized how many people were rooting for her to adopt Dillon.

Spying the batter for the waffles, he hopped down from his chair. With a grunt of he-man perseverance, he pushed the chair to the counter.

"Can I help?" He took the spoon from her hand. "I can make the waffles, mommy. Hey! I want to crack the egg!"

"Do you remember how?" At six, lessons were taught more than once before they stuck.

"Sure I do."

"Okay. Here you go."

He tapped the egg on the side of the bowl. No action. Before she might stop him, Dillon crushed the egg between his palms. Bits of shell and gooey yolk splattered across the counter.

"Oops. I missed. Can I try again?"

Annie slid the waffle batter a safe distance then grabbed a fresh bowl. Another egg? Why not? She'd let the munchkin crack a dozen eggs while she made breakfast.

She gave him a kiss on the forehead. "Go on. Crack 'em all. If you get too much egg on your clothes, you can change before the school bus arrives."

"I can crack . . . all of them?" Dillon grabbed for the carton. "Okay, here goes . . ."

They were still at the counter, with Annie pouring batter into the waffle maker and Dillon creating all forms of chaos, when the doorbell rang.

A rather subdued Michael stood on the other side. "I got your messages," he said.

She pulled him inside. "Can you forgive me? I shouldn't have left you abandoned at the courthouse. It was cruel, especially after everything you've done for us. I should've taken you up on the offer to drive to the pediatrician's office."

"How is Dillon?"

"He's fine. Cooking up a storm in the kitchen. Or so he thinks."

She wove her arms around Michael without invitation. The affection seemed welcome, and he slid his hands across her back in comforting circles. They enjoyed a quiet moment. It was broken by the sound of giggling in the kitchen. They hurried in.

Dillon's effort at cooking had landed several eggs on the floor. "Keep your distance," Annie said to Michael. "Unless you plan to wear egg yolk to work. And don't hug Dillon, until I've checked him from stem to stern. He may be dripping egg in a matter of seconds."

Michael grinned. "Gotcha."

"Oh, I'll be at the office by one o'clock."

"Fine, but you're only working a few hours. This is a day to celebrate. How about if the three of us go out to dinner?"

"We'd love that." She gave him a peck on the cheek then returned to the waffle iron. "Dillon? Where would you like Michael to take us to dinner?"

The lighthearted query was met by silence. Dillon returned to the table and threw his elbows on top.

"Dillon?"

When Annie knelt beside him, he shrugged off her attempt to touch him. "We're eating dinner *at home.*"

Michael approached. "No problem, buddy. Want to barbecue? I can pick up burgers on the way home from work."

"No. You eat dinner at *your* house."

Annie and Michael exchanged glances. They were still trying to work out why Dillon was angry when he faced off before Michael.

"You can go now." He pushed at Michael's legs. "Me and Mommy don't need help making breakfast. We only have waffles for two."

"Buddy, what's wrong? I won't eat all the waffles, promise."

"Go," Dillon repeated, pushing hard against Michael. "I'm not sharing Mommy."

Annie clasped his shoulders. "Sweetie, you know it's good to share. Why don't you tell Michael you're sorry? You aren't being nice."

"Grown-ups don't share. Why should I?" Dillon's eyes glossed with tears, but his face went red with anger. "Tom-Tom and Dianne were crying when I said goodbye. They let me keep the toys, but they were crying."

It was true. After the decision was handed down, the Englands had been devastated. Annie had leaned against Pete with a mix of pity and sadness as she'd watched them say goodbye to Dillon. Tom had practically carried his sobbing wife from the courthouse. Dillon was correct—the adults in Dillon's life had failed dismally at the very human necessity of sharing.

It seemed Michael arrived at the same conclusion and was just as determined to rectify the situation. "Dillon, would you like us to set up a visit with Dianne and Tom-Tom?" He caught Annie's silent assent and added, "We'll drive you to Baltimore whenever you'd like."

Dillon shoved him away. "No. We said goodbye. They can't see me no more."

"We'll try to fix it."

"Go home!" Dillon shouted. "Your talk is hurting my ears!"

Flustered, Michael pivoted on his heel. "Okay, okay. I'm going."

In the foyer, Annie stopped him. "I'll call the psychologist," she said. "Dillon may need to see her several times a week. We have a lot of work to do."

"Call the Englands too. They can't just walk out of his life."

Sighing, she leaned against the doorjamb. "Will tried putting out feelers last week, to discover their intentions if I won custody. Michael, they won't talk to me. For months now they've made it clear if they won, they'd cut me out of Dillon's life. Now they've lost, and they just want to move on."

"What about Dillon's feelings?" Michael raked a hand through his hair. "Should I talk to him tonight? Assure him I won't take you away? He's reacting out of fear."

"Let's give him a couple of days. I'd like to get the psychologist's feedback before we delve into this."

"Meaning I should stay away? It won't help if Dillon thinks he can order me around. He's a child. He needs to know his place."

"He needs understanding and enough space to process everything he's been through. Maybe he isn't ready to see me in a relationship."

"You think I'm the problem?" Disbelief colored Michael's words. "Spell it out, Annie. Should I disappear for a week? A month? Pretend everything's fine at the office, but wait until next year to ask you out?"

"I don't know."

"When *will* you know?"

From the kitchen, Dillon shouted, "Mommy, where are you? I need help tying my shoes."

Annie suffered the sensation of being pulled in opposite directions by the two men in her life. Not that Dillon *was* a man—but he did have male territorial behavior down pat.

"Be there in a sec." To Michael, she whispered, "I can't go into this now. Let's talk later."

"Annie, at some point you have to take our relationship into consideration or we won't *have* a relationship."

"What's that supposed to mean?"

"It means I don't want to stand on the sidelines. We should be discussing how to handle Dillon together, not how you'll deal with him while I'll ride off into the sunset. We should work as a team to help him. Isn't that what couples do?"

She knew she wasn't being fair, but couldn't stop from snapping, "He just became mine. Maybe I'm not ready to share him." It was illogical—and brutally honest.

"No, you're not." Hurt shifted through Michael's eyes, but he fought it down. "I hope you can understand that I'm not ready to assume second place in your heart. Seeing that you don't have room for us both."

Breaking off the conversation, Michael left. When she arrived at Rowe in the afternoon, he treated her with a civility bordering on indifference. There wasn't an easy solution to offer, not with Dillon's unexpected behavior. Annie comforted herself with the thought that Michael was a sensible man. Eventually he'd understand her dilemma and agree to wait a week or two before seeing her again. Surely he understood her need to put Dillon's needs first.

She was mistaken. The following day, Michael was gone.

***

"**W**hy isn't he back yet?" Terrence prowled across her office with nervous agitation. "It's been seven days. I can't possibly work without him. The creative muse has completely abandoned me. I need Michael's input or I'll never create again."

Slumped in her chair, Annie doodled on her notepad. "I don't have any words of wisdom, Terrence. Find a way to work without him."

"We'll be ruined!" She was startled when he wheeled her chair around and grabbed her by the shoulders. "Tell me where Michael has gone. Miriam won't dish. You know how she loves to torture me."

"He's in Marrakesh."

"Where?"

"It's in Morocco." Annie eased out of the artist's clutches. "Last I heard, he's camping in the desert outside Marrakesh."

Michael's sudden departure no longer came as a shock. It no longer made any impact on her ravaged heart. She was empty, void of emotion, far beyond disappointment. She'd shut him out of her life too often, and now she'd lost him for good.

She made another doodle on the pad. "Miriam says Michael is taking an extended holiday. Bill is in charge until he gets back."

"He's camping in North Africa? In the wild?"

"It appears so."

"It's insane."

Annie grimaced. Had Michael thought to pack sunscreen? Or food? Evidently she'd hurt him more than she'd realized when she'd asked him to stay away until she got Dillon sorted out. In retrospect, she should've welcomed his offer to help—not pushed him away.

Terrence snuffled. He seemed on the verge of outright weeping. Before he might launch into tears, he rushed out of her office. Probably to harass Miriam, who was as glum as Annie.

During the last week, the two women had made a melancholy pair. They kept up bright fronts for Dillon's sake. When they were alone together, they talked in worried whispers. They were both heartsick over Michael's disappearance.

It was time to bring him back. Rowe Marketing was his company, after all. Annie knew it wasn't fair to make the boss feel he ought to stay away.

Needing to do what was best for Michael, she balled up the page of doodles and tossed it into the waste can. She opened a Word document and began typing. The tears she'd suppressed built behind her eyelids.

Forcing them back, she composed the letter of resignation.

***

Miriam slid another tray of cookies into the oven.

Her kitchen lay in ruin beneath all manner of baking chaos. A dusting of flour covered the tile floor. Chocolate chips littered the countertops. A gooey pool of caramel syrup congealed on the stove. Given the choice between home or office, she wished she could stay hunkered down in her kitchen for the rest of her natural life.

Since Michael's disappearance, Rowe had come to resemble a morgue. Everyone on staff was either glum or packing tissue for an unexpected bout of tears. Two weeks and counting since Michael's disappearance, everyone on staff had been reduced to a state of mourning for the firm's absent leader. Even worse, Annie had found a part-time IT job at an insurance agency and quit Rowe. She'd cleaned out the pathetic remains of her savings account and left an envelope of cash in the center of Michael's desk. The poor girl was determined to return the money he'd loaned her for Dillon's psychological care.

Last week Miriam had learned Annie wasn't bringing in enough income with her new post at the insurance agency. She was late on her mortgage payment. Miriam had offered to make the bank loan but Annie refused to accept what she deemed was charity.

Which was why Miriam had launched into a non-stop baking spree. As soon as she got home from work each night, she hurried into the kitchen. Bill and Terrence were already grumbling about gaining weight, so many confections were being hustled into Rowe.

And once every child in the neighborhood learned of the baking extravaganza, they'd begun rapping on her door at all hours. Plump Andrew Frost, a freckle-faced boy two doors down, had cornered Miriam this morning in search of a handout.

The oven timer rang. The tray of chocolate chip cookies came out and brownies went in. Stirring the chocolate cake batter, Miriam reflected on Michael's sabbatical and how he'd begun calling her at home at the strangest hours. From Marrakesh, of all places. He'd purchased camping supplies and hired a guide for the trek into the desert. Heavens, would his cell phone bake in the sun?

Twice during their conversations she tried mentioning Annie.

Each time, he hung up on her.

Returning to the oven, she checked the brownies then spied the slip of paper she'd left on the countertop. At the office today she'd impulsively written down the telephone number. It was an invasion of privacy to call a Rowe client for personal reasons, but if she didn't ask Isabel Worthin to intercede, what else was there to do?

With newfound determination, Miriam snatched up the phone. She dialed Isabel's number before her confidence disappeared.

"Isabel? Hello. This is Miriam . . . yes, Miriam from Rowe. I hate to bother you during your holiday but I need some advice. And I need to know if you've had all your shots—for tetanus, Hep B, that sort of thing. Yes—your *shots*. The ones you'll need before traveling overseas. You have? Well, I was wondering if you'd ever fancied a trip to North Africa . . ."

Chapter 35

The camel angled its malodorous snout in her direction and spit a nasty projectile of saliva. After an hour of traveling through desert hills and sweltering heat, it still had the power to sicken her.

Isabel drew herself tall on the animal's pungent and coarse-skinned back. Without ceremony, she thumped the camel on its hump. Her efforts were rewarded with another round of spitting. Then she smiled primly at her Muslim escort, lumbering alongside her on his more mild-mannered beast.

The escort, a lean man who spoke stilted English, wore gauzy robes of the starkest white. Isabel had flung a similar cloth over her shoulders and across her head to keep the fierce sunlight at bay. Trudging along the beautiful hills of North Africa, heat stroke was *always* a possibility.

Thank goodness they were nearing their destination.

The Muslim gestured at the shimmering hills rising on the burnt gold horizon. Squinting, Isabel cursed the hot sun, and focused on the pup tent.

A pup tent, of all things.

It appeared Michael had returned to childhood. He'd become a lonely Boy Scout camping in a foreign nation, nursing his heart in isolation.

The escort shouted in greeting. Beneath her legs, the camel spit.

The commotion brought Michael from the tent, haggard and unshaven. Around his strong neck, a water canteen swung in an arc. He was dressed like the Muslims in flowing, white robes. A thick, brown beard concealed the bronzed skin of his cheeks and chin. He looked like a sheik, sexy and dangerous, and yet . . . sad.

Isabel slid from the camel and nearly stumbled to the ground. "Is that your Halloween costume?" Righting herself, she regarded Michael. The shock registering on his face was no more than he deserved, and she added, "What? You weren't expecting your old friend? I hope you packed enough hot dogs for two."

"How did you find me?" His voice was a low growl of surprise and confusion.

"Do you want the entire itinerary?"

"I guess not."

"Miriam phoned. She asked that I look in on you. Mind you, it took three planes and twenty-two hours to do so."

"She shouldn't have asked."

"Well, she has more sense than you. Once you return to work and your senses, you *will* give her a raise. And buy her some sugar. She's cleaned out her grocery store." Isabel peered inside the barren tent. "What? No marshmallows? I'd hoped we'd roast a few after I take you to task."

It pained her when Michael let the humor pass without a modicum of amusement. He looked haggard and wrung out, with dark circles beneath his eyes. The pity she'd rather not feel—given what he'd put her through—took hold nonetheless.

Sensing her compassion with his admirable sixth sense, Michael folded his arms in a stance brooking no empathy. "Isabel, go home. I'm not prepared for visitors."

"And why not? Hasn't the maid spiffed up the place?" She looked off at the sandy hills. They were miles from civilization in every direction. "All right, then. I'll go. Even though I've spent a ridiculous amount of time getting here."

"I'm sorry for putting you to the trouble of finding me." Michael turned away.

"STOP RIGHT THERE."

Isabel raised her elegant voice with piercing authority. Michael flinched. The escort jumped back in terror. The camels gave out odd, mewling sounds. Then they spit.

She withdrew the letter from her pocket. "I'm not going anywhere until you read this." She pressed Annie's resignation into his hand.

He read, swiftly. "Annie quit my firm? She *quit?*"

"What did you expect? You leave without an explanation and naturally she blames herself. Didn't I tell you to learn a new skill set if you wanted this relationship to work?" He began to explain about Dillon, but she interrupted. "Miriam filled me in. Dillon doesn't hate you. According to Miriam, he's upset by your disappearance."

"It'll pass. He's not ready for a father. He needs time to get used to his life with Annie."

"And so you thought a trip to Africa was in order?"

"It seemed the better part of valor to forget about them both." Sorrow glossed Michael's features. "They need time to become a family, just the two of them. I don't want to get in the way."

"So you're prepared to give up?"

"I'm not giving up. I'm allowing Dillon to have what he needs to heal—Annie."

He started for the tent, but Isabel blocked his retreat. "This is from Dillon," she said, producing the picture the boy had drawn. Miriam, ever efficient, had faxed it along with Isabel's itinerary. "I daresay, you'll feel like a horse's ass once you look at it."

Michael's gaze tripped over the two-part drawing with interest. In the first frame, a couple stood holding hands while a boy flew over their heads like an angel. It was a happy scene with smiling faces and a grinning sun in the background. In the second frame, the boy had crashed to earth and the woman was crying beneath stormy skies. The man in the picture was walking out of the frame with . . . a giraffe.

"He's a smart child," Isabel said. "He knows giraffes live in Africa."

Michael looked up, stunned. The page fluttered to the ground.

"Isabel," he roared, "get back on your camel! We're leaving."

***

Couples milled through the well-appointed aisles of upscale

Nelson Furniture in Baltimore. The showroom carried the pleasing scent of leather; the music drifting through was soothing and classical. Striding up the center aisle, Annie disregarded her misgivings and began searching for Tom England.

A pretty saleswoman with flashing green eyes stopped to greet her. "May I help you?"

"I'm looking for the sales manager."

"Tom? He's in his office."

Following the woman's instructions, Annie wove through the bedding department with her heart beating in her ears. It seemed cruel to corner Tom England at his place of work, but there wasn't a better option. She didn't have the England's home phone number and, even if she did, it was unlikely Dianne would take her call.

Tom stood a few feet from his office chatting with one of his salesmen.

The sight of Annie stole the good humor from his face. Muttering something to the salesman, he approached.

"Why are you here?"

"I need to talk to you and your wife. Please—I just need a few minutes."

"What do you need to discuss?"

"Dillon." It was ballsy, but she took Tom by the arm and steered him to his office. He was pliable to her touch, no doubt too stunned by her appearance to refuse. Once inside, she shut the door and said, "Tom, can you please call your wife? I'd appreciate it if I could talk to both of you about what we can do to fix this."

The suggestion put splotches of red on his face. "She won't talk to you."

"She will, if you insist."

"Why should I?"

"Because you love Dillon and want to ensure his happiness."

Thinking it over, Tom looked past Annie's shoulder, to the arrangement of photographs on his desk. She followed his gaze to the recent shot of Dillon taken during their visit to the amusement park. It had been one of the worst days in memory, and she'd been certain the England's visit represented the end of her life with Dillon. Now, with the adoption complete, she viewed the photograph with pity for the couple who had wanted to adopt him just as badly.

Tom flipped out his cell phone. "Wait outside."

Annie followed his directions, unsure if she'd soon be thrown out of the furniture store. Ten minutes later, Tom reappeared.

"Dianne doesn't want a scene," he said, moving toward the back of the store. "She agreed to meet you in the parking lot."

Dianne England drove up within minutes, her hair unkempt and her face void of makeup. Annie wondered if she'd been drinking—the faint scent of whisky accompanied her to the back door of Nelson Furniture.

"What is this about Dillon?" she demanded.

The speech Annie had rehearsed disappeared beneath the wave of nerves washing over her. The high emotion building between them seemed impossible to surmount.

"Well?" Dianne cornered her against the door.

Annie surprised them both when she pushed Dianne back. "I'm not here to argue. Dillon needs you." She stopped, and marshaled her thoughts. "I know it won't be easy, but I want us to become friends. You don't hate me, Dianne—you hate that I've won Dillon. But he needs you and me, and your husband too. He doesn't understand why adults make all the rules and don't know how to share. He doesn't get why we can't just love him. Because he loves all three of us."

Annie's voice broke, but it was all right. Her words shattered the anger shielding Dianne. Dianne began blinking rapidly, trying to come to grips with the changed circumstance.

She leaned heavily against her husband. "You should go."

"Fine. I hope to hear from you. Dillon does too."

Tom slung his arm around his wife's shoulders. "Thank you for stopping by."

Annie sent him a look of appreciation for his small gesture of kindness. If they needed time to process her offer, she had no choice but to wait. Hopefully they'd come around.

In a shaky hand, she scribbled down her phone number and thrust it toward Dianne. "Call me if you'd like to see Dillon. We can set up a weekend visit here in Baltimore, or you can come down to Fairfax. Either way, he'll be thrilled."

Dianne took the phone number, her expression fluid. Annie had already started off when she said, "Tom and I enjoy golf. Don't we, Tom?"

"I've never played," Annie said, trying to get a handle on where this was going.

"There's a resort in Fairfax we've wanted to visit." The pride in the woman's gaze held a hint of entreaty. "Perhaps we'll come down in early October. Would that work with Dillon's schedule? We can golf in the mornings while he's in school, and take him out in the afternoons. I'm thinking a four-day visit? You know how pretty the Virginia courses are in October."

The gratitude Anne felt tightened her throat. She closed the distance and surprised them both when she hugged Dianne.

***

On her bed, Annie sifted through the photographs. Hours of deep cleaning had left her with a tired back and aching muscles, but she'd made great progress. Dillon had signed up for soccer and was already talking about baseball next spring; soon she'd need every inch of storage for a boy's newfound love of sports.

Moth-eaten toys, long sequestered in the attic, were gently placed in cartons for GoodWill. Old linens were packed up. The task grew easier each day, as an economy of motion took hold. It became an assembly line project: sorting, organizing, packing.

The photographs were the most difficult to manage. She planned to keep them all, of course, but she found herself gingerly settling on the bed to look through them, faded photographs of her parents and snapshots of a Christmas long ago, when she and Toria were children. High School graduation shots. Photographs of her father as a young man working in the greenhouse.

Carefully, she organized them all on top of her bedspread. Then she laid them in the box at her feet. A clean ache filtered through her as she taped the top shut.

She didn't have one snapshot of Michael. Nothing to remember him by except the heartache accompanying her days.

"Annie?" A tall form darkened the doorway.

She drifted from the reverie as Michael stepped inside.

He looked different. Deeply tanned, his dark blue eyes blended arrestingly with the bronzed skin of his face and his coarse beard. He wore a white tee-shirt and faded jeans—and a look of apology.

The urge to rush into his arms nearly sent her across the bedroom. It took all her stamina to resist.

She rose on rubbery legs. "What are you doing here? You're supposed to be in Marrakesh."

His tortured gaze canvassed her face. "Isabel came to Africa. I didn't know you'd resigned from my firm." He studied his feet. "I would've known, if I'd let Miriam tell me. Every time she mentioned you, I hung up on her."

"What was I supposed to do? You left without an explanation."

"I shouldn't have." He rubbed his lips together, failing in an attempt to smile. "How's Dillon?"

"My *son* is managing." Pride and a combative note entered her voice.

"Your son. Right." Anguish ripped through his expression. It was nearly her undoing. Softly, he added, "Our son, if you'll have me. If you can find a way to forgive me."

She wasn't letting him off that easy. "Michael, it isn't a matter of forgiving you. I need to know I can rely on you."

"You can. Always."

"Not if you pack your bags every time there's a problem."

"I need to learn new skills."

"Damn right you do. Did you really think Dillon wanted you to go? Michael, he's just trying to get used to the idea of having a forever family." Annie let out a sigh replete with misgiving. "Listen, it's not all your fault. I had no idea just how much he understood about the court battle. He was worried all summer long, and I didn't have a clue. He'd eavesdropped on too many of my conversations with my attorney, and figured most of it out. He's a smart boy."

"He takes after you."

"He does."

"I didn't help matters by taking off."

Her eyes blazed. "No, you didn't. News flash—parenting is hard work. Dillon will have good days and bad, and on the bad days you learn to stand firm. It's what makes a child feel safe."

The fiery explanation gave him the courage to approach. "Point taken." He blew out a stream of air. "What *did* you tell Dillon?"

"That you were on safari." Her voice grew ragged. "I thought I'd tell him in stages that you were gone for good. I was planning to say you liked giraffes so much, you decided to move to Africa.

Dillon loves giraffes."

"I know." He had the little guy's picture for proof. "He has real talent. We should put him in art class."

"No can do. He's fallen in love with sports." Annie brushed at her damp eyes, but she laughed. "I don't know how I'll store all his gear in a house this size."

"Then don't. Store it at your new home—*our* home."

Michael reached into the back pocket of his jeans and withdrew the small, blue box. Taking her hand, he spread out her cold fingers and placed it on her palm. He would've preferred to put the engagement ring on her finger. Given his recent behavior, he wasn't sure it was a good idea.

Annie stared at the box. When she lifted her eyes, she read the mixture of remorse and passion shifting through his gaze.

An ivory ribbon encased the present. She slipped it off easily.

Inside, a galaxy of starlight beckoned. She brought the ring out on a sigh. Starlight shot from the center of the diamond, filling her with hope and joy.

"Oh, Michael—"

His face swam before her eyesight. She wanted to tell him how much she loved him, too, but she was too overwhelmed.

Catching her around the waist, he pulled her into a kiss that conveyed a wealth of messages: regret, hope, love. Her heart soaring, she went quickly into his arms.

***

Leaping from the bus, Dillon laughed as he landed on the pavement. "Hey, Chip!" He spun toward the bus as Chip jumped off. "Are you coming over to play soccer? My Mom got me a new ball."

"Sure! We should practice so we're the best on the team."

Dillon peered at the house. Annie wasn't on the front steps. "Gee, where's my Mom? She said she'd be home today."

"Better ask her before I come over."

"Okay."

Slinging the book bag over his shoulder, Dillon went inside. Annie was sitting on the couch.

She patted the cushions. "Come here, sweetheart."

He flung the book bag to the floor. Beaming, he ran to the couch.

She kissed him on the cheek. "How was school today?"

"We had lots of fun, with balloons and stuff. It was Bernadette's birthday."

"That's wonderful, sweetie."

"Yep." He studied her face. "Why are you scared looking?"

"I'm not scared, honey." She kissed him again. "But I *do* need to talk to you about someone. . ."

***

The thousand pound gorilla lurked in Michael's thoughts as he waited at the picnic table.

He'd gulped down three cups of coffee, which probably wasn't a good idea, shaved and cleaned himself up in Annie's bathroom then stalked around the perimeter of the tiny backyard, which hadn't helped a bit. He sat back down and drummed his fingers on the picnic table. Hell, he was wound up, and it was almost four o'clock.

He'd really let Dillon down. Taking off for Africa, nursing his emotional wounds and never once considering if the kid would miss him—if Dillon stayed angry for a month of Sundays, Michael knew it was no more than he deserved.

The gorilla threatened to pounce. Throwing him off, Michael wondered: what if the kid wouldn't forgive him at all?

The screen door flew open with a bang. Dillon strutted across the grass with hooded eyes. He wore purple pants, a green belt and a bright red Mickey Mouse shirt. A cowboy hat was planted on his head, and he was fingering the squirt gun in his leather holster.

Michael rose with his mouth gone dry. *Welcome to the Okay Corral. If the kid draws first, you're finished.*

Dillon stopped a few paces off. "Where have you been?" He worked his soft features. "You didn't say goodbye."

"I was in Africa . . . moping. It was a really dumb thing to do."

"What's moping?"

"Feeling sorry for yourself."

"Aren't you too old for that?"

"You'd think so." Honesty seemed the only way to avoid a duel, and he hurriedly added, "I shouldn't have taken off without seeing you. Truth is, I shouldn't have gone at all."

"But you did."

"Can you forgive me?"

"Did you bring me a giraffe?" Dillon stalked to the picnic table. "Chip says Africa is full of giraffes. It's okay if you took one for me."

No gunplay, thank God. Just haul your ass to the Serengeti and steal some wildlife, and you're home free. "I didn't bring back a giraffe. It wouldn't fit in my luggage."

"I guess it's okay." Dillon hooked his thumbs through the belt loops of his pants. Eyes downcast, he added, "I didn't mean to make you go away. I can share my mom. I'm not greedy."

"Don't worry about it, pal. I get it."

Lightheaded, Michael sunk down onto the bench. Jet lag, nerves, half a gallon of coffee—he was too frazzled to think straight. His heart was beating like a jackrabbit on amphetamines, and he *still* had to find a way to propose to Dillon.

"Chip said you'd bring something for Annie," Dillon was saying. "Ladies like presents, you know."

"They do."

"My mom likes stuff. Maybe not giraffes, but she'd like Lucky. She misses your dog."

"Lucky misses both of you, too."

"Did you bring her a ring?" Dillon fiddled with his squirt gun as if deciding if he should fire. "I heard Chip's mom talking to Nana Miriam. They said you'll marry my mom or they'll do things to you."

Beat me senseless, probably. "I would like to marry your mother if it's all right with you."

The cowboy hat joggled as Dillon rocked back and forth. "Do you love her?"

"Completely."

"What about me?"

Michael pulled in a sharp breath. Dillon's gaze bounced off the grass, the picnic table—he was looking at anything but the tension-addled man before him.

Reaching out, Michael rested his thumb beneath Dillon's chin. The boy lifted his eyes. They brimmed with a cloudburst of questions, confusion and a sweet, silent longing.

"Dillon, I love you," Michael said. "I want to be your father. We'll be a family—the three of us. Well, four, if you count Lucky. How 'bout it?"

He waited patiently for the words to sink in. When they did, Dillon's expression crumbled.

Flying into Michael's arms, he whispered, "I love you, too."

***

At dusk, they tossed a few belongings into the Mercedes to spend the night at Michael's house. On the way out of town, Annie suggested they stop at the drugstore.

"While you're in there, grab me a toothbrush," Michael said as she got out of the car. "My suitcase is somewhere in London with Isabel. I got a flight to New York on standby. I left her stranded in Heathrow."

"Is she furious?"

"I hope not."

From the backseat, Dillon piped up. "I'm hungry. Can we get something to eat?"

Michael grinned. "How about hamburgers and shakes?"

"Great!"

"Let's find a drive-through while your Mom is in the drugstore."

A few minutes later, they returned for Annie. Munching on a burger, Dillon chattered the entire drive. He wasn't sure what was going on, but he knew an adventure when he encountered one.

In the front seat, Annie rested her head on Michael's shoulder while he drove.

The grand Tudor came into view from behind a stand of oak trees fluttering in the early autumn dusk. Annie took in the stately house with wide-eyed wonder. Dillon jumped out before Michael had turned off the car's engine.

"Wow! You live here? It's big!" Dillon dashed down the driveway. "Where's Lucky?"

Michael grabbed Annie's suitcase from the trunk. "He's at the kennel. We'll get him in the morning."

"Can't we get him now?"

"Sorry, pal. The kennel is already closed."

"I guess I can wait 'till morning." Dillon ran up the front steps. "This place is bigger than St. Mary's. Do you like school? I do."

"I liked school a lot." Michael crouched before Dillon. "Do you really like the house? There's a stream in back. Have you ever gone fishing? Would you like to try it sometime?"

Damn if he wasn't babbling like a sentimental old fool. Weren't the fishing rods down in the basement storage room? With every baseball mitt he'd ever owned during childhood? And the footballs, soccer balls, and that really neat electric train set he'd once loved.

When Dillon's mouth formed an *O* of glee, Michael asked, "Do you like trains? I do. I liked climbing trees as a kid, too. Come to think of it, there's a big Willow tree on the side of the house. You should check it out."

"Oh, I climb trees every day," Dillon boasted. He waved at Annie, standing with her head angled back as she gaped at the mansion. "Big, big ones. I climb real fast too. Wanna see?"

"You bet."

"Let's go!"

Dillon shot through the foyer without bothering to survey the rich furnishings and sped toward the kitchen. Michael figured he'd find the back door in ten seconds flat.

An hour later, they let Dillon race through the bedrooms upstairs to pick the room he'd call his own. Together, they tucked him beneath the covers. He fell asleep within seconds.

In the master bathroom, Michael filled the Jacuzzi with warm water. "Why don't you soak for awhile? You look tired." He gave Annie a quick peck on the cheek. She was still in some sort of stupor, but he figured it would pass. "I'm going downstairs to start a fire."

"Thanks," she murmured. She was glad for time alone.

After he left the room, she undressed with a sensation of expectancy building in her chest.

The hectic swirl of the last months hadn't given her much time to think. Now, she calculated the days carefully. Yes, it was definitely possible—and was it really a surprise? Given her impetuous behavior with Michael, it was darn near predictable. Shaking her head with bemusement, she reached for the bag from the drugstore.

After a long, luxurious bath, she padded into the bedroom. The mahogany four-poster was gorgeous, the chaise lounge in the corner beckoning with it subtle silk fabric. She began to put on her robe then decided against it. To the right of the bed, a door stood partially ajar. Curious, she went inside and discovered a large walk-in closet bursting with slacks and suits and other male paraphernalia.

A fluffy man's Turkish bathrobe hung on a hook in back. It smelled deliciously like Michael. She shrugged into it.

Downstairs, a fire burned brightly in a living room decorated with rich golds and deep plums. The couches were plump and the lamps set on low. She felt instantly at home. On the carpet before the fireplace, Michael reclined with a pewter platter of cheese, crackers, and grapes.

"Your dinner, madam." Once she'd settled beside him on the carpet, he gave her a long kiss.

Afterward, she reached for a grape and popped it into her mouth. "You've already fed us, Michael. I don't need two dinners."

"You didn't eat the hamburger."

It warmed her that he'd noticed. "It didn't really agree with me." Picking up another grape, she studied it, thinking. "Michael . . . you *do* want other children, don't you?"

He gave look of mingled delight and amazement she knew she'd never grow tired of glimpsing. "I want as many kids as you want." He reached for her hand, and the bliss weaving across his features stole into her heart. "I love Dillon—I'll love all of them. I love *you.*"

"I'm glad." She leaned close, hungry for another kiss. "Because I'm pregnant."

THE END

Book-Group Discussion Questions

1. Throughout much of the novel, Annie keeps secrets while Michael displays an inability to trust. Which character changes the most during the story's progression? Or do they change an equal amount?

2. Annie's sister Toria is never introduced but she provides a strong influence on the plot. How would the plot have changed if she had been introduced prior to her murder? Would her introduction have made Annie a more sympathetic character? Or less?

3. In any novel, secondary characters are often used for a variety of reasons:

—How does the inclusion of Miriam's point-of-view (POV) move the story forward?

—How does Lisbon's POV serve to characterize Michael?

—Why isn't Dillon's POV included?

—Is Terrence used only for comedic relief? Does his character serve more than one function?

4. Much of the novel focuses on Annie's desire to adopt her nephew:

—Should she have mentioned the home study to Michael earlier?

—Does the home study process strike you as harsh? Why or why not?

—Did Tom and Dianne England's desire to adopt Dillon seem logical? Should the judge have allowed them to adopt Dillon? Why or why not?

5. The novel features several parallels:

—How are Miriam and Lisbon similar? Different?

—Both Annie and Michael are healing from past events. Do they need to do an equal amount of emotional work? Is one character more vulnerable than the other? Why or why not?

—How does the depiction of Chip's secure home life highlight Dillon's tragic early childhood?

6. If, like Annie, you had a sibling who behaved recklessly, what would you do? Is there a point when you should walk away from a destructive family member? Why or why not?

About the Author

Christine owned a small public relations firm in Cleveland, Ohio. She closed
the firm after she adopted a sibling group of four children.
Her debut Treasure Me is a 2012 Next Generation Indie Awards finalist.
The Midwest Book Review lists Treasure Me, The Tree of Everlasting Knowledge
and Second Chance Grill as "highly recommended".
She has been writing fulltime since 2004.

Please visit her at
www.christinenolfi.com

Follow her on Twitter at
@christinenolfi

Also by Christine Nolfi

Treasure Me

Second Chance Grill

The Tree of Everlasting Knowledge

Reviews Sell Books

Please turn the page for a sample of *The Tree of Everlasting Knowledge.*

The Tree of Everlasting Knowledge

Chapter 1

Staring at the tables wouldn't put Ourania at one of them.

Nursing a cup of coffee, Troy Fagan wondered if she'd decided to decline the work. Bow out with embarrassment, beg forgiveness—if Ourania didn't come to her senses, he'd fire her.

How didn't matter. He'd find a way.

Resigned to his decision, Troy returned his attention to the crowd of men converging on the lawn. The air sizzled with excitement as carpenters, masons and specialty trades greeted each other before taking their seats. For men accustomed to meager paychecks and unpredictable stints between jobs, Fagan wealth promised to make the pay generous even if the schedule was tight.

Troy didn't share the men's early morning cheer. Remodeling his parent's mansion filled him with anxiety. Thankfully they'd left early this morning, driving through the crisp April sunshine to the other end of the thousand-acre estate, to the factory, where Fagan's Orchard shipped produce and condiments across the Midwest. He prayed the demands of managing the company would keep them occupied as construction began on the mansion.

This would be the first time the stately rooms and antique furnishings were disturbed since his brother's murder fifteen years ago. He worried about sending his parents back into grief. As saws roared and plaster sifted down, would Jason's ghost whisper across the ruins?

One hundred men would contribute sweat and labor to build the mansion's new south wing. The thirteen-course foundation was already in place. The best Amish carpenters in the county had erected the exterior walls and laid five thousand square feet of base flooring. Now the real work would begin, as the other trades jostled for space inside the two-story structure.

Troy was always tense at the beginning of a new project. Today he was worse than usual—a typical construction schedule would increase to warp speed to beat the arrival of his younger sister's baby. Luckily, the very pregnant Dianne Fagan-Zagorski had left the site at daybreak. Given his own anxiety, he couldn't handle hers this morning.

Striding before the tables, he brought the chatter to a halt. He was about to launch into his speech when Ourania D'Andre skirted across the lawn and slipped into a chair in back.

It was odd enough to see a woman in the midst of the stubble-faced trades. What made it worse was that Ourania looked beautiful today.

Troy grimaced. She always looked beautiful.

Her simple blue work shirt and faded jeans were a mockery. With her classic Italian beauty, she caused a stir on any job site. Troy's throat convulsed with sorrow and longing as she took a seat at the table in back, her whiskey-hued eyes dark with worry.

Pulling his attention from her, he launched into an explanation of the construction timeline. Given the size of the mansion's new wing, there wasn't room for scheduling errors. As he emphasized his demand for strict compliance, several of the men shifted uneasily in their chairs.

Finishing, he added, "The schedule is set in stone. Forget about taking side jobs. From now until the finish date, I own you."

At the table in front the lead plumber said, "You don't own my crew. After the 'meet and greet' today, we won't return until next week. I'm taking my men to another job in town."

"Not a problem, Gar. However, once you start here you'll stay put."

"Understood."

Troy looked out over the sea of faces. "We're building the new wing in record time and I expect the best from each of you. If you aren't confident your work will be of the highest caliber, leave now."

Crash, the Amish carpenter who'd lead the main crew, tugged his salt and pepper beard. "My men are ready. What assurance can you give that the others won't hold us up?"

"Any man falling behind will be fired. I have a list of subs waiting to come on board. If you can't cut it, you're out."

"The woman won't get special treatment?" Crash swiveled around to glare at Ourania. "My crew can handle tight schedules. I have twenty men. How will she keep up with only one employee?"

The question provided the opportunity Troy needed. Getting rid of Ourania might be easier than he'd imagined. While the trades enjoyed lusting after her on sites across Lincoln, this time was different. They were being paid top dollar to complete the new wing quickly. They didn't want a woman standing in the way.

Troy drilled her with a hard stare. "Crash has an understandable concern. D'Andre Electric never handles jobs this large. How will you manage?"

Ourania's eyes rounded with fear; but only for a moment. "I've gone over the details with my assistant," she said. "We'll keep pace with the carpenters."

"With only one employee, is that realistic?" Troy asked.

"We'll work overtime if needed." She came to her feet. "We can handle the schedule."

"Naturally my sister likes the idea of awarding the electrical contract to a company run by a woman. But this is a big job. You're out of your depth."

Every man in attendance zeroed in on the woman standing in their midst. Several murmured in agreement. Despite Troy's desire to be rid of her, he felt pity. And respect—damn if Ourania wasn't holding her ground.

"The retainer isn't a problem," he said. "Keep it."

"I want the job." She layered steel on her voice. "Your sister hired me. We're building her new home. Doesn't she have the final say?"

He set his jaw.

Evidently she sensed triumph in his silence. "Then it's settled." She sat. "I'm staying."

Frustrated, he turned back to the others. She'd won—for now. "I want to meet with each trade this afternoon," he said, getting back on track. "Have your timeline ready. I'll need to coordinate schedules. Spend the morning getting acquainted with each other."

Crash sent Ourania a chilly look before regarding Troy. "Where should we have supplies delivered?" he asked.

"Unload them on the south side of the mansion by noon today. My parents and sister will continue living here as we proceed. Keep the front entrance free of materials so we don't disrupt them more than necessary." Troy rocked back on his heels. "That's it for now."

The men dispersed. He was about to do the same when Ourania cornered him.

"Where do you get off telling me to leave?" She appeared ready to take a swing at him. "Your sister accepted my bid."

Her anger came as a surprise. A world of hurt brimmed in her almond-shaped eyes, the kind of pain that brought most women to tears. Yet she'd managed to bring on the fire instead. Did she really want to stay? Her company must be strapped for cash if she'd risk working for him.

"Why did you take so long in supplying the bid?" he countered, and her eyes again rounded. She looked vulnerable and irrepressibly feminine despite the tool belt slung low on her hips. "My sister contacted D'Andre Electric six weeks ago. You waited until the last minute to provide a quote."

"I was rechecking my bid. For accuracy."

"You weren't stalling? Afraid you were getting in over your head?"

"No!"

Her cheeks flamed and he knew she was lying. "I spoke to three of your competitors and got bids within days. The way you held off has me wondering if you were thinking about turning us down."

She rubbed her lips together. From the looks of it, she was having trouble reining in her notable temper. The sharp ring of her cell phone spared her from replying. She yanked it from her pocket and swiveled away.

Troy simmered while she whispered tightly into the phone. Keeping the GC waiting sure as hell wasn't a way to earn Brownie Points. Tapping his foot, he felt his own anger rising.

She snapped the cell shut. "Sorry." The flush spread engagingly across her face. "I have a problem."

"What, exactly?"

She smiled nervously. "Where am I on your afternoon schedule? I have to run a few errands."

The threads of his temper frayed. "Weren't you listening? No one leaves. Have your supplies delivered. Do it this morning."

"It's not about the supplies. They're here." She pursed her lips and the memory of kissing her struck him like a blow. He wasn't prepared for the raw bolt of pleasure that catapulted through his veins. He fled from the memory as she added, "I won't be gone long. I'll meet with Crash before I leave in case he has any questions."

"What about my sister? Dianne wants to meet with each trade this morning."

"I know. And I'm looking forward to meeting her. I'll return before she arrives."

"You aren't going anywhere." Troy nodded at the men merging into small groups on the lawn. "Get up to speed with the carpenters and the guys on heating and cooling."

"It won't take long—"

"You're staying put." He pointed to the men. "Get to know them. As it is, you've already made a few enemies."

Her eyes blazed. The air gelled between them for ten seconds. Then she stalked away.

* * *

The bruises were an angry purple beneath the girl's toffee

colored skin. They marked a passage from her jawbone to her cheek, a distressing series of welts inflicted with brutal force. Sorrow for the child welled in Ourania's chest.

Pushing the emotion down, Ourania glanced at her watch. There wasn't time to feel pity for yet another helpless child dumped into the mire of Jobs & Family Services. There were always children, dozens of them, forced into the system by neglect and abuse. Usually she cared about them deeply. Today would've been the same if her blood pressure weren't approaching dangerous limits after she'd been crazy enough to leave the Fagan job site.

Shuffling down the corridor toward the approaching child, she wondered at her reckless behavior. She was out of her mind. If Troy discovered her missing, the new job would be over before it began.

With a mix of resignation and worry, she let her gaze drift back to the girl. The child skipped forward with fierce concentration, her expression at odds with her carefree movements. The folds of her dress billowed out like a sail. A Barbie doll dangled in her grip. Ourania stepped aside to allow her to pass. Reaching the juncture where the corridors met in a T, the girl paused.

The ceiling's fluorescent lights gave off a nearly imperceptible hum. Footsteps echoed further off. The girl turned toward the sound.

Ourania paused, unsure of what to do. Where was the kid's social worker? "Sweetie, are you lost?"

Out of habit she dug into the pocket of her jacket and rooted around for her antacids. She'd just popped one into her mouth when a woman's voice, soft as rain, called out. The child dashed away.

It took a moment for Ourania to regain her composure. The fleeting exchange was unsettling, an added stress she didn't need this morning.

Grimly, she continued down the corridor. Irritation dogged every step. Not only was she putting the Fagan job at risk. She was doing so because, once again, she couldn't find the courage to stand up to her mother.

In bustling Lincoln, Ohio, Lianna D'Andre was something of

a titan. She managed Jobs & Family Services and championed children's causes before state judges and the media. In a state with more than its share of poverty and drug abuse, the caseload never diminished. In fact, the sheer number of children rescued by the agency increased with depressing predictability.

Which was probably why she'd demanded to see Ourania.

Pausing at the door to her mother's office, Ourania balled her fists. "No. Can't," she practiced under her breath. "Sorry, big job, maybe some other time."

Inside, her mother bobbed between the file cabinet and the paperwork on her desk.

"Pick one," Ourania said by way of greeting. "If I were you, I'd start with the crap on your desk."

Lianna slammed the cabinet drawer shut. "I'm running a marathon. It seems everyone else has crossed the finish line."

"You have a staff. Delegate more."

"My staff puts in the same hours I do." Sitting, her mother unearthed a manila folder. "Ah. The Korchek case," she added, and the heart-shaped curve of her face relaxed. Time left her features like a private beach washed away by the tide.

The transformation always surprised Ourania. In repose, her mother's stern expression gave way to beauty. No wonder children in her care were drawn to her. Kids living in the tumult of abuse and neglect were skittish creatures. They rarely trusted adults, even those sent to rescue them. Yet most trusted the elegant woman who ran the social agency.

Surely Lianna had such a child fixed in her mind's eye now.

No, not a child. Ourania was better with teenagers. Would her mother ask her to provide a foster home for a kid in junior high? It was probably a juvie case. Or a teenager whose delinquency made his parents seek foster care as a last resort.

The particulars didn't matter. Ourania's thoughts veered to the Fagan job and the demands of wiring the new wing of the mansion. There wasn't room for anything else in her life.

Her stomach coiled into a painful knot when her mother said, "I'm sure you understand why I wanted to see you."

"Actually I'm hoping I don't."

"The Korchek case just came in. Wife deceased, husband

clearly grieving—and abusive. I need a short-term foster home while I sort this out."

Ourania studied her work boots. "The Fagan job started this morning. I shouldn't have left the site."

"Well, you're here and I'm glad."

"Mother, I shouldn't have come. I could lose the job." Her comment met with silence. She resisted the urge to glance at her watch. "I can't help now. Ask some other time."

"Don't you think I checked everywhere before calling you? No other foster homes are available."

"Keep trying."

"There isn't a rock I haven't looked under. If your father's health were better, we'd take this on." Lianna released a labored sigh. "You're it, Ourania. At least until Mr. Korchek completes anger management therapy."

"Mother, *no.*"

Disappointment cascaded through her mother's expression, stirring the guilt that had always held Ourania hostage. She'd never measured up—in her mother's eyes or her own. The realization beat against the insulation she'd spent years packing around her heart.

When the silence grew daunting, she said, "You shouldn't have asked me to get the foster-adopt certification." She stopped, despising the contrition in her voice. It shouldn't matter if she let her mother down, but it did. "I'm not parent material."

The small confession eased the burden on her heart. She was surprised by the unexpected void of emotion the words left behind. Disconnecting from the guilt left her momentarily grounded and safe from mishap.

"Your brother and sister have helped in the past."

"Try to understand. The Fagan job is crucial." It was still hard to believe Dianne Fagan had accepted a bid that had arrived weeks behind the competition. If it had been up to Troy, he would've picked anyone else. "If I do a good job Dianne will invite me to bid on the electrical subcontract for the new processing plant."

She neglected to add that D'Andre Electric was bleeding greenbacks. Rent, the cost of supplies, hiring Squeak Grantham, her lumbering if sweet employee—it all added up. Somehow she'd found the courage to take on the residential job for the mansion's new wing even though she'd never planned to visit the estate again. After Jason Fagan's death, she was glad to stay away.

"Fagan's Orchard is building a new plant?" Lianna asked.

"Next year. They'll double the size of the processing facilities." If she persuaded her mother the work was important Lianna might badger someone else into providing emergency foster care. A neighbor or a friend—anyone else. "Residential work's all right. A commercial job is better. It'll turn D'Andre Electric into a real company."

"If you hire a whole crew you'll spend most of your time managing the books. You enjoy the work."

Ourania silently agreed. She loved working with her hands, loved electricity. The heat and the spark—and the danger. She also craved the isolation her job provided, the long hours working alone. The bullet that took Jason Fagan from the world had taken something from her too. In all the intervening years, she'd never repaired what was broken inside her.

Pulling from the depressing reverie, she said, "I agreed to the foster-adopt classes because I knew you'd expect me to help in the future. But not now. Troy is a tough contractor. His parent's mansion was built in 1842. I have no idea what I'll find in those walls, how I'll tie it all together."

Lianna flipped open the folder in her grasp. "Walt and Emma will go directly from school to afternoon programs."

Two kids? Providing emergency care for one unruly teenager was hellish enough.

"I can't handle two teenagers." She gripped the chair's armrests. "One, maybe. For a week. All right—two weeks."

"They aren't teenagers. Walt is eight years old. Emma is seven."

My God. How could she refuse to help children? They couldn't bunk at a juvenile correction facility until a foster home was located. They should be placed with a couple. She was an unmarried electrician with the most important job of her career looming.

"No one would describe me as remotely maternal." Voicing

the truth hurt. She'd lost so much after they'd buried Jason. Her confidence, surely, and her belief in anything but the grind of work. "The next time you need short-term care for a teenager I'll do my bit. Just don't ask me to provide shelter and three square meals for a couple of kids. I wouldn't know where to start."

"I'll help you."

"I'll fail."

Her mother rocked in her chair with an irritating sheen of patience fanning across her features. "For the record, you have maternal instincts even if you hide them behind a tool belt and jeans."

Ourania pushed to her feet before the words caused further damage to her heart. "I have to go."

"Why don't you meet Walt and Emma before you decide?"

She started for the door. "I'll see you later."

"Wait! They're here. Jenalyn brought them to meet you."

She swung into the corridor. "I *had* an appointment with Troy and Dianne. I've probably missed it."

She marched down the corridor with the guilt sending a wave of acid through her stomach. No problem—she kept a jumbo bottle of antacids in the truck.

A secretary approached with a sheaf of papers hugged to her breasts. Ourania skirted around her. If she didn't hurry Troy would read her the riot act the moment she arrived. Or worse, fire her.

He wasn't the type to forgive a subcontractor who cut out on him, and certainly not after he'd demanded she stay on site. The guilt needling her gave way to the anxiety that jolted her whenever he invaded her thoughts. But she'd learned: they were both good at dropping a back hoe's worth of work on top of their emotionally charged past.

This time would be harder. Seeing Troy on his home turf would make the past impossible to avoid. Jason's ghost would haunt their conversations.

Somehow she managed to bury her thoughts as she quickened her stride. At the reception desk the neglected phone blinked with calls. She'd escaped into the waiting room when a voice brought her to a standstill.

"There you are! I thought we were meeting in your mother's

office."

With misgiving she spotted Jenalyn Hampton in the corridor. Yet the lovely Filipino social worker didn't hold her attention. Ourania locked gazes with the girl she'd seen earlier. A step behind, a boy with similar honeyed features gave an appraising look as bitter as winter frost.

Her heart lurched. This close it was easy to see that the children were a stunning blend of black and white with large, expressive eyes as green as emeralds. Glossy curls danced around their faces in a wild chorus of lengths.

"I'd like you to meet Walt and Emma," Jenalyn was saying.

Ourania couldn't hear past the buzzing in her ears. These were the children her mother expected her to foster? Walt was skin and bones and he dwarfed his sister. At best, Emma Korchek weighed fifty pounds. The little wisp of a girl met Ourania's eyes with a stare void of emotion. That too was no surprise—abuse had the potential to cause the death of a soul. A child left in such an environment too long became something less than human. Sociopaths weren't born into the world; they were beaten into existence.

She abruptly withdrew from her thoughts when Emma said, "Why do you wear boy clothes?"

Ourania blinked. "I don't wear boy clothes. These are *work* clothes."

Jenalyn patted the curious girl's head. "Miss D'Andre is an electrician," she said.

The explanation glanced off Emma. "Boy clothes are ugly on a girl." She took an abrupt step forward. "Do you like being ugly?"

"Of course not. I'm just not into frilly chick stuff—"Ourania clamped her mouth shut. The dress Emma Korchek wore was a ruffled mess, circa 1995. No doubt Jenalyn had bought the old frock at the local Goodwill. "Some girls like feminine things but others don't."

"You aren't a girl." Emma held Ourania's gaze hostage. "Girls are small. You're big. How come you don't know that?"

"I do, I just—"

Walt came forward. The gash on his cheek gleamed in the corridor's fluorescent glow. "You don't smell good, either." He regarded Jenalyn. "Get someone who smells nice."

Emma bounced her thumb toward the social worker. "*She* smells nice."

Jenalyn blushed. "It's *White Shoulders*," she confided. "It's not a trendy perfume but I adore it."

"It's nice," Ourania said from behind a manufactured smile. The perfume wafting past was sweet enough to glaze the entire town of Lincoln.

"Worms smell bad," Walt put in reasonably. "Especially after it rains. That's when I squish 'em."

Wincing, Ourania suspected delinquency lurked behind his angelic face. "It's disgusting to squish worms." She imagined the boy trooping through her house with the slimy corpses on his shoes.

He smiled, revealing a chipped front tooth. "That's why I like stompin' on 'em."

"Have any other hobbies? Anything that won't land you on the wrong side of the law?"

He gave her query a moment's consideration. "I throw rocks at squirrels. Chipmunks, too. The squirrels are easier to hit."

Great. Just great. She recalled the case studies she'd read during the coursework for foster-adopt certification. By the time they reached Walt's age, many of the children shuttled through foster care began acting out. Causing harm to animals often led to more serious misbehavior.

If someone didn't teach the boy healthier activities, a few years from now he'd be running over dogs when he got his driver's license. Then he'd move on to breaking and entering. She wasn't the right candidate to keep him toeing the straight and narrow but she *did* possess talents to encourage him toward more constructive forms of play.

"I'm good at baseball," she told him. "I can show you how to play."

Emma snorted. "You *are* a boy."

"No, I'm sporty."

"Boys play baseball. Girls don't."

"Sexism lives," she replied irritably. "Lots of women play

sports. They also wear work shirts and boots. There's nothing wrong with it."

Jenalyn nodded in agreement. "Of course there isn't." She drew Walt forward. "Why don't you tell Miss D'Andre about yourself?"

The boy crossed his arms, mimicking Ourania's stance. "You first."

She peered at her watch then rattled off a quick personal history. The growing unrest on the children's faces merely added to her discomfort. At this rate, she'd never leave. Troy would be livid when she *did* arrive. Forcing a patient smile, she wondered if she should follow up with her Social Security number and her savings account balance. This was worse than taking out a bank loan.

When she finished, Walt said, "Just so you know, Pa wants us back. You can't keep us."

Ourania drew in a steadying breath. She couldn't help but feel sympathy. Walt and Emma were so young. Clearly they'd been through too much. Was it surprising if they weren't delighted to meet her? They'd settle down. Or they wouldn't. Either way, she only needed to provide safe harbor for a short time.

Still, it seemed prudent to take a firm stance. From what she'd learned in the foster-adopt classes, coddling rarely worked. Traumatized children responded more appropriately to firm, consistent parenting.

"I have some rules," she said. "You'll have to follow them."

"I don't eat liver," Walt replied before she got on a roll. "I don't care how many onions you put on top—I won't eat it."

"I don't make liver. In fact, I rarely cook."

"So you'll starve us?"

"I can make the basics. Hamburgers. Spaghetti. Stuff like that."

Emma nudged past her brother. "I have rules, too. No washing floors. It hurts my knees."

Some idiot had made her wash floors? "I don't make kids clean my house." She crouched before them like she'd seen her mother do with other children unlucky enough to be dumped into a foster care system as unpredictable as the world they'd arrived from. "My house is nice. It's on South Street near Lincoln Square."

Emma's eyes grew wide. "Do I get a bed?"

"Don't you usually sleep in a bed?"

Jenalyn caught her attention. "Uh, Ourania—"

Emma cut in to ask, "Can we *always* sleep in the house?"

Ourania came to her feet and regarded Jenalyn. Clearly the social worker preferred to discuss the case privately. But Ourania needed to hear this firsthand.

Running her fingers through her hair, she softened her tone. "Where else would you sleep?" she asked Emma.

The child's bravado slipped. A tremble went across her shoulders as she lowered her head. Ourania's breath caught. Was Emma too frightened to discuss the matter?

She stepped back, distraught by the possibilities. "At my house you'll always sleep in your bedroom," she said, and her heart overturned. "That's the rule. Kids always sleep in a bed."

"There's no barn?" Walt asked.

She froze beneath a sudden wave of anger at the boy's father. Northeast Ohio was experiencing a particularly chilly April. If Buck Korchek had forced his children to sleep in a barn, it was a miracle they hadn't caught pneumonia.

She placed her hand on his shoulder. "I have three bedrooms. You'll each have your own room. Okay?"

They both merely shrugged. At the end of the corridor her mother approached with an annoying spark of pleasure brightening her gaze. Ourania looked from Lianna back to the kids, sizing them up like she'd done with her truck before driving it home from the dealership.

Why consider this? She didn't have the experience to parent one child let alone two. They deserved better. And they'd already made her late for her meeting at the mansion.

The future of D'Andre Electric hinged on her ability to make a good impression on Dianne Fagan while steering clear of Troy. Walt and Emma Korchek didn't factor into the equation. They'd be a hindrance during the most important stage of her career.

All of which swirled through her head as her mother neared. When Lianna came to a halt, Ourania said, "I'll take them."

Chapter 2

"I should've picked the electrical contractor," Troy said as the *rhtt rhtt* of a pneumatic nail gun knifed the air. "Ourania has gone AWOL."

Two-by-fours spiked the air with the scent of wood. Twenty paces off, Crash and the framing crew stood deep in conversation. The mason had left. So had the plumber, after leaving catalogs of kitchen fixtures and brochures on hot tub designs. All of which delighted the abundantly pregnant Dianne Fagan-Zagorski.

At twenty-four, Diane was always upbeat. Today her ebullient mood was a sheer annoyance for Troy, who'd given up on checking for the return of the D'Andre Electric truck. Never in memory had a subcontractor on one of his jobs ignored a command to stay put.

Beside him, Dianne stroked her blossoming belly and swung her briefcase in a careless arc. From the pocket of her blazer her cell phone emitted a barely detectable hum—no doubt their father was calling from the factory on the other side of the estate to inquire when she'd return. Not that Dennis Fagan wouldn't prefer for his daughter to take a sabbatical until after the birth of his first grandchild. Predictably, Dianne had refused. Six months pregnant and sporting puffy circles beneath her eyes, she appeared giddy with pleasure amidst the construction mayhem.

She set her briefcase down in the sawdust covering the sub flooring. "Troy, relax. So Ourania left for an hour. It's not the end of the world."

"I gave her a direct order."

"You're always giving orders but she's a woman." Dianne nodded toward the carpenters. "She won't obey like the men."

"Why are you defending her?"

"Because she *is* a woman." Dianne smiled impishly. "They induct us into a secret society when we reach maturity. That's why we stick together. Didn't you know?"

Troy glowered at the mischief sparking in her green eyes. Of course, Dianne was unaware of his history with Ourania. Nor did she recall Ourania chumming around the mansion with their late brother. The painful events that had propelled Troy into adulthood couldn't mean anything to his younger sister—she'd been in elementary school when Jason died. Sorrow leaked into his thoughts, and regret, but he rose above them.

"Dianne, I'm firing her." He let the pronouncement sink in before adding, "She isn't right for the job. I need a firm with a big crew to keep pace with the other trades."

"You will not. Troy, *please.*" She regarded the men, hauling lumber and setting in windows. "I can't talk to the men. What do they know about decorating or paint chips?"

"Ourania is just like them. She's no decorator, if that's what you're looking for."

"We'll become great friends. I'm sure of it." She gave him a playful nudge. "So it's settled. Ourania stays."

He raked his hand across his scalp. "Don't you have a meeting at the factory?"

"It'll wait. Now, wipe that scowl off your face." She rose on tiptoes to pat his cheek with unflappable cheer, a petite redhead with the luck of the Irish and the good sense to know it.

Fagan's Orchard shipped produce and condiments throughout the U.S. The company had made them all millionaires, Troy included, even though he'd left the family business years ago to pursue a love of construction. Unlike him, Dianne wore her wealth easily while remaining earthy and warm. The diminutive marketing genius gladly sorted Granny Smiths and Macintoshes on the plant's assembly line, smiling whenever one of the workers told a bawdy joke. She wrapped holiday presents for everyone on staff and never missed a birthday.

Troy's parents were the same. They never allowed wealth to build walls around their lives. They remained on a first-name basis with everyone in their employ, from the pickers in the orchards to the executives working beside them on the factory's second floor. Like a couple of cheery elves, their physical size was of inverse proportion to their generous hearts.

Compared to his family, Troy was a giant. During childhood his parents had joked that he'd inherited his height from Scandinavia in a distant past when a Viking ship strayed onto Gaelic shores. Jason, when he'd been alive, enjoyed bragging that his brooding, older brother was Black Irish—and tall enough to prune the apple trees without a ladder. It wasn't true, of course, and before his death Jason reached five foot six, an acceptable height for a man. Troy didn't stop growing until he towered at six foot two. In a family of petite redheads, his physical contrast was another seed of discontent in his increasingly barren soul.

Dianne drew him from his thoughts. "There she is." Outside in the curving driveway, Ourania dashed across the estate's sloping lawn. "You see? She's just a few minutes late."

"I don't need a delay." Troy hooked his fingers through the soft leather of his tool belt. "I'm building your new home at record speed. I can't allow anyone to hold up progress."

"I've heard Ourania is a dream to work with. She never tracks mud or breaks anything. She'll hang my lighting fixtures the same week the carpeting is installed—and the carpet's white. Well, oyster." Dianne patted his forearm, her hand a pale butterfly on the span of muscle. "It's a relief to have a woman here, especially someone with her experience."

Despite his reservations, Troy couldn't fault the assessment. The average electrician left debris in his wake. Once he'd foolishly hired a novice for the electrical on upscale Robin's Gate Drive. The rookie dropped a socket wrench on the master bath's marble steps, chipping them badly. Then he broke the Jacuzzi's sprayer head when he lost his footing.

Troy nearly lost the contract.

He dismissed the thought as Ourania approached with her long, curly hair bobbing in a ponytail. Beneath his anger, desire stirred. It was galling how her beauty affected him. Or perhaps the allure came from the way she ignored the physical attributes she possessed in abundance.

He didn't believe in soul mates but he did believe in fate. Something had always drawn them into a combustible mix. When she'd been little more than a child and he an adolescent, they'd forged a relationship based on hatred. By the time he completed his senior year of high school and she entered ninth grade, Troy worried there was more to it. By then she was gifted with beauty and a body built for sex. Half of the young men in Lincoln had pursued her. Not that Ourania had noticed. Mouthy, with tunnel vision, she'd trod her own path.

She captured his sister's attention, two young women predisposed to hit it off. Dianne offered her hand in greeting.

Clasping it, Ourania made a quick introduction then said, "You've probably received lots of catalogs from the other trades. I work differently. Whenever you're ready, I'll go with you to choose the lighting. It helps to get a second opinion right in the showroom."

"I'd like lighting similar to my parent's side of the mansion," Dianne said.

"You wouldn't want a jarring change."

"I'm not sure how to accomplish it. The mansion's fixtures were installed during the Roaring Twenties."

Ourania trailed her thumb beneath the heart-shaped curve of her chin. "A company outside New York City does wonderful reproductions," she said.

Troy crossed his arms, waiting. Even as she enthralled his sister, her gaze strayed to his. Tired of her unspoken questions—he was livid and she damn well knew it—he finally said, "Where the hell have you been?"

She shrugged. "I had an emergency."

"We've been waiting."

"It won't happen again."

"Get your priorities straight or work somewhere else. Got it?"

The heat in his voice drew a gasp from Dianne. And Ourania looked like she'd been slapped.

In a flash, she dusted off her pride. He sensed danger when she asked, "How's the tooth?"

He flinched at the audacity of the question. Then he remembered. Ourania never had the sense to walk away from a battle.

He swiped his tongue across the false tooth, caught himself, and stopped. "It's fine."

The irritation in his voice increased the mirth on her face. Which wasn't the worst of it. Dianne caught on fast. He sent a few silent curses heavenward when her expression altered from curiosity to delight.

"Oh, I don't believe this." She thwacked him on the chest. "Is Ourania the girl you hated in school? It's been so many years . . . it's her, right? The picture. The darts."

He grappled for control. "Drop it."

She chortled and he glimpsed doom. "She's the pitcher who threw the curveball when you were watching the younger kids play. Big brother, you've made my day."

"Let's move on." He refused to reminisce about the fastball Ourania nailed him with when she'd been in elementary school. Stiffly, he tapped his meddling sister on the shoulder. "Do you have any other questions? I need to check on the other crews."

Dianne wasn't listening. She remained focused on Ourania, whose Mediterranean features went obligingly pink in a way that made her breathtaking. The mellow gold of her skin deepened, accenting the rich brown of her eyes and bringing her rosy lips into high relief. She'd done a hasty job of putting up her hair and a long curl hung loose against the curve of her cheek. She swiped at it, brushing away the barest hint of moisture. Troy forced his attention away.

Dianne smiled at Ourania. "Even if you did knock out my brother's tooth, I can't imagine why the dolt threw darts at your yearbook picture. You're stunning."

The unexpected compliment lifted Ourania's brows. "Thank you."

Troy seared his sister with a look. "That's enough strolling down memory lane."

"We've just started!"

He grabbed her by the arm. "Time for work."

"Okay—I'm going." She elbowed him in the ribs before beaming at Ourania. "It's been a pleasure. I have to hurry now to the factory."

"It was nice to finally meet you," Ourania said.

Dianne waggled her fingers in Troy's face before dashing off, her heels pecking on the sub flooring. No doubt she'd regale everyone at the factory with the story of the girl whose curveball knocked out Troy's tooth.

Ourania wavered. "I shouldn't have brought it up. It was unprofessional."

He studied her features for an under note to the apology. Laughter—something. When it appeared she was sincere, he said, "Your assistant left a dog tied up outside." Why, was beyond imagining. The mutt looked like a burn victim with its missing ear and scar tissue running down its snout. "Mind explaining why Squeak thinks this is a kennel?"

She swallowed. "He brought Princess with him?"

"Princess?" It was the ugliest dog in North America. Troy was about to tell her to get the mongrel off the site when she began wringing her hands. Her sudden vulnerability made him back off. "Just keep the dog outside. All right?"

"Sure," she said, clearly relieved. "I'll tell Squeak."

She walked away, and he meant to get back to work. Instead he watched her move past the carpenters and hurry up the stairwell. He didn't relish having her on the site even if she *was* the best electrician in the county. He didn't relish having her stir up emotions he'd spent years suppressing, the sad and the sweet.

Day by day, her presence would be an excruciating reminder of his late brother. If Jason hadn't been murdered, if he hadn't been in the wrong place when a crack-head robbed the convenience store on Cleveland's mean streets, his relationship with Ourania might have evolved into something deeper. And Troy—he bore responsibility for every misstep he'd ever made with her. He'd bullied her until he'd left for college. It would've been far more courageous to admit that, like Jason, he'd harbored complex emotions for the wild-hearted girl.

His emotions were a tangle, still.

After Jason's murder, Troy had roamed the orchard with his ungovernable remorse. Absolution had never arrived but he'd found a way to go on.

If he walked the orchard now, his self-loathing left a fading taste, like ash, in his mouth as the moon's cold light led him ever higher, to the Great Oak. He'd spend long minutes seated beneath the tree wondering if he'd forged an uneasy truce with his guilt.

Now, lost in his musings, he visualized the Great Oak that spanned the summit above the orchard's rolling acres. Reputed to be the oldest tree in Ohio, it was a sentry of immeasurable power. To this day, couples visited the summit above the tumultuous waters of the Chagrin River and stood in the tree's encircling shade. They came onto Fagan property uninvited because they understood the tree's magic. Beneath the sheltering leaves they voiced their love and let the far-flung branches cradle them in enchantment and dreams.

Yet an agony grew along the tree's roots. Nourished by a thousand tears, it was Troy's alone. Though the Great Oak was a shelter for love, he'd used it for hate when he'd been too young to understand its power.

He'd transmuted good into evil when he'd made love to Ourania beneath its wide-swept arms, not because he'd loved her but because she'd belonged to Jason.